Bella D'Arcy Reed has hac
garden design/history. She
herself using a mobility s(
a writer, and is now con

Previous publications:

Non-Fiction

Gardens of Divine Imitation: a garden design timeline from the Renaissance to the Edwardian era via Ancient Rome.

The Gardens of Easton Lodge: their discovery and Renaissance (with Brian Creasey)

Producer of audio CD: 'Bumps: Gertrude Jekyll and Edwin Lutyens, a lifelong friendship' a play by Sheila Dewey

gardens and people

Published 2017 by
*gardens
and
people*
11 Sawyers Rd, Little Totham, Maldon, Essex, CM9 8JW

ISBN 978-0-9563451-3-4

Typeset by **Biddles**, Blackborough End, Norfolk.

Printed and bound in the United Kingdom.

Bella D'Arcy Reed

The Woman in the Fresco

gardens
and
people

For Jacqui – thank you, and love

Acknowledgements

Thank you to Dr Vicky Ley for checking the manuscript for historical accuracy, any errors in this are entirely due to me for wilfully ignoring a small part of her advice for the purposes of the story. To Em Fanchette for meticulous proofreading, to my friends Jacqui, Stephane, Christine, Tricia, Gill, Nuala and Fran for their eternal encouragement and patience.

This book was conceived while researching for my MA in arts history when I stared at a woman in the fresco in the *Loggia di Psiche* at the Villa Farnesina, Rome, and wondered who she was. Of all the books I read for that MA, the ones I most often returned to for the novel are:

Albert, L. B, trans. Cecil Grayson, 2004. *On Painting.*

Bambach, Carmen C 1999. *Drawing and Painting in the Italian Renaissance Workshop. Theory and Practice, 1300-1600*

Barsali, Isa Belli, 1977, *Baldassare Peruzzi e le ville senesi del Cinquecento.*

Bazzotti, Ugo, 2013. *Palazzo del Te: Giulio Romano's Masterwork in Mantua*

Bedini, Sylvio A. 1998. *The Pope's Elephant..*

Cennini, Cennino. *The Craftsman's Handbook.* Trans. Daniel V. Thompson Jr.

Dacos, Nicole, 2008. *The Loggia of Raphael: a Vatican Art Treasure.*

Gilbert, Felix, 1991. *The Pope, his Banker and Venice*

Hartt, Frederick, 1958. *Giulio Romano.*

Henry, Tom and Paul Johannides, 2013. *Late Raphael*

Contents

Prologue

Mantua, 1524.

On the lower floor of the *Castello Marmirola*, in a room silent and cold with disuse, a servant is lighting a fire on a hearth, then coaxing the smoke to rise up a plainly unswept chimney. Any heat generated from the fire will not stretch across an empty floor to the bed, where I spent a chilled night. Nor will it spread to the unadorned bench which promises to rock when sat upon, or to the large table in similar style, furniture which seems to have been discarded years before. My chest lies somewhere in between; all is dim in the streak of October sky through small windows.

This is the room allotted for me, in the *castello* which I am to restore and embellish. The room is not light enough for an architect, nor big enough to work with the assistants I will need, nor near enough to the activities of the court to provide stimulation for invention. This will need to be changed, but now, I relish the chance to put into order the results of years of work in Rome and to separate out what might be useful to me, Giulio Romano, in my new position as architect and painter at the court of Frederico, Marquis of Mantua.

I pull the table into what light there is, the pull the chest across the floor next to it. I hear a fall of soot, a sneeze, and a muttered curse. As I open the chest and pull out piles of papers onto the table, the servant clears the hearth and starts again. In my rush to leave Rome, everything is mixed up, my plans, my elevations and other architectural drawings, with those of people. He succeeds in building a fire which threatens to heat part of the room, then leaves me with a table covered with unruly piles.

The architectural details of antique Roman buildings, pillars, capitals, cornices, arches and the preparatory paintings for paintings I have made will be useful references for the work I will do for the Marquis. The drawings of people can be copied by assistants and used in the frescos I design. Some of these are crowd scenes derived from the people thronging Rome in the market places, the churches, the streets, or battle scenes from the carvings on ancient Columns. Here are people with mouths open, in anger, in pain, in the trading of gossip, sometimes (not often) in pleasure. Some images are of individuals, drawings of men and women taken from life, to be turned, from the painters, the workshop assistants, and the prostitutes that they are, into gods and goddesses, into saints and angels and endless, painted people. The frescoes of Italy are full of such nameless portraits.

I am sorting these drawings in preparation for my work. That is my reason. It is not my motivation. I am looking for images of a girl, of a woman, one whom I have left behind on the walls in the Vatican and in the loggia of the Chigi Villa.

Cecilia. Ceci.

She is here.

She is here as a child, playing with her cat; here frowning, scrabbling in the dirt at the base of the high column uncovering the ancient engravings. She is here, sitting, squinting at a tiny piece of sculpture, held in hands resting on knees. She is here, grown up, laughing, then serious, modelling for a representation of a statue of Peace, for a Madonna, for a Psiche or a Venus. Other women, not herself.

These I drop one by one onto the fire.

The last one is rolled up, rubbed through handling and faded with kissing. Ceci, after she had given and I had taken her virginity. She is lying on the bed on top of her dress, innocently naked. Her hand is curled at her side, unaware of any need to cover any part of her body. Though drawn in black on white, I know her hair is blond, her eyes are green. Her gaze is a sunray from God; it offers an illusion of gold and red and orange. It is a ferocity of love I had only seen with her, only shared with her. Which I had drawn only once, and which I had shown no-one.

I drop it on the flames. She flares; red, gold, orange. She cracks, black and white, into tiny pieces, into soot.

CHAPTER ONE

The Macello dei Corvi, Rome, 1502.
GIULIO

Time hangs heavy when you have something exciting to tell, and the friend you want to tell isn't there. Niccolò was out on an errand for his father, Angelo, the butcher, whose shop was opposite our house. I sat in some shade and watched people moving about, watched the queue at the baker get shorter as the early morning rush decreased. I saw how the sign over the apothecary was loose on one side and in danger of falling on a customer. I followed with my eyes a young woman going from the butcher to the pastrycook to an old woman selling vegetables, filling her basket so that in carrying it, one shoulder was higher than the other. I sighed. Hours and hours to pass before dawn next day, when my father was taking me with him to work. My father, Pietro Pippi, was the son of Fillipo, the Master Mason. He came from Florence to Rome in the time of Pope Nicholas V. He stayed, and married, so my father and I were born Romans. My father was working for the current Pope, Alexander, in the Papal Palace. It wasn't his work that excited me, for he couldn't take me into the Palace, it was all the places I had only heard about from him and from my mother that we would see on the way.

I started to draw in the dust with a stick, but the sun suddenly struck me as it rose above the rooftops, and I grew hot and restless. I shuffled, about making dips with my heels in the dirt road, then started to chase chickens. They squawked, jumped up and down, and ran around peoples' legs making then sway or trip up, or, as I dodged after them, stop suddenly, and curse me. Their owner shouted out 'find something useful to do, Giulio Pippi' and clipped my ear before rounding the clucking hens into his back yard.

I had to tell *someone*. Then I saw Ceci – 'chickpeas' - the girl who lived downstairs. She was two years younger than me – I was ten – and a girl, so, inferior. She was sitting crossed-legged outside her mother's seamstress's shop, playing with stones. Her fair hair was all over her face and her dress was dirty, the skirt flopping between her knees weighed down by her collection of little stones. She was making a pattern on the ground with these.

She would have to do.

I went over and sat next to her. She didn't look at me, concentrating on the pattern, a cross made with bits of white marble. It had a blue mosaic tile in the middle and she was arranging darker stones around it. She frowned as she sorted those in her lap to find ones the right size.

'I'm going up to the Vatican tomorrow.'

'Oh? What's that then?' She knew perfectly well. I sighed silently and played the game.

'Where the Pope lives.'

'Oh.' She was unimpressed. I would have to try harder.

'And the place where St Peter was martyred - where he was crucified – upside down'

This got her attention. She looked up, not at me, screwing up her eyes until you couldn't see their colour – dark, dark green. She was thinking.

'If the cross was upside down, there wouldn't be enough of the cross to put into the ground. He'd fall over.' She put a stone in place.

Ceci liked to think about things, and sometimes struck me dumb with the results. Like now.

I wriggled. She had taken attention away from my news. I persisted. 'And, I'm going to see the castle where an Emperor was buried,' and wished I hadn't because she said 'Which Emperor?' and I didn't know.

I tried again: 'I'm going to see the Pope!'

'Don't believe you.' She moved the stones into a different pattern. Normally, I would inspect her shape and then change it, then she would change it again; a game we played. Not today.

Why wasn't Niccolò about? He would have believed me.

'And why should he want to see *you* anyway?'

I took a deep breath: 'Because…because my father is taking me to his work tomorrow, and– we'll see lots of buildings, and – and – statues – and the Basilica of S Peter, and where the Pope lives - we'll see - well, lots of things - we're getting up early – it's a long way – and we're taking the mule and food - and – and we'll see a river -' I ran out of words - and breath. I should have known.

'What's a river?'

I'd never seen a river. I knew about springs and wells, and little streams, and the water that flowed out from the fountain where the water carriers filled their barrels, but I knew a river was different. Father had told me about the River Tiber, which he crossed most days, so I knew it was wide; you couldn't jump over it like a stream. You crossed over it on a road above the water, a bridge. But I hadn't ever seen it. And I wasn't good at finding words to describe something I hadn't seen.

I moved a stone with my toe.

'Don't do that!' she pushed it back, and glared at me. 'You don't know!'

I lost hope. 'It's a lot of water.' I muttered.

'How much?'

Too much. I stood up and kicked the pattern to bits.

Don't! Go away!' she threw a stone at me, which hit my chest. 'Loon!' I didn't know the word, but I could tell by the way she said it that it was rude, confirmed by the gesture she made biting her thumb and pointing it at me. She was always rude, even when I first saw her, she was rude.

~

I was eight years old. It was midday, and I was inside, in my stuffy, airless attic room. I'd slept, but was then restless to be outside. I was looking out of the tiny window under the eaves at the familiar scene. A street bedded below a hill, on top, the site of the ancient Roman capitol, and the church of *Santa Maria di Ara Coeli*: altar of heaven. A street where houses were built next to jagged ancient walls, with weedy vegetation rooted in their tops and down their sides. Our house was on one side of a triangular space, next to an archway which cast a moving shadow as the sun turned around the earth. A shadow I now watched travel over pitted dust until it merged with that cast by the opposite wall. As it moved, so did several multi-coloured lumps, rising and settling, rising and settling. Cats. Escaping the intense heat of midday. They formed themselves in a long line against the bottom of a wall, legs stretched out to support noses and whiskers, tails tucked round their behinds. Tail-ends which occasionally twitched, as they chased rats in their sleep, making minute dust hills against the wall of bricks and plundered stone.

Each house had a ground level shop, each with its heavy door and shutters so solidly closed against the heat it seemed as if no one would ever pass through them again. I lifted the oilskin that covered my window, but there was no coolness. Only the stifled air in which hung smells of rotting food with an undertone of effluent from the middens of the human beings who lived there and the animals which passed by. Accentuated by the upright waft of urine from the washerwomen's vats, tinged with the rising sour acidity of the lime-kilns in the nearby Forum. Smells which the residents noticed only when they were at rest, their breaths having nothing else to do (apart from keeping them alive) but inform their minds of the scent.

I imagined that I was aiming a slingshot at them, the cats. I fancied hitting the red and yellow ochre tomcat, the evil one, which always snarled at me when we came across each other.

'Whish!' I dreamt the pebble on its way. I was astonished to see the tomcat suddenly raise its head, ears alert; in fact, the whole row of lumps turned into a row of ears over parallel eyes, all turned in the same direction. For a moment I thought I had created the pebble just by thinking, then I heard the sound which had alerted the cats: the rumbling of a handcart. I couldn't see it but I saw the cats scatter as the sound approached the houses and stopped below me. I couldn't get myself into a position where I could see the cart, but I heard the pounding below on the main door of our house. I heard my mother's footsteps descending, and then I rushed to go down. I stopped at the top of the stairs which led to the ground floor, and sat there where I could see what was going on below. Well, half of it.

I saw the familiar lower part of my mother opening the door, and part of the human being on the threshold. It had skirts, with a smaller skirt attached to it. The skirts entered the house while a pair of drab-coloured hose in dusty boots dragged in a box and two bundles. The boots disappeared; the sound of the handcart started up, then diminished.

I stood up ready to escape back into the attic before the visitors could come upstairs, but they didn't. I could no longer see the big skirt, but if I crept further down I could see a child was looking around. Younger than me, her hair was hidden by a cap: a baby! I was about to lose interest when she lifted her head to stare at me. Clear dark green-brown eyes, like those of the ochre-coloured cat. She shrugged one shoulder, creased her nose and put her tongue out - at me! She then gazed up at her mother with wide eyes.

'Here is the key to the front door, and this is the key to the ground floor which is yours,' My mother was saying. 'The rent is due on this day every month. You can pay Jacopo to bring you water when he fetches ours. You need to arrange to dispose of your own waste away from this house. You may store your fuel at the back away from ours, and you must take care not to set fire to the house. You can wash clothes in the courtyard if you wish but you must not allow water to come inside. If you don't follow these rules, then we will evict you.' The sentences were crisply delivered. Money exchanged hands. The woman's voice softened.

'What is the child's name?'

'Cecilia, Ma'am, she's five.'

'Pretty name.'

I snorted: Ce-ce-ce-ci-ci –li-li - AH!

'Thank you, Ma'am.'

The skirt bobbed up and down in a curtsey, then left the lobby to go into the shop, with the child in tow. I was quite sure that the girl pulled a face at me, but when I focused on her, all I saw was a blank face, then the door was shut.

So they have taken over the shop. I wondered what they would sell. Perhaps it would be a bakery. There had been a great deal of grumbling when the bakery next door did not open one day, nor the next day. And then a smell, bad but different from the usual street scents, was noticed and my father and Angelo had broken in to find the corpse of the baker's stabbed wife under the mixing table and no sign of the baker.

My mother looked up, saw me, and clucked at me to go back upstairs. I resumed my post at the window. The evil cat was back, with four others, lying as if dead.

A pity she wasn't a boy, someone to chase cats with.

'Ce-ce- ci-ci – ce-ci-chickpeas – ci-ci - mrow!' I drew another cat on the wall. It looked like the girl.

~

I wished I had put my tongue out to her then, so I did now. She ignored me.

CHAPTER TWO

CECI

I watched him go off down the road, hugging my knees, which made stones fall out of my lap. I was cross, not because of him kicking the stones, but because Giulio was going to see places away from here (if it was true). And I wasn't. I'd pretended I wasn't interested, but I was. As he disappeared from view, I was jealous, jealous at the way boys could go off on their own, sometimes for hours at a time, and I wasn't allowed to. I had made a promise to Mama not to leave the street on my own, but she had no time to take me anywhere, just to the little church along the street on Sundays. I prayed to Our Lady that, if he was telling the truth, he wouldn't see the Pope. That would be too much.

Would Giulio tell me about it when he came back? I wanted to know how they crucified St Peter upside down. I sat up.

Niccolò was in front of me, with a mule laden down with firewood. He raised a hand at me and smiled. I scowled; Giulio would tell Niccolò, not me. He shrugged and pulled the mule though the alleyway to the back of the shop. Niccolò wouldn't be interested in far-off buildings, not like me. Niccolò was only interested in doing jobs for food, or his cock! I giggled, the thought of cocks always made me giggle, such tiny little wrinkly things! I was glad I hadn't got one, I was nice and smooth and curved there: I ran my hand over myself and felt that little thrill as I pressed it.

Although it would be useful to have a cock just to spray piss away from you instead of having to stand up and get your legs wet and sticky when you couldn't aim straight, or having to bend your knees right down so you could piss on the ground, and fall over into it. Not as bad as shitting though: in that, girls and boys were the same. Boys liked to shit together so they could boast how big their turd was and then push each other into it. Once, Niccolò's mother became so angry, she ordered him and Giulio to strip off their clothes - all of them – and marched them down to the washerwoman, naked for all to see, and made them wash their clothes themselves in her big tubs.

That's how I knew about the wrinkly bits. They'd enjoyed splashing about in the water so much, they often went down to 'help' the washerwoman by treading the clothes up and down. She used to spank their bare behinds when they spilt too much water on the ground, then they'd run back through the streets to dry off before putting their clothes on.

I wasn't allowed to do that, run around with no clothes on. I did once and was spanked and told that girls didn't do that, and I must never, ever do it again. Nobody told me why.

I wished I was a boy.

Mama came out with some sewing. I joined her on the stone sill along the wall of the house and she handed me thread to make a tassel. I was quite good at this; I liked folding the colours over and over the small, smooth rectangular piece of wood until they formed a fat bulk. Then I would carefully push a large needle with the same thread along the top between the wood and the threads, and tie it very tightly so the threads all bunched together. Then I would carefully cut along the other side with large scissors and twist thread round the tied top to form the tassel. I would then cut the other end so that all the strands were the same length. The trick was to get it so level that only minute bits of thread were cut off so as not to waste materials. Making tassels soothed me, and I forgot about Giulio.

Mama hadn't always been a dress-maker. Once, she sewed for pleasure, embroidering beautiful things to wear or to decorate the house. My father was much older than Mama, and I was a bit scared of him. But not so scared as I was of my step-brother, his wife, and their children, who always made fun of me and pulled my hair when Mama wasn't looking. They broke my doll, and would tip a pot so it smashed on the floor and tell Beatrice, the maid and nurse, that I had done it. She always believed them. She told me off and wouldn't give me pudding.

Then my father died, and we left.

I remember arriving here, and seeing Giulio, looking down at me from the stairs, all scrunched up. Lots of black hair, with black eyes. I think I poked my tongue out at him. I'd been practising this for a while, copying what my step-brother's children did to me, but not daring to do it to their faces.

I remember waking up before the sun rose, hearing the sound of a heavy door closing. It wasn't a sound I knew. I hadn't slept well because the straw from the paillasse had been sticking into me all night and I didn't like it. I couldn't see anything in the room in the dark. At home I would see the glow either side of the heavy curtains at the windows, the shape of the linen chest under it, and I knew that the floor was below me, below my bed. Here, the floor was right next to me – if I put my hand out I could feel it. So I would have to get up from the mattress, not sit up and jump down. I lay there and wondered when someone would come in to wash me and put on my clothes. Last night, Mama had taken them off and I had slept in my petticoat. She had gone out for the straw which was tickling me, tying two sheets together at the corners and we had stuffed the straw between them to make a mattress. She had also come back with a broom made of stalks tied to a stick and had swept the room. It was very dusty and full of cobwebs. At the big house, servants did this and I wondered why my mother was doing it here. Why were we here?

I suddenly thought that we'd had to leave because I was so bad, even though it wasn't always my fault. Though once, I had been shut up in a room without food for a day because I had thrown a dish on the floor. But why was Mama shut up with me? What had she done? I heard her get up. There were sounds above me.

There was a clattering outside our door, then footsteps down stairs, then up again, slower, then down, faster, then up, slower. Then down. Mama, who was up, had opened one shutter a little. Curiosity got the better of me and I jumped up to look out: a cart with fat barrels on it. I heard a voice, our landlady: 'New tenants downstairs'. There was a knock on the door. Mama pulled on a shawl and went to open it. There was a big man, standing at the main door. I got behind our door and watched through the gap between it and the its frame.

'Water - Mistress Pietro said '

'Oh yes.'

'Buckets?'

Mama looked round for something for the water and dragged two large pots across to the door; the man took them and filled them. He held out his hand.

'Twenty quattrini.' Mama came inside to find some coins.

Our landlady had come down the stairs again.

'Ten,' she said 'A week.' She looked at our pots. 'For two buckets every two days. Those pots only hold one bucket, if that. One quattrino today.'

The man grunted. Mama looked at the landlady, who nodded, and gave the man a coin. He left to serve people waiting outside with jugs.

'You'll need some bigger buckets,' our landlady said. 'And don't keep the door open when you fetch money. Make sure that,' she indicated the purse in Mama's hand, 'is well-hidden. Try the bricks in the fireplace,' and she went upstairs. Mama closed our door, and she looked so sad I ran across to hug her legs. She picked me up.

'I'll be good, I promise, then we can go home.'

She hugged me.

'This is our home now. You must forget the other place. We can't go back.'

'Why?'

'Because we can't. You must be grown-up now,' and she set me on the floor. 'Now put on your clothes, you have to do it by yourself. There are no servants here. We have to do everything ourselves.'

She shook out the mattress as I struggled into my clothes, getting them all tangled over my head. This made her smile and she helped me. Then she opened the shutters fully and let the sunshine in. It made a splash across the floor and up the wall, showing how bare the room was, with just the mattress, the half-empty box and the bundles.

Mama went to the fireplace, a hollow square made of double bricks with a hook over the top, and felt round the bricks. She found that one at the back was lower than the rest. She pulled out the brick.

'She was right, we can hide the money here, behind the fire.'

She put the bag into the gap behind the fire. With the brick on top it just looked as if a brick was crooked, one side higher than the next brick. Then she made a row of pots from the back to the front at the side of the fireplace, so it looked just like any other fireplace. (Given that I had then only ever seen one, at my old home, which was much bigger than this.)

After that, I wanted to pee, so Mama took me outside and showed me where to do this. She told me that the pee was taken to the washerwomen, and showed me where the midden for the shit was behind a wall behind the houses.

'And don't do either if there is a man out here.'

The bit about the washerwomen was new to me, but I was intent on peeing and any question slipped from my mind.

We sat on a box and had bread crumbled in water for breakfast. She sat, bowed, elbows on knees, her hands over her eyes. I could see water coming between her fingers. She was crying. I was very still. Then she shook her head, murmured 'this will never do', rubbed her eyes and smiled at me. She pulled me towards her.

'We have to shift for ourselves. Come on.'

She took some coins from the bag, and we went shopping. We went to the baker for bread, the butcher for meat, and a stall for vegetables and fruit. I had never been shopping before, and kept close to my mother among the people in the street, watching everything. I saw that coins were given to the person in the shop, and goods were given to us. It was my first lesson in trading.

Back inside, Mama had taken out a cloth bundle tied with ribbon. Inside was a pair of scissors and needles and threads in different colours tied up in hanks. The cloth was an unfinished piece of embroidery of flowers and leaves.

She smoothed it out.

'Will you finish it, Mama?'

'No, it will take too long and I must earn more money. What we have won't last us long.' I didn't understand, but I didn't know what question to ask. She stared at the embroidery and played with the threads. The she got up and asked me to stand so she could open the box. She took out a dress and a chemise, laid them on the floor and gazed at them.

'I can make clothes for children,' she said, and I remembered her cutting out the dress I have on and sewing it with Beatrice. 'I can sell them and I can buy old clothes to cut up too. We are in a shop after all!'

I thought we were in a house.

Mistress Pietro came in at the end of that first week to see how we were. Mama was finishing a dress for a small girl.

'That's very fine work.' She shifted her hips: she was fat. Mama moved onto the floor so she could sit on the box. 'But too small for Cecilia?'

Mama told her of her plan to make small clothes and sell them. Mistress Pietro frowned.

'How long does it take you to make such a dress?'

'A week.'

'Then you should make something even smaller, and quicker, like baby clothes.'

Mama looked at her; it was a new idea.

'I will need such clothes soon, and so will all young women. Why don't you make me a baby shift?'

It took Mama less than a day to make a tiny shift and take it to Mistress Pietro, who paid her, ordered three more and said she would tell her friends about Mama. She also told her about the second-hand clothes shop at the other end of the road.

'It's run by Samuel; he's an honest man and won't cheat you.'

Looking at the remains of the chemise, Mama realised that she could cut more than one at the same time, then sew them so that they would all be ready together. She asked Mistress Pietro if Master Pietro could make her a table in exchange for the three shifts, a table not for eating but to display the clothes at the window. She then finished the first dress, and cut and sewed another two. I was taught to thread needles which I stuck in a tiny cushion so they were always ready for her. She sewed so much that her fingertips were pricked all over and she had callouses because she had left her thimble behind. Mistress Pietro came down one day with one, which made things better. Pietro made a sign to go outside with a picture of a needle and thread and scissors.

On the agreed day, Mama arranged the clothes in the window: two dresses, some shifts and small shirts and some caps. We stood outside, Mistress Pietro and I, to watch Mama lift the shutter to show the clothes, then Pietro hung the sign up. Angelo, the butcher, and his wife came out to see, and his sons, and then the baker and his wife, the apothecary and her daughter, the wine-seller, and some pedlars.

'There's a thing,' said Angelo, standing with arms folded.

'What a pretty dress!' said the baker's wife and started to talk about it to Mama. The pedlar of threads and ribbons gave her a small piece tied in a bow for luck for us (and to ensure future sales).

'I've the best thread in Rome - none of yer rough stuff – strong.' He pulled a long thread several times to show it would not break. Mama nodded and took the bow. 'I'm here every Friday and if you want a special colour you have only to ask me, Pasquale.' He winked at her, and chucked me under the chin. I decided I didn't like him.

The wine-seller brought out a jug of wine for Pietro and Angelo, Pasquale the pedlar of gloves, who had just arrived, and others who had magically appeared, who all toasted Mama and the shop.

On the other side of the street, Giulio had joined Niccolò to watch the scene. People who had come to visit the baker and the butcher drifted across to see what was going on. Mama talked with them and Pietro handed out wine in small beakers, telling them that Mama was the best dressmaker in this part of Rome. Then he had an idea. He made up a new street cry which he taught to the boys and they ran off and could be heard making it into a sing-song: 'New dressmaker in the *Macello*! – new dressmaker in the *Macello*!' as they ran up and down the neighbourhood streets. Mama was so pleased with this that she gave them five *quattrini* each to carry on for the rest of the afternoon and all the next day. It was the next day that Mama made her first sale and took two orders for a dress, and Mistress Pietro asked her to call her Antonina.

~

I was making a second dark blue tassel when Giulio came down the street. Mama smiled and asked him where he'd been, he said, 'to The Column'. I said, 'Niccolò's bac,.' ad smiled. He glanced at me, surprised, then cheered up and went into the butcher's shop to find him.

I asked Mama about The Column, but she didn't know much about it, except that it was covered in carvings and was very, very old.

'Older than Giuseppe?' Giuseppe was the oldest person I knew. He had wrinkled skin and white hair and sat outside the baker's shop run by his son and his son's wife. Mama laughed.

'Much, much older.'

'Older than Giuseppe's father?' I couldn't really imagine Giuseppe's father, who must be dead. People got old and then they died. I knew what being dead meant because I saw my fathers' body, very white and still. He didn't breathe and didn't move when they took him out of the house. I watched him buried. He didn't try to get out when they started to pile earth on him. Mama said his soul had gone to heaven, but I was still puzzled as to which bit of him was his soul and how it could go anywhere without his legs. I knew that there was a strange thing called a skeleton in the painting in the church called Death, but I had never seen a live skeleton. I didn't understand the connection between my father and the skeleton. Perhaps I should ask God. I concentrated hard on asking the question of God. Nothing happened.

There was a commotion, and a dog come running out of the side of Angelo's shop pulling a large bone, followed by Angelo shouting, but the dog picked up the bone in its jaw and ran away. Angelo threw a stone after the dog, and said something I knew he shouldn't, and went back inside. Mama boiled bones for us for soup, and I was sorry that the dog had this one and we hadn't. Then I thought of the bone in the soup, which came out yellowy-creamy coloured and quite clean, and remembered it was a leg from an animal. My hand went to my leg and I felt – a bone! I felt my arms too and under my arms. I had bones everywhere under my skin; if I was boiled I would be like – the skeleton! I grinned. God did answer questions.

Giulio left the butcher's looking glum, went into the house and stomped up the stairs. So, Niccolò hadn't been interested. I was sorry I hadn't been nice to Giulio.

I worked on; a fourth, and fifth and sixth tassel, each one identical, each one the length from the tip of my thumbnail to the knuckle, each one with its own loop. Each one perfect with jealousy.

CHAPTER THREE

GIULIO

'I have to be at the Palace after noon, so we'll have time to go the long way first so you can see the sights, then come back another,' my father said as he ate breakfast.

I didn't want to eat, I was too excited, but my mother made me. Father went to fetch the mule and fixed pouches either side for his tools, food, and water bottles. We were ready. Mother came out to see us go and watched us go up the road.

The sky was pale mauve, still filled with stars, as Father took hold of the mule's bridle and we left the *Macello* and turned right onto the Great Road. Behind us was the hill of the Capitol and behind that the high walls of the Amphitheatre. We had once gone to see the Passion Plays, which made me have nightmares about the crucifixion for many nights. In front of us, the road led to the North, to the major parts of the city that pilgrims came to see, and where Father did most of his work as a plasterer.

Our way was through ruins. Some were low walls, some were high up on hills and, in the three-quarter dark, were big and menacing. Their colours of dark blue and purple with their tufts of weeds and shrubs made them into strange hairy shapes looming over me. There were trees too, dense, tall, and black, which sighed and gave off incense when we brushed past them. Some trees were more fragile; grey and black, with dark vermilion clumps of leaves hanging as if asleep. Some had leaves of dark green and olive. As the sky lightened, these became bright green, and sang as the edge of the world gained a cream, then pink, then yellow glow. The mule stopped to give a loud bray in worship of the rising orange sun-god. It twitched its ears back and forth as it located invisible tweets and trills. Father grinned and slapped its haunch and the sun suddenly warmed our backs. A light, light blue spread over us and the ruins changed their colours into ochres, white and green, and became less intimidating, but still big. We passed between mounds with bricks scattered over them and great round pillars on their sides. Goats clambered onto walls to get at the shrubs on top, and sheep nibbled at the bases.

The ruins became part of houses. And houses became parts of arches, two, three, four storeys high with shops underneath, opening up for the morning trade. Churches, their bells ringing, were either squashed in with entrances between the shops, or took up a whole side of a square. Everything was on a bigger scale than in the *Macello*, except the narrow roads, piled with rubbish smelling of rotting food and dung. Suddenly we were in a queue of travellers, going both ways and being jostled about. Father kept the mule steady and it was us doing a lot of the jostling. There was a tremendous noise of shouting and scuffling, and shrieks when the contents of a water (or worse) pot came down from the high-up windows. I kept as close as I could to the mule's side, holding onto its reins and Father's belt, pretending not to be scared, which I was. My stomach held in, not so much to get through as in fear.

We entered a wider space, with even more people and men in monk's habit coming from a church with a ruined – or half-built – façade. In front of us was an enormous building with arch shapes in curved walls. I looked up as we passed round it; it seemed to have a rounded roof. We went to the front of the building where there was a large space with a fountain and water troughs. We stopped so the mule could drink and Father could fill the water bottles for us. I breathed out and was stilled by the sight of the front of the building. Jutting out from the building, which turned out to be completely round, was another rectangle with pillars holding up a triangle-shaped roof over high closed doors. The pillars were as high as the Great Column at the end of our street, surely? I stood beside the square base of one, and found that it, just the base, was taller than me, and I had to drop my head right back to see the top of the pillar and the inside of the roof. As I did, my mouth dropped open, and I heard my father say, 'It was built by Emperor Marcus Aurelius – it's says so in letters across over the top - "It's a church now – St Mary and all the Martyrs - but people still call it the Pantheon – Temple of All the Gods. You're standing in the entrance – it's called a portico. You've to get used to the proper words soon.'

I was overwhelmed. By the size, by the number of pillars, by the great doors, battered and scarred. Giants had surely lived here. I could see them passing between the pillars and crashing open the doors. This, and the ruins we had passed, gave me the idea that the ancient Romans *were* giants, at least three times our height or more. I was glad the doors were shut as I thought that I wouldn't be brave enough to enter in case the whole thing should fall on me. I turned round and round, staring.

'We must go.' Father took the mule's rein and I walked backwards into the square bumping into people who shouted until he turned me round and we left that wondrous building. I was silent as we walked and then, as if the Pantheon was not enough, another great mass appeared in front of me, and as we got near to it, water, seen moving slowly. The River Tiber. I know I told Ceci it was lots of water, and it was. Lots of water, a wide stretch with a road over it: the bridge.

I stood on this bridge and didn't know whether to watch the water flow beneath it, a boat further upstream, or to gaze at the mighty building, made for the burial of an Emperor. A tomb? Not a bit as I had imagined it, a stone box just big enough for a man. Or perhaps smaller. I'd seen them dug up from the ground, the bones tipped out and then used as water troughs. Sarcophagi. Some quite small really. This tomb was bigger than most of the churches we had passed. knew about Ancient Romans, but I hadn't known they were giants, and the Emperor must have been even bigger. No-one had told me that. The sarcophagi must have been for Roman children. I thought I sounded like Ceci. Not a good thing.

'It's called the *Castello Sant'Angelo* now - your Grandfather worked with the architect Benedetto da Sangallo on the fortifications ordered by Pope Alexander after he was elected - around the time you were born. I was his apprentice then, I plastered some of the inside rooms', said my Father, as we finally crossed the bridge and walked past it.

We went through more streets, houses either side, the Borgo. Then we were in a square, *Piazza San Pietro*: St Peter's Square. Where St Peter had been killed. We stopped in front of a row of buildings and Father explained what they all were. 'The blocky building to our right. 'He gestured to it. 'The Papal Palace, where I persuaded your Grandfather to let me help with the plastering, so I could work with the painters. The chief painter was a man called Pinturicchio - up in Siena now I think. I learned a lot from him. I wanted...' He paused. 'Long time ago. Painters have plastering done by their own apprentices now...' He shook himself and looked at me. 'Besides, there's more money in masonry - when there's work - and you're paid. It's what I've come to see about - the money I'm owed and more work.'

He turned to point to three sets of arches, each set immediately on top of the other. A triple *loggia*.

'That's where the Pope stands to bless the people. Your grandfather, Filippo, helped to build it as a young man.'

My Grandfather had done a lot of important things: he'd built this beautiful building. I had had no idea, no idea at all, that he'd built something so holy, that pilgrims came to see it.

I remembered him as a small man, muscular, who didn't talk much. He would ruffle my hair, divide an apple for us to share. That's all I remember. He died when I was four or five. It was a family story that he had come from Florence in search of an architect, and found a wife, my Grandmother, which was why my father and I were born Roman.

'And next to it is the entrance to the Basilica.'

'Where St Peter was crucified', I whispered, even more in awe, to be so near the place where it had happened.

'We'll have a look inside, if we've time – we'll have something to eat now.' The mule drank at the fountain in the centre of the square as I stared up at the buildings at the top of the flight of steps in front of me. To be a builder of such as these would be something. We found a shady spot and sat on the ground to eat.

'The Basilica has been there for 700 years.' He bit into his pie. I tried to let that number sink in. It wouldn't.

'It's crumbling, you know, the Basilica. The man who designed the *loggia* said that the Basilica walls were some six feet out of true, and that the building would fall down one day.' I was horrified.

'Who said that?'

'Man called Leon Battista Alberti – the architect your Grandfather was looking for when he came to Rome. He wrote a book.'

'What about?'

'Making buildings.'

'So they don't fall down?' I still sounded like Ceci.

He grinned.

'Well the *loggia*'s still standing.'

'That's because Grandfather built it!' I grinned too.

We watched groups of people – pilgrims – standing about looking, going through the entrance to the basilica.

'And over there, behind the Palace'- he gestured to the blocky building 'although you can't see it from here, is the Belvedere, where your grandfather and I did the plastering for the painter Mantegna in the little chapel and the walls of the *loggia*.'

'It's why I've brought you with me today.' I stopped munching fruit: his tone was grave. 'I wanted you to see where I have worked, where your Grandfather worked. I want you to see yourself as the next in a line of craftsmen. You will become my apprentice.'

This was serious.

'It's time, Giulio, now you've learnt your numbers and your letters at school, you're ready to start work.' It made me tingle. He got up.

'Now you take care of the mule while I go over to the Palace.' He walked up the steps and through the archway between the *loggia* and the Palace building. The mule stood in the shade next to me, snorting and tossing its head against the flies. The sun lit up the façade of the *loggia*, emphasising the pattern of the arches with columns between them. As I sat on the steps of the fountain, the midday bell started, the sound coming from behind the Basilica entrance. Groups of people crossed themselves, some knelt in prayer, some passed through the entrance. The sign for prayer, and for shops to close until the heat had passed.

I felt my fingers twitch: I wished I had charcoal between them. They wanted to draw. I felt my hand lift and follow the line of the buildings in front of me. I knew then, without any doubt, that my fingers would remember what my eye could see and I drew. As I drew, I saw it better; I saw the detail my eye had only passed over before. The shapes grew beneath my fingers. I noted how the shadows were made, even in full sun, where decorations came out from the flat surface, where they made black hole of the arches. I noted how the building, the steps had lines, thick and thin lines, strong, confident lies and small, delicate lines. I drew in the air and 'saw' a twin picture. I must have looked like a simple boy waving his hand about.

The sun was beating down; it was almost over my head. I had to keep this picture. I drew it again and again, quickly, more quickly. I sucked the colours into my mind, for there were colours in the stone; yellow, sand, mud, grey, white, black, purple, gold. I shut my eyes and dropped my hand to my knee: the picture was still there.

'Are you alright, my son?' I blinked. A monk. 'I've been watching you, you've been behaving strangely.'

I laughed.

'Yes, I'm alright, Father.' I jumped up. 'I'm waiting for my father, he's at the Palace.' He looked doubtful, shook his head, muttered, 'sunstroke'.

'Why not drink some water?' he said. I agreed I would and he watched me as I took out a water bottle and did so. Then he made the sign of the cross and left.

I closed my eyes, the picture sat in front of me still. Holding the rein in my hand, I slept.

I woke when the mule stirred and brayed. My father was coming towards us, looking stern. He grasped the reins.

'No time for the Basilica,' he said shortly. 'W'll go home.'

Alerted by his tone, I scrambled to my feet.

'Yes Father'.

The sun was behind the Basilica, and the shadows formed shapes on the steps and into the square. The drawing, if I made it then, would be different, with more dark masses, more purples and blacks. I wished I could stay. My father said nothing as we paused to drink at the fountain, then we made our way out of the square to the south. This was a different way home, along the West bank of the river.

For some reason we had to exit through one gate in the city wall and enter through another not very far off. The city walls poked out from the river like two large ears on a, well, a mule. The part between the ears was cultivated with vineyards and market gardens, with fruit trees, maize, melons and root vegetables. I heard Father mutter, 'perhaps this will calm me,' so I sensed his mood had nothing to do with me. I stayed quiet, but allowed myself to be happy, as I was going on the road between the gardens. I liked growing things and watching animals. Father knew the gardeners who were working near the stone walls at the track edge. He waved at them, and our pace slowed. One of the older ones stopped to chat and gave us each an apple fresh off the tree, and a dropped one half-eaten by wasps to the mule. I played with his pigs snuffling under the fruit trees while they talked about the Jubilee two years ago, and how much trouble the pilgrims caused in the gardens.

'We 'ad to keep watch all night, but we still got stuff taken,' the gardener told Father. 'They would sleep here and crap all over the place.' He sniffed. 'Pope's got a lot to answer for.'

He bought soft pears and a melon from him to take home, then we walked through another archway into the cluster of houses which formed the settlement of Settimiana. We passed by the shops, including the wine shops where banter was exchanged with the drinkers along the lines of 'it's a'right for some', 'no work then?' and crossed a bridge named for Pope Sixtus.

We dawdled on the bridge to watch the boats and the fishermen for a while. I was struck by the boat with a mast and furled sail which was being rowed downriver. My Father explained they rowed because they were aiming to dock on the East bank, where there were other boats, rocking gently. 'See the sail, rolled up at the top of the mast. They'll lower the sail when there's wind - the wind'll fill the sail. Look ahead, there's one.'

I gasped as I saw a boat far ahead with a sail like a sheet on a line, but with the ends tied down. It made a curve which changed as they pulled into the centre of the river. I watched it move through the glints of sun on the water, water made of crystal and gold, belying the filth that flowed through it. The colours, the sky, the water, the clothes of the people flowing across the bridge, filled my mind. My Father, seeing the sun lowering, said, 'Come on' He had lost his sternness, but still looked unhappy. We both mounted the mule to continue at a faster pace through the ruins of the *Campo Vaccino*.

Walls of stone and brick had been picked over for the construction of shelters. Great arches, which looked to be half-buried deep, stood alongside mounds and piles of rubble over which the mule was more sure-footed than we would have been. Ruins, my father told me, that my Grandfather had contributed to in the past with limekilns set up to convert the stones, and especially the marbles, into material for mortar and plaster. So we lived off the creations of the past generations, the old consumed by the new. The work of craftsmen destroyed by craftsmen.

The remains were covered with vegetation and inhabited by the homeless, common prostitutes, thieves and bandits. They were there, singly, or in groups, eyeing up the travellers. Not necessarily to steal, though that too, but to sell the coins and small artefacts they found in the rubble to the pilgrims come to see the past, for they had once been an ancient meeting place of grand buildings.

'Sometimes, I buy good pieces and resell them to rich collectors,' Father told me, but nothing was offered that day. We crossed the lower region of grass, goats, sheep, and cows grazing, after which the field – *Campo Vaccino* – was named, watched by several herdsmen, and then we were home.

~

My mother asked if I had enjoyed my day, and I told her yes, very much. I wanted to tell her about my fingers, how they wanted to draw, but I also wanted to keep it to myself, it was such a big feeling. We sat down to eat, I was so tired, my head was drooping.

'You've worn him out, Pietro!'

'Yes, perhaps I have. He's seen so much today, haven't you?' I nodded, spooning up some stew. 'I'm afraid that after being in the Palace, I wasn't much company to you.'

'What happened?'

'Nothing. I wanted to see about the payment for the last contract, and when work would start again. Johannes Burchardus, the overseer, wasn't there, and his assistant didn't know when I'd be paid for that last lot of Jubilee work. I said it was nearly two years now. He just shrugged, said it had cost a lot and I wasn't the only one.' He chewed bread.

'And the rooms in the Pope's apartment won't be finished. All the work Pinturicchio left drawings for were done last year - he's been back at Siena three years now, working on a big project, and unlikely to come back.' So that was why he looked so unhappy.

'Is there no more work for the Pope?' He shook his head.

'No. Seems he's lost interest in building or decorating. That's why the painters, the good ones, have gone elsewhere - this isn't the time for Popes and Cardinals to stop having ideas!' He chewed again for a while.

'I saw Giuliano da Sangallo on the way out.' He was the Pope's architect.

'And?'

'He's done the plan for *Maria dell 'Anima* for the Germans, there may be work there and there's talk of the Cardinal Riario wanting a villa, but nothing more. I'll keep an ear open though, as I'll bid for the construction project and get a licence for a limekiln.'

'And will Master Giuliano aid you?'

He shrugged.

'The architect is likely to be this new fellow, Donato Bramante, come from Milan and Urbino. Seems Riario brought him here to do it. He's planning to build something up at San Pietro in Montorio, I've heard. I'll see if he wants help on that.'

I felt unhappy because he was not working, but what I wanted to do was draw that picture, on my wall, before I forgot it.

'So you get off starting to work for a bit, but you can still go on with abacus school. I'll arrange with Fra Bartolomeo - improve your reading and writing all to the good.'

I nodded.

'Perhaps I could take you to the limekiln, to see how mortar and plaster is made.'

Mama protested about the limekiln - it was the hottest month of the year, the place was full of ghosts, the fumes would hurt my throat...

I knew that when the wind blew from the *Campo Vaccino* to our house I felt a scratch in my throat which didn't clear with coughing. I knew that the scratching got worse the nearer I got to the *Campo*, near to where the stones of the old buildings were crushed and burnt in an old building turned into a kiln. I thought, for the first time, that perhaps it was the scratching that made Father's voice so rough and was why he coughed a lot of the time. I didn't tell them that I had already got quite close to the limekiln in my forays to look at ruins and knew how it affected my throat, making it sour and dry. I had been forbidden to go under the arch dug out from the mound of rubble and earth as a cover at the back of our house because of the stored lime and mixed plaster there. A stricture strengthened by the fact that everyone who lived around us avoided that arch as an evil place.

'He must know how things are done, soonest learnt, better for him.'

'It's all right Mama, I want to go.'

My mother looked at me without her usual smile and I saw an expression I didn't understand. My father said, 'that's good, then we go,' and to her, 'he's no child now – it's time'.

My mother, without looking at him, got to her feet and started to clear the table.

I yawned.

'Off to bed, Sunday tomorrow,' said my Father.

~

There was enough light in my attic room to allow me to wipe the wall clean of cats, brushing away the charcoal marks, making a pale grey surface.

I held a charcoal stick in my hand, and shut my eyes to concentrate on bringing the image back to my mind. I started to draw. I drew until the light had gone and I could see no more. I couldn't see what I had done.

The next day, when I opened my eyes it was to see the light through the window shining on a half-finished picture, the Basilica entrance, part of the *loggia*. It was waiting for me to finish it.

As I drew, I understood how the arches of the *loggia* stood on top of each other. I saw the differences between it and the building either side. I saw how the Palace was at an angle to these buildings. I remembered how I could see the wall on my right looking angled, even though I was sure it was built straight on. I didn't understand that, but I drew it as I remembered.

I sat back, frustrated. I couldn't do it! It wasn't right! I heard

Mother calling up the stairs saying she would put the breakfast away if I didn't go down. I shouted that I wasn't hungry.

'Then get dressed for church!' she shouted back.

I didn't know then about perspective, and all the other techniques that later on became second-nature. I just knew it was wrong. The joy stopped, that joy I had when I saw the picture for the first time had gone. The light had shifted right away from the window and, apart from the wall being wrong, the drawing was dull, grey, black. It wasn't what I saw in my head. It wanted colour; I wanted colour. I was saddened in a way I had not had felt before.

Yet, I had been absorbed in the drawing, enjoyed the physical act of drawing, the feeling of the charcoal, the act of touching it to the wall. I observed the slight difference in pressure needed to make the lines of a different thickness, without breaking the charcoal. My former drawings of cats and faces had just been simple outlines. This was different. I realised then that the light from the window had been important to how the drawing looked - but surely in a good drawing that wouldn't matter? I was dissatisfied. I wanted to be better.

Mother was calling me again, it was time to go to church.

CHAPTER FOUR

CECI

We used to go to the little church on our road, but that was being pulled down to begin a new one. We went then with Giulio, Master and Mistress Pietro to Santa Maria dei Aracoeli on top of the Capitol, the hill behind our street. I liked it there. The priest wore more colourful clothes than the one in the little church, and there were boys to carry the cross and hand the priest things when he wanted them. I liked listening to the melody of long lines of strange words called 'Latin', and looking at the faded pictures on the wall. People with names: lots of names beginning with Saint (which must be the Latin for Signor); a woman (the only one) called the Madonna or Our Lady, a man called Joseph and a baby called Yesu. Then there was someone called Kyrie Eleison and the man hanging from a cross was called Christus.

I had learned when to bob up and down, when to make crosses over my body, when to say 'amen'. I would try not to cough when clouds of smoke, which smelled like cypress trees, drifted over my face and made the whole thing totally mysterious and lovely in the dim candlelight. I liked it because Giulio walked next to me on the way there and on the way back, although we were separated inside because the women went to the back behind the men. Which is why we didn't see much of what went on at the front, and especially when the priest went behind the screen. Mama said it was a special act when the Priest turned a cup of wine into blood with a lot of words – a magic spell I suppose. I didn't know why they had to do that; they could have got a cupful of blood from Angelo. Bells sounded when this happened, otherwise, we wouldn't have known it had. The bells made us all go silent and make crosses wildly over our bodies, and be very solemn. The blood was supposed to be from the man on the cross. I used to watch to see if blood flowed from him, to be collected into a cup, but I stopped doing that and just accepted that it had happened. I had stopped trying to work this one out, but why the priest was drinking the blood of a dead man, the son of God, I still wasn't sure. It was beyond me: another question in my long list to ask God when I met him.

~

It was one of those things you accept in the end. Church was something you did, without thought, alongside everyone else. I did not properly connect Yesu as the baby Jesus, and that he and Christus were the same person until I stood in front of Michelangelo's Pietà in St Peter's. Mary holds her adult son in her lap; the sculptor had made her larger than him so that she can contain him completely within her whole bowed body. Her face is silent: she knows that what the angel told her about Jesus being the Son of God and a King is a lie. She will never speak again.

~

On that Sunday, Giulio trailed behind us and was told off for being slow. He didn't talk to us either, and was then told off for being 'rude to our neighbours'. Master Pietro told him to 'smarten up' and frowned at him. After church, when the men went off to the tavern, he walked in front of us scuffling his feet in the dust. Mistress Pietro told Mama that he'd got up late, had no breakfast, said nothing about his day out, and she feared he was sickening for something.

When we got home, I went straight to the back of our house to look at the kittens I had found yesterday. There were four of them, little scraps inside their mother's legs, sucking. She looked at me and twitched her tail. I sat a little way off to watch them. I hadn't been so close to kittens before. The cat watched me all the time as the kittens finished feeding then curled up together and her tail went round them, her head dipped to meet the end of the tail, so they looked just like one large furry lump. She kept her eyes half-open, slits of light, on me, so I thought I should leave them so she could sleep too. I went into the house to get some water, picked up an apple and heard voices raised upstairs. Pietro shouting at Giulio, Giulio not saying anything, Antonina sounding angry, Pietro thudding downstairs. Then Giulio sulking downstairs. I went into the street to eat the apple and to find out what was going on.

Giulio was sitting outside on the stone sill, eyes on the ground. I sat down beside him.

'Hello,' he said, not looking at me. I was encouraged.

'Hello.'

We sat. His black hair flopped over his eyes and I couldn't see them properly.

'What happened?'

'Father got angry with me. Then I got angry, then my mother got angry and sent me outside.'

'No – why?'

He shrugged.

'Oh. I don't know.'

'You don't know? What sort of answer is that?' I bit into the apple.

'I couldn't tell them - what happened – I wanted to, but I couldn't.'

'What happened? When?'

'The day before.' He didn't answer the 'what?'

I pressed on.

'You went to see the Pope, to see St Peter, you told me!'

'I didn't see the Pope, I didn't see St Peter – well, I saw his basilica. And I saw these huge buildings.'

He waved a hand high in the air, then looked at me for the first time.

'Did you know the old Romans were giants?'

I shook my head.

'How do you know?'

'The size of the buildings, the doors, tall as a house.'

I looked across the road, tried to imagine the door the height of the house, then the house around it. My eyes lifted upwards.

'The house must have been huge.'

'It was – but it wasn't a house it was…' he hesitated. 'I don't know, it was a round building, like the amphitheatre, but whole.'

I had seen the amphitheatre walls far off down the road, high with pieces broken off, mostly concealed by houses. But I didn't know it was round.

'Father said it was called the Pantheon, a temple for all the gods.' The apple stopped halfway to my mouth.

'I thought there was only one God?' Had I missed something important?

'There is – now. In the old times, ancient Rome, when all the ruins were whole buildings, they believed in lots of gods.'

'Why?'

Giulio shifted, and shrugged. *He didn't know…*

'I saw the Papal Palace, and the Basilica - the entrance to it, and the *loggia*.'

'What's a basilica? what's a *loggia*?' I said with my mouth full.

'Buildings – like…' he stopped. 'I'll show you. - come with me.'

He got up and led me back into the house. We went up the stairs past their apartment to the attic. I hadn't been there before. I stood in the doorway; a window in front of me, a bed on one side, and on the other side - I stared, apple to mouth, teeth caught in the flesh.

'Come in'

We stood facing a wall with a picture on it. My eyes fixed on it, chewing, as he pointed to each part in turn, telling me what it was. I listened and looked.

I swallowed.

'You drew this?'

I had only ever drawn shapes with white chalk in a piece of cloth, to cut out the pieces for Mama to sew into clothes.

'All of this?'

'Last night and this morning. It's what I saw.'

I had to sit down on the bed, mouth open, the apple clutched in my fingers, forgotten. Giulio picked up a stump of black stick, turned to the wall and, where there was a space, used the stick to make marks on the wall. Marks which turned into a picture of pillars, a triangular roof with doors under it. He made lines either side to show that the building behind was wider and taller, and had a curved roof. I gaped. It was magic, that Giulio could make this happen.

''s'what I was telling you. The giants' house.'

He drew a tiny person at the base of the pillar.

'That's me.'

He stood back.

'Words, I couldn't do it in words, I have to draw.'

I looked at what he had just done. He was right, I hadn't understood the building with the big doors when he'd tried to tell me. Now I could see it. Giulio had made lines which showed it to me. I was more impressed by that than the actual building.

'Do some more, make another,' I urged.

He started again. The lines made ears, a body legs, a mule! I laughed!

'I'll draw you.'

It appeared – a face, with curly hair.

'You!' he said.

'Me?' I didn't know what I looked like. I got up, touched the picture. 'Me?' He laughed. My finger had black on it, there was a smudge over the eye.

'It comes off!'

'Yes, it has to be fixed. I don't know how.'

We stood back and looked at the wall.

'That's not all I don't know – this part, here, at the side – the drawing isn't right. It's a wall that should look as if it comes towards you, I can't get it.'

He sat next to me.

'When I was there, my fingers – they tingled – they moved – they wanted to draw. They want to draw now – real things, real people, things in my mind – they want to make pictures.'

'Like in the church?'

'Yes – no – they don't look like real people do they? There's no buildings, they just hang in air. I want to paint people as they are, as you see them in church – not all straight and stiff. I want to paint the sky, the trees, the clothes rich people wear. I want to make colours like mosaic colours - I don't know how to do that, Ceci!'

But he'd only just started – he'd have to practise. I'd been clumsy when I started to sew, and Mama told me to practise, and I would get better. I did. (but I still didn't like it much).

'My grandfather made those,' he told me, 'the one with three sets of arches, each one is called a *loggia* – they are corridors open to the air. The Pope appears in the arch to bless people. Look I'll draw him in.'

He did this with a few strokes, a curved shape with a face on top and a cone on top of that. I was amazed.

'He's so small!'

'Yes, the little Pope shows how big the *loggia* is.' I frowned.

Then I remembered looking down the street and watching people walk up towards me. How they got bigger until they stood over me. I hadn't thought about it before. Was this the same? No. Because the drawing was on a wall, like the pictures in church. Some of the Saints were smaller than others. Why? I was about to ask a question, but Giulio started taking again.

'Father makes buildings, then inside, the walls get decorated. Plaster is put on the walls and painters put colours on it – he's told me. I can't remember how - the colours they use – the paints - but I haven't seen any. I don't know what they are - I'm sure he told me - why didn't I listen when he told me?'

He was rambling, talking to himself, not to me.

'The people that use them, that's why they're called painters -'.

He stopped.

It seemed simple to me. I always asked Mama if I wanted to know something, and if she didn't know, I'd ask God (not that he ever answered).

'Why don't you ask your father to tell you again?'

But Giulio didn't ask questions, and I wasn't sure he listened to me when I was telling him something I'd found out. He was usually making marks in the dust with a stick, drawing, I now realised.

'He'll tell you - he might even get you some.'

He didn't answer. He was very still.

I shuffled my bottom on the bed. I realised then what my mother meant when she said 'it's like getting blood out of a stone' (easier to get it out of wine…) I tried again.

'So you can draw.' I pointed to the wall.' But you can't paint?'

He stared at me now. His eyes dropped slightly down at their outer edges - I hadn't noticed it before. I was beginning to be uncomfortable, and cross, and the unfinished apple was now brown. I'll try one more time……

'And that's what you want to do?'

'No, Ceci. It's what I want to *be*. I want to *be* a painter.'

His eyes were wide open. The hot air hummed. Solemn. Like that moment in the Mass, when the priest held up the cup, and the wine turned to blood – he had said something important, but I didn't know what it was.

'What if I'm not good enough - I don't know– what if I'm never good enough.'

He was scared. I'd never seen him scared before. I was lost. I didn't know the difference between wanting to *do* something and wanting to *be* something. Except that it was important enough to make Giulio scared.

We heard footsteps, Mistress Antonina. I got up.

'Tell them, Giulio' I said. *'Be a painter' I thought, 'make this drawing coloured like the pictures in the church.*

She came in. She looked at me, then at the wall.

'Giulio did it,' I said, and left the room.

~

Downstairs, Mama was smoothing out a skirt she had unpicked from a dress with a hot iron. She had made pattern pieces from a coarse cloth which she used all the time to pin on to the better cloth. I was learning how to pin this pattern for her, and was waiting until she thought I was old enough to use the big scissors to cut the pieces out. I picked up these scissors – they were still too heavy for me. She put down the iron, placed the material on the table and the pattern pieces on top. I held the little cushion of pins and handed them to her one at a time. As we worked I told her about Giulio, and the journey, and the drawings.

'He says he wants to be a painter.'

She put two pins into the top of a sleeve.

'Antonina once told me that Pietro wanted to be a painter, but he wasn't good enough.'

'How did he know?'

'Someone told him – a famous painter - Someone he admired.'

She put a pin between her lips to adjust the material. It was a dull pink, with little raised flowers. She liked to make sure the flowers when seen were whole. Her next words were spoken over the pin.

'I can't remember his name - Antonina did tell me.'

'And then?'

The lips were released.

'Then he just went on working with his father.'

The man who had built the *loggias*.

'And with the painters?'

'I expect so.'

'But what if the painter wasn't right?'

She shrugged.

'He trusted the painter I suppose.'

Another pin between the lips.

'Or he just knew the painter was telling him the truth.'

I knew then why Giulio was afraid.

CHAPTER FIVE

GIULIO

I was watching Mother prepare vegetables when we heard my father come back. I didn't look at him. She put down her knife.

'I've something to show you.'

She took my father's hand and led him up the stairs. I followed slowly. I leaned on the door post and looked at them both. They weren't saying anything; he was looking at the wall, she was looking at him.

'This wall here… 'he pointed 'it's not right. Pass me the charcoal.'

I quickly gave it to him. He leaned forward. He drew.

Where I had the top of the wall and the bottom in lines both drooping downwards, he changed the top to one which went upwards, so they were diverging. The lines stopped at a point one above the other; he joined them vertically. That was all. The wall came towards me, just as it had in reality.

'It's an illusion, called perspective – the way you translate what you see, which is three-dimensional, to the wall or the paper which is flat – two-dimensional.'

He was using words that he would use to a grown-up. I wasn't sure I understood the words, but I understood what he had drawn.

'You see, if something is actually far away, you make it small, something near, it's large. If it's a wall coming towards you, the end nearest you is taller than the end further away, its top is higher than at the start, the bottom is lower. It's to do with the way you draw things to seem real. The way you make space in a picture, the way the hand makes the illusion of space.'

I stowed away those last words – I liked the sound of them – 'the illusion of space' even if I didn't understand them then.

He sat on the bed.

'You think of the old pictures; the way everyone is in a line – it's called being on the same plane.'

He drew his hand across the air in front of him. 'A hundred years ago – less – a painter called Masaccio painted pictures differently. He started off like the old paintings, but then, he made a picture of the Holy Trinity which had Christ on a cross behind an arch, with God behind him. These were against a vault which went backwards, becoming smaller as it receded so it gave an illusion of reality. That's perspective.'

'You've seen it – the painting?'

'I went there when I was young with a friend – It showed me why I couldn't be a painter.'

He stared into the air. As if seeing the painting. I almost expected him to raise his hands and to draw as I had done. But he didn't.

'The painting - it's in Florence – in the church of Santa Maria Novella. He painted it in his late twenties, a year or so before he died – he was only 27 years old.'

He paused, and shifted his stance.

'Then we went to the Duomo to see the dome made by an architect called Brunelleschi. The dome! That is something wondrous! It can never be repeated. It's said that perspective in drawing and painting was invented by Brunelleschi, who made the dome. Masaccio would have known him.'

I hadn't ever heard him talk like this before. Of course

he must have talked about painters before, but I just hadn't heard. Now they were magic: Brunelleschi, Masaccio, and the ones he'd spoken about in St Peter's Square. Mantegna, Pinturicchio. The names sang together, they had a rhythm, a melody, like a prayer chant. Perhaps if I repeated them enough - He got up to look at the drawing again

'Your lines and your shading, they are good. Your observation, yes, it is what you saw.' He stroked his beard, a habit when he was thinking. I waited.

'You need to draw some more.' That was all he said.

It was enough – for now.

'Let's go and eat.'

My Mother smiled. As they went down the stairs with me following, I heard her say, 'it's a long time since you talked like that, husband.'

~

The next day, when Father came home, he dropped his pouch on the table and reached inside.

'Here.'

He took out a dried chicken carcass, too dry to use for soup.

'What's that for?'

'Wait and see.'

He took out three smooth wooden panels about eight *onzie* by twelve *onzie*[1] and a small bunch of silver wires. I picked up a panel and smoothed my hand across it. It was fine close-grained wood. 'It's made of box, nice and smooth and dense - for painters to work on.' My heart speeded up.

'For you to draw on – properly, with a metalpoint.'

He indicated the wires, and I saw that there were six, three

1 1 *onzia* roughly equivalent to an inch

pairs of different widths. 'You draw on the panel with these.' Pietro took up one of the wires, and passed it into a tube made from a bird's feather's quill until it is stuck fast with only its top showing. He put it in my hand.

'And the chicken?' Antonina asked, stirring the stewpot, although her voice told me she knew.

'Ah yes the chicken. No - hold it like this – that's right. You see, you have to prepare the panel. If you draw straight into the wood, you either won't make any mark or you will scratch a hole in it, then you can't use it again. So you need to make a surface for the point to make lines on. And when you've finished, you can scratch off the surface and the drawing and make another one.'

'But that means you lose the drawing!'

'You'll be glad to lose the drawing because you'll be dissatisfied. That's how apprentices work - you need to see your mistakes and learn from them. When you can draw well, you can use paper, but this way, you save on the paper.'

Antonina was cutting bread.

'But you still haven't told us about the chicken – or do we wait until after we've eaten?'

Father took up the chicken carcass, pulled off the wings and threw them onto the fire.

'The stew can wait – if you can?' said Mother. He grinned.

I was surprised: having given me the metalpoints he was now going to make charcoal?

'We burn the bones to make them into bone ash - like this' he pulled out a scrap of cloth inside which there was a pile of powder and bits of bone.

'This makes a surface, for the panel, that you can scratch lines on.'

He produced a small smooth slab of stone and half a large pebble, with one flat side and the rest rounded to fit the hand.

He placed the stone on top to grind the ash down. There was a cracking as the tiny pieces rolled together and were flattened against each other, then a rasping as these pieces became tiny morsels the size of sand, then softer continuous sounds as the whole is melded into a very fine powder like flour. He then made it damp with spittle, and wiped the substance across the panel making a smooth covering.

'I'll show you later how to make rabbit glue from the skin to mix with the bone, but this is a start for you.'

Father prepared the first panel himself, then, leaving it to dry, he passed the grinding stone to me. I grasped the stone in both hands, struggled at first, the stone slid about.

'I can't do it!'

'You will – a little every day and you'll build up your strength, and then you'll have the way of doing it - and you'll be ready to grind materials to make paints.'

'Make paints?' My eyes widened. Mother fetched a pot with a lid to store the powder in.

'There – you can keep it in your room, and fill it up every time we have chicken'

I touched the prepared panel.

'Not yet – a couple of hours to dry first.'

'Oh!'

'We'll eat now.'

I sat spooning stew into my mouth and chewing bread, very fast, as if by doing so I could speed up the chicken process. I was finished long before my parents and watched the fire and the carcass, anxious lest it burn away.

Father decided that the bones were ready when they had stopped crackling he pulled them out and put then on the table. Then he finished his meal.

Mother cleared the bowls away, and Father fetched a small hammer tapped the bones, and they fell into pieces.

'Go on, grind!'

I started – the bones crackled and split beneath the grinding stone. Father started to sing and I fell into the rhythm of the tune and thence into the knack of the grind. After a while my hands were aching. Mother inspected them.

'Hm – blisters.'

'He must do this every day to get hardened.'

'Yes but today, enough!'

I picked up the metalpoint and pressed it against my fingers, making a tiny imprint on my skin, then I tried the other wires, making a small imprint, then quite a dent.

'They're for different lines,' explained Father. 'You make the drawing out of different width lines, and cross the lines over each other to make darker patches. It's called cross-hatching.'

He demonstrated this on the table with his little finger, and I watched him making invisible marks: left to right, upwards and then downwards, crossing diagonally, and I imagined the lines piling up one on top of the other.

Then he picked up his pouch and produced the last item. It was a panel with a drawing on it already, of a young man, drawing with his head down. A man, drawing a man, drawing. I gasped.

'This was done by the older apprentices in the workshop at the Vatican, under Giuliano da Sangallo. This is what you might do one day.'

I was transfixed by the portrait, the delicacy of the hair: each single hair next to another. The face of a real person, made of lines. A single line to make the shape of the head, delicate lines to make the eyes, the nose, and the mouth. There were shadows to make the folds of his tunic: the cross-hatching Pietro had demonstrated. Feather strokes made the form of the legs, one bent at the knee with its foot on the bench supporting the panel, the other on the floor. I could even see a little fold in the boy's hose make by the slightest of lines. Just a few stronger lines made the shoe on his foot. I held it in both hands, its base on the table, and looked and looked. I heard Mother say 'You've done a good thing, Pietro.'

He nodded.

'When the panel is dry you can start to copy this one. Apprentices always start by making copies of the master's drawings.'

I picked up the wire in the quill and held it over the panel, using it to follow the lines without touching. I tried to control the different strokes and angles, it was awkward.

'It'll take practice, that's why you start with a panel which you can re-use. When you're good enough to make real drawings, drawings that are kept, you'll use paper – like this.' He produced several pages of different sizes. 'Offcuts from a printer I know – don't waste it. Practise on the panels first.' I put down the panel and took the paper. Smooth, like flattened linen, but firm. I ran my fingers over it.

'Oh go on – draw something!' and he passed over some new charcoal. He arranged some fruits on the table. 'Draw these.'

The paper was smooth under my hand, it was flat on the table, not upright like a wall. My hand with the charcoal was not raised at an angle from my body, it was parallel to the table.

'Look at them first.'

I looked at an apple and then drew it from memory. Then I looked again and drew it without looking at the paper. I drew the outlines of the other fruits, looking up and down: at the fruits, at the paper. I drew shading: cross-hatch lines. The charcoal wouldn't do the fine line I wanted, not on this small area. I used a knife to sharpen the end, as if I knew what to do. They watched me.

Father looked over me. 'H'm.' He took some charcoal and

made a few strokes. They made the apple become round, and alive. I imitated what he did on the pear, and that lived too.

Over the next few days, my Mother had to chase me outdoors for air.

CHAPTER SIX

CECI

I would take bits of meat to the cat and the kittens. I watched them playing all over the back yard, except one. It stayed by the wall, frightened. The other kittens ignored it and pushed it away when I put food down. I tried to give it meat, holding the others away, and it ate, looking round all the time. I picked it up and stroked it, it trembled, its tongue came out a little way and I knew it was anxious. I petted it and gave it water on the palm of my hand, which it lapped, then settled against my arm. It was black and white and orange with big green eyes – like mine! When I put it down, it ran to a dark corner.

I was sad when they all disappeared. I looked round the yard but they'd gone – except - I heard mewing and there was the little one against the wall. I picked it up and took it inside and offered it milk on my finger. It lapped up and mewed for more.

'She's very pretty,' said Mama.

'Can we keep her? I can train her to catch mice.' She smiled.

'I don't think you'll have to train her. What will you call her?'

'Prettycat.'

She stayed and slept beside me and even though she would go outside, she always came back. Sometimes with a mouse.

Once, when she was older, she dragged a rat in and Mama had to take it out as I was scared of such a nasty thing.

It was because of Prettycat that my scratchy feeling for Giulio changed to adoration.

I was dozing outside with her in my lap, or so I thought, when I heard the shouts of boys.

'Go on! Get it!'

I opened my eyes and at the same time realized my lap was empty and across the street Prettycat was hissing, her tail up against the wall, and her fur standing out all over, making her twice her size. Three boys, including Niccolò, and his big brother Giorgio, were surrounding her with stones in their hands. One of them threw one as I scrabbled to my feet

'Stop it! Leave her alone!' I rushed forward. Giorgio caught me while another threw a stone which hit Prettycat who fell over. I screamed and struggled, I saw Niccolò go towards Prettycat.

'No!' I tried to bite Giorgio.

'No you don't, bitch!' he twisted my arm behind me.

Then a shout of 'leave it –leave her!' It was Giulio.

The boys stopped and I squirmed away and ran to Prettycat, knelt down and protected her with my skirt. I was sobbing.

'You've killed her.'

They protested. 'Only a bit of fun.' 'It's just a cat.' 'Come on, Giu'

'It's her cat.' said Giulio so sternly that they went away, even Giorgio who was older and much bigger than Giulio. He glowered as he went. Mama was in the doorway shading her eyes to see what was going on. Giulio picked up my cat.

'They've killed her!' I gulped. Mama ran to us, and took me in her arms. 'Oh. Ceci!'

'No, she's breathing,' he said, 'but her ear is split. I think she's just stunned.'

I pulled away from Mama and went to him. He carried her into the house, motioned me to sit down and put her gently onto my lap. Mama got a damp cloth and he cleaned Prettycat's ear. She stirred and mewed. I touched her gently.

'She'll be alright. Just wipe the blood away till she heals.' he said.

I took the cloth from him.

'Thank you,' I whispered. I adored Giulio unquestioningly from that moment on.

~

I also wanted to leave my bit of the *Macello*, to explore others places, find pretty stones and pieces of carved marble. I started by following Giulio, just so I could say I wasn't on my own, I was with someone. Besides, I wanted to see him draw, to see what he drew.

I heard him come down the stairs, and out the front door. I went to watch him around the door jamb. He had his pouch in which I knew were drawing panels, a water bottle and food. I stayed a little distance behind so he didn't see me, although I saw from his stride that he was only interested in where he was going. He went across the street and down the lane towards the *Campo Vaccino*[2], over the mound of rubble towards where the three pillars stood up.

We crossed away from the limekilns and towards three high arches with dirt gathered up the brickwork and plants growing from every crack. This was further than I had been before on my own, except that I wasn't on my own, was I? Giulio settled himself down in front of the arches and took out a hat to shade his eyes, a panel and a thin straight quill. Because of the

2 Now the Forum

slope up from the arches I could sit above him and although I couldn't see the panel, I could see him make marks. He didn't look at the panel much, he looked at the arches most of the time as his hand moved over it. It was as if his eyes were telling his hand what to do.

I wished I could do that with scissors, I had just started to use the big scissors. Mama had given me odd scraps, with shapes drawn on them with chalk, so I wouldn't spoil her cloth patterns. I had to look carefully at the shapes to get it right. I wondered, as I watched Giulio, that if the shape was on the wall and I looked at it rather than the fabric, whether my hand (and the scissors) would obey my eyes. I doubted it, and didn't fancy the telling off I would get for 'not concentrating'.

I looked at the arches and tried to draw them in the dust with my finger without looking down. When I did, all I could see were two arcs crossing each other, and a very wide gap between two arcs that should have been next to each other. I decided that I definitely wouldn't be trying this with scissors.

I crept down towards him a little more, and could just see the panel but not the picture. I inched to one side and then I could see it. It looked exactly like two of the arches in front of us, a smaller version. I looked up at the arches and then down to the picture. I thought of the tiny Pope, and tried to understand how Giulio had made the great arches so small that they fitted onto the panel. Also, I didn't think he had drawn any of the plants. As I squinted to see, I leaned forward and nudged a stone with my foot so that it rolled towards Giulio. I held my breath, but the stone stopped before it reached him and I breathed again. I watched as he made more marks and completed the third arch. He was so serious, so absorbed; he seemed to look much older.

He stopped to take out a water bottle.

'You must be thirsty, Ceci, why don't you come and sit next to me?' he said without looking round. I blushed and then, because I was thirsty, I scrambled down to do as he said. He handed me the water bottle and I drank, looking up at him over the lip of the bottle. Under his hat, his hair was very black and curly, with dark eyes under even darker eyebrows. He smiled, which gave me a funny feeling under my ribs.

'You'll get sunstroke without a hat.' He took a kerchief out of the pouch and gave it to me. I tied it over my head.

'I wanted to see where you were going.' I could have said how excited I was when we passed over the Great Road, and that I had felt such fear when we did. I could have said that if Giulio hadn't been there I would have turned and run back home. But I didn't say either of those things.

I said 'How do you make the arches fit onto the panel? How do you know how to make them small?'

Giulio looked at the arches and then at the panel.

'I've not thought about it – I just do it.'

'Would the arches be bigger if the panel was bigger?'

'Yes, they would.'

'And if you had a big piece of paper, ' I spread my hands wide - 'would you draw them the same size as they are?'

'It would have to be a very big piece of paper, bigger than the paper makers could make.' He laughed. I looked at the arches again. They towered over us.

'I can only see them all if I turn my head from side to side. But you weren't doing that.'

'My eyes move though.'

I make my eyes move.

'But when my eyes move to one side I can't see the other.'

Then I remembered seeing his picture with only two arches.

'You draw from side to side - a bit at a time.'

Giulio thought, and looked at the arches.

'No, my eyes move all the time.'

'Do it now – let me watch you.' So he turned the panel over and started to draw while I watched his eyes. Yes, they did move from side to side and he had started making the marks of the middle arch first.

I tried to imitate him but I couldn't watch his eyes and move mine at the same time.

I giggled.

'I've gone cross-eyed!'

I blinked and flicked my eyes even more. Giulio looked at me and imitated me, making his eyes wide and his eyebrows stand up. He started to giggle too and then we both fell over and tears were falling down my cheeks from my screwed up eyes and my tummy hurt as we both shrieked with laughter. The laughter ended in hiccups and tummy jumps, then we lay side by side looking at the sky, watching birds fly.

Giulio sat up and took food from the pouch.

'Here.'

We ate and later, after he had added the plants to the first picture, he put his things away.

'Let's see what we can find.'

He turned over some pieces of marble and showed me the patterns on them, explaining that they decorations, part of an old building.

'An antique – that means very old, built long ago by the Ancient Romans.' 'By the giants?'

'I don't think they were giants – they just liked building huge things! Some of the ancient ruins seem to be the remains of little houses, just the right size for us.'

I was a bit disappointed. I liked to imagine giants striding across the land.

'Sometimes you can find pieces with paint still on them, or if you're lucky, coins.'

'Will we find some here?'

'We might.' He put his drawings things away as I started to search, picking over earth and stones, which nibbled away at my fingernails, filling them with dirt. Then I yelped with excitement when I found several pieces with decorations carved on them.

'The pilgrims buy these as souvenirs.' Giulio said, taking them from me and examining them.

'D'you sell them?'

'No I keep them.'

'But you could sell them?' I was alert at the prospect of trading.

'I s'ppose. But I'm not sure I should…'

'Why?'

'Because I don't need too – I don't need the money – besides, it's how the poor folk who live in the ruins earn money for food.'

I turned the pieces over in my hand. Mama and I had to earn money for food.

'I just like looking at them and drawing them to see if I can add to the little pieces and make them into bigger pieces – see where they might fit onto a building…'

I had stopped listening.

'I could sell them in the shop – 'cept that pilgrims don't come into the shop. Or I could sell them at the end of the Macello on the Great Road.'

Giulio stared.

'You couldn't!'

'Why not?'

'You're a girl.'

'So? Women sell from door to door don't they?'

'You're not a woman, you're a girl, and you couldn't stand in the street - selling things! It wouldn't be right'.

There it was, because I was a girl, I couldn't do something.

'But you could –'

'Of course, I could, I …oh, no Ceci!'

'I could collect things while you draw, I'd sort them, you could stand up and sell them - they'd think we were brother and sister.'

He shook his head.

'That's what they'll see – a girl sorting things sitting on the floor, her brother talking and taking the money…' He shook his head.

'We should go home,' he said and started off. 'Come on.'

He sounded like a brother, telling me what to do, but I followed him.

After that, I often went with him. He drew, I found things. I made quite a collection. And I persuaded him.

We did sell them. At first I sat meekly on the ground, hair hidden under a large cap, eyes down, silently setting out the pieces in front of me. I rubbed my hands on my face, the dirt sticking onto my cheeks. The pilgrims would look at them, then at me, mutter 'poor child' take a piece and give Giulio some money. He was very surprised but after this happened a few times, he started to laugh.

'It's you – you sit looking so sweet and dirty and forlorn! They buy the pieces because of you.'

I grinned.

'You see I can sell without standing or saying a word!' I rubbed the dirt off my face. Still laughing, he shared the money.

My mother knew that I went out with Giulio, but I don't

know if she knew how far I went with him. I had heard her talking with Mistress Pietro, saying that she wished I could be friends with Isabella, a girl in the next block, who 'plays nicely' and didn't get dirty. I wasn't sure really what 'playing nicely' meant, but I didn't like the sound of it, as Isabella wouldn't come out to play at all – she said she would get her dress dirty. And she didn't seem curious about anything. Then Mama would sigh and Mistress Pietro would laugh and say that I was safe with Giulio, who wouldn't lead me astray as all he wanted to do was draw. They agreed we were like brother and sister. Mama said that it was alright as we were children, but it wouldn't be long before we couldn't be together anymore. Mistress Pietro nodded. And I wondered where Giulio was going, and when.

~

I crunched my skirts up like the washwomen to climb over the ruins, but they would catch on something and fall down. Sometimes I would trip over them, as I did that day, and ended up on the ground. 'Ouch!' a piece of sharp stone was sticking into me.

These skirts get in the way. I wish I were a boy.' Giulio pulled me up and looked me up and down as I brushed the back of my skirt.

'You could pass for one - if you had breeches!' He laughed.

'I could, couldn't I? I could wind up my hair under a cap.'

'A girl in boy's clothes? You'd be taken for a heathen.' He sat and started to draw me.

'Not if no-one knew.' I leaned against a broken wall and started to pick off the weeds.

'I could borrow breeches from you, we could hide them, I could change clothes out here.'

'Hmm.'

'Just think how much easier it would be – how much freer I would be. We could go further, I could search further.'

'Your mother would be horrified – all the women would be horrified. You'd end up in prison, or be whipped out of the city.'

Not if they didn't know.

'Please. Giulio.'

'No. Mother would notice if a pair of breeches had gone.'

I pulled out a while clump of weeds which dropped dirt and little stones down my dress.

'I wouldn't make my dresses so dirty.'

'Then your mother would know something was wrong… keep still.'

I glowered at him.

'There – that's what you'd look like.' He passed the paper to me. It was a boy, with my face, but a boy, leaning against a wall, looking cross.

'You'd have to cut your hair a bit.'

'I could push it up into a cap.' I was absorbed by the picture. I sat down as Giulio started another drawing, of the pillar this time. I had an idea.

'Giulio - you're growing – what happens to the clothes you grow out of?

'Mother keeps them – for the next son.'

'Where does she keep them?' He looked at me.

'No, Ceci - oh no, bad idea.'

'You don't want me to come with you.'

'Not like that! We'd both get into trouble.'

'Giulio, please.' He shook his head and went on drawing.

'It wouldn't just be breeches would it, you'd have to have a tunic, a shirt' he mumbled.

He was thinking about it. I kept quiet. I looked him from time to time, but he wouldn't look at me. I sighed. His eyes flicked towards me. I made my cat-pleading-for-food eyes.

'No!'

'No-one would know.'

'I would.'

'You told me you liked me coming with you because Niccolò wasn't interested and I was.'

'Only 'cause I couldn't stop you. Go away, Ceci, forget it.'

He really looked cross so I got up and left.

But I didn't forget it. I tried to think of how I could get some boys clothes. The washerwomen were eagle-eyed and knew every piece they washed, so I couldn't get any from them, and it would be stealing. Samuel – Mother always checked what we bought. I kept coming back to Giulio's mother and her stock of clothes…

~

I was working with Mama.

'Mama – why do women wear skirts and men wear breeches?'

She looked startled.

'I've never thought about it – they just do.'

'But why? In the old mosaics they both wear skirts.'

She paused.

'I hadn't thought of that – yes they do.'

'And now, the priest and the monks - they wear skirts. So, why can't we wear breeches?'

'It would be unseemly, we would be showing our legs. Soldiers couldn't wear skirts, men on horseback couldn't wear skirts.'

'The soldiers on the Column wear skirts…and women ride

horses - they ride mules, with both legs on one side – I've always thought that awkward. It would be easier in breeches.'

'Women are not men, Ceci, it's wrong to even think about it. It would be improper and against the law of God.'

I had heard that before, so much was deemed to be against the law of God.

'Why does God makes one law for girls and one for boys?'

She got cross. She always did when she couldn't answer the question, or she didn't want to discuss something. 'Ceci, hold your tongue! And don't let others hear your loose talk. Nor me either!'

I held my tongue. I was learning that there were things you could only talk about inside your head, where you couldn't find the answers to the questions anyway. I stored up all these things I couldn't answer, or talk to myself about, to ask, when I met God.

Once I had started thinking about what I could and couldn't do, the ideas wouldn't go away. But I knew better than to raise the subject again. Until...I was sitting there with pieces on the ground, not able to speak to or bargain with the pilgrims, listening to Giulio and getting annoyed.

'You let the last ones go too cheaply – you give up too soon.'

He didn't like me telling him off – I didn't do it often.

'I could get more – you know that, you've seen me with the customers in the shop.'

He sighed.

'Ceci, we've had this out before. You're not in the shop, we're on the road. If you stood up to sell they'd think you were selling something else.'

I knew what he meant but I wanted him to say it.

'What?'

'You know …'

'I don't.'

'Yes you do - they'd think you were a whore.'

'They wouldn't if I looked like a boy. We'd make more money.'

'Sometimes Ceci you're really, really annoying. Why can't you be like Isabella?'

Isabella - she had a smile that was like eating too much honey, and she would look up through her eyelashes. Except at me. She looked down her nose at me, eyeing my dirty skirt, and not speaking. Nasty prissy little thing. But everyone praised her. Even Mama once or twice had asked me why I couldn't be like her. I sighed.

I don't see you taking Isabella out with you, I thought but didn't say. I knew that the boys all thought she was wonderful and gazed at her with cow eyes. Even Giulio.

I'd rather be me.

'And we ought to move further down, towards the Amphitheatre, before the pilgrims meet the Campo sellers.' I grumbled.

Giulio just looked at me. I could read his mind. Yes I know. I couldn't be away from the *Macello* out of sight of Mama and the neighbours.

When we met again, nothing more was said. I'd given up. I was a girl.

CHAPTER SEVEN

GIULIO

A man came to talk with Father to offer him work in Sant'Onofrio in Trastevere.

'Painter called Baldassare Peruzzi, I haven't come across him, comes from Siena I think. He's not been here long – yet to establish a full workshop of his own – just the one apprentice - so it's a plastering job.' He looked pleased. He'd be working with a painter again. He's finishing the work – you remember, I did the repairs there and the plastering for Pinturicchio for the apse – Peruzzi's doing the frescos on the wall behind the altar. I'm off to meet him there tomorrow.'

I listened. A Painter. Please take me with you...

Mother gave Father his food.

'And Giulio, you can come with me – real painting!'

I woke before dawn with a sense of something new about to happen. I usually lay there trying to remember my dream, but that day I was up and pulling on clothes. I heard my father and mother and tripped over my feet in my urgent need to join them. I was afraid that my father might have forgotten he was taking me with him.

We went the way we had returned from *San Pietro*, over *the Ponte Sisto.* There were people everywhere, carts, mules, chickens. I wanted to stop and draw a mule with its load of kindling bush wood. I wanted to watch, and draw, an altercation between two clerics, whose voices rose in irritation with red faces and swift, vivid gestures. A church bell started to toll and the sky turned gold.

We went through the Porta Settimania and up an overgrown track to the church of Sant'Onofrio. Inside, some walls were painted, some were bare, but ahead of me was - I stopped. A vault, startling with gold and bright colours such as I had never seen. Such as I wanted to paint. Reds, blues, pinks, all shining as water in the sun, thrusting out above me, striking inside my head like trumpets and drums, like the noise of people at a festival. These were the paintings of Pinturicchio.

At the top a bearded man, God, and beneath him, angels playing instruments: a lute, pipes, a harp, viols. In the centre, angels were singing from a long sheet of paper. Perhaps they had paused between melodies: their mouths were closed. All of them were standing on clouds, against a background of gold.

Below the angels was Our Lady with her hands together looking down. God was holding a crown over her head, surrounded by cherubs and seraphim, with gold halos and a big gold light behind them. The painting was high as the sky, bright as the sky; dazzling as the sun. As dazzling as Heaven should be. I stretched my neck towards it. I forgot to breathe, I felt dizzy. I leaned against a pillar. I stared, I gazed: tears rose in my throat. I gulped.

'Giulio!'

I reluctantly changed my focus to my father who had reached two men kneeling in front of the apse. They weren't praying, they were examining large sheets of paper stretched out on the floor, talking and looking up at the bare walls below Heaven. One of them got up when we approached. He held out a hand to my Father.

'Baldassare Peruzzi,' he said, 'Pinturicchio recommended you.'

My father was pleased.

'Yes, I did this plastering for him here.'

He indicated the vault frescoes and shook the offered hand. The two of them, my father, recommended by one painter to another, were caught for a second as part of the representation of Heaven. The other man on the floor completed the composition, and I was the painter.

Peruzzi was about the same height as my father, but slighter in build. A face younger than Father's, with a wide smile, and long dark brown hair, reaching below his shoulders. He wore a paint-splashed scruffy tunic. The other man, still on the floor, was older, with greying hair cut to the end of his ears and a beard. The fingers on his left hand were curled over as he leaned on them on the floor. This did not alter when he raised the hand to sit upright. The first finger and thumb remained extended as if holding a beaker as his hand dropped into his lap, and I realised they were frozen like that. He glanced up, waved his right hand, which looked intact, and stretchy, and nodded.

'This is Perino, who will do the *cartone*.'

'My son, Giulio, it is his first day to work.'

Master Peruzzi smiled at me.

'You are very welcome, Giulio Pippi,' he said, and shook my hand.

This hadn't happened to me before, and I felt very grown-up, but shy of saying anything. Master Peruzzi turned to Father and I looked down to see that the pieces of paper were drawings, very detailed drawings. Master Peruzzi picked up a sheet, and showed it to my father.

'There are three large sections to be painted at the base of the wall. The subjects are the life of Mary.'

This paper showed the sections, with sketches of figures, but I could see that the one on the floor was a detailed drawing of the central sketch. 'The arches over the windows either side, and the columns, have to be painted as well.'

'Will you be painting all of it?'

'I will be doing the pictures and Perino will do the arch and column decorations, and the lettering above the bottom row.'

I noticed now that there were upright squiggles in a line above the pictures, although I couldn't read it all. I knew some Latin. But not much.

'Perino, spread the *modelli*[3] out.'

Perino sorted the sheets into a line. I gasped at the pictures, so much more detailed than the ones already painted on the wall, with many more figures behind the main ones, and landscapes behind. I hadn't seen such drawings before, not like this

Master Peruzzi grinned.

'Do you like my camels?' he pointed. I laughed, they were such comical creatures with bulges on their backs, long necks and fat lips.

'They're real, I've seen them, real ones, in Siena.'

I wasn't sure whether to believe him, as his eyes were twinkling.

'And painted ones, in Florence, in a wonderful painting of the journey of the magi – leopards and monkeys too.'

I liked drawing animals, but this drawing - how much better than my attempts!

'It's all right, come closer,' said Perino. 'You can look at them but don't move them.'

I knelt down to look at them in detail.

While Father and Master Peruzzi talked about the work to be done, Perino explained the story of each picture. He also told me that these drawings, the *modellos,* were to show how the pictures would be and had been passed by the client. He explained that these would be made bigger – the *cartone* – to exactly fit the spaces on the wall and that was his job.

---

3 *Modello,* plural of *modello*, the drawing agreed with the client.

'You see how the space we're painting is curved, well, I have to make sure that the pictures fits exactly, so that it looks almost flat.'

'How do you get it onto the wall?'

'Well first, the plasterer makes a coating on the wall, quite thick and rough, the *trullisatio,* that is, plaster and horse-hair, which fills in any imperfections of the stone wall, whether it be brick or stone. Then he follows this with a finer plaster called the *arriccio.* The *cartone* used to be drawn directly onto this surface, with red chalk, to show the positions of all the main features – this is how the frescos we see in the old churches were done. But now, with the more detailed pictures like these-' he pointed to the *modelli,* '-and the fact that paper became cheaper and available to all of us, the *cartone* is held on or stuck against the wall and pounced, so that the painter can follow the lines.'

I was puzzled.

'Pounced?'

'The picture is pricked all along the lines, and then fine chalk in a little mesh bag is pressed against the holes and leaves a mark on the wall. You'll understand when you see it done.'

'And then?'

'The painter comes to do his work. The final coat, the *intonaco,* is done ready for when the painter comes in each day just enough wet plaster for a day's work – the *giornata.* He works out how much he can paint in a day and the plasterer puts on just enough plaster for that work. If a painter can't finish what he thought he could, the plaster will dry and have to be scraped off.' He shrugged. 'A painter who does that has either been taken ill, or doesn't know his job.'

His expression was such that I wouldn't want to be that painter if Perino was around. I struggled to get this into my mind as I listened.

'You understand?'

'I will when I see it done, and do it myself.'

'You want to paint?' I nodded.

'Then you need to be apprenticed to a painter, join a workshop.'

I need to be apprenticed to a painter – Master Peruzzi had only one apprentice. Father said...

Master Peruzzi and Father had moved nearer to the apse. They were talking about the day the plastering would start, the day the *cartone* was to be pounced, and the days for the *intonaca* - already I knew the words and the sequence. It was as if another part of my mind had been opened, and I couldn't wait to fill it with more and more.

Perino drank some water, offered it to me. I took it, imagining that I was his assistant, and he was sharing a break with me. He told me the stories of the drawings.

'This one, with the camels in the background, is when the Magi come to see Jesus, see, the shepherds – here- and the three kings – here.'

There was water behind, and on the other side, a walled town, its towers reflected in the water. People, in a long trail, were coming down a hill.

'This one is of Joseph with Our Lady and the baby on a donkey escaping to Egypt when King Herod ordered the killing of the babies. You can see the soldiers, the mothers and the babies here.' The background was of a river with bridges, like the Tiber, with men fighting on them, one bridge had fallen into the river, like our Ponte Rotto. The towers in the landscape had strange tops, cones with spindles on top. To the side was a very detailed palm tree.

'The palm tree indicates Egypt,' explained Perino.

Father was calling me.

'Come here, Giulio, we are talking about the scaffolding.'

So I went to join them with Perino, and listened while they

talked about the height of the scaffolding, whether it needed to be fixed to the walls or freestanding, and how many ladders there would be. Father drew a little sketch on a thin sheet of white wood, made and noted measurements. I recognised that he was making calculations of the wood he would need, and what I had done at abacus school as exercises suddenly had a meaning.

'We'll need to move the altar.'

'Yes, the brothers know that. They will do it for us; as you can see, it is not stone but wood. They will make sure the space is clear.'

I gazed up at the bare wall and tried to imagine what it would be like. I tried to convert the drawings into colour, to match those already there. I saw that there would be no gold background, the landscapes replaced that. It would make the pictures more real, have more depth.

'Will Giulio be helping us?'

'Yes,' said Father 'he will.'

We made a pact with our eyes. I know my eyes were shining as I looked at them all.

'An eager apprentice,' said Perino.

'Yes indeed,' agreed Master Peruzzi and shivered, 'Let's finish our talk outside; Perino rolled up the *modelli* and tied ribbon round them.

We went outside into the warm, where then men took out their food and we shared it. I almost couldn't eat. Almost.

Afterwards we shook hands again and Father and I went next door to the monastery to talk with the Prior about arrangements for deliveries and storage.

My mind was buzzing with words and realisations – and the paintings, so that I was quiet all the way home. But when I got there, I was bursting with it all and spilled it out in incoherence to my Mother, until they both laughed at me and told me to stop and eat.

CHAPTER EIGHT

CECI

Giulio then went to work with his father every day, and some evenings he would sit with me and Mama while we worked, and tell us about it all, drawing the street and the people, the animals, especially the cats. He drew me a long line of cats in all positions: lying paws in the sir, sleeping; sitting, washing playing, with Prettycat looking at them with a disdainful look on her face – as well she might, being the only one who had a real inside home. This was my treasure: it cheered me up if I was sad, which wasn't often I admit. On Sundays, after church, we went out together for him to draw and me to search for coins. It dropped into a pattern, he with his work with his father, me with my work with Mama.

Every week Mama and I went to the second-hand shop, where we turned over the clothes, looking for dresses with big skirts that would make more than one dress for a child. She looked for tough material to make jerkins for boys, and soft material for shirts. Even though the clothes smelled of their previous owners, and were often stained and torn, I enjoyed looking through them. I liked the smoothness of satin and silk, the sumptuousness of brocade, and the softness of velvet. I loved to discover the patches of embroidery, left over when the main parts had been cut away; the cording and the scraps of beading with their delicate shapes and colours. Quite often you would see women with these patches and scraps sewn into a dress or skirt for festival days. But I knew that these fabrics were not suitable for children's clothes, and had to put these aside to search for linen, cotton and wool.

The shop was always surrounded by women sorting through the clothes, the smells of their bodies strong as they stretched across each other. Their flaring up at each other, and language which Mama told me not to remember – or use. I didn't understand the words, but I did understand the expressions that went with them; the snarls, the gestures, even spitting – though if the spit went on the clothes, Samuel would march them to the door. (They always came back and were tolerated until the next explosion). I stored the words away in my head in case I would need them one day… (and I did.)

Once, instead of using the words in front of Mama, I bit one of the women. She had seized on a dress that Mama already had hold of.

'Hoi, that's mine!' she said, pulling the fabric. She had black and grey hairs escaping from her cap, sleeves rolled up showing fat arms, a torn apron and she was sweating unpleasantly. She had another dress under one arm. Mama took the bulk of the skirt in both hands so as not to damage it, and pulled.

'I had it first!' I was still surprised how quickly Mama could change from a quiet, patient and friendly seamstress to an aggressive cat (and how quickly she had learned the words herself.) The woman shifted until I was between the two of them, the fabric tight against my face.

'*Puttana*!'

I heard her say, as I struggled to get free, and saw Mama, with a cunning look in her eye, let the dress loose, as if losing her grip. The woman's hand softened, then Mama gave a big pull and the woman's arm came across in front of me. So I bit it. It tasted very nasty. She howled and dropped both dresses, Mama quickly bundled up hers and went to bargain with Samuel, the shop owner.

'You little cow!' (only she didn't say 'cow').

The woman raised her hand to slap me but I dodged under the table and came up the other side. I stuck my tongue out at her, and she shook her fist. Another woman took advantage and grabbed the first dress as it had dropped from her grasp to the floor. The first woman turned on her with rage:

That was mine!'

'Should've kept hold of it then, shouldn't you?' The second women came to make her own bargain.

'I'm bleeding!'

'Don't you bleed on the goods!' Samuel, who was a big man, caught hold of her and pushed her out of the shop. I'm not sure what difference a bit of blood on the worn and dirty clothes would have made, but still. As he gave Mama her change, he winked at me.

'Glad it wasn't me,' he said.

The second woman smirked.

'Serve her right, she's a big bully that one, Serena, ha!' She sniffed at the inappropriateness of the name. 'But mind yourself when she's about, she'll have it in for you.'

We left, laughing.

'Well, Ceci, why don't you buy the thread for me?'

Mama gave me some coins and we crossed to the pedlar selling thread. She watched as I matched the hanks to the dresses and chose the exact colours.

Five *quattrini,*' said the pedlar. I looked at him.

'Too much. Two'

'That's less'n I paid for it'

'It's what I will pay for it'

'Three'

'There are other pedlars,' I said, remembering what Mama said and waited.

'Two?' it was a shame he had made it a question. I had him!

'Two.'

He held out his hand – I'd won! I grinned as I gave Mama the threads, and I skipped along beside her, very proud of myself. She bought me an apple from the fruit-seller.I put it in my pocket, for later. This was my first experience of bargaining.

Samuel, as well as selling second-hand clothes, acted as a pawnbroker, and I learned about the quality of goods, what set the price, and what Samuel would offer. Goods would be 'sold' to him for coins, and then, when the seller had money again, or something else to exchange, they would go to Samuel and redeem their goods. The links of Mama's necklace found their way in and out of this shop. I noted that the price we paid to get them back was more than the money given to us for them, and I learned from Samuel that this difference was called 'interest', and was part of how he learned his living. If the goods weren't redeemed after a certain time, he sold them.

~

I'd watched how the boys got things. They ran errands, carried stuff, worked for the baker and pie maker by taking food on a tray to sell to the pilgrims on the Great Road. They got things in return; bread, pies, a chunk of meat, vegetables from the gardeners who come down to the piazza to sell their goods. Sometimes the received coins, but these were often in short supply as the mints ran out of metals, especially silver, so if they worked for the non-food merchants, they were often 'paid' in small objects, and, like me, they searched for ancient coins in the ruins, all of which they could also sell to the pilgrims.

So I learned about bartering, agreeing rewards for work, the street trade, buying, selling, and dealing in a pawnshop, all exchanges of money and goods, trading. It fascinated me. I persuaded Mama to let me bargain with Samuel, pointing out bad stains or tears to get the price down. It started as a game between him and me and his eyes twinkled as we, apparently, thrashed out a price. At first he was humouring me, an eight-year old child, but then, he took me seriously and started to argue a case in earnest as he did with the adult women. I learned to say no when he insisted on a price I wasn't prepared to pay, and to walk away. I knew that he would never let me have a piece below the price he was willing to sell it for, and we had to reach that point. Through this, he taught me, not just about the game of bargaining, but about quality of cloth, about its street value.

Sometimes I went to the apothecary for remedies for aches and pains. The shop was full of shelves of jars with patterns on them, some of which I knew were words, telling you what was inside the jars. I couldn't read them, and wouldn't have known what some of the words meant anyway. There were baskets of dry crackly leaves, seeds, twisted papers with unseen objects inside, dried petals and fruits, bones and skins and other strange things. Bundles of soapwort, pots of ointments, small jars like jugs with corks, with oils inside, smelling of roses, wild flowers, lemons and oranges, and piles of tallow candles. The shop smelled of flowers, must, hay, with an undercurrent of an acrid smell which I couldn't identify, but was always present and on its own would be unbearable.

The shop was owned by the Apothecary, Vittorio, who was crippled – some said by soldiers, others in a brawl, no-one really knew. He was also blind in one eye, but he saw well enough to choose and measure ingredients for potions and oils. He was not seen much, in fact, I had not seen him at all, but I knew he was helped by his daughter, Adelina. The shop was run by his wife Nunciata and her daughter Adelina, who were also the midwives for the *Macello,* and they mixed simple remedies themselves from herbs. They both knew a lot about which leaves or seeds to pound together, or which elements – they didn't say what these were – to make into syrups for whatever was wrong with you. They looked like each other, with the same crooked nose, the same eyebrows that met in the middle, the same shaped ears, the same lack of chin, so it seemed their faces grew straight into their necks.

I was fascinated to watch their mouths open to speak, as their lower lips would disappear into their necks, then reappear to join their upper lips in two thin straight lines. The only way you could tell them apart was that Nunciata's lips turned down at each side, and she had more wrinkles than Adelina, wrinkles which started below her eyes and continued down her cheeks and neck in parallel lines.

They had the same way of bundling their hair into nets under their caps, and wore identical dresses, and, although they were called ugly, their appearance in those dresses was always neat and smart. When people talked about them, they called the daughter 'poor Adelina' because 'with that face, she would never find a husband'. And they were sorry for her, that she was getting old (she was about seventeen) and would never have a child.

Then one day the gossip changed to whispers about Adelina expecting a baby. She wasn't married, they called her *puttana,* whore, a word they said in a nasty way. So I got the idea that a 'whore' was a woman having a baby before she was married and was something wrong, something which was frowned on. Especially here where they said Adelina should be 'put away' and there she was still serving in the shop. Some of the women stopped going there, or, if they went, it was to tell the others how big Adelina was getting. They liked talking about it, even if it was wrong.

I thought about it a lot, this baby business, how when the mother was married, she was expected to have bay after baby. As I knew nothing about men and women, I worked out that babies must come at a certain time in a women's life, and if she wasn't married by then, she would be a 'whore' and people would be angry about her. I knew Our Lady was told by an angel, before she married Joseph, that she was to have a baby. So I assumed that Adelina had been told by an angel too, but why didn't the angel tell someone to marry her like he did after he'd told Joseph? Perhaps he did, but no-one would obey him, because Adelina was ugly? Which Our Lady wasn't, she was sweet and kind in the pictures in the church.

I didn't think that was fair. It wasn't Adelina's fault she was ugly. I was upset that an angel couldn't make someone marry her. Perhaps Adelina's angel didn't try hard enough, which was a shame because I had thought that angels looked after people. I told God that this wasn't kind, and continued to be nice to Adelina.

The story of Our Lady worried me a lot at that time. What would have happened if Joseph had refused to marry her? Would the angel have had to find someone else (and punish Joseph for disobeying him)? What if he didn't find one in time? Would that make Our Lady a whore? Then she would have been talked about as Adelina was talked about; but she wasn't. And I did worry about me - would I get a husband before my body produced a baby? Or would I too be a 'whore' and shunned?

Adelina disappeared from the shop for a while, and returned, thin once more, but there was no baby. When I asked Mama where the baby was, she told me 'not to talk about it - we don't talk about it'. Then Vittorio died, and we all went to say a Mass for him. Everyone expected the shop to close down, but it didn't. They rented out the top floor, and lived in the shop, as we did. Although they couldn't make the potions that Vittorio could, because they were women, and the Guild wouldn't allow it, they still went on with their remedies, their sale of scented waters and oils, their tallow candles, and still delivered babies.

Everyone went to the shop again and it was as if nothing had happened. Until Adelina started to grow her stomach again. She was again spoken of as 'the whore Adelina', and I was even more worried as I worked out that once the babies started, they obviously kept on coming. I also thought when Adelina disappeared again and came back without a baby that babies only stayed when there was a husband, and I wondered where they went otherwise. I thought Our Lady was very lucky that Joseph agreed to marry her, otherwise there wouldn't have been a Baby Jesus. I was very impressed with Joseph and thought that he was much ignored and should be treated better, so in church, I talked to him, and asked him to find me a husband before I became a whore.

The 'whore Adelina' disappeared twice, then her stomach swelled again, and that was absolutely scandalous, the height of deliciousness for the gossips, and shaken heads and smirks from the men. Her mother died unexpectedly and Adelina, who was quite big at the time, closed the shop for several days, and then there were the sounds of a baby. This baby stayed. Customers flocked to the shop. The baby had a chin and was called Faustina, and was in a cradle in the shop. She was adored by her mother, whose lips turned up at the corners all the time. She never disappeared again, and she became Signora Adelina and was liked by people because she was clean and smart and a good mother and nice to everyone. There was some talk of Nunniata's unexpected death and the fact that no-one knew what might be in the remedies Adelina knew how to make, but that died down, as her goods and her skills were necessary. No-one called her ugly anymore and her daughter was beautiful.

Mama and Antonina were both with her during her birth days, and when she insisted on re-opening the shop, Mama suggested that I helped her. We went to the shop together, and it was arranged that I would work for Adelina for a few weeks, sweeping, setting things out, keeping customers happy while she dealt with the baby. We agreed that I would do this in exchange for things from the shop when we needed them. She would make a note of the time I was there against the things I would take, and she produced a book of paper to keep track of this.

This was the first time I saw that bargains could be written down. I was intrigued by this and asked her to teach me numbers and how to keep simple accounts. She taught me how to write down the words for things in the shop, to count hem, and to know when we needed to buy more supplies. I loved making these lists, and I loved working out the prices for Mama's work. I started to make such a book for Mama, what we bought and how much we paid, and what we sold, and for how much; and how much we needed to sell to buy food, wood, candles for ourselves. I also made a book to list all the coins and pieces we sold, and found then I could work out what raised the best prices, against the time spent looking for them. I was beginning to be able to sort out the coins which brought in the most money by watching the eyes of the buyers to see the initial glint before they shut down the eagerness in their eyes.

I loved being in Adelina's shop, I loved being with the customers who came in all the time, not just now and then as in ours, when they came to order things from Mama. Soon Adelina was happy to let me run it on my own for half-an-hour or so.

So I took over dealing with Mama's customers, discussing what they wanted and price. She soon left all that to me, and it also got me out of sewing so much. This, of course, made Mama cross at having to sew for longer, and wish she hadn't suggested that I help Adelina.

'But I suppose it won't be much longer, she said she would find someone to help soon. She knows I need you here.'

I knew that Adelina had put the word out for an assistant. I knew that the woman she had for a week on trial had messed things up and had left. I also knew that I wanted the assistant to be me. I had learned the words on the jars, I could make the bundles and fill the little jars from the big amphorae of oils without spilling a drop. Once, instead of keeping a customer talking until Adelina re-appeared, I actually served them with what they wanted, shaking dried herbs out of a jar onto the weighing scales, twisting them into a screw of paper and asking for the correct price. Adelina was standing with the baby in her arms; she had not come forward to take over but had watched me.

'You did that well.' I blushed with pleasure. 'I know you are young but you work well and the customers like you. Would your Mama allow you to work here, with me, as my apprentice, my assistant?'

I didn't want to say it, but I had to.

'I don't think so, she needs me to sew for her, things are getting behind.'

'Oh, what a shame, but I can see that. Perhaps I shall find someone soon.'

At the evening meal I was silent, which was unusual.

'What's wrong?'

'Nothing.'

'Yes there is. Tell me. Have you quarrelled with Giulio?'

I was startled; Giulio was far from my thoughts.

'No.'

'What then?'

'Adelina asked if I could be her assistant, but I can't.'

'No, I need you here. You spend too long there as it is.'

'But I would be an apprentice, I would learn the trade, I'd learn to read and write – I am learning to read and write!'

'You want to leave me - whatever are you thinking of?'

'But you could get an apprentice, someone who could really sew, better and faster than me.'

'And where would I get one of those? If you applied yourself, you could sew better and faster.'

'I don't like it!'

'We all have to do things we don't like, Cecilia.'

'But you like sewing!'

'I liked sewing before, in a nice house, with a servant, without thinking where the next meal was coming from.' She said this quietly.

I had forgotten that house, I had forgotten we had a servant. I never thought where the food came from, it was just there. Mama had not forgotten.

'We lived in a house near Santa Maria del Populo, on three floors, your father, your step-brother, Matteus, and his family. I'd married your father, Francesco, after he saw me in church – and, like the foolish old man he was, he fell in love with my pretty face ,and body). I had been living in a convent, an orphan, since my parents died of the plague when I was nine. I was just fourteen when we married.

'You were just five years old when your father died and we were thrown out. I told you we had to go away, for a while, and we had to pack things to take with us. I told you we were going on a magic journey. I was folding things up to take with us, and you came into the room dragging a woollen blanket.

"Mama, you've forgotten this' you said.

'Your fair hair, like my own, like a lot of the Lombard line, should have been covered by a cap, but that has been lost, as usual, and your hair was in tangled curls waving over your head and across your shoulders. Your bright green eyes were shining at thought of 'an adventure'.

"We can't take this; we can only take what I brought into the house with me. This belongs to Matteus.'

''But it's my blanket' you protested. I took the blanket from you and pulled you in my arms. At least I have my daughter. His son, Matteus, who had always disapproved of the marriage, because convent girls were thought to be lower class; even though Francesco never treated me as such. Nor did he want a another girl-child to find a dowry for – he had two of his own. He told me that he wanted us out of the house because he needed all the rooms for his own family. He would find me a home. There was nothing I could do, you see, as Francesco had not made a will.

'Beatrice, my maid, appeared in the doorway.

"Master wants to see you.' she said curtly, no need to be polite anymore, no longer the servant of the widow, but angling to stay with the Master. She left without a glance. I sighed and raised myself from the floor. The sooner we could leave the better.

"Sit down Ceci - sit on your blanket. Stay here.'

In the downstairs room, Matteus was waiting There was a paper on the table.

"The place is part of a house on the *Macello dei Corvi*. It has two rooms on the ground floor, once a shop. Here is the contract, which you must sign, or make your mark.' Matteus, a notary, had taken so little interest in me he didn't know if I could write.

''I can write my name,' I said, and did. I signed the name of my mother - Antea Arditti, widow of Francesco ...

"No. not that.' said Matteus, and scrawled out 'the widow of'.

'I had chosen the name right. I was on my own.

'He rolled up the document.

"I have been looking at the dowry list'

'Well, there wasn't a lot there. I waited, preparing myself to argue for my clothes.

"It seems that you brought so little into the house that you will sore-pressed to make a home.'

'I was surprised he cared. But no, not for me. For himself, his reputation. He coughed. I said nothing, unprepared to make things easier for him.

"I have therefore decided to add to your possessions.' He stopped, as if having second thoughts. He called for his wife.

'Emilia.' He coughed again. 'My wife – she will tell you. Emilia –' and he left, with no great reluctance.

"Madama,' started Emilia, even though she was at least twenty years older than me. 'I have chosen some chattels for you – dishes, pans, to take. And of course all your clothes and those of your daughter.'

'I was surprised, for I assumed these would be reused for Matteus' family.

'Thank you.' I said.

'Emilia ignored this, intent on what she was to say next.

"It is hard for you to have to leave so soon after the death of my father-in-law.'

'Her words were muttered and I could tell she had had words with Matteus.

"But you are to leave this afternoon - so I will not be looking for your bedclothes, nor for this.' She handed me a small, quite heavy, drawstring bag. 'I have ordered a cart for you within the hour.'

So that was it.

"I shall miss you,' I think she said, and she was gone. Miss me? Miss the sarcastic way she addressed me when Francesco wasn't there. Miss the wheedling, fawning of me when he was. Miss the hoping I would not have a boy and cut Matheus and her children out of the inheritance. Miss me? Like the devil she would!

'Except – she would miss all the sewing work I did – the linens, underclothes, shirts. She would have to do this herself, and teach her awful girls properly … and none of them as good as me… pleasurable thoughts…

'I took the bag upstairs, and told you 'you can keep the blanket'.

'I took it and all our bedclothes and pillows and rolled them into a large bundle. Beatrice came in with dishes, plates, knives, pans and beakers which she put on the floor with a disapproving sniff.

"I'm to bring you a box for these.' and she swept out of the room.

'You and I placed the things into the box, together with two dresses each, while linens and your clothes were tied into another bundle. Into the centre of that bundle I had tucked a rolled-up linen cloth tied with ribbon. When we had finished, I took the bag from my pocket. Inside was the gold necklace that Balthazar had given me on our marriage and coins. One looked like silver, no two, three. I heard footsteps and quickly put the bag in my pocket. It was Beatrice

"The man's outside for you. Andrea!' she shouted for the house servant 'get these things downstairs!'

'In the hall below, you and I, now in our own cloaks, looked round, but there was no-one to say goodbye to. Beatrice and Andrea had disappeared. The man with the cart was waiting impatiently outside. Then Andrea returned.

'Master says to take these ladies to this address – you'll be paid when you return.'

Well, at least I would not have the carter running off with my belongings and leaving me to be molested in the street. Together we left the house. From the window upstairs, I saw Emilia watching.

'We walked together, we didn't speak. The carter only made a sound when the cart struck a rock and he had to manoeuvre it backwards and forwards again to free it. You were silent, but excited. You were holding my hand, your eyes huge at all the new things you were seeing. You twisted round to follow the movements of people, mules, dogs, but were jerked back by me until you learned to simply walk and dart only your eyes at what you had never seen before. We followed the carter along a narrow street with houses either side, then curved round the edge of a mound with ruined arches on top, an equally ruined tower behind. Then we went across a square filled with traders of all kinds, shouting their wares and bargaining with their customers. You kept close to me, holding my hand tightly.

"Hi, pretty one, some ribbons for you?' The carter growled at the trader, and was sworn at.

'I knew I should have to shift for myself. I fingered the bag in my pocket, and realised I was free, of the old man, of the house, of his stuck-up family … I was tingling – with fear? Yes, but also - all at once I could be myself. As a widow I had a better status than a single woman, as a widow with a child, I could make my own way. Me and my daughter. I swung your hand in naïve joy, and laughed. I felt I had sprung out of a chrysalis, I was flying!

"It is an adventure!' I was just nineteen.

'We turned into another street and stopped at a wooden door on which the carter knocked. This door.'

There was silence between us. The sun had left the window and it was cooling. I went round the table and knelt by my mother.

'I'm sorry – you had to give up so much.'

'No, I'm not sorry. Although I missed the comforts for a while, and sometime do even now, I was often lonely. Matteus and Emilia weren't friendly, their children were rude. I couldn't go out by myself. The sewing passed the time, but I did it mostly on my own. The windows were always closed. I only saw your father at the evening meal, and he rarely spoke. And then it was to Matteus about work. It was better when you came, but even then you were with a wet nurse, and Beatrice looked after you. But here, I am lucky. I'm not alone; I'm helped by Antonina, Pietro, Adelina, our other neighbours. And I have you.' She squeezed my hand. We sat together.

She didn't tell me it all, how he came to her bed, did what he wanted and went back to his own. How he chose her clothes and inspected her when they went out, telling her what to say, who to talk to, who not. Who allowed Emilia to run the house, so that the servants took little notice of her, the second wife, even more so after I arrived. His disappointment when the baby was a girl, and the glee of her 'step-son'. There was a silent battle between the son and the father – who would get a boy first. A wife who must be 'protected' at all times, in a beautiful prison with jailers who obeyed him and ignored her – a woman without family, with no woman to call a friend.

I learned this afterwards, when I knew how things went for married women, and however hard my life was, it was preferable to this gilded, empty, cage.

'I won't leave you – ever - I promise - and I'll try harder with the sewing' I said, and we hugged each other.

Oh. Mama...

I told Adelina that I would still come for a couple of hours each day until she found an assistant, which she did, a young woman who had learned about herbs at a convent, and who was pleased to have work and a home in the attic. And I, with the knowledge I had gained from Adelina, was content to be my mother's assistant, to find pleasure in buying and selling.

What I didn't learn then was that I would grow to have something else I could sell.

CHAPTER NINE

GIULIO

We did go to the limekilns. We went to the Amphitheatre where there were piles of rubble which had been made, not by the natural vagaries of time or earthquakes, but by the deliberate act of demolition of part of the walls to use, either directly as blocks or through crushing to make mortar, in the repair of churches and to make new houses.

'Kilns are placed when there is a demand for lime and mortar. Small ones keep going for the repairs and re-making of houses, and restoration in churches. Large kilns are made when there is a lot of demand, which usually comes from Popes and wealthy families and Cardinals. Then a master builder, like my father and grandfather, would work with an architect and hire or make a kiln to produce what they needed.'

We had reached the Amphitheatre, and walked round to a large kiln made out of an old building on the other side. It was about the height of ten men standing on top of each other. It was also not in use.

'Now, there are no large building or restoration projects on – the Pope has lost interest. They say he's dying - who knows who the next Pope will be. Some old families are moving out of Rome because they think his son Cesare will take everything and leave, and there will be no money in the Papal coffers, no chance of influence, and no work for artisans.'

Father now talked to me as if I understood what he was saying.

I did understand some, as I now listened to the conversations between him and Mother. It seemed that Father belonged to a group of builders who worked on the major projects, and that these seemed to be only created by important people, especially by the Pope.

To we children playing in the *Macello dei Corvi*, 'The Pope' was a mysterious being who was 'god-on-earth' and lived in a Palace on the shores the great river far away on another side of the city. He was a being of great power and was served by a great many men: Cardinals (in big red hats), priests, monks, nuns and clergymen, and whom great numbers of people called pilgrims came to see. These whom we saw around the place and on mules going up the Great Road to see the Pope. So, the Pope was important, in a vague way. Now I saw that the Pope was important in a very particular way: to my family as the provider of work.

The large kiln had a slope built up its side, at the bottom of which lay piles of stones lending places for weeds to grow.

'These stones would be broken up into smaller pieces by teams of stonecutters, then they were carried up this slope by boys hauling baskets. If a man came upon a piece of marble, it was put on that pile over there to be burnt in a smaller kiln for fine lime. We'll see that in minute. If the marble has an inscription on it, it would be reported to the overseer who would take it to the Master to be sold to the collectors. Sometimes there could be forty to fifty men working here, and great numbers of carts going round the Amphitheatre to pick up the big stones. You always build a kiln as near as possible to the stone you are quarrying and you have to be careful when taking the stone that you don't cause a downfall – two men were crushed to death last year when the tops arches fell on them because they taking down a pillar without thought.'

We turned to the smaller kiln, where men were working. Father spoke to the overseer, and passed him some coins, and we were allowed to go up ladders to look over the top. There were men inside stacking the stones, carried up on the ladders, it being much smaller than the big kiln, and each layer of stones was separated from the next by layers of wood. The kiln was nearly full.

'When it's full the wood is lit through this small entrance here.' Father indicated a space like a bread oven which already had straw and kindling laid. 'Once the kiln is full, the fire is set, then they have to keep building it up night and day to keep up the temperature high so as to burn the stones.' Father explained.

'Then when the stone has diminished, and is ready for use, the ashes are raked out and the powder that remains is filtered to be used as mortar and plaster. This kiln is for pure marble, which makes the best plaster for the *intonaco* which is why this one is working because we will need good quality lime for *San Onofrio,*'

'How long does it take?'

'A kiln this big will take a week to fill, to burn and rake out. The big kiln would take three weeks.'

'Then you come here to choose the lime you need?'

'I do.' We climbed down our ladders. 'One day I will do a whole project again, like my father - work with an architect, hire my own kiln and workers.' This was said quietly, so I made no reply. Shortly after the men came out from the inside, and others joined them all round the top to seal the kiln.

'We timed it right, they're going to fire it.'

We sat out of the way and watched. The overseer lit the straw and bent down to watch it take. Then he signalled another to push in some smaller branches.

'There she goes!' he cried. The fire would leap up through the layers catching and making hot embers.

'Eight or more men will sleep here, and keep the fire burning for the next three days -it can't be let out, it can't be allowed to burn down or the stone will not change.'

We watched as the men shovelled continually. Two at a time, while the others waiting their turn, pulled stacks of wood closer. A boy was sent off.

'He's going to start the trail of cartloads of wood which'll go on all the time, and tell the women who bring the food and water that it's started.'

The overseer picked up a small piece of marble with an inscription, or part of one, 'u-p- e- r,' read Father. 'Perhaps Jupiter?'

The overseer shrugged.

'Master only wants long words or pretty women – sell better. Let the lad have this.'

He passed it to me. I pulled me fingers over the letters. To me, they were VP then a crack, then ER I would give it to Ceci and tell her it was an inscription to the god Jupiter and she would say 'it's a V not a U' and I would tell her that it was Latin and they wrote like that. I smiled.

'Thank you' I said and Father put it in his pouch, shook hands with the overseer, and wished him well until they next met. We walked back up the Great Road, followed by the beginning of the acrid smell.

~

I woke before dawn with a sense of something new about to happen. I usually lay there trying to remember my dream, but that day I was up and pulling on clothes. I heard my father and mother and tripped over my feet in my urgent need to join them. I was afraid that my father might have forgotten he was taking me with him.

When he saw me in the lifting light he said, 'you need to wear a jerkin, you must look like an artisan – you must look like my apprentice.' My mother had one in her hand, a leather garment that I hadn't seen or worn before. It was supple and felt good.

She handed me a water bottle and food wrapped in a cloth, enough for two, which went into the pannier along with the bags of tools. She stood in the doorway, and there was a scuffle as Ceci pushed past her and Antea looked over her shoulder.

I was already sitting on the mule. Ceci came up and stroked the mule's ear.

'God be with you, Giulio,' she said without looking at me. I was embarrassed, then Prettycat jumped up onto the mule's neck, which made it toss its ears and stamp its feet. Ceci reached up and took her in her arms.

'Silly cat – you're not going!' We all laughed and she caught my eye then, and mouthed, 'Be one!'

Father, or Master Pietro, as I must now call him, took the rein and we set off under a violet-grey sky where a few stars could still be seen. We passed the local shops being opened and exchanged greetings with Angelo, the butcher, who had already collected carcasses from the abattoir and was hanging them up on hooks.

Time then?" he said, smiling at me. Master Pietro nodded and grinned. Angelo nodded too, then picked up his knife and his sharpening stone. Giorgio, heaving a carcass, didn't look at me but Niccolò gave me a wave. The baker, Tommaso, was pulling his first batch from his oven, and already customers were waiting. We joined them to get our own fresh bread and paid his wife. She gave the bread to me.

'There y'are, apprentice".

That day was special, it was powerful. They seemed to know that, everyone knew. The sky knew too, it was shading grey and pink, waiting for the momentous moment of the rising sun. An apprentice. Today. To start in a great church, to work and to be able to watch a painter. The walls we passed, once the walls of a palace, or a great villa, became coloured in the light. Colours – yellows, oranges, browns, whites - colours I magnified in my mind: my colours.

Father glanced up at the sky, pink and pale violet.

'We must hurry,' he said, "before the blue truly comes'.

Workers were already unloading the scaffolding beams and planks into the church when we arrived. Buckets filled with lime mortar, which Father has brought up some days ago to settle, stood ready for use at the back of a bare-walled chapel close to the apse. They were covered with cloth and wood lathes to keep the dust from their surfaces.

'We don't take them near the wall we are plastering until we've brushed it down and swept up all the loose bits and dust.'

He took the wood and the cloths from the buckets.

'You see how this plaster has bits in it and this one has less, while this one it quite smooth. We make layers, each one smoother as we go.'

He crossed to a trestle and unloaded a large bag he had carried in.

'Here are the tools, these are yours.'

He placed two sets of tools, floats, trowels, plaster boards, brushes. One float, trowel and plaster board were smaller than the other, made by him especially for me. I look up at him. He grinned.

Come on, water first.' He picked up empty buckets and gave me one.

There was a lot more grinning from the workmen as they came into the church.

''e's no more bigger than 'is bucket!'

I knew I was small for my age.

''e'll never carry that back when it's full,' from two men at either end of some scaffolding poles.

'Master Pietro's new 'pprentice eh? Welcome lad. I'm Fabio.'

This from an older man who rubbed the hat on my head and left it over one ear.

I blushed and staggered on following Father. The bucket was heavy on the way back, and I had to put it down once or twice. The scaffolder nodded up and down at me.

'Mm, said so but not unkindly

'Leave 'im be,' said Fabio, 'e'll grow. Take no notice, lad.'

My father used a long brush on the wall and got me to sweep up the bits that came down. Then the scaffolding went up, tied securely. Two planks, paint- and plaster- spattered made each of two platforms, with a short ladder between them so that the plasterer could reach the top of the unpainted wall. Then he swept again to make sure there was nothing loose on the bare surface, which had one coat of plaster on it done years ago. I took the sweepings outside and dropped them amongst the trees which grew thickly round the church and down the hill. When Master Pietro, by rubbing his hand over it, was satisfied with the surface, he said to me,

'now for the *arriccio*.'

He signalled the older man, Fabio, to wet the walls. Fabio flung water from the bucket at the wall and Pietro made sweeps with a wide brush to make sure the wall was covered. Fabio let me throw half-buckets onto the lower half of the wall, much of it went straight onto the floor until he taught me how to angle it properly. The other men had to make the water journey three or four times before Pietro was satisfied with the wetness of the wall. 'We need to do this more in the summer or the wall will dry out too quickly. In the winter we can use less water,' he explained to me.

The next part was to put the first layer of plaster, the *arriccio,* on the wall. My father put a lump of plaster on his board and I copied him on mine. He took the float in his right hand, balancing the board on his left. Then he stood on the scaffolding and I watched as his right hand swept across the lump and then straight onto the wall in one swing. It looked easy. I started to swing my float in imitation of him towards my left shoulder, twist my wrist and flatten the float onto the wall. I tried this several times, then I tried with the plaster. I had to balance the board on my left hand and pick up plaster onto my float and then attach it to the wall. I moved the float across the plaster, and pushed it all onto the floor. Fabio came forward, took my hand and showed me. We did this several times before I found the right pressure to ensure that the plaster stayed on the float, not the floor. Master Pietro looked down from the scaffold to watch without losing the rhythm of his work.

'Now pick it up and press it down on the wall and sweep. There at the side'. I did so but could not get the float flat and the plaster fell off the wall.

After a few tries, my muscles did as I wanted them to, or I thought they did, and I tried again with plaster and there, a sweep of plaster was on the wall. I grinned and continued. After several minutes my wrist ached and I started to drop plaster again.

'I can't,' I wailed, forgetting I was an apprentice. Master Pietro frowned.

'No such word,' said Fabio as he replaced the empty bucket at Master Pietro's feet with a full one.

I tried again, and again. My patch of plaster was lumpy and uneven, and Fabio scratched it off.

'Don't waste anymore plaster, practise without it.'

Fabio and Master Pietro continued the work across the wall, and I practised the sweep. It was easier without the plaster and after a few passes it became mechanical, and the ache crawled up my forearm. I wanted to stop. It wasn't fun anymore. I was tired.

Master Pietro came down from the scaffolding which was

then dismantled and he started on the lower half. Master Pietro said to me,

'Don't worry, a little every day and then you will do it. Sit and watch'.

The workmen then went with the scaffolding, and I sat and wished I had a panel on which to draw Master Pietro at work as I am sure I would have understood the technique better. As it was, I followed his movements with my finger, but that ached too. So I examined the paintings above him. From my place on the floor they seemed even higher, and in my mind, the angels sang, and I painted as they did so.

~

The days were filled with fetching and carrying, and practising on the walls of the stable next to the church. Fabio supervised me, patiently but sternly.

'You're not looking at the wall – look where you're putting it, not at the tool, or the board or the plaster.' Or 'The movement is from the board to the place on the wall where it's going - the wall, Giulio, look at the wall! – don't look at the plaster on the board!' Or 'Giulio, your weight should be on both feet not one – you'll get a bent spine that. way' Or 'Stop scrunching your shoulder - it's only the arm that moves.' Or 'Get into the rhythm, if you don't you'll tire yourself out – hum, or chant if you like.' Or 'don't go over it again and again – you've to join the plaster not lump it up!' Or 'Follow through - the action to put the plaster on the wall then continues to pick up the next plaster – all in one movement - don't pause in between!' Or 'Don't drop your wrist Giulio!' Or 'You haven't cleaned this board – or this trowel – or this bucket – properly. Do it again!' Or 'Watch the amount you're using – there's a bump here - it's got to be the same depth of plaster over the whole wall.' 'Or 'Rhythm, Giulio, rhythm. Why don't you sing?' Or 'A bit dry this plaster – see it's lumpy.'

Or 'Go and tell the others there's food ready…'

What?

I fell asleep as soon as my head touched the bed, but dreamed of plaster dripping from the wall, making puddles which became pools and crawled up my feet and legs as I tried to push it away. Every time I put plaster on the wall, it fell off, or it grew until it was as thick as the wall itself and I was told to do it again – after I'd rebuilt the wall, which had fallen down when I wasn't looking. I dreamed of carrying buckets of water from the river, up the hill to the church, to find them empty when I got there.

CHAPTER TEN

CECI

I was restless.

I'd finished all my chores indoors. I'd scrubbed out the stewpot, raked out the wood ash from the fire, and taken our urine to the washerwomen and our shit to the common cesspit. I'd stuffed the mattress covers with new hay, and swept the floors, throwing all the bits and the ash outside. Mama was resting, Prettycat had gone off mousing. Giulio had gone with his parents to pay their respects to an uncle – or someone, or something.

It was just after midday, and hot, not that that bothered me. I sat outside, wanting something to do. I looked up and down the street, no-one was out, no cats, no dogs. A movement catches my eye from the Great Road, a couple of mules piled high with sticks trudged past led by a man with his head down. I leaned back against the warm wall, and gazed upwards over the houses to the top of the Column. It shimmered against the sky, hazy, like the air around me. I got glimpses of the Column when we went down to Samuel's and knew it had carvings, but I didn't know what of.

Today, I would find out, I would go to see the Column up close.

I made my way up the street, past the closed shops. Adelina's, three bakers, two for bread and one for pies. Prettycat was sniffing round these. I called her, but she ignored me. Angelo's butchery, the cobbler, the draper who sold cloth when he could get it, but really had his shop full of trinkets and cheap items mostly for the pilgrims. Further down there was another butcher and more food shops. I carried on.

I passed the little chapel built of brick with its door set between two stone pillars, where there were two men sleeping against the shaded wall, and Samuel's shop. I had not been further than this. I knew that there, where it curved towards the Column, were artisans' workshops, from which you could hear sounds of hammers on marble, metal upon metal, but in the afternoon, it was silent. I was a little scared as I passed an abattoir and a tanner. It stank a lot there of fish glue, fresh meat, blood and animal skins, to be made into leather, and the sour smell of goat and sheep skins for jerkins. I was careful to avoid the dogs scavenging for scattered animal parts, and the droppings from animals and people. I half-turned round, and as I did, I could see The Column in its full height, just a bit further on. Beyond it were fallen fluted stone drums of great width, tall pillars and half-collapsed buildings, then a semicircle of houses built over a foundation of half-buried arches. Further off I could see smoke rising and get a whiff of the sour smell, a lime kiln. If I shade my eyes with one hand, I can see clusters of men and carts going to and fro. Looking out over that space cluttered with the strange shapes of ruins, some blackened, most of them with bushes growing out of the tops, and the pall of smoke, I felt a flush of fear, but I was too near The Column to turn back. I stretched my eyes to look up to the top where there was a lump that I couldn't make out. I could see that the carvings were made in spirals all the way to the top.

Even though it towered above me, I was no longer afraid of the Column and I went right up to it. It appeared to grow out of a mound of rubble banked against its sides. I climbed up the mound, found a firm foothold, put my hands on the pillar and stretched them as far as they would go, hugging the stone. But I can't really hug it as it was as wide as a house. It was warm against my face and I could feel the dips and bumps of the carvings against my cheek. I stretched my neck backwards to look up, the top is far, far up there in the sky. I wouldn't have been surprised to see angels there.

I dropped my head and pulled back to look closely at the surface. I couldn't make anything out at first, so I rubbed my hands over the surface. I could feel curves and knobs under my hand, and could trace a line going round the pillar, a spiral. I rubbed at it with my skirt, and a figure appeared. I rub some more, and there is a man with a bull and a man with a sheep, and men blowing trumpets. I grew excited and rubbed some more. Men on horses, a standing man, houses. Then, a break and another picture: men carrying poles and round things, all standing in a row. I began to see how the pictures stretched round the Column, its base sloping from left to right, and I followed the slope and saw how the pictures followed each other up and up and up. It was as if you could strip them off to make one long, long set of pictures. I wondered if the pictures told a story. With my fingers, I traced the outlines of a man in a skirt and a strangely-shaped tunic with a cloak across his shoulders; I liked him, he looked strong and dependable. Then, because I couldn't reach up to see further, I got down on my knees and scraped away the earth from the bottom, and found pictures of houses, and two men loading barrels into a cart without wheels. These looked just like any of our neighbours working. There was a roof on top of four pillars, just like the ones at the doors of the chapel, and some more houses going up a hill and suddenly a huge man from the waist up, with a beard and corn in his hair looking up at another row of men going downhill. Then a horse, going uphill to join the pictures I've already seen.

I was so absorbed in the excitement of these discoveries that I didn't realise that someone else was there until I saw a shadow on the ground. I started back, lost my footing and slid down the mound, turning head over heels, and landed on a pair of feet.

'Ouf!' I looked up. It was Giulio, sitting there, drawing. I get off his feet, and sit opposite him shading my eyes with my hand.

'How long have you been there?' I was cross, he had disturbed me.

He shrugged 'as long as you, nearly.'

He was still drawing. 'I saw you go down the street and I followed you.'

'Why?'

'To see you were alright.'

I dropped my eyes from his face.

'You sound like Mama – of course I'm alright' I rubbed earth from my hands. 'I can look after myself.'

He raised an eyebrow. I slapped his arm, he grinned. I turned and slid away, with my back to him. I could of course have gone back to the Column, but… I could hear the scratch of chalk on paper. I wanted to know… No, I didn't. I would go back to the column. .

I crawled next to him and sat hugging my knees.

'Can I see it?'

He turned the paper towards me. There was part of the Column, and there at the base was a girl, bottom up, head on the ground. Next to her were other girls, one with her hands stretching up the Column, one with her hand holding her skirt against it, and one on her knees peering at something.

'It's you,' he said.

I was astonished. The little pictures were like those round the Column, one after another.

'I wanted to get nearer to make your face more real, but then, you would have stopped doing what you were doing.'

'It's so clever.'

'It's not right though, I haven't got your arm right - here.'

He pointed to one of the drawings.

'You moved too quickly. Sit still.'

I did as I was told, and as he drew. I thought of the church pictures in the church. Someone made them – but were they drawn from real people? Was there someone like Giulio in the stable, or at the Crucifixion, drawing? I thought about that, I knew there were pictures and carvings of a man with his arms out in front of a cross, which I found scary. If is it was *real*, that man was a person, a person dying, and how could anyone have sat in front of it like Giulio and just drawn it? It couldn't be right. So I thought about Our Lady and the baby, they were much nicer. I opened my mouth to ask a question but shut it again. Keep still! I started to think about the pictures on the Column. They weren't drawings, they weren't flat, they looked like little people – had they been real?

Giulio stopped.

'There.'

I crawled to his side. And there I was, just like I sat, knees up, arms round them, head on my knees, and my mouth open. I stared. It wasn't just the drawing. I had no idea what I looked like. Curly hair I knew I had, light eyes because Mama told me, but not my nose, my ears, my whole face. I looked at the feet, they had the same earth stains as in the drawing, so did my dress, dirty and crumpled – and torn. I hadn't noticed that. I didn't know what to say.

'The mouth's a bit funny, you opened it, then closed it, so it's sort-of halfway.'

'It's me - I look like that?'

He frowned.

'Yes, but it isn't you. I can't get you.'

'What do you mean?'

'It's a girl, she looks like you, but she isn't you.'

I shook my head, not understanding.

'It always the same!' He got up and screwed up the paper.

I screamed.

'Don't!' and snatched it from him, smoothing it out on my knee.

'Let's go and look at the Column.' He stomped off. Now he was cross. I tucked the paper under his pouch, got up and followed him.

He stood, looking down. I wanted to break his mood.

'See here what I've uncovered – men loading barrels into a cart.'

'It isn't a cart… it's a boat,' he scowled.

Then he went down on one knee.

'See, these wavy bits underneath, that's water, that's a river. You see there are several boats here…and here above them are soldiers lined up and this one, he's the Captain. They must be getting ready to get into the boats.'

He stood up.

'I must draw them, I've drawn the ones above up to here –' he stretched up –' the soldiers on horses going to war, but I can't get up any further. If I go backwards I can't see the detail.'

He'd stopped being cross.

'Lift me up,' I said.

'What?'

I brought my skirt up between my legs and tied it at the front.

'Lift me up, on your shoulders – then I can see and tell you. You can draw what I tell you?'

'Yes, of course I can,' he said with the expression of someone not telling the truth because they don't know (which isn't quite the same as lying).

'We'll find out.' He helped me climb onto his shoulders, and I stood on them, steadying myself with my hands against the Column.

'It's soldiers, fighting' I tell him. 'all mixed up and yelling. 'There's a - '

'Hoi! What's going on?'

It was Pietro, coming towards us. Guilio took my hand, bent his knees and I jumped down. I untied my skirt. I suddenly felt the enormity of what I had done; not just go as far as the Column, but raising my skirt, showing my legs, not least being so close to Giulio's body. I blushed, felt embarrassed and ashamed. I waited to be told off, I waited for anger at what we had done.

'We were just – looking at the pictures,' I said as if it's the most natural thing in the world. Giulio explained.

'I wanted to know what was further up, so I could try to draw them. I can make them up from what Ceci tells me.'

There was a silence as Master Pietro stared at us. He frowned. I waited, eyes down. I would go to prison, I would be whipped.

There was just the sound of breathing, three of us. I looked at Guilio under my eyelashes, he was as pink as me. A horse snorted, tearing at the grass not far from the Column. I could see its feet and its mouth and tongue. We both had our hands behind our backs. Master Pietro made a sound: Hmm: it sounded like the beginning of a laugh, then became a cough. I looked up – I could see - he was trying not to laugh.

'Well you won't be able to draw with a girl on your shoulders. And it is not proper.' He coughed again.

'I can do better than that. We'll get a scaffold up as far as we can then you can draw them.' He turned to me.

'Your mother's looking for you,' he said. 'I just came down for a walk.'

'Giulio's drawn a picture of me – show him.' I pointed to the pouch.

Giulio took up the drawings and handed them to his father.

'It's not right – it's not her.'

Pietro studied it.

'It's good.' He looked at Giulio.

'It's very good,' then at me, 'make sure your mother sees it – now – go home!'

A few days later, early in the morning, Giulio and Pietro and some of Pietro's assistants went down the road with planks and poles in a cart. I followed them to the Column with, Mama, Antonina, Angelo and Niccolò, and watched the scaffold go up next to the Column as high as it could with steps up to the first planks then up again and again. Giulio climbed to the top, and we left him there to draw. He insisted on sleeping there, and was joined by one or two of the artisan's apprentices to make sure no-one stole the scaffold. He was there for four days, the boys bringing him food and drink from Antonina. Then we watched the workmen take the poles and planks away. That evening, we sat outside looking at Giulio's drawings.

Master Pietro said 'I shall show these to Master Peruzzi.'

~

The next day, news flew through the city as fast as a magpie onto a dead rat: the Pope was dead. The funeral, the second magpie said, was a shambles. It was never finished; halfway though, soldiers arrived. Or it might have been the Palace Guard, or his son, Cesare's, men. The Pope was left, for days – weeks, said the third magpie. He stank, worse than a newly dead rat! He was squashed into a coffin too small for him.

Mama and Mistress Pietro were horrified.

'Although he was not a good man, he should have had a proper burial,' they agreed.

The fourth magpie told us that a new Pope, Pius II was elected, the fifth told us he had died, and the sixth told us Julius II was now Pope: all in two months.

CHAPTER ELEVEN

GIULIO

The apprenticeship with Master Peruzzi was arranged, My Father talked to him, showed him my drawings, and of course, he had met me. A contract was drawn up: I was to stay with Master Peruzzi for five years, starting on my eleventh birthday at the end of the year. A sum of money passed to him from my father and I would stay in his house, eating and being clothed by him, working for him and learning. I would go home on Sundays to spend time with my family. In the months before my birthday, it was agreed that I should work at St Onofrio for both my father and for Master Peruzzi. My father told me and my mother that day after it was agreed.

'It is good that he will have a training, and he will be taken care of. With the new Pope, I have no idea what will happen after the St Onofrio job. But I hope that with this connection with Peruzzi, I will be close at hand when any building work is planned.'

Although she agreed, my Mother was quiet, but I didn't pay much attention. I was too full of what was to happen.

~

It was the day the *cartone* was to be prepared from the *modelli*, after which it would be transferred to the *arriccio*. Perino arrived with a pile of papers all of a similar size, the *modello* of Flight into Egypt had been sized up on the different sheets which were to be pasted together. Perino had brought the modello to show me how he had drawn squares on it and had then enlarged them onto the sheets of paper – each paper having four squares. 'We'll paste these together on the floor of the church - it takes up a lot of space - and we can make sure it fits where the wall is curved,' he said. He checked the measurements on the side of the apse where the painting was to go, then drew these with chalk, muttering. Fabio boiled up water in a pan and added wheat flour finely ground to make paste.

'The paper will be stretched in certain places, to fit the space on the curve, so that the illusion is that the painting is flat.'

I had no idea what he meant but watched as Perino started in the bottom left-hand corner with one sheet pasted to the floor so that it was just over the chalk line. He and Fabio used flat brushes to edge the sides of the papers with paste, which were then stuck carefully together. He then dampened the pages and carefully stretched them, holding them down at their edge with his left hand and smoothing them with his right.

When the paper became one large sheet dried out, I sat back on my heels in amazement. It was an exact huge copy of the *modello*. Each time I learned something or saw things fall into place in front of me or in my mind I felt a thrill and a sense of satisfaction. And, then, as now, a feeling of wonder.

Another boy appeared and he and I were given the job of pricking, all along the lines of the drawing, following then exactly. As I took care to make the holes the same and follow the lines exactly, I suddenly thought of Ceci using her needle, and how she would have hated this process. When I had only done a tenth of it, I hated it too.

'I know it's boring, but you must concentrate and not be careless. The painter follows these outlines on the wall. If you get even one prick out of line, you will spoil the fresco. It won't be like his *modello*,' the boy, Laurentio, told me. That frightened me, the thought of spoiling the painter's work. 'You must get into a rhythm.' Rhythm. I had heard that word several times recently. It was true, doing repetitive work, it was necessary. They got me to practise on a sheet of paper, just the movement, and when Perino was satisfied, he put me onto the real thing. Perino watched me like a cat watching a mouse; he hummed under his breath. Stressing each beat. Rhythm.

Pouncing: not quite like a cat on a mouse, I thought, but it was as short and sharp a movement. The *cartone* had placed against the wall and secured with tiny nails. Perino smoothed it against the curve so it was taut. Fine cloths full of black dust, tied at the top to form a handle to be held between first and second fingers, were bumped against the line of holes to make marks through them onto the plaster. On-Off –On –Off. The movement was the one the cat makes, suddenly, before the mouse is aware. I've seen them, the cats, playing with mice – pounce – pounce – delicate and fast.

I was slow at first then realised that it was the fast action that made the powder go through the hole and make a mark on the wall. Laurentio was so fast, the bag and hand blurred and I couldn't see the movement at all. Just like the cat's paw. Only faster. I got a little faster, my arms ached, and I had to stop because of cramp.

'It'll come,' said Laurentio, 'Just watch.'

Fabio and Perino joined, and I was fascinated by three blurry hands going up and down the lines on the paper. They changed hands and were just as fast with both of them. I joined them; when I had finished my wrists were encircled with pain. The paper was carefully removed and there was the picture in black outline on the wall.

It was ready for the Painter.

CHAPTER TWELVE

CECI

It was Sunday. We were sitting outside the house after church, and Giulio told me about the arrangement with Master Peruzzi. He glowed and grinned and I glowed, and wanted to hug him, but was shy. So he hugged me instead, and picked me up and whirled me round as if I was his little brother!

We sat. He wriggled his wrists. One inside the other, then the other way.

'What's up?'

'My hands hurt.' He held one up limply, I sat down next to him.

'Where?'

He curled the fingers of one hand round the wrist off the other, 'Here,' and twitched his second and third fingers, 'here' he bent his head down and touched the back of this neck: 'here - and my knees.'

'Poor Giulio' I simpered then giggled. 'Tell me.'

He looked offended, then he told me: the water carrying, the practise on the stable walls, kneeling on the stone floor, glue under his fingernails. Powder everywhere.

'Why?'

He twisted his shoulders. And told me about pouncing.

'Show me!'

'Can't haven't got any fine powder.'

She frowned.

'Tell me about the other boy then.'

'Laurentio.'

'How old is he?'

'Fourteen. And he doesn't paint yet.'

'Why? Isn't he good enough?' He shrugged.

'If I have to wait three years before I can paint - three years Ceci! – I shall be nearly a man!"

I got up and placed a large stone about three paces in front of us.

'So - you spend them learning.'

I started to pick up smaller stones – the game was to see which of us could hit the big stone and make it move. I sat down again next to him, and frowned at him.

'Don't you?' He mumbled.

'Yes I s'pose.'

'Good.'

'Yes, but' he sighed. 'It's so slow.'

'You've not been there five minutes. And you're not living there yet. Learn from your father.' I threw a stone; it bounced off the big one and rolled away.

'All I want to do is draw. I want to learn that from Master Peruzzi."

He threw, didn't touch the stone, fell short.

'You're saying he's better than your father?'

'No – yes – no - - he is.'

I threw. Close.

'The building, the plastering - don't you think you'll be a better painter if you know what goes on underneath the painting?'

'Yes.'

He threw. It knocked the big stone and stayed there, but the big stone did not move.

'You want to paint – you said so. So learn. Put up with it - stop moaning.'

I threw. Nowhere near.

'You've got that chance. More'n I have.'

He sat up, astonished.

'You want to a painter?' I raised my eyebrows.

'No. Course not.' I told me about Adelina and the shop, and what Mama had said.

'She's right she does need me. But… '

'You think you can do something better than Antea, better than being a dressmaker? Ceci?'

I wriggled. He threw a stone; just missed

'Oh I didn't mean that - no-on is better than Mama! Just…'

'Just?'

'You're learning to do something you want to do – I don't want to be a dressmaker.'

'What do you want?' I shrugged. 'Dressmaking is useful.'

I threw the next stone so hard it bounced across the street, and I was yelled at by a man.

'Painting on walls is useful?'

It was his turn to wriggle.

'No -yes – '

'So, I could be a painter?'

He laughed and threw a stone. Missed.

' Course not, you're a girl! You'll get married, and have children and… '

I stood with my arms on my hips.

'Why?'

'Why what?'

'Why can't I be a painter?'

Giulio looked uncomfortable; I could see him struggling. This was a question he had never, ever thought about – of course!

'Girls – they don't draw or paint – they don't have ideas like boys, like men do - they don't need to read or write, not to look after a family…' He tailed off.

'Mama has ideas; she looks at a big dress then works out how to make a smaller dress out of fabric. She does it in her head That's an idea isn't it?'

And she had a baby. I threw, and hit the stone. It rolled away. Game over.

Giulio shrugged.

'I've got to go.'

I sat for a while, looking at the women on our street. Adelina, outside, holding her little one's hand as it tottered about: no husband. Her assistant, a widow, would be on the streets sleeping rough, begging if she hadn't found Adelina. Mama, turned out after my father's death to look after herself, and me. Antonina, who didn't have to work because of Pietro, but had had no more children after Giulio, who kept the house clean and cooked, she could afford a maid, but wanted to do things herself. Angelo's wife, who was rarely seen, and whose name I didn't remember, with two great men and Niccolò to look after. The baker's wife, who worked as hard as her husband and looked after his father too. The washerwomen, who had no husbands. All so different. All working hard. None of them painters, or builders, or notaries – or Popes. I wondered why God made it so?

No wonder he didn't talk to me – I was a girl. He was too busy making different men, different lives; women to serve men? I kicked the stones on the ground. I listed a question for Him – Why? No answer. Not a flicker. I sighed and went indoors.

~

Some months later, one Sunday when visiting from his work, and we were out drawing and searching, Giulio took a bundle out of his pouch.

'Here. We'll find place to hide them.'

A pair of breeches, a tunic, hose, shoes, and a cap.

CHAPTER THIRTEEN

CECI Rome 1506

The clothes made a great difference. My hair, which was down below my shoulders, had been plaited into a single tail for some time. I simply wound it around my head and pulled the cap over it tightly, leaving a few short curls at the front. I could go off round the ruins farther away, picking things up, and scramble into caves, which were really parts of houses underground. It was there I could find could find coins which only needed to be brushed off to be ready for sale. I could go further when Giulio was there, to scrabble about while he drew. Mama had made me promise that I wouldn't stray to where Giulio couldn't see me. I did make sure I could see him – most of the time.

We went out on Sundays, after church. He would tell me about his work that week on the way, then he would settle by an interesting building or in front of a herd of animals, or by the side of the road where people went back and forth. He would draw while I went to see what I could find. Sometimes he joined me; sometimes we found big interesting pieces which he would take home. The smaller pieces were for sale to the pilgrims, and now, as Tommaso I was able to bargain with them, honing my skills to get the best price. We were sometimes chased off by the more hardened sellers, and once, a very large man knocked Giulio down, and threatened to do the same with me, so we handed over our money and our pieces, and retreated. We then got very good at sensing a malevolent approach, whipping our pieces off the ground in their cloth and making off for home.

When we made sales, we would share the proceeds; mine would be saved to give to Mama, and Giulio would spend his on honeycakes from a pedlar for us to eat on the way home, after the clothes were stored in their hiding place. Mama thought that I found the pieces and Giulio sold them.

One Sunday in January, one of those cold, bright days that make the inside so murky and dismal you want to be outside, we agreed to go out as usual. I wrapped myself in woollen clothes, including short stockings, with a thick woollen cloth around my head and shoulders, and we promised not to be out long. It was the beginning of one of those days that you look back on as momentous, the first major time of emotion in growing up, though I had no idea about that as I waited for Giulio at his door. Mistress Antonina was there, big and breathless. She smiled at me.

I put my arms round her belly: there was no way my hands would meet at the back.

'Not long now I think,' she said. 'He's still kicking, that's a good sign.'

Mama had told me that Mistress Antonina's her first baby after Giulio had been a fine boy but died of the plague when he was two. The next two had lasted one month and two months respectively and the last had been born dead. I hoped this one would be alright, and prayed alternately to Joseph and Our Lady. I hugged Mistress Antonina.

'You won't have it when I'm out will you? I want to see it come.'

'No, I promise!'

'You coming?' said Giulio, pouch hanging from his shoulder.

'Yes. Bye.' We left, Giulio grunting a farewell to his mother.

Mistress Antonina went in to pass the rest of the day with Mama, sewing and talking.

We decided to go to the area of the vineyards to the north-east of the huge remains of the amphitheatre hoping to find some interesting pieces. It was a place where a lot of ancient stuff was being found. After turning myself into Tomaso, I had wrapped the woollen cloth around me over my boy's clothes for warmth, and had cloth bound round my legs and hands. I felt my cheeks glow and the freshness of the air on my face contrasted with the warm me inside the wrappings. I left Giulio to himself when he found some interesting column bases with curly bits near a ruin, and wanted to draw them. The sun shone clear and bright as if it was summer, but the air was chilly.

I scrabbled up the hill towards a vineyard, turning over bits of pottery and stone, and found a long straight piece with a regular pattern of circles and triangles. I sat down to clean out the dust and dirt when I heard shouts from above me. I put the piece in my bag and crawled up the hill, keeping low and dodging from tree to tree until I could see that the shouts had come from workmen digging a hole for foundations of a new house. I inched forward on my elbows and knees as near as I could to hear what they were saying.

'It's a big one, look at that shoulder.'

'Ay – be careful – dig down that way a bit.'

I heard shovels full of earth and stones landing on the ground, and inched forwards between the bare vines, aiming for an evergreen bush.

'Let me see what you've found.' A finer voice was approaching in good quality clothes. The man was accompanied by another with the air of a servant.

I saw that they were all turned away from me so I took the chance to run like a ground bird towards the evergreen and hide in its lower branches. Now I could see several men standing round a hole watching the master lowering himself into it. His head went down until it disappeared.

'It's a fine statue - we must bring it up carefully. But we must tell Master Giuliano.' He looked up to the servant.

'Go to the Vatican to the architect's office and find Giuliano da Sangallo, tell him what we've found.'

The servant nodded and left. The man hauled himself out of the hole with the help of one of the workmen, as the others stood aside.

'It's gonna be a heavy one, Master. We should dig around it a lot more to see how we go about it,' said a workman, obviously the foreman, as they both stood together looking into the hole.

The man, who must had been the owner of the vineyard, got down onto his haunches.

'It's a beauty, a real beauty. We must be very, very careful.'

'This part – a boy I think – looks as if it's broken away…'

'That can be repaired. Make sure no-one, no-one gets near it without my permission.' He stood up. 'Three of you must be here all the time, to keep people away and warn me if anyone tries to… ' He laughed. 'Well, there's no way anyone can steal it.'

The workmen laughed dutifully.

'I trust you to sort that out?'

'Right you are, sir.'

It must be important to send to the Vatican, Giulio must see this. I took a chance that no-one would notice me and scuttled off to find him. He was where I had left him, measuring the columns now and writing down figures on the drawing. I told him what I had seen and his eyes brightened.

'Come on, I'll show you.'

I led the way back. Giulio wasn't afraid of being seen, and

nor I was I, because I was with him. He walked straight up to the men and said:

'Hear you've found a statue - could we see it?'

'You from the Vatican?'

'Yes, from Master Peruzzi, from the Architect of the Pope.'

I was impressed by his manner; he did not sound like an apprentice at all. I didn't know then that this was how he had been taught to announce himself when Peruzzi sent him on an errand.

'And this is my apprentice, Tommaso.'

Cheek! Yet I was proud and stood up straight. The foreman frowned.

'You may let me see it, then I can report to my Master.'

Very Impressive. The foreman must have thought so too. After all, only they and their master knew about the find.

'There's a ladder, and room for one,' said the foreman.

My heart beat faster; what could be in the hole? Giulio crouched at the edge, and I joined him. We looked down on a head, on curly hair on shoulders, one higher than the other, covered in dirt. Below these were other shapes, smaller figures, snakes. Giulio swung his legs over and started to descend. Half way down, he turned on the ladder.

'You be careful,' said the foreman. 'We don't want it damaged.'

Giulio gave him a look.

'Give me that small brush, over there.'

I handed it down and climbed to sit on the second rung of the ladder just over Giulio's head. He took the brush and started to clear the head of dust. The heavy brows were furrowed, and the eyes below them brows were sad. Giulio cleaned the nose and mouth and it was indeed a face of suffering. I gasped.

'Poor man,' I was going to say, then remembered I was an apprentice and said nothing.

'It's wonderful.'

Giulio ran his hand over the face. Then he descended to the base of the ladder where the lower half of the statue was still covered with dirt.

The workman tutted, anxious, he wanted us out of there. Giulio, and I, were intent on the statue. After several minutes, he took out paper and chalk from his pouch. There was just room for him to lean against the sides of the hole and draw. I got out of the hole and shuffled round the top to see it better. A powerful man, who seemed to be being crushed by a snake, with a child - his son? The other side of the statue had broken away, but seemed to be another child and parts of another snake. It was strange. Why would anyone want to make a statue of such a thing?

The men, reassured that Giulio wasn't going to knock off any pieces, sat back, drank water and talked amongst themselves. We stayed like this for some time. The sun passed from one side of the sky to another, and was beginning to descend. Giulio went on drawing and passed the sheets up to me. I could now see the face full on. It was the face of a man who knew, despite his strength, that he would not win.

The bells for vespers sounded across the air, the lowered light caused a shadow of the stature to be projected onto the side of the hole and I could see the shape of the head, turned in anguish. There was a sudden shuffling as the men get to their feet. I turn round and see the Master, and behind him two men and a boy.

I hissed 'Giulio, come out! The Master's back with some others.'

He scrambled out, and I feared for us. He bowed to them 'Master Giuliano, Master Michelangelo.'

He stood aside as if in reverence. I did not know the men,

though I had heard their names, and knew they were important. I shuffled backwards and pretended to be with the workmen.

The owner of the vineyard indicated the hole and stood aside. They stared into it, then Master Giuliano beckoned to the boy with them, and Master Michelangelo started down the ladder as the other two knelt at the top of the hole. Apart from a shuffling inside, there was silence.

'It's magnificent,' breathed Master Giuliano. A growl came from the hole.

'What is it, Father?' asked the boy.

'It seems to be a statue of a man and two boys and snakes.'

Then his face lit up.

'The priest and his sons being killed by serpents sent by Athena. I can't remember his name!'

'Why did she send serpents?'

'I can't remember.'

There were more growls from the hole.

'The right arm is missing, have those men broken it?'

The voice was deep and magnified by the hole. The men looked at each other in alarm.

'No, no, there was no arm.'

I wanted to laugh and turned my head with my mouth in my hand. I glanced at Giulio, who was twitching, refusing to look at me.

Then a head appeared and Master Giuliano and his son stood up to let Master Michelangelo come up. He rubbed dirt off his hands.

'His name was Laocoön. Pliny wrote about this statue, it was made by Athenodorus.'

'Then the Pope will want it,' said Master Giuliano

'Ay. And I to study it.' He gazed into the hole.

I hadn't understood what they'd said, but it was obvious

that the statue was important if the Pope wanted it. Master Giuliano turned to the owner, who was looking anxious.

'I will report this to the Pope, he will want this.' The man started to speak. Master Giuliano waved a hand.

'We will agree a price.'

'The cost of moving it will be very high.'

'And there'll be danger if it's done by people other than stonemasons or sculptors.' Master Michelangelo said, scowling at the workmen. He turned to the owner.

'And it must be guarded - we don't want bits chipped off do we?' The man shook his head.

'No, no I will arrange it.'

'Humph.' He crouched down to look into the hole. He was rather frightening. I sidled towards Giulio.

'Who is he?' I whispered.

'Shh!' So I shushed.

Master Giuliano spoke to the owner.

'Ah, your name?'

'Felice – Felice de'Fredis.'

'Felice? Happy man to have found this on his property,' he laughed.

'I haven't had the vineyard very long, I was digging foundations for an extension to the house.'

He didn't look happy when Master Giuliano told him he would supervise the removal himself.

'We will remove it to the inside of your house – for safety.'

The man looked even less happy. It wasn't exactly a table ornament.

'Who will pay?'

'For the removal? You will.' The man's face fell towards his boots. 'But you will be pleased to, as you will be keeping it for the Pope.' The face couldn't fall anymore, so his eyes did.

'You're sure the Pope...?'

'Want it? Without a doubt. It is one of the most famous statues ever made. It belonged to an Emperor and now it must belong to a Pope. You may allow visitors to see it while the Pope makes his decision. You can re-coup the costs that way.' The man' face brightened. 'After all, it is yours.'

Until the Pope takes it. I hoped the man would get a good price. I hoped he would charge people a lot of money to see it. Master Giuliano bowed to him. 'Good day. You will hear from me.'

'G-good day.' The man bowed in return.

As the two men and the boy turned to go, Master Michelangelo got to his feet, spotted us and said,

'You two- you keep quiet about this!' And he stomped off.

'Yes,' said Master Giuliano, 'perhaps it's best just for now.'

'Yes, Sir,' said Giulio, and I nodded.

We watched them go.

'Who were they?'

'The one who did all the talking is Master Giuliano, the Pope's architect, I told you about. I've been in his office with Master Peruzzi. The gruff one is a sculptor. He made a statue of David more than three times life-size – double the height of this one.'

I looked up trying to imagine such a statue.

'You're making that up.'

'No, I'm not, Master Giuliano told me – and Father said it was true.'

'Has he seen it? Master Giuliano?'

'I don't know – It's in Florence – I expect so – he comes from there.'

'Ah. Does he live here? The sculptor? What's he doing?'

Giulio didn't answer; he didn't know then. He went back to the hole to look at the statue again. You'd have thought he would have known it by heart by then; it was very life-like I thought, but very sad.

Felice de'Fredis, associating him with the Pope, bowed to him and assured him he had organised the men to keep guard in shifts. I saw Giulio bow his head quite graciously. I was impressed; but I wasn't going to let on.

'Race you down the hill!' I called out. He looked annoyed, Felice puzzled.

'Come on, 'brother'!' I got him off the hook. He grinned.

'I'm staying here! Tell them at home, Tommaso!'

I waved and ran off, skipping down the hill. I had been inactive for too long. I changed my clothes. The sun was low, the clouds around it grey and sending out streams of cold air. The shadows of the houses were dark, creeping towards me and swallowing me up. I shivered. As I entered the front door, I called out.

'Mama! Mistress Antonina!'

They weren't in our room; sewing was on the floor. I sensed another kind of cold… heard shuffling above, a baby was crying. I raced up the stairs, and pushed the door.

'You didn't wait for me!' and I laughed. 'The baby is it boy?'

No-one laughed with me. There was a smell in the room and Mama and two women turned to me. Their faces made the blood run from my cheeks. The other kind of cold crept up behind me.

'What's…' I saw between them. The bed was red. I was sure the cover was blue. But it was red. Then I saw.

'Out!' said mama sternly and took my arm.

'Mistress Antonina?'

'Out!'

She pushed me through the door and shut it behind her. I caught a whiff of the smell as the door wafted it through. I knew it was blood, and something else.

'But the baby, I heard a baby cry.'

'It's a girl. She's fine.'

'Mistress…'

'She's dead, Ceci.' She pulled me out and shut the door.

'Where's Giulio?'

'He – stayed.'

'He's not with you?'

'No – he…'

'You must go and fetch him, he must find Pietro. Go!'

'Shall I tell him?'

'Of course you must tell him! Tell him his aunt is here. Go – go!'

She pushed me so I nearly fell down the stairs.

'Out of my way! I must get some water!'

She hustled me down and out of the front door. Only the tip of the sun remained.

~

The funeral was held the following day. Mistress Beata, her sister, was upset that Antonina had not had any rites said over her before she died. Although she had said prayers during the birth and after the death, it was not the same thing as she had not been able to confess or be shriven. Mistress Antonina was buried with her parents. Mistress Beata, her sister, had taken the baby, found a wet nurse, and would keep the child whom I hadn't seen. Master Pietro did not talk of his wife, or of the child.

The house became very quiet. Pietro often did not come

home at night; he slept at his workplace. He was engaged in a major project, the extension of the Belvedere and a new sculpture court, where the statue we saw, the Laocoön, would be housed alongside others the Pope had collected. He was working with the architect Donato Bramante. I remembered the joy when the contract was signed, not just that he would be Master Mason for the work, but it was next to where his father had been the builder. We didn't see him on Sundays, he attended St Peter's. Giulio was at Master Peruzzi's all the time.

I still went out 'excavating' and recruited Niccolò to help me carry the heavy pieces. He was sworn to secrecy about Tommaso and stood with me as I sold. Niccolò was bigger and stronger now, and was better at fending off other sellers. He was also very quiet, not like Giulio.

Adelina came to see Mama more often with her little one, Faustina, and I persuaded her to teach me about account books. I made one for myself to record the finds and sales, and to make sure Niccolò got the correct share. Sometime I would sit with Prettycat and stroke my tears for Giulio into her fur, which she licked. Only she knew how much I missed him.

CHAPTER FOURTEEN

GIULIO

I didn't go home on Sundays any more. I slept in a room at Master Peruzzi's home, the ground floor of a house in the Borgo, sharing with Laurentio, and another two boys, Pasquale and Benedetto, both a year older than me. We had straw mattresses which were pushed to one side in the morning to make space to work at a large table in the centre. We slept, ate and drank plaster, paint, chalk and paper. We ran errands, bought food, and fetched water. And drew, drew, drew. I learned to grind minerals into granules, then into powder to mix them with water for the painting on the *intonaco*. I, overseen by Perino, learned how to calculate the exact amount of paint needed to complete that day's *giornata,* how much painting could be completed in a day. I took measurements, I copied plans. I pricked and pounced. And drew.

I was introduced to Giuliano da Sangallo, and to Donato Bramante, and I was allowed on the site of the Belvedere to see the start of Bramante's new buildings to take note of how foundations were laid and to watch the masons at work; work supervised by my father. I went into the Belvedere *loggia* and chapel, which my grandfather had built, to see for myself the frescoes of Mantegna, which my father had prepared the plaster. As I prepared plaster, I thought of my father and grandfather doing the same thing as I was, and how the techniques of plasterwork had not, and would not, I thought, ever change no matter what the painter put on top of it. (I was to be proved wrong when I later worked with a certain Giovanni da Udine, who finally worked out how to make the purer white plaster he had seen in the *domus aurea* for use in the modelling of stucco decorations.)

I was dazzled by the Mantegna frescos, and visited church after church to see the work of others, and began to see how one painter differed from another. How the painting of people were conventional in some frescoes, repeating a pattern for say, the Madonna, that had been used for years, some older ones where she was pale and unearthly, and the newest frescoes where she looked like a real woman you would see in the street. I saw how used colour was used, how the picture was designed in the placing of its elements: the spatial relationships of the people depicted, and of them and their surroundings. I learned how differently painters depicted the stories of the Bible; how, in the Belvedere, they represented what they could actually see, through the painting of the houses, streets, towers of towns and cities.

I did know then that painting was changing, and worked hard at perspective in my drawings. I saw that architecture was changing from the solid walls of fortified villas, with just a few windows facing outwards and turrets to the delicacy of the arches of Bramante.

~

I was tidying up the workshop and stacking drawings when Master Peruzzi, followed by Perino, came in with a roll of papers. He was fizzing with energy.

'Something to show you!' he said and threw the roll onto the table, standing over it as we took out places by his side.

'The Chigi villa!' Agostino Chigi, the banker who had brought Master Peruzzi to Rome from Siena, the banker who was a friend of Pope Julius. Now I was fizzing!

'It's based on exact proportion, and has the *loggia* as the central idea.'

He rolled out the drawings, separated them, and put stones on the corners. The plan looked very simple: a rectangle with two outstanding wings on the North side making a U-shape. There were dots on the North and East sides: arches. I looked, and saw that it was not symmetrical.

The arches on the North side were exactly in the centre, inside the two wings. The five Eastern arches were the width of the rectangle, ending before the North-East wing began.

'The *logge* are on the ground floor. The old buildings and castles had *logge* on the first floor, so you get the fresh air and see the view, but you couldn't actually walk into the view directly from the *loggia*'

'Like the Belvedere?' I said.

'Exactly. I've done a couple of ground floor *logge* for houses in Siena for the Chigi family, but they were really just an entrance way, a kind of internal portico, but not extending out. This is different.' He leaned over to indicate parts of the plan, which was laid so that the East was at the top.

'The walls with the arches face the gardens - the greater part of the land North and East - here and here.' He drew a wavy line for the river to the east of the plan, and then the boundary of the site to the North.

'The *logge* are on the coolest side. The West and South sides, - the sunniest, hottest sides - have windows which can be shuttered against the heat. The *loggia* with five arches on the North is protected from the winds in the winter by the projecting wings, while in Summer they give a shaded space for parties, festivals, plays.'

I was listening with ears wide open, learning about how the open sides were situated facing large garden spaces, how the weather, the climate, the winds affected his choices, how the sides with windows were those nearest to the walls of the land next door, on the South, giving a small intimate garden space and that of the *Via Lunghara* on the West: the arched sides open to wide space, the closed sides (one with a door) facing the much smaller spaces.

Master Peruzzi continued.

'The North *loggia* is also the main public entrance; people arrive at the stables up here in the North, then walk through the gardens,'

'Looking at the sculptures!' I said. He nodded

'And go up a flight of steps in the centre to be greeted by the host. Both *logge* have a great depth so that they are as big as, or bigger than, most main halls, with high vaults. The *loggia* on the East side is more private, for small dinner parties, and where guests can walk in and out of the garden as they please.'

'With the sun behind them.' He smiled. I was pleased with myself. Perino, who had been listening impassively, but staring at the drawings like a kestrel at a mouse, spoke for the first time.

'Two floors, divided into rooms.' Master Peruzzi nodded. 'With a wide staircase – all the walls to be frescoed?'

'Every inch, inside and out.' My mouth dropped open, as Perino's eyebrows rose.

'Outside?'

'Yes. The whole of the outside will be painted in *chiaroscuro* – light and shade - to represent carved sculpture all over, swags and cherubs, garlands and urns.' He unrolled a drawing of the North façade.

We gasped and then were silent.

The drawing showed the symmetry of the windows and the arches. But the decoration! I recognised the triangular pediments over the windows, which I had copied a hundred times. These were divided by pilasters, which were repeated between the arches. I saw the reference:

'The Amphitheatre!' The Master smiled.

These drawings showed details of the antique ruins, imitated and transformed into a new elegant style. There was a small sketch of cherubs holding a swag of laurel, to go over the windows: another detail I had copied. The outside walls all to be decorated in *chiaroscuro* to represent carvings.

'The outside is monochrome, the inside colourful,' he said. 'And inside – inside, the *logge* vaults will be painted so they relate to the sky outside - the night sky in the East *loggia*, the daylight sky in the North. And on the first floor, at the top of the staircase, the main hall will be frescoed as if it is a *loggia,* with arches, facing out on three sides, all painted with the view you would see if there were real inside/outside arches.'

He sat down, his eyes sparkling. My mind tried to grasp this concept, totally, totally new. I could see Perino taking it in.

'I will show that perspective can work to make an illusion; I will make what the ancient writers described. A painter painted a curtain so well that someone tried to lift it to see what was behind, and drew grapes so real that a bird flew down to peck them. This room will be so, but much more, much, much more.' He grinned.

'Like the frescoes you've described that Pinturicchio painted in the Siena Library?'

'Yes. But more than that – it will not be a series of perspective drawings inside arches, each picture different. This will be a whole room, a room open on three sides, with widows along the back. The spaces between the windows will be painted as a continuation of what you see through the windows and when you shutter the windows and light the candles, you will think you can walk out onto the balconies, feel the breeze, and see people in the gardens and on the river.'

The idea of the *logge* real and illusory, would integrate garden and living indoor spaces into a whole, a freedom of movement in air, not boxed in like the fortified buildings. Chigi's villa would be the first in Rome that was not a fortress,

It was new, it was exciting, and I was to be part of its making.

It would be a first realisation of the discussions of the artists and architects around me, of how the antique style, the 'Old' Rome, would be used in creating the 'New' Rome'. A revival, yet re-imagined. It made me see that a painter could be an architect; and, as I grew within that workshop, I saw how being able to draw meant we could draw designs for plays, festival arches, costumes, silverware, anything at all in the world. Whatever the wealthy and their love of show could desire.

Perino stretched his neck and back. 'It's a good lot of work,' he said.

~

There were other things I was learning. Drink and Women, and what you did with them. I joined the other apprentices at the inns in the Borgo for drink and sing bawdy songs. I was a frequenter of prostitutes whenever I had money or goods to give. I had started going with Pasquale and Benedetto, the other apprentices, just after I joined Master Peruzzi' s workshop. They had both discerned I was a virgin and were determined to put that right. The first prostitute took my money.

'Just in and out then?' It was over very quickly. 'If you slow down you'll enjoy it more. Come back and I'll show you.'

So I went back, on my own, and she was right. She wasn't pretty, so I changed to another house, went less, and paid more. This time, the girl had large breasts, which she wanted me to stroke. She then taught me, at a price - I had to borrow the money - how to make a girl happy.

'So that when you marry, you won't be stuck with a miserable wife.'

I forgot about these encounters the next day, or, rather I forgot about the women. I remembered the explosions and the relief. Then I realised the opportunity to draw nudes. I made them pose, on their own, once or twice with men. I drew them in the positions of the sexual act. The start of a collection that was to cause so much trouble later.

CHAPTER FIFTEEN

CECI

I was sewing a piece of decoration onto a cap; it needed big stitches, which I could do. I couldn't do fine sewing like Mama. She knew, and ignored, that I hated sewing anything. I did it with an ill grace as I would rather be selling. Urging customers on market days to look at the ready-to-wear garments, the fine sewing, telling them that she could alter things for them (she did a lot of that commissioned work now), bargaining on prices. We should have been resting at midday, but there was so much to do. She had just finished a dress for a small girl in pink and grey brocade cut out from an adult dress we got from Samuel in exchange for three tall wax candles, which we had received for two adult shirts. She wrapped the dress carefully in a length of cotton cloth and tied it with a cord. She then looked out onto the street to find a boy to take it to the customer who lived on the other side of the church of San Marco. She saw Niccolò helping a carter unload wood at the baker's, a task which he did in exchange for a small loaf, and called him over.

'Will you take this for me to the street opposite *San Marco*, the house with the heavy door and Our Lady over it,' he didn't smile (this is the game), 'for two *quattrini*?' he grinned, grunted as the carter called him back and promised to do it when the cart is unloaded.

I protested, 'I can go.'

'No - those caps must be finished today. They're being called for after vespers bell.'

I sighed. I hated sewing, have I said that? She looked at my work.

'I know there are several thicknesses, but you could make neater stitches,' and she undid all the work I've done. 'If you take more care, you'll finish sooner.'

If it's needed this evening, why don't you do it? I thought, but didn't say. I glared at her and she gave me a look which got me threading a needle. I prodded through the fabric; needle up, needle down, needle up, needle down. Rhythm. Mama nodded and smiled.

'You see? If you stop dreaming and just concentrate, it goes quickly.'

Needle up, needle down; needle up, needle down… humph…

Niccolò came in.

'Wash your hands,' Mama instructed pointing to a bucket. Niccolò grimaced but did as he was told, as he was always told before he ran such errands for Mama.

'The price is five soldi, which they have promised on delivery. You will bring back the cloth and the cord.'

Niccolò nodded, took the package and left.

We sewed in silence. Prettycat, too adult to do anything like jumping on us and pulling threads – unless she thought we weren't looking - lay asleep under the window, snoring slightly. My annoyance was lost in timing my stitches to those snores. Needle up (snore in) needle down (snore out)…From outside we heard sounds of shops opening again, street cries, and snatches of gossip on which we commented with eyebrows and grins.

Niccolò returned; he was still carrying the package

Mama, about to bite off a length of thread, frowned at it, then at him.

'What's wrong?'

'They wouldn't take it.' He held it out.

'Why? They didn't like it?' She put down the thread and took the package. It was in the cloth exactly as she had tied it. 'It looks as if it hasn't been opened.'

'No, they just said to bring it back, it was diseased, they said.' I stopped sewing, mid-snore.

'Diseased? What did they mean?'

Niccolò shrugged.

'Dunno. I waited for the payment, like you said. The maid came back with it, ever so upset. Said if she caught the plague from, it she would curse you and all your family.' He emphasised the word 'curse' with open eyes and a thrust of the head.

We were startled.

'The plague?' said Mama. 'Why on God's earth would they think this would give them the plague?' She crossed herself and I followed, stabbing both shoulders and almost getting the needle in my eye.

Niccolò shrugged one shoulder.

'Dunno. ''Swhat she said.' He shuffled his feet 'Do I get paid? Wasn't my fault.'

'Er, yes.' Mama was perplexed. She handed him one quattrino, he looked, understood, and was out of the shop before she could change her mind and take it back.

'What was that all about?'

'I have no idea. Antea looked uncertainly at the parcel. 'Folks do get some strange notions.'

'But there isn't the plague in Rome now is there? What gave them that idea?'

'It's a made-up piece of nonsense, I should've known she'd

cheat us. She was so insistent on the 'right colours' - wouldn't have it till I showed her an exact sample – and I had to show her three before she would order – and then she changed her mind. After we'd cut it'.

The dress she had ready for sewing next was the rejected sample.

'Now I've got two unordered dresses to sell!'

'Perhaps Niccolò made a mistake.'

'Why would he bring it back unopened? I shall have to go there myself.'

I got up immediately and put my work down.

'I'll go Mama; I know my way better than you. I'll make her pay for it.'

'No, Ceci'

'You know I'm good with the customers, about prices and payment.'

'Yes. I know, but -' I took the package and set off. Niccolò was hanging around hoping for another errand from someone.

'Where you goin'?' He looked at the parcel 'you goin' for a ruck?'

His eyes gleamed at the thought of some drama.

'Can I come with you? – you should 'ave a man with you.'

Niccolò, the thin beanpole who can't be seen from the side, and wafts in the breeze. I was about to say no, then thought I might have need of a witness.

'A'right.' I started off ' Com'on then.'

Niccolò ran after me, grinning.

We marched through the streets, and when we got to the house I pounded on the door. There was the sound of a latch being slid back over the tiny hole in the door and a female voice asking for my name and business.

'Cecilia Arditti, dressmaker.'

'If it's about the parcel, Mistress doesn't want it.'

'I want to talk to her, I'm sure there's been a mistake.'

'No mistake. We don't want the plague here. Go away.' The latch slid back.

'Why do you say that? There's no plague in Rome.'

There was no reply. I pounded on the door again.

'Please, tell me why you think that?'

There had been nothing said on the street, gossip like that would have spread like fire.

'Please,' I shouted, 'I want to know'

The latch slid again and a man's voice said,

'Mistress knows where you get your fabrics – secondhand.'

'Yes, everyone knows we re-make clothes.'

'Well then.'

'I don't understand.'

'Mistress saw you buying, at the Jew's shop. She says it's the Jews' fault, the plague. They bring it in on the clothes. You buy them.'

He slid the latch shut with a large clack and I heard his footsteps as he walked away.

The Jew's shop? Samuel?

'My uncle says Jews are bad people.' I stared at Niccolò.

Samuel, a Jew? I thought of Samuel, with his black ringlets and his little black hat. I knew he didn't come to church, and didn't buy or sell on a Saturday. People made rude remarks about him, but it didn't stop them trading with him. I had heard people being nasty about Jews, but it had gone over my head. I had not connected the man I knew with those remarks.

'Do you think Samuel is a bad person? You run errands for him.'

'Yes, but my uncle says the Jews killed Jesus, and one day they will kill us all and take our money.'

'That's nonsense!'

'It's what my uncle says.'

'But your uncle pawns things with Samuel.' Niccolò shrugged.

'Uncle says you wouldn't catch Christians doing – what he does.'

Niccolò can't think for himself – then he does.

'But I won't run errands for 'im again, not now I knows about the plague'.

Two men nearby had stopped their conversation to listen. I've had enough. I dropped the package and boxed Niccole's ears.

'Don't be so silly! There isn't a plague. I like Samuel, he saves the best clothes for us, and for a fair price.'

He howled, and backed away, hands over ears. One of the men spoke.

'Don't you stand for that, lad - from a girl!' and he chortled, while the other said

''E don't deserve that, little shrew, e's only tellin' the truth. Them Jews!' and he spat on the ground.

I turned on him.

'So you've been spreading rumours.'

The man shrugged.

'No rumours – we all know who's t'blame for evrythin' - them Jews. Rob you blind they do giv'n 'alf a chance.' A woman joined in.

'Take stuff from poor folk and if they can't buy it back put up the price so they can't ever get it back. Unchristian it is.'

I recognised her: the arm I had bitten in Samuel's shop. She gave a grin full of black teeth and malice.

They all looked at me. Others stopped.

'And did I 'ear you standin' up for a Jew?' The man leered.

'Maybe she's a Jew 'erself', said the woman.

The man laughed and came towards me. His friend watched, eyes narrowed.

'Jew-lover!' someone shouted. More people stopped to look.

I was nervous. I was not from this district, no-one knew me except the woman, and she wasn't going to help me.

Niccolò looked from me to the men, pale-faced and afraid. I bent to pick up the package and the man who spat on the ground came up behind me and grasped my buttock. I felt sick. I flicked my eyes to see where I could escape to. I saw Niccolò run away. The man seized my chin and forced me back against the house door. I could see spittle on his lips.

'Now, what's a wench like you doing out on 'er own then?'

'Whore! Jew-whore!' I could hear the cries, but kept my eyes on him. He pushed me against the door and thrust himself forward. I felt something hard against my stomach, pushing against me.

'Now, don't spoil the fun.'

The man's hands were sliding up my legs, pulling up my skirt. He put his mouth on mine and tried to part my lips with his tongue. I twisted my head, pushed my hands against the door. As one hand squeezed my buttock and the other fumbled between my legs, I brought my knee up between his legs with all my strength. He screamed and backed away, bowing over. There were roars of laughter. Then I saw Angelo, holding a meat cleaver, come charging round the corner followed by Niccolò. Angelo approached the still-bent over, groaning man and brought his hand with the handle of the cleaver down onto his head, catching his shoulder with the sharp blade. He roared and thumped the man in the face. The man was on his back, rolling on the ground trying to get away. The crowd was roaring too, no, cheering. There were cries of 'Grounded by a lass' 'and a butcher!' Shouts of laughter and applause. I was panting.

These people who watched him with me, who did nothing for me, are now applauding me, and Angelo? I spat on the ground, to get rid of the man's saliva, and at them. Angelo came over to me.

'You alright, Cecilia?' The man's friend is hauling him up from the ground, laughing at him. I spat again, in their direction.

'Come on.' Angelo, turned me round, I was shaking.

Niccolò picked up the package and we all three walked back to the *Macello*, Mama ran to meet me and threw her arms round me. I start to cry, in rage and fear. Through my sobs I heard Angelo tell her what happened.

'Next time,' said Angelo, 'wait for me or my son Giorgio and take one of us with you.'

The story spread through the *Macello* and beyond. Not the story of a girl who was attacked, that was a common occurrence, but the part of the story with the word 'plague' in it. Orders were cancelled, and the two small dresses remained unsold. Fewer people visited Samuel's shop to buy clothes, and only those truly desperate for money arrived to pawn household goods. They too stopped after one of them was attacked and left bleeding in the street, and a woman was dragged into an alley and raped by several men. Our shop remained closed after we found excrement smeared over our door. We were afraid, and stayed in the house. Angelo and Adelina got food for us, and it was Pietro, home one day, who told us that someone had set fire to Samuel's shop and that neighbours failed to save the house next door from the fire. Two children and their mother who lived in the attic died. Their artisan father had both his hands so badly burned he would not carve again.

'Next day they dragged Samuel's body through the streets and threw it into the lime quarry.'

I shuddered.

'And us?' asked Mama.

Pietro hesitated then said 'I think you must burn all your fabrics outside so that people see, and you should curse the Jews.'

Mama was shocked.

'Curse Samuel?'

'You must…' He paused. 'Angelo told me that when he got to you some of the crowd were yelling 'Jew-lover' and 'Jewess'. You must convince them that you are not. You must pray in the street to the Lord, you must be seen doing so and that way you may be safe.'

'May be?'

'You may have to move where no-one knows you.'

Mama was silent. Then she picked up the dress that was the start of it all.

'Tomorrow at midday, we will make a fire. We'll do as you say and we will make penance at *Santa Maria*.'

Pietro nodded.

'I will help you, and spread the word'

The next day, dressed in sackcloth, at Pietro's insistence, we carried out all the clothes: those waiting to be used, the new-made caps and the two dresses. The pieces already cut out, the ribbons and threads, even though those were not bought from Samuel.

The neighbours glanced at us, but said nothing and got on with their work. I don't know who blamed us, who approved of what we did. I didn't know what anyone felt about us. It was as if we were strangers, unwelcome strangers. A woman, who sold herbs round the district, came into the *Macello*, looked at us and said, 'You have poisoned the air – you should leave.'

Indeed, the air was heavy, not just with the usual smells but with anxiety and fear. Our fear of the people; theirs of us. Except for Pietro, who laid the kindling under and around the clothes, and Adelina who lent us two large crosses made of wood to hang round our necks, and Angelo who added fat to the pile to make it burn. Giorgio leant against the butcher's door and watched. He caught my eye and his expression changed to a twisted smile that I had to look away from. More people came. A priest arrived, and made the sign of the cross over the pile, and, as Mama bent to light it, he shouted,

'Cursed be the Jews of this city who bring infection, and who killed our Lord!'

Mama and I kneeled and crossed ourselves, as did the crowd which had gathered around us.

'Blessed be these women who have been led astray.' He made the sign of the cross over us. 'May they repent...'

Repent? What for?

'...and live only for the Lord.'

Was he suggesting we become nuns? He looked at us.

'We repent!' cried Mama, raising her hands. I followed her lead.

'We repent! We repent!' The fire flared up, the fat had done its work. The priest backed away.

'Thanks be to God!' he cried. 'These women are absolved in the name of the Lord. Amen!'

'Amens' ran through the crowd, some of whom were kneeling, everyone crossing themselves. I didn't see anyone I knew from our street.

We got up off the floor and bowed to the priest. I see Mama pass something to him.

'For the Virgin,' she said aloud, and I saw it was two links of the necklace. We had one left. He took it and disappeared.

We looked into the fire, at the sparks made by the heat on the gold and silver threads, at the brocades turning to grey ash, at the fine fabric for chemises crumpling as if melting and sending off flecks of white ash. Mama turned away but I watched as the dress which caused all this, curled in on itself then devoured itself in a flash of flame.

'What about that they're wearing?' demanded the herb-seller.

'They are wearing sackcloth,' replied Pietro 'as they should, and they have been blessed by the Priest so there cannot be anything for you to fear.'

The herb-seller sniffed.

'Well, you live next to them… we shall see', and she trundled off.

See what?

Then I was inspired. I went down on my knees, raked out the cooler ashes at the edge of the pile, raised my alms and dropped them onto my head. I remembered a chant from penitents outside a church (even though they were hanged afterwards.)

'Mea culpa! Mea culpa!'

Give them a good show. An old man came up to me.

'Bless you my child', and others murmured the same. Well, that was something.

We doused down the remaining flames and swept up the ashes, collecting them to take to Santa Maria's to make penance.

That evening, after brushing out the ashes from our hair and changing into simple dresses, two we had saved from the fire for modesty's sake and had hidden with Adelina, we ate in silence. I was lost in thought.

That day had had nothing to do with God or Our Lady. It had to do with people. People who watched the man assault me, who then applauded when Angelo came. People who spread hatred of the Jews, who demanded we humiliate ourselves and who destroyed our business. People in the *Macello* who avoided us today. People from outside who came to see a show. People for whom we were entertainment.

We made a show, to save ourselves from people, from what they could do and from what they did. Through that show we saved our lives.

I thought of Samuel. What had he done to deserve his shop being burned and his body dragged through the streets? Nothing. Samuel was a fair man, he didn't cheat anyone. He wasn't responsible for the Jews who killed Jesus. I worried about Samuel being in Hell. Why would he be in Hell? Just being a Jew condemned him? I'm sorry God, but I liked him. Why was a good Jew worse than the man who wanted to rape me? Why? Why?

I thought of the few people who were our friends: Pietro, Angelo and Adelina, perhaps Niccolò who went to fetch Angelo, but he was a child. I was a child no longer. And Giulio. And Giulio?

The next day, Mama gave Pietro the last gold link and asked him to change it. We counted the coins he gave us, as we had counted coins when we first arrived. The joy I felt then for the pretty shiny things and in learning to count was something far away. Something in complete contrast to what I had learned in the past week. Now I knew what the coins meant, I knew exactly how much we had and I knew long it would last.

I asked the same question Mama asked then; how will we live? I know now that Mama was happy; she had hope, and excitement in being her own person, her power to control her own destiny. But I saw no hope in her face then. Her joy in sewing, her pride in her being able to provide us with a living had gone. She was shocked into silence and her power had gone.

We went to Santa Maria, offered the ashes and made confession. Of what? I made something up about being ashamed of dealing with a Jew, and promised not to do it again. Mama simply mumbled. I prayed for Giulio to come home, to talk with me. But, in that church, I knew what I must do. I had to look after Mama. I had to find someone who needed a servant.

~

But I didn't find work as a servant. Neither did Mama. No-one in the district wanted a 'Jew-lover'. Mama went to the Palazzo Colonna next to the church of the Apostles to offer her services as a seamstress, but they said they did not need her, their work was done by the nuns at the nearby convent. She went to the convent to offer herself as a novice, but she was poor and had no family to pay the convent the 'dowry' for her admittance, so she was refused. I went, as Tommaso, to the gardeners at the Palazzo Colonna and the Palazzo Venezia, and asked for work but they told me I didn't look strong enough for a gardener's boy, and anyway, they had enough boys. They only have work for weeding women. So I returned in a dress a few days later. The Head Gardener looked me over, pulled his hand up one arm, across my chest and down my other arm and pinched my buttocks. He slapped them.

'Not much muscle, but good legs. Start tomorrow, at the Colonna garden on *Monte Cavallo*, before sun-up.'

'How much?'

He looked surprised.

'For weeding? Three *quattrini* per day – or two and a bag of vegetables.'

I said I would take the two, and the vegetables.

'And anything else – a bit extra.' I knew from his look what he meant. The man who wanted to rape me had suddenly opened my eyes to men's desires. I stared at him until he dropped his eyes.

'Perhaps,' he mumbled.

I went home and told Mama that I had a job, one that will bring in coins and food. She was stirring something in the pot, a large bone with scraps of meat on it. She told me that Angelo had given it to her, and Adelina had asked her to make lots of little drawstring bags for her goods, and would supply the materials. She had arranged to help at the bakery in the early morning, hidden from view at the ovens, during the pilgrim season in exchange for loaves.

'We shall survive!' she said and smiled with her mouth.

So the whole summer we worked. At first, I had an aching back every day and struggled to get up from the mattress each morning, but then, my muscles got used to the bending and carrying. I came to love it, outside in the sun, in the vineyard and the vegetable garden. I grew brown and my legs and arms become stronger. At midday, we women sat in the shade of the fruit trees, eating and drinking and telling each other stories. When I first arrived and spoke, they taunted me for being 'above myself' and 'trying to be a lady' so I listened, and started to imitate their dialect until they forgot I had ever spoken differently. I learned new words – rude words – and how to make crude jokes, even though I didn't totally understand them. Nor did I understand the lewd remarks to and from the male gardeners but I laughed because everyone else did. Sometimes, one of the younger women 'went missing', as the older women put it as they cackled. One of them said to me and to two other girls my age, 'go and see what it's all about,' and they roared with laughter.

'I dun need t'' said one of the girls. 'We all sleep together, and Ma and Pa are at it every night.'S'noisy an' I can't sleep.'

The younger one said 'my brother tried to do me, but 'e got

whipped by Pa – 'e 'as t'sleep outside now.' So it's only me who doesn't actually know what 'it' is; there is only my mother, no father and no brothers, no-one to watch.

One evening when I was later than the others to take my basket of weeds to the compost heap, I heard giggling, and followed the noise round to the other side. The girl who 'went missing' and one of the gardeners were rolling together on a pile of straw, he tickling her and she crunched up over his hands on her stomach, laughing. She gasped and as he raised his hands, she twisted under him and pulled his face to hers, his mouth on hers. Her skirt was up round her thighs and his hand was between them. I watched; she raised her knees and they writhed as if joined together; then I saw that they were, as he raised himself and I saw his cock, upright and huge. I blinked. Like the goats, and when the ram came to the sheep, was she going to turn over? No, they stayed face to face, mouth to mouth. Then he pushed his cock against her and into her, and bounced up and down, while her hands were on his bare buttocks as if helping him.

I wanted to giggle, but her face, mouth open, stopped me. It had an intensity I had never seen, and perhaps knew, for it seemed to match what did to myself in bed at night, and what was now fizzing between my own thighs. I longed to be touched. There was a lot of writhing and then a shout and a shudder and a cry from her. He fell on her and rolled, she was whimpering. I couldn't see what happened then, but she gave a cry arced her back, and they lay together, panting, and looking at each other, smiling, and smiling. As they rolled apart I could see their full nakedness from the waist down, and the fizzing was unbearable. My hand reached down then I too was panting and had to stifle my own cry at the explosion of feeling. I thought they must have heard, but they were too absorbed in each other to pay attention to anything else, murmuring, kissing. Looking at her all the time and she at him. Then he gently smoothed her skirt and covered himself. As I slowed my breathing, I felt empty, I felt so sad. I curled up close to the heap of fresh leaves, and, as I heard them leave, I was bereft.

The shade came suddenly as the sun was blocked by the cypresses and then the olive trees, and I felt a chill, but did not move. I tried to work out what I had seen; I thought that it was what Mama had told me about how babies were made. As she had spoken, I thought of the goats and sheep and even horses mating, imagined men and women in the same positions. I had thought that it was just an act when people wanted children. I hadn't connected it at all with the physical relief I felt in bed. I remembered the man in the piazza, who had touched me *there* and how, while I had hated his tongue in my mouth, hated his smell and his hand on me, I had, for the instant that he touched me felt a brief thrill of excitement that I had then refused to acknowledge. Today, though, I had seen something else. Not just the position, face to face, but something else. Not just pleasure, or even happiness, an absorption in each other bodies and in each other, the way they shared their eyes, it was joy that I had seen.

I sat up straight. My body was longing for a man on it, for a man's hand on me, but only in this way. I wanted that joy.

Giulio. Giulio!

I got up and ran, faster and faster, all the way home, and arrived panting and laughing. I had stopped thinking of Giulio with a childish admiration, I thought of him quite differently. My dreams of him changed from me just looking at him, to us together, like that!

It made everything brighter, it made me hum. I didn't mind when the head gardener came amongst us and hit our buttocks with his stick to make us work faster. I enjoyed the sun on me, I enjoyed the physical work even when it was tiring. I found that pleasure in the body was not just contained in that one spot, but everywhere, as my back bent, my arms stretched, my shoulders bearing panniers of weeds. I slowed the movement when I pulled my fingers through my hair, enjoyed its softness either side of each finger and the slight shiver when it fell on my back, moving my head so I could feel that gentle tickling of hair against skin. I enjoyed the difference between stroking Prettycat's fur down her back, the slight movement of the velvet on her nose and the skin of her ear; the sun's warmth on my body, the shade at midday. I liked turning fruit on my tongue, the feel of it, the texture, the taste; the pleasure of sinking my nose into orange flowers, and crushing lemon and mint leaves; trailing my hand across thymes. I loved the earthy scent of the weeds as they came out of the soil, each one different; of my own sweat at the end of the day.

I watched buds change into tiny fruits that grew and grew; grapes come onto the vines; vegetables in rows growing from tiny leaves to wide leaves, tall stems, miniature trees. I liked to hear sheep eating grass under the fruit trees, and the goats scrunching the thorny bushes and the scrub at the edges of the gardens; breathe in their musty smell; hear their bleating, the sound of the birds and to watch their flight from tree to tree.

I wished I could set seed, dig purple carrots and green turnips, gather honey from the hives: only men did these things. But we women, in twos, in the late summer, carried big baskets of grapes down to great tubs to be trodden down for wine. At this time of the year, we were all put to this task, men and women together, with bare legs and feet, we with our skirts tucked up getting green or red juice up our legs. We pounded the grapes, we wore out our feet, then washed them afterwards, to feel clean and pure. I felt that the men treading with us were angels not devils as we all sang to keep the rhythm of the tread. We laughed, not at crude jokes, but just laughed. I loved the bright colours, greens, reds, yellows, purples, colours so much brighter than the pictures in the church. Colours that made me think of Giulio. I wished he was a part of all this, sharing this joy. I went home tired, hoping to find him, knowing I wouldn't, but still sharply disappointed.

I filled the Giulio-shaped space with yearning for the meeting with him that I was quite, quite sure would come. I wanted to be, I would be, part of him. I just had to wait.

~

The weather got wet and cold, and the weeding stopped. The pilgrims diminished in numbers and neither Mama nor I had work. I brought the boy clothes home, and turned into Tommaso, without Mama saying anything; to raid the hills, the gardens and the tree clumps for firewood, to forage for herbs and leaves and to search the ruins for coins. Bones still came from Angelo's, sometimes with a lot of meat on them. I thought how generous he was, but then he was always kind to us, perhaps because he had no daughters of his own. Even so, I travelled to the market places in other districts to pawn the pots and pans, until we had only one pot, two knives and two beakers, nothing to buy things back, and no coins for the rent.

Mama was always coughing, she become pale and thin. I realised then how small and delicate she was; how much stronger I was. Every day I tried to find work, but there was none. I went up to the gardens on Monte Cavallo, but only the head gardener was there, who didn't recognise me, dressed as I was as Tommaso, and sent me away. Then, searching further afield for coins, I got nearer to the limekiln, and I asked if there was work there. The foreman looked at me, saw my strong legs and said

'Where've you worked?'

'At the gardens.'

He laughed then coughed. I waited.

Then he mumbled 'a lad – cheaper than a man. I'm one short' Then

'You c'n load wood – once a week, mind, for a meal and a place by th'fire'

'I want coins, I have my family.' He laughed coarsely which

set off more coughing. 'Think you're a man eh, got yurself a babby?' and he laughed and spat at his feeble joke. I stayed silent.

'You're a pretty boy, if you want money, you should take that mincy bum down to the sailors! There'll be coins there! Be off!' and he hit me across the face and pushed me to the ground.

That winter we huddled together, me, Mama and Prettycat, under the one blanket we had not sold, and a pile of straw, but sometimes it was too cold to sleep. Mama started to cough and cough, and her throat was so swollen that she could not eat bread, what bread there was, stale at the end of the day. The meat bones continued, but less often, and our meals were bones in water and whatever I could scavenge from the gardens, and the hedgerows. Pietro, when he came home, did not visit us as Antonina had, and Giulio did not come home at all.

My dreams about him stopped. I was wrong about him, about him and me. There would be no blissful meeting. Now he was a man, now he was working in important places for important people, now he was doing what he wanted: drawing, painting. He would have forgotten all about me, the child on the ground floor. However could I have convinced myself otherwise? I concentrated on being Tommaso and not Ceci. I was ashamed of her: I couldn't bear to be her. I ceased to listen to the remarks of the neighbours, most of whom now shunned me and Mama. I was rarely seen on the *Macello*. Elsewhere I was just a boy, with long hair. A boy who learned about what 'pretty boys' did, and managed to avoid it; I was a 'street child': up for errands, but not for poking.

I found out when market days were held round the city, and I learned to steal food, and, when the sellers were packing up, fight off other children for the dropped leaves and mouldy vegetables that were left on the ground. I learnt to always have my knife with me, but even so, I lost out to the little boys and girls who could dart round me or the bigger boys who would swipe me, or cut me with their own knives. I often went home with blood on me and bruises. I dropped into dialect and used the words I had learned in the garden, now knowing what they meant, and picked up more to use as insults.

I forgot all about the summer, about the happiness. The aches and pains were of suffering, not of joy. I slept from the exhaustion of being out every day, from lack of proper food, and from the cold, not from the wholesome tiredness of that time, in a different country. With a different sun.

I forgot I was a girl. The only time I wore a dress was on Sundays, when we went to church for the warmth of being in a crowd of people until Mama could not walk so far. Then, I went on my own, to the further church of San'Apostoli, as Tommaso, to queue for bread with the beggars. Wood appeared most days, from Angelo, as sometimes when I set out I met his son Giorgio coming out of the butchery with a pile of wood.

'This is for you – I'll take it over shall I,' he would say and I would smile; I didn't like him, the smile was for Angelo.

After that I often saw Giorgio go into our house with something when I was on my way out. It was good of him, of Angelo, to help us like this.

Mama seemed preoccupied and didn't ask what I did when I was out, Adelina was too busy with Faustina and her increased stock: she was now selling oil and perfumes and silver jewellery she and the widow made themselves. Prettycat left us as we had no food: I saw her fighting other cats for a mouse, and sometimes, when there was sun and I sat outside, she would come to sit with me which made me sadder, but she didn't come into the house, too cold.

I was thirteen, nearly fourteen. I had forgotten how to laugh.

Mama had to tell Pietro that she had no money to pay the rent. He didn't seem to be worried; he waved a hand, and didn't ask us to leave. It was Advent, and people were talking about Christmas and the Glory of God, and good will to all men. Pietro came down the same day with a hamper of food and a pile of firewood. He told us that he was sorry he had neglected us, and that he would make up for it. I was glad to eat properly again, and not to have to go out scavenging so often. I suppose he hadn't helped us before because we reminded him of Antonina; whatever the reason, I was grateful.

We made oatcakes and cooked them over the fire, where they sat on the griddle and dripped through the bars catching fire. We ate them, warm and charred, with melted cheese. Pietro told us how Giulio was doing in Master Peruzzi's workshop, and asked Mama if she would clean the house for him, as he had neglected that too. Angelo came across with bones and wood as well, grumbling about Giorgio not wanting to do errands anymore 'because he was a man'.

'He's right, so he does a bit at the abattoir,' Angelo told us, 'which means he can put aside better meat for the shop.'

He grinned and wished us a happy Christmas. I wished his wife (whom we rarely saw) would die and he would marry Mama, so we could have meat and wood every day, and could buy vegetables.

The bells, which I realised I had stopped noticing, rang out on Christmas Day, and we went to church, me in a dress, where people smiled at us, or seemed to. Pietro went to St Peter's Basilica for Christmas, but gave us some wine before he left. He began to come home more often; he gave us food all through January and February, and Mama began to look better. I hadn't seen Giulio for over a year, perhaps I wouldn't recognise him. He was someone I used to know.

The Spring came, and with it a wedding.

CHAPTER SIXTEEN

GIULIO 1508

My father had made an arrangement to marry again. He wanted the dowry to buy some land, and he wanted another son. I understood that: I did not want to be a mason, I did not want to take over his business. I wanted to be a painter, an architect, the one who worked with the mason. Now he was a full-time contractor like my grandfather, he wished to, and should, advance his status.

The chosen woman was Graziosa de'Antonii, a fifteen-year old, the link with whose family would enhance our own. The settlement contract was made in February, but the wedding was celebrated in March. It was a bright, if cold to start with, day. The family had adorned the street with flags and Father's workers had painted arches with scenes of flowers and garlands of leaves. There were musicians, with pipes and drums and singers. The sun shone to honour us, and it became a sweet Spring day.

My sister, the two-year old Gerolama, whom I had not seen since her birth, and then only for a second, was dressed like a miniature lady. She looked like a delicious, absurd marionette, fussed over by my Aunt. She would be coming back to the house to be cared for by her new mother; I noted that my Aunt appraised Graziosa with a long up-and-down look. Her expression showed her view that such a little stick as she would not be capable of caring for the child, even with the nurse whom she was handing over along with Gerolama. I got the impression that the Aunt would be a frequent visitor, not to see Gerolama, although that would be her reason, but to assert her authority over the 'stick'.

Pietro told me he had invited Antea and Ceci and had given them lengths of material so they would look nice for his wedding. He wanted them there, he said, because they had been good to Antonina, and to him. 'And if anyone thinks they shouldn't be here, you can say it is my wish.' I thought back to when Ceci and I used to go out, and smiled at the childhood memories. I had been fond of her, enjoyed her company and wondered if she still wished she was a boy.

Pietro had put up a canopy stretching across the street from our house to Angelo's, tables were laden with food, including sugar delicacies made into animal shapes, fruit and flowers from the confectioners in the Borgo. These were the attraction of the tables as many of our neighbours had seen nothing like them before. Wine had also been brought from the Borgo, but Pietro had bought food and wine locally so no-one would feel put out. The local baker had made special wedding loaves decorated with leaves. Musicians with lutes, woodwind, drums and trumpets for the ceremony and for dancing had their own canopy. All our neighbours at this end of the street were invited, and when they realised it wasn't going to rain, they hung carpets and coloured cloth over their window sills, as they would for a carnival.

As it was mid-April, garlands of leaves intertwined with wild flowers, violets and oranges and lemons decorated the tables and were hung over the door to our house. Pietro had hired serving men and women, and the house was full of the smells of hot food and people coming and going. There was even a basket of presents to distribute to the guests. It all showed Father's new status, a successful man allied to a family with wealth, with the promise of a large family through the young bride. It was chaotic, noisy, exciting and magnificent! I had brought Master Peruzzi and Perino with me. We were filling our wineglasses, when I saw Antea emerge from the house, and behind her a young woman, in a cream silky dress, loose golden hair, adorned only with fresh flowers, She was enchanting, an angel in a Peruzzian Nativity. She looked around her smiling with delight. I saw her green eyes, and her smile. I was startled, and gazed at her: Ceci?

About to approach her, I was stopped by a huge cheer and applause, and the musicians started to play. A fanfare on the trumpets, a roll of drums, then a lively tune on the other instruments. Horses came into the street from the Great Road with a party of people in rich colours, the women's dresses glittering in golds and silvers, jewels round their necks and arms. At the head was a man in satin and furs, next to him a pretty horse on which was the bride. Pietro greeted them as the man got off his horse, and watched his daughter being helped down from hers. Her hand was taken by her father and given to Pietro. Everyone roared.

She was of middle height, with black hair and a pale skin. Not pretty, but with a pleasing figure, a little thin. Her dress was ill-chosen, of a richness and colour that made her pale face sallow. She looked tense and awkward, did not look at Father but nervously behind her to a woman whom I presume was her mother. 'Graziosa Cole Antonii, my wife, welcome to your home!' More applause.

'Giulio! May I present my son, to you, my wife.'

I thought of my mother, Antonina. I bowed to Graziosa and kissed her hand – a trick I had got from watching the court people. She blushed, and pulled her hand away, a tiny pillow with baby fingers. Father grinned at me.

'You see what courtly manners my son has!' and he clapped me on the back.

She returned a small smile, her lips soft like two smaller pillows. I was quite sure that there would be a baby in a year.

The father-of-the-bride was rather pompous, and did not smile. He was one of those who think that if they are unsmiling, they are seen as stern, as someone not to be crossed, as respectable and to be revered. It merely looked as if everyone else was causing a bad smell under his nose, and he was avoided. Her mother had a permanent smile under raised eyebrows which did not leave her face the whole day, continually looking at her daughter, nodding, and altogether like a parakeet.

My father led her and us to a long table covered with a Turkish rug, with a line of leather stools with backs, which he had hired for the immediate family. This was set up just outside the house, making a u-shape with the tables set up for the friends and neighbours, and special guests such as Master Peruzzi and Perino, At these tables the women sat at one, facing the men on the other one. We sat, the guests sat, and Father made a signal to the *maestro di cerimonia* who bowed, and dishes started to whirl out from the house. Everyone started to eat, holding out their beakers for wine. I was sitting at the family table: I looked for Antea and Ceci, and saw them sitting with Adelina. It was obvious that she was pleased with the dress, I supposed it was the first one made of new material that she had ever had. She kept looking at it and feeling it, with a face that smiled and smiled. Little Faustina was sitting between Adelina and Ceci, who was feeding her little pieces of food. She was enchanting. On the table opposite were Angelo and his sons, I frowned when I saw the way Giorgio was looking at her, drooling, smirking, looking at her through her dress. I shuddered at the thought of him touching her. That joy should belong to me, was the unbidden thought which rose in my mind and would not leave it.

Only Father at our table, and Graziosa's mother, seemed to be truly enjoying themselves. Graziosa nibbled and played with her food. I tried to talk with Graziosa's brother, and we talked of Trastevere where they lived, and I tried to engage him about the work we had done at the church, but he didn't know it and didn't seem interested in painting. I let him talk about his horse as I gradually turned my chair until I got a full view of Ceci. I watched her as I chewed and drank, and half-attended to the story of the horse. When he had nothing more to tell me about it, I knew so much I could have drawn it on the spot. The flow of dishes had slowed, and everyone was pink with wine, and my Father had returned from making the rounds of the tables to welcome his guests, I turned to him.

'That young woman, she is - Ceci - isn't she?'

'Yes, she's grown into a pretty lass.' He laughed.

'I should greet her. Will you excuse me Father, Madam?'

'Of course you must!'

As I crossed to their table, people were beginning to stand, to stretch and to talk with others than their immediate neighbours. I caught Angelo's eyes, who looked puzzled then beckoned me so I had to cross to him and shake his hand across the table.

'Giulio! In heaven's name!' He touched my face. 'Look at you, a full beard, what a young man!'

He took my hand in both of his, and yelled across to Giorgio and Niccolò who were now leaning against a wall talking to some other young men.

'It's Giulio!' Giorgio glared at me and held Niccolò back from coming across. We talked for a while and then I crossed to the women's table, where some were standing and sitting on the other side. Ceci was standing with Faustina in her arms, trying to stop her playing with her hair. Adelina was admonishing her. It was a pretty picture.

What a Madonna she would make!

Antea saw me first and greeted me. I smiled, and was close enough to ruffle Faustina's own hair. She squealed and started to cry.

'You're used to babies?' She was looking at Faustina not me.

'Draw then all the time! Cherubim!' Faustina wailed.

'Let me take her. 'Adelina did so, and she and Antea tried to distract her with a piece of sugar. She stopped crying.

'You have a beard.' Ceci said unnecessarily.

'And you – ' *have the loveliest face, not pretty but – beautiful, fresh* 'have become a – lady.' I spoke the words of a courtier, and felt a fool.

She shook her head, but her lips twitched.

'That is Master Peruzzi?' indicating him with her eyes.

'Yes and that is Perino with him. They teach me everything.'

'And you learn everything?'

'As you once told me.' Ceci hesitated, and dropped her eyes. I asked permission and sat beside her. I talked about the work, the villa, the plans for the new Basilica that the Pope wanted to build. She listened, and I thought of the tough little girl, and perhaps regretted her slightly. I asked her in a low voice what had happened to Tommaso.

'Oh - he grew up and went away,' she said.

'So, you've decided to be a girl.' I laughed. She looked into my eyes, but before I could register the slight shadow that crossed them, she nodded and looked down at her hands. They were roughened, the nails short. I assumed they were so because of all the sewing and housework she did.

The eyelashes rested on her cheeks.

The wedding party went inside, and the musicians struck up with country dance music. Men and women could dance with each other, touch hands. Perino, once introduced, partnered Adelina, and Master Peruzzi, Antea. Faustina was asleep in a little cot in the shade. Just the two of us at table.

'So, you are a painter.'

'Not yet, but I will be.'

'I am glad Giulio.'

We were sitting next to each other, miles and miles apart. I wanted to hear her teasing, telling me off, asking questions.

'And you Ceci, how are you?'

She shrugged – as you see.

'And Prettycat? How is she?' Why was it so hard?

'She left us. I see her sometimes.'

'Oh I'm sorry – when?'

'When we didn't have enough to eat.'

'Ceci? When? Why?'

She told me the story, and I felt guilty because I hadn't noticed. That Father hadn't told me. No. I hadn't thought to ask. I hadn't thought about her. I hadn't taken in that the room I glanced in as I went up the stairs wasn't full of materials and sewing.

'Oh Ceci, I am so sorry -' for what happened, for not noticing, for not caring enough.

'It's over now, I shall go back to work in the garden. Oh Giulio, you should see the garden... but I suppose you see lot of gardens now.' She dropped her head. There had been a touch of the younger Ceci; I wasn't going to lose it.

'Yes, but tell me about this one.'

So she did and as she spoke the colour came into her cheeks, her eyes sparkled and she was laughing. Then suddenly, she stopped, blushed deeply and said no more. I thought, she has someone – a gardener! She's too good for a gardener. I felt disappointed, angry, how dare she! How dare she love anyone but me... I got up.

'I should go back to my family.'

She nodded, still pink, I didn't move. Then Master Peruzzi and Perino came across to bud me farewell and we stood talking a while until they left. The noise level heightened, people from further down the street crept up and started on the food, what was left of it. The sugar confectionaries had long gone.

I glanced across to see Ceci with Niccolò trying to teach him dance steps, which of course he couldn't do. They were giggling, and at ease, I flushed, and I went across to offer my hand. She caught my eye, but before I could get to her, Giorgio had taken her hand from Niccolò and was pulling her into a space to dance. It was absurd, Giorgio so big and clumsy and she, so light and bright. I barged across.

'Excuse me. The bride wishes to meet Ceci.'

Giorgio wasn't pleased but allowed me to escort her away. For the sake of truthfulness, I took her up the stairs towards Graziosa and introduced them. Ceci did a little bob, and my father complimented her on how pretty she looked. Because it was hot and crowed, we went out to the stairway and stopped, facing each other. Our eyes locked.

I took her hand and led her up to my room in the attic. Clean, new, bedcovers. The drawing still on the wall, faded. I shut the door and leaned against it. The sounds of the party below, the music, welded together into the buzzing of bees. She stood before me, wisps of hair dancing in the light. I knew what I wanted to happen. I couldn't move. She reached up and stroked my beard.

'It suits you.' I took her hand, kissed her palm, her eyes sparkled. She knew too.

'I'm glad I'm a girl.' She tilted her head and we were kissing. She kissed me as if she was thirsty and welcomed my tongue in her mouth. I slid my hand down to her waist, to her buttocks. She whispered my name then drew me towards the bed. I was uncertain, had she done this before?

As if she guessed, she said, 'no-one else. I've been waiting for you, I dreamt of you in the garden.' So there was no gardener.

'I want you Giulio.'

I was afraid of hurting her, I was hesitant. This wasn't a prostitute; this was a virgin. This was Ceci and I wanted *her*.

'Please.' She lay back on the bed.

I felt myself harden and I knelt beside the bed to kiss her, to untie strings, to open her dress, to caress her with my hands and with my lips. She murmured. She drew up her skirt, and took my hand downwards towards hair as soft as sable. I stroked her and felt the sable part beneath my fingers. She fixed her eyes on mine, green eyes darkened to malachite, her lashes brown like wet sand and I knew that the tears which made them so were in my eyes too.

'Are you sure?' She answered by pushing herself to me, and freeing my clothes so that our skins were touching. Her hands were on my bare back as she opened her legs to draw me in. She cried out and I knew I had hurt her, but It was too late. I started to withdraw. She drew in her breath and grasped my head, her fingers clutching my hair.

'No! No! Stay there, stay there!' she hissed, commanding me, clasping me to her and sinking her tongue into my mouth where it flicked from side to side like a lizard's tail. Reds and oranges and purples crashed into my head: we were like two streams flowing into a fast-flowing river, leaping, sparkling over pebbles and stones.

We were both panting. I grasped her shoulders and put my head against her neck. She pulled her legs up around me and held me as close as she could. She was sobbing, tears drenched my cheeks, some of them were mine. I raised my head.

'Ceci – Ceci did I hurt you?'

'Yes; she laughed, still sobbing, 'but I don't care. It's where I want you to be!'

We lay together, gazing and kissing. I had once thought that I wanted to have her, simply to have her before anyone else in the street. I had felt she had belonged to me and that it was my right. I hadn't expected to worry that I would hurt her; that thought had never come into my mind with any girl. I had never asked a girl if I could, I had just ploughed felt the physical exhilaration and left her - after all they were all prostitutes - without a further thought. It's how men were. You tried to get it for free, otherwise you paid for it, and you wanted your money's worth. You could even, as I had once or twice, perform the act with boys. But this…

I was completely shocked, at the feeling within me. Not just physical pleasure, but something - something which made me want to be with Ceci, and only Ceci, like this for ever. I thought of the songs of love and the stories of lovers and ecstasy we bawled over wine, the lewd remarks. Never again. Not even the poets, their ardent words, their sighs, could describe this. This! This was seeing that first painting, the queen of heaven – this was she, on earth, human, with me. Not for the love of God, the love of Ceci – I whispered her name.

She stirred, and sighed.

'I didn't know it could be like that – I have seen others do it, and I have seen how happy they were. But I didn't know it would be so – it hurt, but it was having you inside me - to be so close. I wanted to pull you in further and further until you were part of me.'

She pressed herself against me, and I felt myself subsiding and withdrew.

She gave little cry of disappointment.

'Ah! I didn't want you to leave me!'

I kissed her.

'I – I have no words.'

'Your eyes have words.' She held my face between her hands.

I had drawn this face so often, and I will again, but I will never be able to draw this moment.

I caressed her body over and over, with my hands, with

my tongue, removing her dress completely, and saw the bloodstain.

'I've spoilt your lovely dress!'

'No – it's a trophy! A banner to my first time – a banner that it is you.' She laughed 'Two virgins deflowered on the same night! Oh, Graziosa, may your first time be like this!'

We laughed, uncaring, selfish, as lovers are, heedless of what might have been happening on the floor below. Greedily I kissed her ears, her eyebrows her nose and her mouth and she imitated me.

We slept. Through the late hours of the wedding party, through the taking in of the carpets and clothes, through the wine sellers collecting up the jars and beakers, through the closure of the front door after the last person left.

...and through the gulping, stifled crying from the marital bed...

CHAPTER SEVENTEEN

CECI

To wake up next to Giulio, to stretch my naked body on a mattress, not clothed in linen on a bed of straw, to gaze at his face, at his long eyelashes twitching slightly in tune with his breath – how can I find words to describe how I felt? My hand hovered over his beard, over his moustache, over his red lips. I kissed the air over his nose, not wanting him to wake, as if in waking he would deny me. His left arm was across the sheet, holding it down on the bed, covering his legs but showing the black curly hair at his groin. My hand wanted to follow that hair under the sheet. A hand that was instead placed on the bed next to his right hand which was an inch away from my thigh. I prayed for the sun not to rise, for the day not to begin, not to take him from me. I watched his chest rise and fall, and imagined it still, his heart stopping and mine too so we could enter Heaven together.

His face was as close to me as it could be without losing focus, and then he raised his eyelids and the line between his brown irises and my green ones was the line of a light ray from God to the earth.

'Hello,' he said and smiled. He turned over and his left hand came to my face and he kissed me and his right hand curled under my thigh and scooped me towards him. His leg between mine. I felt sore, but would not have denied him. He seemed to know, s we stayed, skin to skin, rocking and caressing, and murmuring each other's names. The sun rose, and he did not deny me.

'This is what the poets write about,' he said. 'This is what they sing.'

'What do they write?'

'They write about love, they sing of their mistress, how fair she is, how much she is desired, how they suffer when she isn't there.'

'And will you suffer when I'm not there?'

'I'll tell you! But you are here – let me draw you!' He jumped up to find paper and chalk and I understood the pain of his body's absence, and knew I would suffer when he was not with me. My heart already felt a stab of coldness, I had already lost him. I pulled the sheet over me.

'No! Don't cover yourself, I want to draw you as you are. Lie back – look at me.' Where else would I look?

His eyes were on me, they moved as he drew, they met mine, but focussed elsewhere. He was looking at me, but not in me, as he did. Dispassionate. I shuddered inside.

'There! I will have this with me always.'

He showed me the drawing, I was smiling as I knew I had smiled when he opened his eyes, and the eyes I saw there in chalk were, I knew, the eyes he had seen then.

'Oh!'

The picture showed my passion, it was too strong. It shouldn't be drawn like that.

'Don't show it to anyone!' I was alarmed, not at my nakedness but at the look which betrayed me.

'No – you think I want to see you look at anyone else like that?'

He put down the paper and I could see he was aroused. He fell on me, my body responded, but my heart did not, until he said 'I cannot hold a picture in my arms, I cannot make love with a picture, I cannot kiss, I cannot enter a picture. I love you Ceci, I love you as no other.'

It did not occur to me that there was any other. I did not know the difference between lust and love. I believed this new word, 'love' was Giulio, was something I had not seen, had not known, something beyond the girl and the gardener, something unreal and inexpressible and frightening. I was too young, too small for this, too weak for this.

That earlier cold clutching of my heart was, of course, simply the lack of the warmth of his body.

'I have you, you are mine,' he said holding me so tightly I could scarcely breath. 'No-one else will see the picture.'

I wanted, then, to dissolve, to get off this dizzying height before I fell.

I clung to you. I could not speak – 'I love you' was not enough. 'I love you, I fear you,' was what my older self would say.

~

Pietro had bought a horse for the wedding; Giulio took over the mule. I wanted to ride to church, me in front, both legs over one side, Giulio's arms either side of me to guide him with the reins. A knight and his lady! Angelo would wave, Adelina and Faustina would wave... everyone would smile to see us. Except that they wouldn't. It was impossible, to be seen so would blight me in the *Macello* – people who thought me wild already would label me a whore, even my friends would be appalled at such a breach of decorum. My mother would not smile; I didn't even think of what Mama thought of me not sleeping downstairs. I didn't think of Mama at all.

We went to Santa Maria d'Aracoeli that Sunday, because our church had been demolished and a new one was being built. There, I dedicated myself to Giulio before God. On my 'wedding' dress, I sewed a patch of silk in the shape of a flower over the bloodstain, the only time I enjoyed sewing. Mama asked me why there was a patch on my dress, and I told her I had torn it. The first lie had been told.

'You've never mended a tear before.'

'The dress is special, I want to look after it. I'm growing up'

'Yes.' She looked sad.

A few weeks after, I knew I had grown up. The blood started. I wasn't a girl any more. I was a woman, Giulio's woman. When I showed Mama she said 'thank God' and crossed herself, then she taught me how to fix the rags.

'Now, you must be careful.'

I thought she meant not to let the blood drip out.

CHAPTER EIGHTEEN

GIULIO

'The head's not right.' Master Peruzzi squinted at my drawing. 'In fact the head isn't at all like the statue. It looks real. Are you thinking of someone?'

Perino came across to have a look.

'Hmm. He's been in a bit of a dream all day.' Master Peruzzi and he exchanged looks as I blushed. 'Ah!' Perino caught on 'Special one, yes?'

At that the other stopped drawing and looked at me curiously. I nodded. I think my whole body was red. Perino and Master Peruzzi exchanged smiles, they had recognised her.

Benedetto came over.

'Let's see.' He frowned. 'It isn't any of the usual – Pasquale, do you know her?'

Pasquale ambled across and shook his head.

'No - new to me, nice and fresh-looking. Has Giulio found a virgin?'

'Who is she, can we share her?'

'She's not a prostitute!' I bent my head over the panel and started to scrub the face out.

'Ooooo! He's in love – look at him!'

'No I'm not.' The first lie. 'She's just someone I saw in church, rather pretty, I don't know who she is.' The second lie.

They didn't believe me.

Pasquale said, 'Did she like it?' Master Peruzzi cut in sternly.

'Enough. Get on with your work' They went back to their places, sniggering. 'Now get the head right.' he turned away. Perino shook his head and went back to measuring a *modello*.

I was ashamed. Of drawing her face at all, of lying, denying her. But I wasn't, I was keeping her to myself, I concentrated on the head of the statue while my mind held the image of Ceci, and that look.

Pasquale and Benedetto kept glancing at me. I knew that they would get at me after the session. I also knew that I was no longer content to draw statues, cold and stiff, so unlike living, breathing Ceci. I thought of the picture rolled up in my pouch and feared they might find it if they decided to rough me up. No-one else should see it.

With Ceci, the actions were the same, but in a whole other world far, far away from the prostitutes – as remote from them as the angels of heaven from the demons of hell. I wanted it to happen all over again, felt I couldn't wait until Sunday.

Head down, I took up another panel and placed myself in front of another sculpture, this one had no arms, but a beautiful face, the face of Apollo. At the end of the session in the sculpture garden, I braced myself. But Master Peruzzi lined up the panels from us and he and Perino studied them.

Pasquale's: 'Good, accurate, the folds of the garment are not quite right.'

Benedetto's: 'Her shoulders are not accurate, see? The curve on the sculpture starts lower than you have drawn, and her legs are too short.'

Pasquale giggled.

'She's a dwarf!'

'You need to study anatomy more. Try drawing real people.'

He probably knew that Benedetto did no drawing outside

of work, he didn't care about painting. It was his father who had apprenticed him, Benedetto really wanted to work with horses. Master Peruzzi was very patient with him.

'Giulio, your woman is accurate, though the face is a little faint. The man, though, he is good. Everything is exactly right. We will start you on *chiaroscuri*.' In effect, he had promoted me. 'You can start practising for those on the Chigi house. So, Pasquale and Benedetto, you must repeat the exercise, and Benedetto, perhaps you might think whether you truly wish to be a painter?' He said this kindly, for Master Peruzzi was loath to be angry at someone, or to chastise them.

'Giulio, you will come with me to the villa. Chigi has purchased some more sculpture. You will make a record of it.'

The joy of Ceci had been continued in my work, the world to me was perfect. She had always believed in me, encouraged me. Now, she was my charm, my talisman, my inspiration. My work would be better because of her. She was now the whole of me. I adored her. I smiled, I grinned, for her and for the work.

As we went towards the villa, Master Peruzzi talked to me about the work he had done with Pinturicchio in Siena, the decorations of the library there.

'The vault and the decorations round each fresco were taken from real antique art,' he told me, 'copied from the grottoes, near the Amphitheatre - Nero's *domus aurea*. Pinturicchio went down a shaft under the ground to see them, and I want you to see them - real Roman art - because clients will want us to use these in our designs. Are you alright in tight spaces in the dark?'

I had no idea.

'Yes,' I said. After all, I hadn't been scared of heights when up a scaffolding, so it was unlikely I would be scared of this.

'I don't mean going in the ruins, I mean really underground.

We have to lower ourselves on planks, crawl through small tunnels and light our way with torches. All day.'

It sounded like an adventure.

'We'll take Pasquale and Benedetto, and there may be other painters. We need a good group of us to help each other out. Would your father like to come? Have you any friend?'

I thought of Ceci, her wonderment at the Laocoön, her delight in searching under arches and rooting around for coins.

'I don't know about my father, but I do know someone. Tommaso. He comes with me on expeditions to find stuff. He's used to scrabbling in the dirt.'

'Good. That's five - Perino will come and stay on top in case we need help - I think we need a couple more.'

We had reached the villa, where the first floor had been completed, and we walked round so I could see the *logge* on two sides, with their arched entrances and the precision of the holes for the windows in exact order on the other two sides. It was precise and clever, and, although I had seen the plans, and copied them, totally unexpected.

Master Peruzzi produced paper and chalk and sat me down in front of three sculptures, or rather, three parts of three sculptures.

'I need to have copies so I can design them into the garden.'

He went off to talk to the builder. I could draw quickly and soon had the sculptures on paper from all sides. Then drew the building so as to compare it with the elevations, although I knew there would be no differences. No fortress this, no turrets, no blind walls to the outside. Already because of the vines and the vegetables, it had a garden, but I knew Master Peruzzi would re-plan it to work with the building, to make his vision of 'inside/outside' evident and complete. It was new, exciting, and totally replaced Ceci in my mind for the rest of the day.

CHAPTER NINETEEN

CECI

We met at sunset on Saturdays beyond where the *Macello* led into the Great Road. He would lean down and pick me up to sit before him on the mule, and we would go to our own place in the olive groves. On Sundays, we went to Santa Maria, he with his father and Graciosa with me and Mama: Mama did not exist until I accompanied her to church. Afterwards, Giulio and I stayed together until he had to leave before sunset to get back to his work.

One Sunday he had talked to me about the trip to the *domus aurea* and persuaded me to go with them.

'Master Peruzzi asked me if I had a friend who might want to go, and I thought of Tomasso.' I was excited; at last I was to be included with the painters. 'He suggested Father but I think he is too old to go down into caves – it will be dark, we'll be going through tunnels – will you be alright?' I nodded. Nothing would stop me joining Giulio – not underground, not into caves: into the mouth of Hell if need be.

Early the next morning, I was up and away to where the clothes were hidden. I waited at the roadside until Giulio, Master Peruzzi and Perino and the two other apprentices with two mules loaded with planks, ropes and panniers of food, oil lamps and tools met us. We walked past Santa Maria, towards the Amphitheatre, then turned off just before that great building, eastwards, where there was a large hill topped by enormous ruins. Master Peruzzi told us they were of the buildings of an

Emperor Titus, below which were the paintings we were going to see. The ruined walls were high and my heart thumped at the thought of going underneath them. It was said that the paintings were discovered when a boy fell through a hole, and I hoped no hole would open up under us, or worse, on top of us when we were underground.

As they were preparing the ropes, tying one round a pillar and testing it, I caught Perino looking at me. He spoke quietly.

'Are you sure you want to go down… Tommaso?' I nodded. 'You can stay up here with me –'

I shook my head. He shrugged.

'Giulio,' he shouted, 'you make sure this lad is alright.'

Giulio turned, his eyes sparkling. 'Indeed I will!'

Master Peruzzi was let down first, then Giulio, then me. Perino lowered a bag with lamps, paper, chalk. Then Benedetto. Pasquale would wait in case one of us needed to be hauled up quickly, but would change places with Benedetto later.

I wasn't afraid of the dark, and, as lamps were lit, Giulio squeezed my hand quickly.

'Stay close to me.'

Master Peruzzi had been there before and led the way to where we could all stand up, and we held up the lamps. The ceiling and walls gleamed with colour, more and more pictures revealed as we turned round and then travelled through gaps in the wall for more. There were strange images: women with tails instead of legs, bird's heads on lion's bodies, men becoming candle holders, horses with serpents' tails. We stopped; Giulio and Benedetto started to draw. The light flickered across the images, broken-beamed as their heads moved up and down. I could see that above us were curved vaults, painted within frames of squares and rectangles; shapes filled with animals, leaves and flowers, or people. I recognised men as soldiers with spears, women with their hair in ribbons and with draped dresses. There were women naked to the waist with wings instead of arms: angels, but not angels. On the walls, painted garlands and tassels fell from arches made of very thin upright poles, doors and balconies with guards made of poles forming an X.

The colours were reds, browns, blues, yellows, greys like silver, and gold, glittering in the lamplight. Giulio and Master Peruzzi talked excitedly about the vault, how the curve was made, how the decorations were in lines and how they must extend into the earth beneath us. I noticed that many of the women were naked, or had a thin veil over part of their bodies; one was lying as I had done for the drawing Giulio had made, and I felt a shuffling behind me and he appeared. Head to head, we looked at her and smiled to ourselves. She was surrounded by regular patterns on a white ground.

'Not as beautiful as you,' he whispered, then laughed. For my face must have been like his, dirty and streaked, our clothes filthy. The laughter echoed in the space. We crawled on hands and knees through another hole, and there were many strange creatures, half-animal and half-human, besides pictures of perfectly ordinary people.

'The rooms must have been much, much bigger – taller – they've somehow got filled up – there must be more paintings underneath.' Giulio was excited, but suddenly I felt overwhelmed by the paintings, the experience of being underground, and began to feel uncomfortable. I felt the chill air, and shivered. Giulio told me to go backwards and suggested to Master Peruzzi that I went up and swapped with Pasquale, which, relieved, I did.

After we had let Pasquale down, Perino took out a water bottle and food and we sat in the sun together. I needed to warm up.

'You're not a boy are you?' He knew perfectly well that I

wasn't. 'You have the eyes of a cat, I saw them at the wedding.' I blushed, and saw no point in lying.

'Cecilia' I said.

'Giulio's special lady.' He wasn't mocking me. 'Who wanted to see the paintings?'

'Yes.'

He raised his eyebrows and drank.

'And what do you think?'

'They are strange, some of them are funny, some – some make me feel scared.'

'It's the lamplight, the shadows and the dark that makes you feel that you're somewhere else – the underworld – a world from long ago. Until that boy fell into the hole no-one had seen them for centuries – they were painted before Jesus – so I'm told.'

I found it hard to think of a time before Jesus.

'The time of the Garden of Eden maybe?' I took this literally.

'But there was only Adam and Eve – they couldn't have painted all that. Besides, the rooms belonged to Emperor Nero.'

'Aye. The antiques – the old Romans. All the statues we find - graven images, which God didn't like. So He buried them. P'raps we shouldn't be digging them up. Maybe He didn't like painters either.'

I was puzzled. I didn't know what he was talking about.

'Y'know, the ten commandments?' I shook my head.

'Well, it's things that God told us not to do, one of them was not to carve images – statues, sculpture.'

'But he didn't say paintings.'

'No, he didn't say paintings. And it was before Jesus, who

didn't say anything about it at all as far's I know. I'm alright with paintings - ' I was relieved.

'But wouldn't God like the paintings in the churches? The ones of Our Lady and of Jesus.'

'No-one knows.'

'He must do or he wouldn't allow them in the churches.'

'Yes, there is that.' He paused and drank again. 'Mind you, there are carved images in the churches.' I thought of Christus on the cross, made of wood.

It was a strange conversation. Especially so as it was between a young girl and an older man. I used to worry so much about understanding things, about questions to ask God, and it could have been that Perino could have answered them. But I had forgotten what the questions were, and thought only of Giulio. Yet the paintings had taken a place in my mind, and I wanted to know how Giulio saw them, if they would affect the way he drew. I wanted to know why the Romans had painted half animal, half human shapes. I imagined myself with a tail.

Perino and I were silent for a while. I took out my knife to cut up an apple, and chewed as my mouth filed with sweet juice and I daydreamed of another mouth.

Then there were shouts from below, and one by one the men appeared each one as dirty as the other, and we all stood and laughed at the sights we were.

~

As we lay together again, Giulio talked and talked about the paintings – Perino had collected the drawings and taken them with him, but I could see them as Giulio talked. And I could see him longing to paint them on the walls of a villa.

'And I shall paint you there too, like the women in the caves.'

'But you don't paint women like that, without clothes.'

No. I just draw them. I'd admit to one.

'I've drawn you, so why wouldn't I paint one? Just because no-one does it now.'

I wasn't sure about this, if no-one had done it must be wrong. I wish he hadn't drawn me. But I didn't mind him seeing me so.

I watched him go up the Great Road as dawn began until he was out of sight. I was reluctant to go indoors, and walked in the half-light along the line of houses and unopen shops. I saw Prettycat in an alley and turned down it, she jumped into my arms and I leaned against the wall to stroke her. Then she stiffened, yowled and jumped down, scratching my arm. I saw a shape in the space between the walls blocking the light. It was Giorgio. No wonder Prettycat had run off, Giorgio was a tormentor of cats. He leaned his hand on the wall facing me.

'Hello Giorgio.'

'You're out early – or are you late home?'

'I'm going to work,' and made to pass him.

'Stay and talk to me Ceci'

'Yes, but not here.' I felt a chill. The light behind him grew but here it was dim and Giorgio's face was in shadow. He seemed bigger.

'So– the little virgin. But you aren't one any more are you?'

I was startled.

'I saw your cat just now, leaving you – I saw your tomcat, Giulio.'

He caught my arm.

'My father thinks you will make me a good wife, Ceci. He's waiting until you're ready.' The last word was a snarl.

He was hurting me.

'Let me pass, Giorgio.'

He put his mouth to my ear.

'But I don't want second-hand goods…not for a wife… but a playmate, who knows want to do…' I was pushed further into the alley, up to the dead end where he held me by both arms against the wall.

'Pretty, pretty pussy…Giulio's prettycat!' His breath stank. I pushed him. He held me tight.

'You like to play the boy - Tommaso isn't it? Is that because Giulio likes boys? Likes to take you from behind?'

'Go home Giorgio, you should sleep it off!' and struggled. 'Let go!' I twisted and tried to bite him.

'Oh, pussy's got teeth – and claws – ' he grasped my wrists 'not like her mother – soft – soft paddy paws - soft tongue.'

He put his lips against mine. My cap fell off, as I twisted and his mouth hit my ear.

'Perhaps Mummy will let her daughter share me – one in front then one behind.'

He put one hand under my tunic and grasped my left buttock.

'Nice and soft; like Mummy like daughter'.

The words meant nothing. I had to get away. I tried to scratch his face.

'Ooh, claws, not like Mummy, she has soft, soft paddy paws, and a soft mouth.'

He held my arm against the wall, pushing me. His hand moved forwards between us and I felt his cock against my stomach as he pressed himself against me, making my ribs squash my lungs. It was a choice between rape and being strangled. I felt my knife sticking into my side. I relaxed my body suddenly, whispered,

'Let me help you Giorgio.'

'That's more like it, let's see what Giulio has taught you.' He allowed my left hand free so I could take his cock in my fingers. I would not let it go into me, not violate Giulio's place.

'Both hands, Giorgio, better with both hands,' and he allowed space for my other hand, which held the handle of the knife. He was breathing hard. I squeezed him, and as he was about to penetrate me, I penetrated him - in his side. He cried out and twisted so I could slide out.

'You bitch! *Puttana*! Cunt!' Anger flushed through me and I stabbed again. He fell against the wall and I stood back. I drew breath. The words he had said suddenly showed a meaning: my anger dissolved into ice - he had insulted my mother.

'For Mama,' I hissed and with two hands on the knife handle stabbed again at his heart once.

'For Giulio.' Twice.

He slid down, gurgling, then nothing. I felt the sun behind me. I heard someone pulling up shutters, I stared. I pulled up my hose but couldn't take my eyes off him. I stood still. I heard a 'good morning' called. I had to leave; blood was on my tunic, not much. I threw down the knife. Picked up my cap and scrunched my hair into it. Listened. Looked out. Two men buying bread, backs to me, obscuring me from the baker's wife. They laughed. I ran quickly past them, not looking. Round our house to the empty stable behind, and there, in the animals' trough, I washed the blood from my hands then crept in through the back door into the hall and into our apartment. Mama looked at me started to smile then stopped.

'What?'

I was trembling, panting. She took me in her arms. I told her what had happened. I told her I had killed Giorgio.

'No – no you didn't kill him – you didn't see him – you've been here all night – ' she shook me. 'You hear me? It didn't happen.'

I was shaking my head. She slapped me.

'Cecilia! It didn't happen! Get those clothes off!' and she pulled the tunic over my head and pulled off my shoes, the hose, the torn braies. Then she pulled me across to a bucket of water and washed me, tidied my hair into a plait. She took me into her arms again holding me close as she had when I was a child and had hurt my knee.

'Shush, shush.' The more she cuddled me and stoked my cheek the more I cried.

I cried because Giorgio had touched me where only Giulio had touched me. He had spoilt it – I began to shake, and couldn't stop. She drew me down onto her mattress and rocked me until the shudders subsided and I slept. I thought I heard her say 'Giulio will make it better, Giulio will make it go away.'

She knew. Of course she knew! Giorgio knew. Whatever made me think that no-one knew – in the bubble I had created around us, I had assumed – no I hadn't thought – I hadn't bothered to ask myself if anyone knew…if it mattered if they did… I would tell her when I woke… I would… 'soft, soft paddy paws…soft tongue'…what was that? mummy and daughter…

~

I heard the cries outside as the body was found, and Mama.

'Shush! Shush! They've found him, they'll bury him.' I clung to her. 'I shall go to Angelo.'

'No – let me go – I'll tell him.'

'Stay here! You'll tell no-one! Drink this'. It was water with some herbs and it made me sleepy. The dreams came, bad dreams: the door was ripped open as Angelo stabbed Antea; 'I was me!' I screamed and felt someone choking me; someone was holding me down. Giulio, he had found out and would never see me again. I awoke to tears and the heat of midday. Mama was cooking something.

'The funeral this evening, we shall go. Word has been sent to Pietro.'

She didn't mention Giulio, and neither did I.

The vespers bell tolled. The neighbours stood outside as the cart went past, but only Angelo, Niccolò, Pietro, Mama and I followed it to the burial ground.

'Why just us?'

Pietro was stern-faced.

'He wasn't liked.'

That I knew, but it didn't normally stop people attending a funeral.

After the body had been buried, I went up to Angelo, shaking slightly. He took my hand in both of his and thanked me. I lost tears for Angelo, the man who was kind to us, who had rescued me from an assault, and had lost his son through me.

'Don't weep, Cecilia, he was not a good man. I have Niccolò, a sweeter boy. Giorgio was a bully.' I was surprised.

Niccolò came up to Mama and me.

'Thank you for coming. He didn't deserve it.' and he spat onto the ground which covered Giorgio. 'I'm glad he's gone. I wish I knew who'd killed him, I would thank them.'

He turned to me.

'You didn't know him, he wasn't just a bully, he made me – people - do things they didn't want to.'

'What?' the word just came out before I could stop it.

'I can't tell you.'

He trudged of after Angelo and Pietro, and joined them to drink.

Niccolò was happy from that day on, he chatted more, he stayed awhile when he brought supplies for us. He grew muscular and people liked it when he was in the shop. He became my friend again. I stopped going out alone, Mama told me not to, but I didn't want to anyway. Tomasso was folded away, and I brushed my hair every day. When the sun had warmed the earth, I returned to the garden. Niccolò insisted on walking with me there and meeting me in the evening.

'You ask me if you want anything, Ceci,' he said. He accompanied us to church, with Adelina and adored little Faustina; playing with her. On Sundays, when Giulio was there, he smiled at us and left us alone. He was my protector, my brother.

It was as if a shadow had lifted, one that most of us in the street had only been vaguely aware of. I sometimes dreamt of the killing, but I also day-dreamt of Angelo and Mama marrying. Another false idyll in my head. It didn't last long.

CHAPTER TWENTY

GIULIO

Father told me about Giorgio. I was glad.

'He won't be missed.'

'No. Niccolò seemed as if a load had lifted from his shoulders.'

'It would have.'

'Mm - he was overshadowed.'

More than that. Niccolò had told me. We had been sitting outside doing not very much, watching Ceci and Antea sewing, sitting on the stone bench.

'I wonder who'll have Ceci first?' he said.

'What?'

'You know' – he nudged me.

'Ceci? She's a little girl!'

'She's older than me. Giorgio says she's ready for it.'

I stared at him, at Ceci. I formed an idea of her and Giorgio, and it made me sick.

'Don't talk about her like that!' I pushed him over and slapped his face hard on both sides.

Antea looked across and shouted.

'You two – stop it! Giulio – Niccolò! get up!'

We obeyed. Ceci laughed at us, and bit her thumb. I had to grin.

'It'll be Giorgio,' Niccolò said mournfully.

No – it won't. It'll be me – no-one else. I was startled by the idea, and sat down, unable to look at her.

'He'll bugger anything that moves, Giorgio: sheep, goats, market girls and little boys. He hurts people - he hurts me - he buggers me - since I was little.'

A memory. Emerging suddenly like, a slap in the face. A child. Me. Peeing under a tree, being grabbed from behind. A struggle. A pain. Blood. Crying into the dust.

Yes, it was good that Giorgio was dead.

~

Pasquale and I were copying *chiaroscuri* in the Santa Maria del Populo, painted by Pinturicchio. Groups of people in a frame like a relief, with benches on four legs, little pillars with shadows to one side according to the light from the other side. Astonishingly three-dimensional in the dim candlelight, I had to really look to see that the benches were painted, with a touch of colour to make them look like marble. On one bench there were two books, incredibly real. Four benches in all each with its own relief and each framed by lovely reliefs of women. As I drew, I was amazed at how the shading, the perspective deepened each relief. One seemed to have a depth greater than the others, purely because of the angle of the lines of a wall, and where the feet of the people were placed. The image was flat, I kept telling myself, but could not be convinced until I drew it. And there, beneath my hand was a relief, a model stage with marionettes. If you squinted, the marionettes seemed to move.

I enthused about it to Pasquale, but he was stolidly copying – perfectly, but a pale imitation of the original painter, who used the various shades of black, white, brown and grey to make the scenes look real. Pasquale did not notice these subtleties.

We stopped to eat and drink, sitting on the floor in front

of this chapel of Girolamo Basso della Rovere, relative of the current Pope. We gazed at the picture of the Madonna and her baby on a throne, and disagreed about the saints around her, the raising of her to heaven, standing on a cloud, in a narrow horseshoe decorated with cherubim. I especially liked the little bald one at the bottom, gazing down happily, with his wings folded like a neat fur collar. There were cherubim with musical instruments above. Very sweetly pretty, but what interested me was the landscape in the background, and the fact that the more I looked at it the more I thought it wasn't actually by Pinturicchio – or the top of it wasn't. It seemed to be of copybook figures while the bottom with the landscape seemed to be taken from real people. Pasquale was unimpressed.

'What does it matter? You just get the figures together, and the decorations and paint them.'

Pasquale was a stolid person, but at least now that Benedetto had gone, returned home, hopefully to the horses, Pasquale was less inclined to sneer or made crude remarks. He was rather dull, and I couldn't engage him in any discussion on our work, but at least he was conscientious, and painstaking. Where he had made one drawing I had made six.

He did, however, keep his ears open.

'Bramante's brought a new painter into town,' he said over a mouthful of bread and cheese.

'Oh? Who?'

'Raffaello Sanzio. He knew him in Umbria, think they're related.'

It's being part of a family that got you work. I had heard the name.

'Don't know what we need more painters for. There are enough of us here already.'

Us? I called myself a painter, but I knew that I couldn't say that I was. I was an apprentice still.

'I've heard he does panels and easel pictures, not frescoes. So he won't be getting in Master Peruzzi's way.' Pasquale was complacent.

I had seen many easel paintings; in churches, panels of wood on stands, which could then be hung in a church; they could be quite big. Painted with colours mixed with oil, not water. I didn't know much about that. I shifted my behind which was getting numb. I'd better get a move on, persuade Master Peruzzi I was ready to paint real walls, real pictures, not just details.

And if Bramante, the Pope's Architect, had brought Raffaello to Rome, then it had to be for important work. Would he be a rival to Master Peruzzi? In which case, I needed to be around him. I needed to work with the most important painters.

When we got back to the workshop, I asked Master Peruzzi if he knew Raffaello.

'Not yet, but the Pope has agreed that he paint a wall of his new rooms.' I knew it!

'Will he need assistants?'

'I've been asked to make suggestions.' He said no more. Sometimes Master Peruzzi could be too diplomatic, too reserved. Too modest to push himself - or me, if he didn't think I was ready.

'I've heard he doesn't do fresco.'

'Well, he'll be doing it now.'

He took my drawings up.

'I'm working on the design for the exterior of the villa, come and see what you think.'

He had the original *chiaroscuro* drawing made bigger and more detailed. A design with garlands, cherubs, caryatids and other images taken from the caves. It was to be repeated around every window on every wall.

'Each window is the same for complete symmetry. Perino

will draw the design up and when the exterior building is finished, you and Pasquale will paint the walls.' I was excited, but fearful, as when I counted the windows I could see there was a lot of repetitious work. He guessed my thoughts.

'By the time you've finished the paintings, you'll be an expert in *chiaroscuro.*' His eyes twinkled. 'Then you can take up the coloured stuff.'

He was pacing me, I know that now, but I was impatient. If Raffaello wanted me, I would go – I thought I was ready. I ignored the fact that I was contracted to Master Peruzzi.

Perino asked me to detail the design into a *modello*, and I did so using everything I had noted from the Basso della Rovere chapel. I wanted the paintings to make observers think that the walls were truly made of carved marble right to the point of entry – and even then. I didn't want them to know until they were told. When I had finished, he nodded.

'Good - we will use that for the *cartone.*' He stowed it carefully away.

'I'll be a month or two yet. Just keep practising.'

It being Saturday, I travelled home full of my success, wanting to tell Father, wanting to draw the design for him and for Ceci. Ceci? I had to refocus, had to take out the drawing of her, and as I got nearer to the *Macello* I thought of her and felt I had been away from her too long. Raffaello was put to the back of my mind.

On Sunday, I was not only commanded to church with Father and Graziosa, I was summoned to a special meal afterwards. While it took me away from Ceci, I was glad because I wanted to talk about the work, about Raffaello, to see if my father knew him.

He was ebullient that day. Graziosa was very quiet, like a mouse, Father did the commanding of the servants. I felt a bit sorry for her, Father was kind, but he had got a bit overwhelming in the confidence of his enhanced stature, shown in the new costly furniture and the new tapestry on the wall, and the appointment of a man to do most of the supervision of the site-work. He made visits to check on the quality, and to pursue the next project. He spent much time at the Papal court, and keeping his eyes and ears open.

He talked: yes he had met Raffaello, a charming young man, yes he was very well thought-of, but he didn't know his work – his Father was a painter, he had studied with Perugino who had worked for the last Pope. Oh, and did I know that Michelangelo had moved in down the road? A house as part payment for painting the ceiling of the Sistine Chapel…

'But he's a sculptor!'

'Well, maybe the Pope knows something we don't.' He beamed.

After we had eaten, he made a sign to Graziosa who got up, bowed and left the room. I smiled at her, intending to cheer her up, but she wasn't looking at me. Now, I could tell Father all about my successes.

'There is something I want to discuss with you.' He poured more wine and looked uneasy.

'You're a grown man, Giulio, and who you spend your time with is your business, but you are my son, my heir.' He looked grave; whatever he wanted to say was something he didn't want to say, but had to. I thought of my companions, was there something about Pasquale?

'Ceci. Cecilia.' I was taken aback.

'She's a lovely girl, I'm very fond of her. So was your mother.' He drank. Would he come to the point?

'But she is poor, she has no dowry. Her mother is…' He coughed and drank some more.

'The thing is, if you get her with child - you cannot marry her. You have to marry a girl – a virgin – from a good family – with wealth to match our own.'

Marry? It hadn't entered my mind. But marry – Ceci? Of course I would marry Ceci! I gaped.

'I know you two are – uhh – but it must stop before anything happens. You must stop seeing her, stop her getting ideas.'

'No - I love Ceci!' He interrupted.

'Love – love is all very well, but it has nothing to do with marriage.'

'You loved Mother!'

'Yes, well-enough, and she brought a decent dowry. Then.'

He started to suck on a plum.

'I married Graziosa for her dowry, and because she is young, we can have children, the ones Antonina couldn't give me. You are my only heir, what happens to my wealth if I outlive you?'

This was something I had never considered. I remembered that after the wedding, he didn't go drinking with Angelo. He spent time with the notaries at their houses, not at the wine-seller. He consorted with Pope's secretaries, with Cardinals.

'You think Ceci is beneath me.'

'Yes. And I think you must stop for her sake, don't give her false hopes.'

I was quiet, I was seething; I didn't like this change in my Father. Of course Graziosa would not have been chosen without the money. This was something I knew, but I had not thought of it in connection with Ceci. What we had was apart from this world, she was a part of my drawing, painting, of art, not of alliances, contracts, status. She did not belong there.

'You are my son, I can command you to do this.' It was said quietly. 'You could, of course, keep her as a mistress when you are married…' I started, how could he regard her so? A strumpet? I felt my anger rising.

'Though that would be a shame – for her.' His voice rose: 'And to make sure, I will be giving Antea and Ceci notice.

Graziosa is pregnant and we will need the rooms.' So the family had been started! I was on my feet.

'You can have my room – I'll live at the Borgo! I'll look after them!'

'With what? What money do you have beside what I give you?'

'I'll earn money – I'm good enough now. I'll work for Raffaello!'

'You're contracted to Peruzzi.' He pulled some skin from between his teeth. 'You're saying you won't give up Cecilia?' My knuckles on the table were trembling.

'No!' He leaned forward.

'Then I must tell you – '

He hesitated. He looked uncomfortable.

'You'll tell me nothing!' I turned my back on him.

'Giulio –' I wanted to shout, but he was my father

I'd tell her this afternoon. That I loved her, that I would look after her. That I would not give her up. I needed time. I turned round.

'At least let them stay until near the birth, time to find somewhere else...'

'I don't want to quarrel with you Giulio, if you will stop seeing Ceci, then I will agree to that.' He looked old. I nodded.

'I loved Antonina very much.' I thought I heard as I left the room.

I didn't tell Ceci any of this. She had been subdued the night before, perhaps she knew? That afternoon, as she lay in my arms, she told me about Giorgio, about what happened. The anger I had felt with my father rose again - if he had not been already dead, I would have gone then to find him and kill him myself. The picture in my head of Ceci and him.

'No, Giulio, he didn't come inside me, he didn't take your place. No-one will.' I held her close. Let Father make another heir. I would be a painter for the Pope, and she, she would be my wife.

CHAPTER TWENTY-ONE

CECI

I was waiting for Guilio. I sat by the fire with Mama, and I saw two things. One was her beauty. In the flickering light, she was like the Madonna in the church, the old church before it was pulled down, where the pictures were not as old as the ruins, but were different from the ones Giulio drew. That Madonna was dark with the smoke of years of candles, with a little gold coming through from the background. Mama's face was long like hers, her eyes narrowed and slanted, eyebrows black in contrast to her pale skin. Her white hands and long fingers like those which held the Christ child, held against her stomach.

She moved these to bend towards the pot to stir it, and I saw the second thing. The folds of her skirt had bunched up over her stomach, but when she put her hands back, the folds did not collapse, instead, the stomach formed an extension beyond her hips Like the people I had seen who were starved, whose bellies pumped up with air instead of food and fat. Or… as if she was with child. I looked at her and she met my gaze. Then lowered her eyes, to her hands, and smoothed the material of her skirt over the bump.

How was she pregnant? Of course I knew how…but Mama? My mother? With a man? I stared.

'Mama – '

She nodded.

'Yes.'

'Who?' She shook her head. No…she wouldn't tell me… or she didn't know. I shook that thought from my head, my mother wasn't a whore. But it bounced back. I fought it with trying to imagine my mother in love, like me, but the picture was crooked. She sighed.

'Where do you think the food, the wood, the clothes came from?'

I hadn't thought, only that the neighbours were very kind to us. Master Pietro had been kind to us, Angelo had always been kind to us….

'They didn't come through the good of people's hearts. Don't gawp! I paid for them.'

'What with?'

'You see only Giulio, you think you're in love - you give yourself to him for nothing! He takes advantage of you – you're lucky you're not pregnant!' Her anger changed her face. The beauty of the Madonna was gone, the long thin face was a skull under skin, the hands and the wrists were bones, with the flesh so thin I could see the blue veins.

'I am a prostitute.'

I froze. She had cut into my dream. I would leave. I would leave her to cope with the child, with the censure of the neighbours, with the fact that Master Pietro would throw her out. Pietro? – No that was unthinkable? Others? How many? While I was happy in the garden, happy with my discovery of sexual pleasure, ecstatic over Giulio, wrapped up entirely in him: my mother performing the same act for money. I felt I was choking.

'Did you expect me just to sit here and starve? Did you think you were the only one who could get food and money? I started with a pedlar, for bread. I could do it, after all, it was exactly as it had been with your father, a few unpleasant moments endured. Then Giorgio because of the meat and the fuel, he became a regular. Then the priest, and the notary, and…' she looked me straight in the eye. 'And if they didn't withdraw, I got twice as much.' She laughed mirthlessly and slapped her stomach. The silence in the room thrummed between us.

'Don't judge me!' she shouted. 'I had nothing else to sell!'

I had something to sell. I could have sold it to the gardeners. I didn't. I kept it as a dream, which came true, it was beautiful. I suddenly understood many of the remarks of the old women in the garden, about my body and how it would make my fortune.

'You could have sold me.' I whispered.

'No. Not you, with your joy and your dreams, and your innocence. How could I. I didn't want you to learn how horrid it can be with a man. Not yet. I see how you are with Giulio. I didn't want to stop you because of the beauty of you both. I worried every time you were with him. I waited in terror for your next blood. I wanted you to keep it a little longer, that dream, that love I dreamed of, but never had. That most women never had.' She was no longer angry. 'He will never marry you, he can't, his Father will have other plans for him.' She was weary.

In my love with Giulio I had never, never thought of becoming pregnant. Never. The idea of sex to have a child wasn't the love we made. It was as if what we felt, what we did, was different.

All the ideas of men and women, of sex, of marriage, of motherhood were jumbled up in my head. As if, absurdly, I still believed that old idea I had worked out that children came after marriage, or rather I hadn't believed anything at all. My life was constricted to one thing only, one person. My mother was there only to serve me – and she had! A laugh turned into a snort turned into tears that I held in my eyes.

But I couldn't touch her.

'After Samuel died, no-one wanted sewing from me. You got work in the garden, then, you were out either getting food or with Giulio. So it was easy. Adelina found the notary and the clerk so I wouldn't have to go out on the street.'

Adelina?

'Sometimes, women help each other. Only she knew.'

'And Giorgio, he would have told.'

'No, he didn't want his father to know he was using the deliveries, Angelo's gifts, as bargaining tools. He wouldn't hand them over unless…'

'You should have told Angelo!'

'How could I shame him?'

'His son shamed him! You let him!'

'We were hungry, Ceci.'

'I'm glad I killed him!'

'He isn't the father Ceci. I know.'

I was rigid as I understood. Without knowing I understood. I remembered learning about the 'pretty boys' and how men and women did it that way, and how the Church condemned it. I shuddered and heard a mangled cry coming from my throat. The image was too terrible.

'I'm sorry Ceci. I want you to know. The father is a respectable man!'

'Respectable?' I snorted and mucus flew out of my nose onto my mouth.

'He – they – weren't married…'

'So' a touch of hope 'one of them can marry you?'

'No. One is married to the church, the other has since become a husband.'

She was so sad, but I still couldn't put her before my own reactions. I had to strike her. I stood up and snarled.

'And who else? How many others fathers could there be?' She sat still, sorrowful. Why didn't she fight back?

'It will have a mother. It will be your brother or sister.'

'I don't want a bastard for a brother or sister!'

She looked at me sharply.

'It is a baby, it will need me and you to care for it.'

I can't believe she was being so, so – stupid!

'You should have got rid of it months ago, Adelina could have managed it, she's had a lot of practise hasn't she? Now, you'll have to stay home until it is born. Then we give it away.' Another realisation - like Adelina did. 'Let God look after it.'

'Adelina's mother forced her to give herself, then the children away, she didn't want to.'

'Adelina? Her mother? was a prostitute too?'

She said nothing.

'You'll be saying that you were visited by the angel Gabriel next. You're not the Virgin Mary!'

'That is blasphemous talk, Cecilia, I won't hear such words in my house!'

'Yet you had sex in this house, you made a child in this house.' I was ranting, sobbing. 'A child who has nothing to do with us, who will cost us to feed. You will have to have more clients to do that...Or do you want me to join you?'

I might as well have hit her.

'I did it for us, Ceci, for you!'

I knew. I don't know why I was being cruel. Yes I did. I was jealous. I didn't want to share my mother with a child. I just wanted it to be me, her and Giulio – and Prettycat, who had gone. I knew my dream had broken. I sobbed. I was afraid. Afraid of being a woman, afraid that the baby would kill my mother. Afraid that I would have to become a whore myself. How could God let this be?

I must have said it out loud.

'When Matteus told us we had to leave, I prayed to God

that he would change his mind. But he didn't, so I thought that it was God's will. But when I couldn't make enough money sewing, I thought I could be a servant in someone's house. But I found that no house would take a servant who had a child. I had no dowry left. All I had was you. I didn't know what I had done to offend God, I find it difficult to believe that what has happened, what other people suffer, is His will. Yet it must be.'

'Oh, Mama. Why? Why does he make women suffer?' I went to her. She rocked me. I prayed for the baby to die.

~

Giulio and I met away from the house, so nothing changed. He didn't tell me about the quarrel, or his father's decision, he didn't tell me about Graziosa, though I could soon see that for myself. I didn't tell him about Mama. We both cocooned ourselves once more in our own little bubble, whose skin was made of paintings, of colour, of fantastical beings, of the villa being built and the gossip of the painter and the world of the Cardinals and the Pope It was full of the plants and trees, our garden. It was more real to me than the house and the street. He promised I would be part of that world as soon as he was an artisan, a painter worth paying. The skin, unseen by us, was stretching, thinning to transparency.

~

The night of the birth arrived, Mama was in pain for hours, Adelina came with drugs, and told me to call her when the waters broke. But I didn't. Mama was muttering between cries, calling names – mine, Adelina, Pietro. Mine. Pietro, Pietro. The baby emerged. It didn't cry, and I pushed a blood-soaked cloth into its face to make sure it didn't. I cut it from Mama and wrapped the wizened, bloodied body in the cloth. I noticed it was male.

Then I cleaned Mama and she slept. I carried the bundle

into the night to drop into the quarry where they had dropped Samuel. I did not pray for its soul. On the way back I suddenly thought of the picture Giulio copied to show me, the Killing of the Innocents. God sent an angel to warn Joseph to get the baby into Egypt. He didn't prevent the massacre of all the others, he just saved the one, his son. He didn't care about the rest of us, of Mama, of the baby, he let me kill it.

I stumbled back, I lay beside Mama, without changing into a nightshift. Her breathing was soft. She said something, but I couldn't hear what. I took her hand and slept.

The dark was lifting, another day, and no third mouth to feed. I stirred, and my hand was aware of something sticky beneath it. I opened my eyes and found myself staring at a hand covered in blood. It was on my clothes, underneath me. I jumped up to see that it was all over the lower part of the mattress. It was not on Mama's shoulders or her face. A pale face, a motionless face, when I touched it, cold, with no sound of breath. I remembered Antonina. I screamed and clutched her in my arms. I rocked her. I rocked her and I cried. The warmth of my tears did not warm her. Her eyes were opaque; I could not see into her soul – I could not see if it had gone. I howled. Rocked. Howled. She is at peace; she is with the Virgin.

Neither is true. She is dead.

I heard a knock at the door.

'Ceci?' it was Adelina.

I could not stop my sobs.

'Ceci? I'm coming in.' She did, stood. I could not look at her. I felt her kneel beside me.

'Ceci… Ceci….let go.'

I clutched Mama even closer, her head to my chest. Adelina put his arms round me and tried to pull my arms away.

'No!'

But at that moment, she was stronger than me. Mama's body fell to the bed, and holding my wrists, she pushed my arms so that they were crossed over my breast and hers were round me. I leaned my head against her shoulder and sobbed. I don't know how long she held me like this, but I knew she was rocking me as Mama had rocked me, gently, saying nothing.

When I had stopped crying she said,

'Come, sit over there.' She pulled me up and sat me on the bench by the now cold fire. Then she left, to return carrying a blanket, a bucket of water, a cloth and a dress.

She helped me move Mama from the bed onto the floor where I washed her, crossed her arms on her chest. She hauled the mattress outside to be burned, then helped me to wrap her in the blanket. Then, she undressed me, washed the blood away, and pulled her dress over my head. She put my dress into cold water so the blood could soak away.

'The baby died. I took it away.'

She nodded and caressed my cheek.

'Stay here, I will get a priest and someone to take the body away.'

A body, not Mama; Antea is not there, it was a body, much smaller that her, with a face – I knelt beside her, pulled the blanket from her face, stroked her cheek as she had so often stroked mine. Her mouth was open, I could not shut it. It looked as if she was screaming. But now there was no intake of breath, no pulling of me towards her.

A Priest came in and muttered over the body. It was then put on a cart and I watched it trundle away. I saw Angelo watching it too, looking at me, then he came across. I could not bear him to speak, He didn't know about his son. I killed him. I killed my brother.

I cannot be with people. Mama is dead, Prettycat is gone. Giulio is not there; he is with the painter. He loves his art; he does not need me. He only came home to see me. He shouldn't do that; I don't deserve him. I have killed, twice now. I am not a person he should love.

I returned to the *Macello*, I opened the front door slowly, heard Graziosa upstairs talking, probably to their servant. I prayed for her as I filled a water skin, added a knife, and the remains of a loaf. I chopped off my hair with the sewing scissors and changed into my tunic, stockings and heavy shoes. They still fitted me. I left Adelina's dress on the bench. That was all there was now the mattress has gone. Just two beakers, two dishes on the floor, the cooking pot over the cold ashes in the fireplace, a bundle of cloth.. Some specks of blood on the floor. I touched them; they were dry. I thought of my 'wedding dress': it was in that bundle of cloth. I reached out – no - leave it – leave it with him – whose face had faded.

When the shops shut at midday and everyone was indoors, I picked up my small bundle and left. I went down the *Macello*, past the workshops, round the Column and through the ruins towards the vineyards where we saw the Laocoön. I crossed to where there was a gate in the city walls, and followed the wall until I found a place to hide. A ruined house filled with rubble, I spent the rest of daylight hauling stones around, making an inner wall, a cave I could crawl into. I kept awake after dark in case there was a returning inhabitant, but no-one came. I stared into the darkness all night, curled up with my arms around the bundle, as if it were Prettycat, imagining Mama beside me. I thought of her as she slept – I heard her voice.

'Ceci – Pietro – Pietro.'

What was she telling me, that Pietro was the father? The food before Christmas, the dresses for the wedding … the unmarried man who married someone else, with a dowry… Pietro… Pietro… I had killed Giulio's brother?

The stars were bright, bright in the sky. I wanted to pull down the stones over me, block out the stars. It was warm, I was sweating. I was cold. Cold. Cold.

CHAPTER TWENTY-TWO

GIULIO Rome, 1509

When Ceci did not meet me at the end of the *Macello* that Sunday, I waited for a while: not long, as I was impatient to see her, then went towards the house. The shop was shuttered as I would expect, but the walls seemed to exude emptiness as if the rooms themselves were shuttered on the inside. As I went through the main door, I had no sense of Ceci or Antea, and opened their door to a dust-filled silence which seemed to have been there for years. The room was empty. The fire grate had only cold grey ashes. I lifted the stone at the back, nothing. No clothes no trace of women. It was as if they had only been there in my imagination.

I went upstairs to be met by a woman I didn't know who looked at me suspiciously and stood firmly at the tops of the stairs. Who are you?

'I am Giulio Pippi, son of Pietro, the owner of this house. Who are you?

'I am maid to the mistress.' She did not give way.

I decided formality was the best way forward.

'May I see your mistress?'

She turned and went into the apartment I heard voices murmuring and then she came out and indicated that I might enter – my own apartment! Or was it anymore? The woman who greeted me was, I was glad to see, Graziosa, certainly the woman my father had married. And certainly pregnant. She was stiff and waved me towards a stool. Uncertain of me, but recognising me. I asked after her health.

'Where are Antea and Ceci?'

'Antea died and her daughter left the same day.'

'Died?'

'Yes. You should ask Adelina.'

'And Ceci?'

'No-one saw her after the body was taken away, no-one knows where she went.' It was clear to me that Graziosa did not care. The door below opened, heavy footsteps came upwards – my father. I rose from my seat. He was taken aback to see me.

'Giulio?' his tone was uncertain. We had not spoken since the quarrel. I made no greeting.

'I have heard about Antea, where is Ceci?'

He shook his head.

'Didn't you look for her?'

He shook it again.

'Of course you didn't, you want the rooms back, don't you?'

He made no answer.

'Does Adelina know?'

'Adelina arranged the burial. I don't know what else she knows'.

'Then I will ask her, I am getting no answers here.' I paused, but no further words came. 'I shall find her.'

'Wait.'

Pietro walked to a chest and opened it. He took out a bundle and unwrapped it.

'You may want to look for Tomasso' he said. I showed my

surprise at this knowledge. He nodded. In his hand was a hank of pale gold hair.

'All that was left was a dress and a bundle of cloth which Adelina claimed as hers, and this.'

I took it. Handled it. Her precious hair, divorced from her face, her ears, her shoulders. I wanted to caress it to sink my lips into it, but, in front of them, did not. I took the cloth from Pietro, wrapped the hair back into it and put it in my pouch. I should have thanked him, he could have thrown it away. Our eyes met, and a moment of almost understanding passed from him to me, but was quickly broken by the lowering of his eyes and a slight nod. I turned and left the house, made for the apothecary, and thumped loudly on the door.

Adelina told me the story of Antea, the birth and her death. How she had helped Ceci, had lent her a dress. How Ceci had not followed the cart with the body and only she, Adelina, had watched the body being tipped into the mass grave and covered with quicklime. I listened to this, head bowed, eyes tipped with saltwater as I tried to imagine why Ceci had left her mother.

'I don't know. She told me nothing. I came back to find her, but all I found was the dress I had lent her, and the one she had left behind.' She went into the other room.

'I washed it, and kept it for her.' She handed it over. It was the dress she had worn at the wedding, the dress I had carefully taken from her when she had given me her maidenhood. The maidenhead that Adelina had washed away. I held it.

'And her hair.' Adelina looked puzzled. 'She'd cut if off. My father found it.' I showed her the bundle.

'Ah. Completely Tomasso.' So, they all knew.

I rolled up the dress and put it with the hair back into my pouch.

'Find her, Giulio.'

Before I left Adelina, I drew a picture of Ceci, no, of Tomasso, with cap and shoulder-length hair. I would need this.

I planned my search: the place where we hid Tomasso's clothes, everywhere we had searched for small antiquities, everywhere I had drawn and she had watched, everywhere we had explored, everywhere we had made love. I followed this way whenever I could, every hour of light I had. I went into shops, shouted to gardeners, enquired in churches, showed the drawing to pedlars. I was met with indifference, with shrugs, with unhelpful lies, with negative responses. With ribald faces and remarks about my 'lost boy' accompanied by a smirk, and offers of 'a much prettier boy', for a price.

After six weeks, the drawing was dirty and torn. The face creased and worn away. After two months, the face had almost disappeared. After three month, the dress and the bundle of hair were removed from under my pillow and hidden at the bottom of my chest. After four months I stopped actively searching, and after six months I stopped looking at every face in the crowd, watching every exit from a church. My drawings of women resembled the model I was using at the time and no longer had any semblance of Ceci. My hands forgot the feel of her skin, my nose, her scent. My penis rose and fell in and out of other women and forgot there was ever a home where it was loved.

CHAPTER TWENTY-THREE

TOMASSO

I lay there in a fever, alternately hot and cold, in and out of nightmares, tears and cries of pain, light and dark, until I was conscious of smells: urine, earth, the dust in my nose: of limbs which ached, and of a spider running across my face. I batted at it and sat up suddenly, banging my head on the stone above me. I then remembered - and wished to die. It wouldn't be a nuisance; my body would be hidden here and could rot into the rest of the ruins. Then my body sagged and I went into almost dreamless sleep to be woken by the arrival of hunger. It nagged at me, telling me my body wanted to live even if my mind wanted to die. It wanted food and drink, my tongue was dry, it imagined water; my mind could only see the death cart rumbling. Eyes shut, as if not wanting to relinquish that image, I slid out from under the stone, and opened eyes gummed with tears, to find myself lying amongst goats snuffling at the scrub. The nearest goat bleated in surprise and sprang away, then went on eating.

The warm air was filled with the smell of goat. I must be like a goat; I had been startled, cried in alarm and now should eat. So my body told me. I stood up and looked around me. The goatherd was sitting on a pillar and far beyond him people were trudging up and down the hills in one and twos, on foot, on mules, pushing carts. The scene was like the background to a painting, moving, past me, as if I wasn't here. It was an ordinary day, but I wasn't part of it. Even the goatherd seemed not to see me, did not even turn in my direction. Perhaps

I wasn't here, perhaps I was dead; perhaps the trudgers, all going the same way, were the dead walking to heaven, and I should join them.

I approached them, stopped where I could hear as well as see them. They didn't look happy as they should, surely, if on the way to heaven? They mostly looked careworn, walking a trail they were so used to they didn't need to use their eyes to see where they were going, except for a few children who ran about until told crossly not to. These people were pushing animals, birds, carts filled with vegetables or fruit. I was near enough to see an apple rolling from the top of basket; my body leapt towards it then sat at the side of the road, its teeth sinking into the flesh. The juice was balm on my tongue, and the fruit itself released its aroma when bitten. It was chewed slowly and swallowed, and showed my taste buds were not grieving. It showed that I was not dead, and helped me to remember where I was, close to a gate through which people came from the gardens and little farms outside the city walls to sell the animals and foodstuff in a market. No-one looked at me. I ate, my hand and mouth continuing on their own without my direction. I watched the human trail, a haze of movement, a mixture of sounds, which then turned into words and footfalls. They were alive, I was alive. Think of the sun! Look at the sky! Imagine Giulio painting it – no, don't think of him.

He doesn't exist. Mama doesn't ex…I do.

I found myself on my feet and going forward to join the uneven line of walkers. I caught the eye of a young girl on a cart, who grinned at me. Then she blew a kiss, and I remembered I was Tomasso, not Cecilia, as her father (I suppose – or it might have been her husband) cuffed her and scowled at me. I threw aside the broken parts that were Cecilia, lengthened my step, pulled back my shoulders and left the now-crying girl behind.

I was following a flock of geese, (at a safe distance – geese and I don't get on), when the sound of hooves came from behind me and, as I stood aside, two horsemen whipped up their horses with whooping yells and galloped forward, scattering hissing geese in all directions. The herdsmen, taken by surprise, shook their fists then started to herd the geese back together. Some took the opportunity, (guessing they were on the way to market?), to escape into the ruins, some ran backwards when the men tried to catch them, some just stood hissed and squawked. People around me woke up and ran to throw themselves at a goose and either get it round the neck or be left with feathers in their hand and bites on the shins or wrist. I joined in, not to catch one, but to look as if I was. I saw a goose harrying a child which I took into my arms and carried to the side of the road, where it yelled and screamed, and struggled, and I wondered what to do with it. A woman had successfully caught a goose. Instead of shushing it towards the herdsmen, she wrang its neck and pitched it onto a cart, then looked round and came up to me to snatch the child away.

'Give me 'er – I've 'eard about young men like you!' And she scurried away to join the cart which moved swiftly on.

The more honest walkers, whose trek was enlivened hugely by the incident, including myself, eventually formed a circle around the remaining geese, which were counted by the herdsmen. They looked at each other sorrowfully, while the eldest yelled obscenities into the distance as he realised the number of geese were less than they had started out with. The younger herdsman dipped his hand in his large pouch and scattered seed, which calmed the geese and brought a couple more back from the side of the road. Buoyed up by the jollity of it all, I shushed these two back into the herd and said, in dialect, 'Want my 'elp to market?' He looked dubious, and the older man scrutinised me

'Why'd we want 'elp? We've less of 'em now.'

'In case another 'orseman…?'

He swore and spat, and turned away. The younger one, I suppose his son, said 'can't pay you'

'Don' want payin'.' I dropped into the dialect. 'Just a crust and water.' He considered this, and glanced at his father, who grunted.

'Aw'right," he said and I became, temporarily, a geese-herder.

We entered the market, crowded with more people than I had ever seen in one place, this place being an area of flattened earth, hard a stone, surrounded by houses leaning against each other, a church, and a small fountain. There were stalls as far as I could see, with pens for sheep and goats and cages full of chickens. I could see groups of trestle tables near the pens had foodstuffs, while on the other side of the piazza were stalls of gloves and hats, hose and stockings, tools. Mules were being unloaded and goods being placed on trestles. There were cobblers, cloth-sellers, pedlars with food or trinkets pushing past. The noise was tremendous: shouting, men and women negotiating to hire a trestle or a pen, grunts and squeals, quacks and gobbles.

We crossed towards these and while the older man, Nino, haggled, the younger man, his son Franco, herded the geese into a pen. There were a lot of people just standing around, not doing anything except chatting to each other, or eyeing goods. Then a low bell pealed and those standing around began to converge on the stalls and the pens. I heard music playing and people calling out. To me, the din, though alarming in its volume, was exciting. Franco and his father started haggling with customers and I pricked up my ears to listen. A woman tugged my arm.

'You gonna sell me a goose 'r what?'

So I turned on the charm, and haggled with her for a fine fellow with a good stomach. After the sale of three birds, Franco said to me,

'You've got th' touch, the women like you. You've got more for the birds than us.' I was about to say it was because I was a woman, then, remembered,

'Women alwus 'ave liked me.'

The older man, Nino, looked over.

''Cause you're a pretty boy'

'Will you stay?' asked Franco.

I spotted another woman checking over a goose, and advanced on her, saying 'yes' over my shoulder.

The market carried on all day, but the geese had all been sold by the time the sun started to descend. Nino bought pies and mixed wine for us and we sat on the shady side against the walls of the permanent shops and ate. The taste was delicious, and my empty stomach responded with a rumble and a belch.

'Looks like you've not eaten for a while, ' said Nino.

'I'm always 'ungry' I said.

'You've made uz back th' money we lost to them youths.' Nino made the last word sound like a swearword. ''ere's some for yersel,' and he handed me some coins. Enough to buy me food for three days, if I was careful, even at the prices here, which were much higher than in the M*acello*.

'Yu be 'ere next market?' I didn't know when the next market was. 'We be coming with the pigs.'

I said I didn't know where I'd be, but if I was, I'd find them. I stowed the coins in my pouch, keeping my hand on it, said goodbye and wandered off to see the rest of the market. I bought a new pouch, a new water bottle, and had my knife sharpened. As I was waiting for it and not paying attention, a hand punched me in the stomach making me drop my coins, which were swept up. I coughed.

'Good job you paid me already,' said the sharpener, handing me my knife. I couldn't answer: I was winded. 'Best keep your wits abou' you boy' he said.

~

I learned a bit more with everything that happened. Sometimes I had food, by stealing or by earning, sometimes I was hungry for days, living only on water and scraps. I got thin, my monthly bleeding stopped. At times, I was caught stealing and beaten, sometimes I was just tripped up for the fun of it, or chased by youths bigger than me. I slept anywhere I could find that was small and enclosed. Places that were often damp or hot, dark and, nearly always, smelly. Quite often I would be woken by another body squeezing in, or one that pulled me out, swearing and sending me on my way. I lined up for food from the monks, but if I went into a church to rest, I got thrown out. I was dirty, my clothes torn. No different from any other street boy, except that I learned to squirm away from men who approached me with a leer, knowing that one day I wouldn't be able to.

That day came. I stole a cheese from a stall, and was being chased by a youth who saw me and wanted want I had. I found myself trapped in an alleyway, the cheese in my right hand, and I fumbled with my left hand for my knife. He was quick, seized the cheese, chopped at my left-hand so that I dropped the knife. He grasped my tunic and drew me to him. I raised my hands to batter his face as he twisted his hand through a tear in the tunic, and exposed one breast which brushed his hand.

'What'?'

He ripped the tear down to show both breasts, then grinned and put his hand between my legs, pushing me against the wall. Suddenly, I was too tired to struggle. It would be over quickly if I didn't. Then he pushed me to my knees, and took his cock out.

'Go on!' I realised what he wanted and for the first time, I opened my mouth. There was smell and a thrust that nearly choked me, and a taste. Then he was gone and I was vomiting, and crying. I crawled next to the wall and stayed there.

I am no-one.

I stole a dress. I got used to being abused by men. I lay down and just accepted what was done to me. I then scrabbled after the coins which were thrown at me. My knife was ready if the demands were too extreme, or no coins came, when I would leap onto a back and stab arms and faces. I did not speak or talk, I spat and scowled and cursed. I stole another tunic, and hose. I was a girl, I was a boy. I was Tomasina, I was Tomasso.

The winter was the worst. I remembered the limekilns and those who used to sleep by them to keep warm. I would go into the Camp Vaccino, wait until dark, then creep as near as I could to the warmth, trying not to get near to those already there. I got used to waking before dawn so as to leave before the workers came, who would flog people to make them go. In the coldest months of January and February, I wore the dress under the tunic for an extra layer of warmth. At times, I snuggled against a cow which had not been gathered in, and sucked milk from her. I got into gardens and picked vegetables to eat raw, and slept in the piles of steaming compost.

In the spring, I cleaned myself and my dress as well as I could and, and made my way to the Palazzo Colonna gardens to seek weeding work. Across the road from the entrance I paused. I watched as chattering women entered, one or two of whom I recognised, including the girl whom I had watched with the gardener. They entered together, smiling, she with a baby in her arms. It was too bright. I couldn't move forwards. I couldn't be part of them, I wasn't worthy. I slumped against a wall and watched the metal gate clang shut behind them.

~

I don't know why my body did not just lie down and die: I had no energy to make that decision. It was all spent on the physical actions required to exist, and that was all.

~

Until.

I was hungry. My belly hurt, I was dizzy. I'd had only water from the fountain for…I don't know how many days. I'd tried to steal food, but I'd been caught, and had been whipped for it. My back hurt, my feet were bare and torn. I wore only a shirt and torn breeches. I was dirty and smelly. It was March, and the weather had changed to warm rain and some sunny days, I think, but I had stopped noticing. I hung around the markets, but others were stronger than me and beat me to any left-over food.

I was sitting at the side of a fountain, not able to move, when a man came up to me. 'I've been watching you. Yer're 'ungry ain't yer?' I said nothing. 'Yer want some food don't yer?' I had a foreboding, but I didn't move. He sat down and stared into my face.

'Reckon you'd scrub up well, pretty lad like you.'

I was aware of what might happen next, but I didn't care. When he found out I was a girl, he'd leave me alone. He might beat me up, so what?

'Food in exchange?' I looked at him.

'Food first.'

He grinned.

'Come with me.' I thought he would lead me to a dark space without any food.

'Food first.' I said staying where I was.

'Alrigh'. Stay 'ere.' He crossed to a pedlar of pies, watching me all the time, and brought back a meat pie. I stuffed it into my mouth, gagging on it, coughing.

'My, you are 'ungry.'

When I had finished, and felt queasy after eating too fast, he said quietly, 'Payment.'

He led me into an alleyway, to a dark narrow space between houses. He pushed me ahead of him and we went right to the end. There, amid the shit and the rubbish, he shooed off the rats and told me to lie down, on my stomach. I did as he said, listless, with my stomach in pain from eating the pie too quickly. He was on top of me, pulling up my tunic and my breeks down. Then I realised. Too late. He held me down with one hand and pulled down his own breeks. He pushed himself against me, a hard thing, then pulled my buttocks apart and plunged his cock into me. I gasped at the pain as he pumped up and down. Then he left me. He swore.

'A bloody virgin – blood all over me.' He swiped at my head. 'I should fuck you again for that.' He got up, kicked me, and left.

My face was in a pile of dung. I felt sick and vomited over it. This made me raise my head from the mess. I turned over and pulled up my breeks, seeing the blood on the rubbish and feeling the pain. I put my head in my hands and sobbed, tears falling over the shit on my fingers. He hadn't even noticed I was female! I started to laugh. I leaned against the wall. *An angel hovers over me, I say 'take me now,' and put up my hands. The angel shakes his head and flies away.*

'Mama!'

'Ceci – Ceci – stay calm now'

'Mama!'

'I can't come, Ceci – you know I can't – Giulio wants me.'

'Giulio?' I can't see him, can't make him out. A shadowy figure – he turns. It isn't him, it is the man who had assaulted me. Then it is him. 'Giulio!'

Giulio turns his back on me, takes my mother's hand; they smile at each other and walk away. I can't get up. Rats run round and round me, rats bigger than human beings. I scream then all is silent and dark.... I am in a wood, where the sun comes though the leaves and sits in bright pools on the ground. Someone is laughing, a male laugh; it's the person holding my hand. I turn to look at him, to laugh with him, to say his name, 'Giulio', but he's disappeared. I am alone; then I'm not.

I am lying under a tree, in one of those bright pools and he is caressing me, stroking me, and as he strokes, my pain increases and I cry.

I was lying on a bed, and someone was washing me. I had to leave, no-one should find out I was a girl. I moved to sit up but I was lying on my front. A hand stopped me. 'Shush child.' I realised it was a woman, wiping my back and behind. I looked at my shoulder; where my dirty clothes had been there was a clean white cloth.

'There.' I felt her pulling down the cloth. 'You might be able to turn over now. I'll help you'. I felt strong hands pull my shoulders and my hips and turn me gently. I whimpered, but I was on my back. The woman was a nun. She pulled a sheet over me and smiled.

'You are at the hospital of Santa Maria de'Angeli. You were picked up by the corpse collectors who thought you were dead. Then one of them saw you breathing and they brought you here. I am Sister Beata.'

'You cleaned me?'

'Yes, and found you were not a boy after all. I shall ask no questions, not yet. I will give you a little food and then you must res.t'

'My clothes?'

'They have been burned. We will find you new ones when you've recovered.'

Another woman in a plain dress came in with a dish. Sister Beata took it from her and sat next to me. The other woman put pillows behind my head so I could eat. It was a kind of porridge, which was spooned into my mouth bit by bit. It exhausted me, so although it wasn't empty, she gave the bowl back to the woman and took the pillow away.

'Sleep now,' she said.

I don't know how many days I spent in that bed. They didn't tell me.

~

It was warm. I was sitting up, then standing, then able to eat two meals a day. I visited the chapel every day and said my prayers for my delivery, but I no longer believed in the love of God, just His vengeance. I believed in penance and asked if what I had suffered was enough for what I had done. I feared that it wasn't. I had been injured, I had starved, but I was still alive. Perhaps not enough payment for two, no, three, deaths, for I was now sure my actions had killed Mama. Perhaps God had made me well to suffer again, until all was equal.

I grew a little fatter, my limbs were pinker, my hair was clean and down past my shoulders. They gave me a patched up skirt and blouse. The stride of Tomasso, the attitudes, the 'freedom' – all were lost in this skirt. I got used to it. I liked it. I was able to help with the cooking and the washing, and enjoyed the little enclosed garden while weeding among the herbs. Lewd words retreated in my head, and my former manner of speaking returned, the dialect softened, and then was lost. Just before I had an idea this might be for always, Sister Beata came to me, with a cloak over her arm and a pouch.

'You are well enough to leave,' she said. Fear flooded through me. 'We only have room for so many patients, and we need your bed.' She gave me the cloak, worn and patched but clean, and the pouch.

'This has food and water for two days, three if you're careful.' She gave me a veil for my head.

'Where will I go?'

'God will show you the way.'

That was what I was afraid of – why hadn't he just taken me? Why had the corpse collector not just ignored my breathing and left me to die in the pit? We got to the door to the outside.

'Remember, God made you a woman, do not go against him and dress like a boy. It is not what He meant you to be; you must accept who and what you are.'

I walked through the door.

'I will pray for you,' she said, and I heard it shut behind me.

I pulled my veil down and the cloak around me. I didn't know who I was. I picked at the skirt. In the street, I wanted the cover of being a boy. I needed a knife. I needed the protection of boys' clothes. I would be going against God. So be it.

I wandered aimlessly that day, I saw nothing to steal. I slept in a dark corner. I felt unsafe, unsure, and hid. The food ran out, and when it did, I found myself walking down a street when a group of soldiers came by. One of them stopped, came up to me and raised my veil. He whistled, and took hold of my chin. I was back in the square; there was no Angelo to save me now. The other soldiers went on laughing.

'Your cock'll wear out!'

'How much?' he said.

I named a price, he halved it. Enough for a meal. It was over quickly, up against a wall. And he paid me; an honourable man. As he straightened his clothes he said, 'Hope to see you again, my lady', and bowed. It wasn't so bad.

I went into a tavern, ordered food and wine and water. I went to a table to wait, and looked around. There were both men and women there, together, eating and laughing. It seemed safe. The food came and I started to eat, slowly.

I was concentrating on the food, and was startled to see a woman sit down opposite me. She was plump, grey and wrinkled, but her eyes were sharp and there seemed to be some vestige of beauty in her face.

'You've been drawing attention,' she said. I started to get up.

'I'll go.' She leaned forward to stop me.

'No, not that kind of attention. Admiration, from the men.'

I looked round and noticed that a couple of men were looking at me, exchanging words and smiling.

'Don't stop eating.' I obeyed.

'You're wearing patched up clothes, so I guess they're handouts.'

'From the Sisters.' I don't know why I told her that. She nodded.

'So you have no money, you're not a servant or you'd have a livery, and you're on your own. He beat you didn't he?' I was puzzled.

'Your pimp – left you for dead, the Sisters found you and now you're free of him, unless he finds you.'

'He won't - there wasn't a pimp.' She raised her eyebrows.

'I was dressed as a boy. Some of the time.' I swallowed some wine and water. She looked me up and down and laughed.

'Well, I can see how that might be. Small, slim, pretty, shortish hair – yes, a boy.'

'I need work,' I said. 'Can I work here?'

She leaned across the table.

'Well, let's see.' She stared at me; and I stared back. 'Small, slim, pretty – you look like a virgin, which you're not, of course.'

I realised then that any work would not be merely as a serving-maid. But what could I do? I continued to stare.

'And you're bright, I can see that.'I went on eating and drinking as if I were just a customer.

'Very bright.' She nodded approvingly. 'I think Vanozza would like you for the parties.'

'Vanozza?'

'Vanozza dei Cattenei, she owns this place, and that one over the road, and one near *Santa Maria del Popolo*, for her richer customers.' I had no idea who this Vanozza was.

'Mistress of Pope Alexander, mother of Cesare and Lucretia, they say.'

I had heard stories of them. I finished my food and sat there, waiting. So was she. To offer, or be offered? I stood up and took up my pouch.

'The food was very nice. Thank you.' And I made for the door.

'Wait!' I turned round.

'How old are you?'

'Fifteen.'

'Shrewd.'

'I've learned.'

'On the streets. Yes. Better to be in a warm place with regular food.'

'That's a nice dream.' I noticed that people had stopped talking and were watching us, enjoying the silent battle.

'With a little money to spend, and clients vetted – and parties.' I waited.

'Cardinals, and merchants, Rich guests - they like parties with pretty women - who can talk, and speak poetry, who can read and write, as well as smile.'

I could do all of those things. Once. I made my offer.

'I can do those things.' She sat up straight.

'Come with me,' she said, and made a signal to a man slouching in a corner, watching us. Outside, a smart cart came out of nowhere and we journeyed to a house in a quiet street not far from *Piazza del Popolo*.

She knocked and we were let in. She told me to wait and went up the stairs.

There was a chair with carved armrests and back, with shabby velvet on the seat. Once very expensive. The carpet on the floor was worn, but also of a price. The woman called me from the top of the stairs.

'Come up.'

I did so. In a large room where there was other worn furniture, a woman sat upright on a velvet seat. She was thin, old, in an old-fashioned dress, and cap. A blanket lay over her lap and fell down to the floor; a richly embroidered blanket in red and gold. She raised her eyes; they were as faded as the furniture, and one had a milky film over it. The other was rheumy, but the expression was sharp. I felt an urge to curtsey.

'Name?' The voice was so clear and arrogant that I was glad I hadn't curtsied. Name? What was my name?

'Tomasina,' I said, as coldly as I could. She raised her chin.

'Take off that cloak and turn round.' I did so.

'Again.' This time I twirled so my skirt flew out.

'Walk across the room.' I drew myself straight and walked with a sight bounce. 'Come here – kneel down.'

She looked into my face, put her hand on my breasts.

'Stand up,' and she felt all the way down my legs. 'Pull up your skirt.' I did so. She opened my breeks and looked down at my pubis. 'Hmm.' She touched the hairs there and slid her hand across my vagina, then removed it.

'Keep your skirt up and turn round.' She felt my buttocks. 'The Sisters made a good job. Put your skirt down and sit over there.' I sat. She made me read something and write, and asked me questions about the Papal court which I couldn't answer. She looked at me for a long time. I kept eye contact with her.

'You want a roof over your head? Food and drink every day? You want to go to parties? You want to have clothes and jewels? You're willing to listen and learn about the gossip, and keep your mouth shut when necessary? You want to be fucked by rich men?' Something she knew all about, this woman, who had been a Pope's mistress, who had mothered that Pope's favourite children. And who knew about torture, death and trading. I lowered my head in acquiescence, without losing eye contact. There was a moment's silence. She broke the contact with me and took it up with the woman.

'Good. Serafina, set her up. You are to do everything Serafina tells you, and you will live here, in the *Osteria del Orso*.' The Bear Inn. Her best hostelry.

She waved us away, and I saw a servant come out of the gloom, pull up the edges of the blanket over her, and go behind her. It was then I realised the chair had wheels. My body dipped as in a little curtsey; she had gained my respect if not my liking; she had survived. But she didn't see it.

I became a prostitute, not a common one, an 'honest' one. My mother had done it; why should it be any different for me? The act of sex wasn't the act of love. What I had done with Giulio was a world apart, a dream, something hidden in my head, not to be looked at, not thought of. Being fucked by rich men was a different thing altogether; different as the sun from shit. But as least the shit would not be in the street now; I was to join a high-class establishment. I would no longer be hungry, I would be a girl in nice clothes. A 'virgin', until it was known that I was not. It might physically hurt occasionally, men wanted strange things sometimes. As I was well-fed, the bleeding came back, so I was careful not to get pregnant, not to get a sexual disease. It was better to suffer in comfort than in the street. God's will.

Tomasso was gone. Ceci was gone. Tomasina would survive.

I shared a room with Ginevra, who was my own age, and who had been rescued from the streets like me. She had been left alone when her parents had died of the *mal aria* when she was twelve and no-one else would look after her. Her father had been a musician and her mother a dancer, she had taken her flute and a drum onto the streets, to play and sing.

'I was thrown out of the rooms where we lived, so I slept where I could, in the soldiers' barracks a lot of the time – in return for favours. Serafina found me when I was performing with musicians in the market.' The only musicians I had ever seen were at Pietro's wedding.

'Vanozza liked me because I could play and dance.'

She would play and dance for me and the others, she would play dance music on the flute then take up the drum and dance in time with it, slow first, then faster until she was whirling round, skirts flying, while we clapped in time and cheered when she had finished. Vanozza often asked her to play for her. This was her skill. Mine was in recitation, and I was given Latin poetry to learn. Ginevra – Ginetta - and I devised a performance where she played and I recited. This proved very popular, so we were sent out together. It also earned us small jewels and presents of silks, and beautiful cloth, and gloves. These were all given to Vanozza, who turned the fabrics into clothes for us and sometimes gave us a small jewel back to keep, or to spend when we went out in groups to go shopping.

I had not had girl-friends before, and I grew to love Ginetta, her laugh and her funny stories. I felt happy with her and the others, and the men at the parties were, mostly, satisfied with the basic positions, and, usually, smelt better than those on the streets. Those who wanted more than the basics, we would refer to Serafina and the price went up for them. At first our clients were those who frequented or stayed at the *Orso*, then, when we had learned the most refined of manners, and the court dances, we were sent in groups to parties at rich men's houses. It was the ambition of all of us to attract and retain two or three men for whom we would be exclusive lovers, for then, we could be released from the *Orso* and live our own lives.

It was at a party hosted by Agostino Chigi that we met Raffaello, who came to the *Orso* to draw us both, bringing with him his assistant Gianfrancesco, who fell for Ginetta and was a regular visitor. From him we heard about the painters and their work, and gossip from the Papal court. From him, I heard the name 'Giulio', which tore through the carefully constructed barrier in my mind like a musket shot, throwing me into a past which I had not wanted to remember; which I had 'forgotten'.

That evening, I told Ginetta my real name.

'Cecilia, that's so pretty! Much better than Tomasina, much higher class!' And she started to call me that when we were on our own.

CHAPTER TWENTY-FOUR

GIULIO Rome, 1511

I was working with Master Peruzzi on the frescos of the east-facing *loggia* of the Chigi Villa when I met Raffaello properly for the first time. I was painting the decorations on the pilasters either side of the arches, while Sebastiano, the painter Chigi had brought from Venice, was painting the lunettes beneath Master Peruzzi's ceiling. We were engrossed in our work, Sebastiano high up on the scaffolding, me at the mid-point of a pilaster between the arches to the garden, painting in *chiaroscuro* with touches of gold and bronze against a blue background. Women with curly tails, men with the hind-quarters of goats, boys climbing spirals and holding up plaques. There was a clatter of feet, voices and laughter, and Chigi burst in with the painter and several followers. They stood in the middle of the room, ignoring us, looking at the bare wall opposite.

Chigi waved his hand across the wall.

'You see, Raffaello, here I want a series of goddesses or nymphs: Venus, Calisto, Galatea – tasteful –'

'Nude,' said Raffaello

'Yes – tasteful.' Raffaello grinned.

Sebastiano had stopped painting and was looking down with a frown. Clients (well, Pope Julius) had been known to request Raffaello to paint over the recent work of other painters, although he had refused to paint out those in the Papal apartments by Perugino, who had been his teacher.

'Below the lunettes,' said Raffaello, and threw a glance at Sebastiano, who continued painting. 'Over the line of the doors, five of them.' Chigi rubbed his hands.

'Five!'

'I will do some drawings, suggest some suitable subjects, and' he signalled to one of his followers -'Gianfrancesco will arrange a contract to be drawn up with you.' He then turned to look at the paintings we were making. Chigi, swelling with pride at having Raffaello accept his commission, decided to introduce us.

'Sebastiano di Piombo – I brought him back with me from Venice.'

'Yes, I see the Venetian style. And you?' He turned to me. I wished I was painting a picture not just the decorations, so that he could see my worth.

'You work for Master Peruzzi do you not?' I nodded. 'And you painted the *chiaroscuro* figures outside?' I was surprised that he knew.

'They are very fine. – Giulio, isn't it?'

'Giulio Pippi'.

'Ah yes, it was your father who told me.' He turned to Chigi.

'I am about to work on the second *stanza*, the drawings are all made, so I can start on your commission while the *sinopie* are done. And Giulio, I will need some *chiaroscuro* statues on the lower level, I am not happy with the ones in the first stanza. I will talk with Master Peruzzi.' He smiled. I smiled – was it that simple? I was nineteen; last year I had finished my seven-year apprenticeship with Master Peruzzi, so I was free to leave him if I wished. Sebastiano had stopped brush in hand, and looked angry as Chigi guided Raffaello from the *loggia* into the villa, followed by two of his followers, while the rest went into the garden.

'*Chiaroscuro*! He didn't even look at my paintings!' It was true, he hadn't, he had looked away after the remark about Venice. Sebastiano threw down his brush and climbed down the scaffolding.

'And you,' he hissed at me, 'a maker of decorations and false statues! Not a real painter at all!'

He stomped out of the room. I hoped that Raffaello, charming as he was, had not just made a passing remark about me that he would forget by the morning. I went back to work, paying more attention to it, in case Raffaello came back in. But he did not. I heard them all leave, chattering and laughing.

I climbed up the scaffolding in front of Sebastiano's unfinished fresco, which would have to be erased and re-done because of the drying of the plaster. The lunette next to it was bare, and on it I drew a face of a beautiful young man, just to show I could draw, in case Raffaello came back. I knew that it would make Sebastiano angry and he would plaster and paint over it, but it was satisfying to make my mark, show my drawing skills, on a real wall inside: in truth, for the sheer pleasure of it. I also wanted to show up the upstart from Venice, who had been promoted over the rest of us to do his own work on the lunettes.

The next day, Sebastiano did not come in, and I painted decorations alone until the afternoon, when Master Peruzzi appeared.

'Sebastiano is not here?' I shook my head. He looked up at the unfinished lunette, frowned, saw the drawing beside it, and frowned again.

'What is this? He leaves his work unfinished, but draws a head on the next lunette? I gave him the work because Chigi asked me to - he wastes paint and time, and he isn't here.' Master Peruzzi was not often angry, only when people let him down or work wasn't to schedule. He had employed Sebastiano as a favour to Chigi, and he could foresee a problem not just with the painter but with the client. I had to own up.

'Forgive me Master, I drew the face at the end of work yesterday.'

He was surprised. 'Why?'

I explained that I couldn't resist the urge to draw something of my own on the wall. I didn't tell him that I had got tired of the seemingly endless *chiaroscuro* outside, and inside, nor that it was done out of jealousy of Sebastiano. Master Peruzzi looked at it again.

'Raffaello came to see me this morning.' I held my breath.

'He came to ask me if I would allow you to become an assistant to him. I told him you were no longer in thrall to me.' I put down my brush, and crouched on the scaffolding to be nearer to him, not to miss a word.

'There is no doubt that Raffaello has become a favourite of the Pope, and that it would be good for you to work with him.' I swung down to the floor.

'You have done well, Giulio, you have learned the skills of a painter. You've been with me long enough – Raffaello will be getting the major commissions now. You will want to be with him.' He smiled, as I did not reply.

'I can see by your face that you do – and your drawing -' he indicated the face ' -shows you are ready. I will not hold you back.'

'Master, thank you.' I could say no more.

'Your master is Raffaello now,' he said gently. 'And the drawing – I suggest you paint it before Sebastiano covers it.'

He grinned, and I knew that, kind though he was, this was not just a boost for me, but a dig at having to employ a painter he had not trained over one of his team. I came in the next day with a bucket of plaster, and painted the face in *chiaroscuro*, to show up my skills, and to pay back the sneer about such work.

I was told that Chigi liked it, and that Master Peruzzi had told him it was done by someone who had the favour of Raffaello and would be one of his major painters in time. I expect that Chigi liked that and that he had got a painting for free.

Sebastiano returned the next day to start his lunette again, tapping his paintbrush against his arm while an apprentice carefully scraped off the unfinished work for him to start again. He glanced at the head and glowered at me. There was no greeting for me, and he did not speak to me unless he had to.

Later, he sided with Michelangelo in the rivalry which developed between him and Raffaello, and became a bitter denigrator of his – of our - work. Although I supported Raffaello in any dispute, I did admire Michelangelo's work in the Sistine Chapel, which I gawped at with everyone else after it was unveiled. It was monumental, and it was delicate at the same time. No-one had ever portrayed God as a flying grey-bearded man of such physical strength, and no-one had painted such a beautiful male figure as Adam; more beautiful than any ancient sculpture I had seen, though it was known that the sculptor and painter, Michelangelo, had modelled Adam on a Roman torso, which stood in the Belvedere alongside the Laocoön.

I then knew Raffaello had seen the paintings before that opening of Michelangelo's Sistine work, for some of Raffaello's work in the *stanza* showed a robustness not seen in his painting before. I was to learn that Raffaello absorbed the work of others and skilfully turned it into his own, as he absorbed the details of the antique architecture to bring it into his own designs, in which I was to follow him, and develop it further.

~

When the decorations were finished, I was given the task of working up the *cartone* from the *modello,* made by Gianfrancesco Penni, of Raffaello's first fresco in the *loggia*: Galatea riding the sea on a seashell pulled by dolphins surrounded by nymphs and sea-centaurs. A Galatea with her head turned to one side, her body *contrapposto* - shoulders one way, legs another - her hair blowing in the wind, of such great beauty I was afraid of spoiling her. Her arm covered her breasts in a way that was so natural to her movement that you didn't realise this was Raffaello's way of combining nudity with modesty, together with the cloak draped so cunningly around her lower body, framing her torso and face and echoing the direction of her hair. There had been many statues of Venus that I had copied where her nudity was tempered with a well-place cloth, a hand, or a dress which revealed one breast, but I had never seen this used with such movement, such skill, such sublime beauty in painting. I saw the delicacy of the colouring of the bodies, the sky, the water and how the red of the cloak did not just draw the eye to Galatea, but brought the composition together to focus on her, the centre of the picture, her obvious command at the centre of the story, her strength in both mind and body.

When it was finished, I was invited to live in Raffaello's house alongside Gianfrancesco, who had become *fattore* - project manager. I became Giulio, the Roman, to distinguish me from other Giulios from elsewhere. Giulio Romano.

~

Rome 1513

Raffaello had been ordered by the Pope to paint a Madonna for his family church of San Sisto in Piacenza. This was in honour of the family patron saint, and of his uncle, Pope Sixtus IV, who had built the Sistine chapel and for whom the bridge was named. On a worktable, Raffaello was assembling his drawings to make the composition: a Madonna and child, St Sisto, and St Barbara, whose relics were held in the church. He called me over to work with him. The picture was large; a rectangle of string formed its size, twisted at the corners around pins hammered into the table. He held several drawings which I knew he had done at a recent session with models. He placed the first one, the Madonna holding her child, at the top, explaining that there would be an object, he did not yet know what, repeated either side of their heads to allow focus onto the faces. There would be a neutral background and she would be standing on clouds. Usually his Madonnas were tender and loving, clear-eyed and content, but this one's eyes were open wide, making her look fearful. I pointed to it and asked him why.

Painters always asked questions such as how high the picture would be, what size the space it should fill, where the light which reached the picture was coming from. Raffaello also insisted on knowing what the picture would be facing, especially when, as in this case, the place was too far for him to travel. He wanted to know all the surroundings, what other paintings there were, who by. He would ask for a local painter to make sketches for him. This was indicative of the care he took to make the painting a part of its surroundings, and especial care was taken for this one, an altarpiece in a church unknown to him, a painting that must shine out from any others.

'The picture will be hung facing a large crucifix,' he explained, 'so they are looking at the future, which they cannot avoid, and will always be there.'

So the Madonna was fearful, the baby too had an element of fear, but he plainly did not know why, he had caught the tension in his mother's arms. Once again, I was impressed by Raffaello's ability to portray the essence of a Madonna picture in the relationship with the baby. This mother and child were trapped forever, not able to take their eyes from that terrible fate; the painting would be powerful when in its place.

In counterpoint, at the bottom of the picture, he put two cherubs looking up, not fearful, but apprehensive. Their expressions made me laugh.

'They look a bit worried – as if they are asking each other if she is going to fall on them!'

'They were actually looking up from a table at their mother, wondering when the food was coming!'

He still held two papers, and put one down. This was St Sixtus, a model I knew well, whom we had drawn in different postures many times for various frescos. His name, appropriately for many paintings, was Joseph and he was one of the Pope's gardeners. He was pointing out of the picture, a fine piece of foreshortening.

'He's looking at her and pointing at the crucifix.'

'As if she couldn't see it herself... '

'Emphasis, Giulio, for the people and the pilgrims, to make sure *they* see the crucifix,' he told me, 'and an excuse to use the technique!'

Gianfrancesco came to join us, as Raffaello re-adjusted the position of the saint and in doing so, put the Barbara on the table. Raffaello and Gianfrancesco dissolved, their voices lost in a roaring in my ears. The room faded around the drawing; I had to put my hands on the table edge to support myself.

'Giulio?' Raffaello's voice was distant. 'Giulio? Are you alright? You've gone as white as marble.'

I muttered something about my head, the amount I'd drunk the night before (although I hadn't had much). Raffaello clapped me on the shoulder, I winced. He went back to the composition, picked up the Barbara and placed her on the right hand side so she was looking down at the cherubs, her face calm and serene.

Ceci.

The mist cleared as I looked. Her hair, her face, her eyes downcast, so that their intelligence, their fire was unseen. She was gentle, this Barbara, a gentle Ceci.

I cleared my throat.

'The model – I've not seen her before.'

'I've drawn her once or twice, but yes, this is the first time I'm using her in a painting. I saw her at one of Chigi's parties, and thought she would be perfect – lovely isn't she?' Gianfrancesco nodded. I stared. Chigi's parties – what was she doing there?

'Chigi is very taken with her,' he laughed, 'but Francesca keeps them apart!' Francesca was Chigi's mistress that he had brought back from Venice, they already had one child. Francesca had been a prostitute – my face went from white to red, I could feel it. Gianfrancesco teased.

'I think Romano has just fallen in love! I can introduce her if you like, she lives with Ginetta, my girl.' Ginetta was one of the many pretty girls whom Chigi welcomed to his parties for entertainment, for sex with his guests. I shuddered. I wanted to ask…

'What's her name? I've forgotten,' Raffaello asked

Ceci! My mind screamed.

'Her name is Tomasina.'

'That's it! Tomasina.'

My knuckles were white. Tomasina – Tomasso. So near – known to them, seen by them, not by me, I wasn't privy to Chigi's parties.

They went on talking and I tried to concentrate, to join the discussion of the exact positioning, of what would frame the Madonna. Usually a Madonna would be flanked by angels, Raffaello gave his Madonnas landscapes.

'Too distracting this time – not enough room.' I heard Raffaello say. He wanted no background, just a framing device. A decision was made for curtains; I don't know why, I'm sure I spoke for clouds, but perhaps I didn't. Raffaello drew a quick sketch of the composition and left it with Gianfrancesco who started to draw the *modello*. I recovered myself, and went back to work on the *cartone* for the expulsion of Heliodorus in the second Vatican *stanza*, where I would be painting the *chiaroscuro* statues under the paintings, and helping with the backgrounds. I worked mechanically, with only half my mind.

That afternoon, Raffaello having gone to Papal Palace at the behest of Pope Julius, was one of working quietly. Giovanni da Udine came in to show his large book of drawings of birds to Gianfrancesco, and talked about his failure to reproduce the pure white of the stucco found in the *Domus Aurea*. I didn't pay that much attention. Then Raffaello returned and I had to watch and listen as he looked over the *cartone* and altered some details, then he left me alone to work.

All the while, the thought of Ceci was foremost in my mind.

I went to the tavern with Gianfrancesco and Giovanni, the former then leaving to visit Ginetta, asking if I wanted him to arrange an introduction to Tomasina, explaining to Giovanni that I was befuddled with love since seeing one of Raffaello' drawings and hadn't been myself all day. This was followed by ribald laughter; I shook my head and Gianfrancesco left. Giovanni took up with a good-looking young painter, and became so engrossed in a discussion on pigments that he forgot he wanted to seduce him. I drank without joining in, and a woman whom I knew and whom I visited frequently came to sit on my lap and caress my face. I pushed her off, finished my drink and left.

The cool air hit me; any desire to sleep had fled. I walked to Raffaello's house and sat in the garden, which I didn't see. I saw only memory after memory of Ceci which came leaping out of the darkness of my mind where I had supressed them so long ago, when I had lost her. And I was angry - angry that others knew her and I didn't, angry that she was a prostitute, that she had abandoned me. I howled with that anger, and swung my hands across my face trying to sweep her away, to drown her in the pool in front of me, to throw her to the wolves that crept into the city.

'Go away!' I heard my voice say as my hand covered my mouth to stop the sobs which erupted from my throat, which covered my eyes in tears. Tears that had not escaped my eyelids since the days I searched for her. I gasped and wished that Raffaello had never met her, never drawn her. I cried out in jealousy and pain and indecision. How dare she come back! How dare she not find me! How dare she betray me – how dare she forget me!

I awoke under a tree, wondering why I could see the sky, not a ceiling. My back was aching from sleeping awkwardly across its roots. I got up and stretched, feeling wretched, and staggered to the fountain for water to splash my face and drink. Trying not to recall my dreams, I staggered into the workshop. No-one was there yet, so I turned towards the table I was working on. I had to pass Gianfrancesco's and was drawn to the *modello*. He had drawn the Madonna and child, and started St Sixtus. There was a space where the Barbara would go. I pulled Raffaello's drawing towards me.

I knew it was her – I had to know it was her. I had to know how she came to be what she was, where she was.

Gianfrancesco came in and grinned to see me.

'Are you sure you don't want an introduction?'

'I think I knew her – once. I think she lived in our street.'

'If you knew her, good reason for meeting up with her,' he said, sitting down at his work.

'Don't tell her that – tell her I want to draw her – don't tell her my name.' He pulled his face back in puzzlement.

'I can't not tell her – the dragon Serafina won't let any strangers into the house.'

'What?'

'The old woman who looks after them, who vets the clients.'

I winced 'She's a good sort, she won't let in anyone out of hours except the 'special ones', as she calls them. That's me, as Ginetta's lover.' He started to sharpen a stick of red chalk.

'Does - Ginetta – does she have others?'

'I can't afford to keep her just for myself.' He bent his head to work, conversation ended. I went to my table.

'Tomasina hasn't got a special one.' He muttered after an hour or so.

I did not reply; this was no comfort. It meant that she … entertained – no, had sex with - different men, many men. Played with them as she had…I tried to dismiss the image. She was just the same as the woman I had pushed off me last night, as all the women with whom I spent night after night… she must have coarsened. I would not want her now, but the drawing did not show her to be. And surely Gianfrancesco would not have such a relationship with a common tart.

We worked in silence. I became engrossed. Tomasina the whore was not Ceci, my beloved girl. There was a dull ache under my ribs. Tree roots.

For several days I worked, as many hours as there was light, and completed the *cartone*. Many pieces of paper which all needed to be pricked along each and every line before it was assembled on the wall and pounced. Raffaello spread the sheets out on the floor and made some changes, then nodded his approval.

The job of pricking was given to four young lads, and I was to oversee this, on my own, without Raffaello. They crouched over the sheets with a mixture of eagerness, concentration and boredom, as I had. When it was finished, we made our way to the Papal Palace, I in apprehension and anticipation. The scaffolding was up. We laid the pieces of the *cartone* on the floor and pasted several together, then stuck these to the wall, stretching the seams against the curve of the painted arch. Two of the lads started pouncing as the rest of the *cartone* was pasted and carefully stuck to the wall. The concentration of making it accurate was intense, both on my side and that of the lads, so the work was done almost in silence. At the end of the day, it was complete, and Raffaello came in to check. He walked across in front of it, ascended the scaffolding and inspected it minutely, then turned and grinned down at us all.

'Good, very good! To the tavern!' I glowed with pride. I clapped the lads on their shoulders, and accompanied Raffaello to his favourite tavern, too expensive for me, where he ordered wine and food to celebrate my first unaided supervision.

'To Giulio Pippi, great painter!' and told me of a commission that he would secure for me, just me, to paint under his name.

She came to me in a dream, and I awoke sweating. I had to get rid of this, I had to lay this ghost. I needed to concentrate on my work. I had to see her.

CHAPTER TWENTY-FIVE

CECILIA

Ginetta had told me that Gianfrancesco wanted to bring a friend to meet me, as a possible model, and was that alright? I said of course, and we told Serafina that there would be two painters that afternoon and she was to let them both in. She knew Gianfrancesco of course, as Ginetta's lover, and trusted that this new one – what's his name? – would be bringing food supplies. The artists paid us as models, but not for anything else. If we took up with one, it was accepted that he bring us food and wine.

What was his name?

'Giulio,' said Ginetta. I felt a lurch in my heartbeat, which then went faster. Would it be him?

I dressed simply, so that if he wanted to paint me nude he could see how my body was shaped through the lightness of the gown. My hair was in a single braid, so he could see my face. I sat waiting, while Ginetta talked, I have no idea about what. I turned myself away from the door, so that I would not see this Giulio, so I couldn't betray myself to him. Shock? Disappointment? I found I was twisting the end of the girdle of the dress. I forced myself to stop. There was a knocking at the door; my heart jumped. Serafina opened it and I could hear low talking. She would be taking the baskets of food from them, then conducting them to the room. I heard the door open. She spoke two words - 'The painters' - and shut the door behind her.

Ginetta jumped up to kiss Gianfrancesco and take him to her own room. Silence, but for a bird twittering outside. I felt a presence but did not turn to look. My heart was beating so loudly I was sure he could hear it. I could bear it no longer. I rose and turned to face him.

Giulio.

It was her.

It was him. I couldn't speak. My hand to my mouth, an expulsion of air, I had been holding my breath. I gasped and sat down suddenly. I couldn't look at him.

'Ceci?'

His voice was a little deeper. I raised my head. His eyes were bright but there was a furrow between his eyebrows, and a line beneath his eyes as if he had not slept. His hair was longer and fell either side of his head; his lips were red in the centre of his beard. I swallowed.

'Ceci.' He came towards me. 'Ceci, what happened? Where did you go? I looked everywhere for you!'

I shook my head. He stood still, raised a hand to me, then dropped it.

'You know,' my voice rasped. I coughed. 'You know what I am.'

'Yes.'

'Then…'

All my anger has gone, she looks the same, as she was; but her eyes are sad. I want to take her in her arms and chase that sadness away. I don't move.

'Then you know I am not what I was, my body has been used by men, it is no longer mine –' (or yours - as yours has been by many women, taken and paid for, I thought,. So where was the difference between us? Oh, yes, you choose, I don't.)

'I am no longer a young innocent, Giulio.' I gasped as I said his name, aloud.

'Say my name again,' he said. I looked at him.

'Giulio.' It was whispered, and followed by tears. 'Giulio!'

He knelt in front of me and took my hands. I saw his eyes too were wet.

He kissed my hands; I snatched them from him.

'No! No! I am not the same, Giulio, I am Tomasina, a prostitute –'

'A model for Raffaello – he made you a saint, he didn't care. Ceci, whatever happened, it's over, it's gone.'

'Yes,' I thought 'it's over, it's gone'

'Ceci –'

'My name is Tomasina… Please, go, or if you wish to use my services, talk with Serafina and arrange a time with her.' I could feel myself quivering as I said these words. Please go, before I break down, I thought.

Her words hit me, so cold, so dismissive. My anger rises. I stand up.

'You didn't come to me – your mother died and you didn't find me. I spoke to Adelina.'

I thought, yes, Mama died, because of our brother. Because your father used her: you are all the same!

'Antea became a prostitute, to earn money and food to keep us alive. While I was tied up on a bubble with you, I didn't see. I didn't see what she was doing. The baby was born and then Mama died, in our bed.' The memory, which I had held back for so long crashed into my mind with such force that I stepped backwards my eyes staring past him to find her.

'The baby?' Why had he come, why could he not have left me in peace? I locked my eyes into his.

'I killed it.' Silence. 'I killed it before Antea died, so we wouldn't have another mouth to feed. It was easy – I'd killed before.' Silence. I held his eyes. 'Giorgio. He tried to rape me. You found him.'

'You didn't tell me. You didn't tell me!' He dropped to his knees. 'You didn't trust me to know – you didn't find me.'

I wasn't going to let him go where only you had been. I saw he was going to embrace me. No.

'I killed my brother – I killed our brother.'

The space between us was riven with those words, they hung in the air like a dead man from a gibbet.

'Pietro, before the wedding, before Christmas, the food he gave us, the fabric for the dresses. He was her lover. He didn't marry her because she was poor.' I froze. I heard the echo of Pietro's words to me. The image of him with Antea. The image of me with Ceci. The image of a baby tying us all together. I rose slowly, away from the images.

'You see, Giulio, you see what is between then and now.' I sat. Three paces between us, each the distance between the earth and the moon. He opened his pouch and took out a bundle. He threw it to the floor. A dress, crumpled around - a bird's nest?

'Yours. You cut it off. You left the dress. I took them both.'

The bundle lay between us. Not a nest, hair: mine. I stared at it, a barrier between us. If I stepped forward to pick it up, I would be a breath away from him, in a place from where I could touch him. I did not move. I could not take that step. The bundle looked like a dead child.

You kept these? I thought, but I must have said the words aloud.

'I kept them under my pillow, then I put them in my chest, then my work made me forget them –' 'And you,' was implied.

I remember the effect seeing Raffaello's drawing had on me. I look at the woman in front of me. I cannot leave. The image of a dead child:

my father, her mother? She didn't find me because she thought she had killed my, and her, brother –because of what my father did. While I was doing the work I loved, learning, drawing, painting, she had been suffering. I was ashamed.

'Ceci – look at me.'

If I looked at him, I would be back there, on his bed, under the trees, among the ruins. I could not go back into the dream; I could not drag him down. I could feel his eyes upon me, pulling me back into the dream as if it was real. I turned away.

'You are a painter - you are what you said you would be. I am pleased for you. I am no longer the girl who wore that dress. I no longer belong to you, I belong to the men who want me. If you wish me to model for you, then I will, and you will pay me. If you want my body, then it is not for sale, not to you.'

Her voice is one I do not know; cold, empty. She has turned from me, as she never had before.

I heard him leave the room. I heard the main door open and shut. Tears falling down my face, I knelt to pick up the bundle. I held it in my arms, buried my face in it. The door opened slowly and Serafina came in. She would have heard everything, she always listened in case a client became forceful or violent and then she intervened. She knelt and gathered me in her arms.

'You knew him.' My head was against her shoulder, but I nodded. 'More than that.'

'Yes,' and she cradled me in a way she had never done before.

CHAPTER TWENTY-SIX

GIULIO

I left, my mind screaming. I walked without knowing where I was going, entered a tavern I did not know. I accepted a girl with blonde hair, coarse through being dried in the sun, oranged with some unknown treatment. I bored into her without preamble, again and again, front and back, crushing her breasts until she cried in pain. I slapped her, abused her, scoured her with my fingernails, twisted and pulled her hair until lumps came out, covering her mouth when she screamed. When I had finished, she was pale and bloody and frightened. I threw every coin I had at her and left, filled with terror at what I had done.

I went into a church to find quiet. I knelt in front of Christ on the cross and fell to my knees in despair - 'forgive me, forgive me' - for what I had done to the girl, for my use of an instrument of pleasure as a weapon. That I could use what once had been an expression of love as a sword. I had destroyed love. I thought Ceci had rejected me, betrayed me, but I had done more. She had become a prostitute to survive, as had that girl. She had killed for self-protection. Tonight I had killed whatever was good in me, whatever she could have loved in me.

I asked for pity, for mercy, for myself (not the girl, not Ceci,) vainly hoping Christ would give me absolution, despising myself. It was the whimpering of a weak man, who thought that by admitting his transgressions he would be given peace. I was not. My hands curled against my face, my eyes screwed up against the images of the girl, of Ceci. Christ was silent. Ceci had turned away. I lay, her name beating at my head like a bell tolling for the dead.

I walked though streets where bare-branched trees stood, uncertain of when to leaf, and still, dark cypresses were held stiff, waiting for a blue, warm background of sky before they allowed themselves to spread their needles and grow. It was as if I too was dormant alongside them, in tune with the dark grey coldness of that February pre-dawn. I shivered as I made my way between house and shops, passing wrapped-up figures on their late way home or early to work. I would submerse myself in work, subdue myself in paint, plans, design and execution. I would work all the hours of the day and night into exhaustion, I would visit no taverns, no prostitutes. Work would be my life.

I noticed that there were many clergy scurrying past me, then a sudden bell, out of time, too early to summon people to church, to wake people for work. A tolling which echoed that inner tolling I had felt in the church. Another bell, another and another. The air of Rome was filled with the singular tolling of bells. I stopped a priest rushing past me by catching his sleeve.

'What has happened?' He looked distracted.

'The Pope is dead. Julius died this night.' He pulled himself away from me.

Doors were opening, lights appeared in windows. Neighbour called to neighbour – what is it? The Pope is dead!. People crossed themselves, knocked on doors to tell others. The dawn arrived to reveal shocked faces, tearful women, people kneeling in the streets to pray. I hurried to our house, to find Raffaello in a cloak lighting candles, waking others, a hubbub of soft chatter and half-dressed painters and apprentices.

The death of not only the Pope, the leader of Christendom, but of our major client. Would work at the Papal Palace stop? Would the building of the new Belvedere halt? Would contracts fail and money due be unpaid? Questions were hurled at each other, raising new questions, no answers. Raffaello and Gianfrancesco decided to go to the Palace, so everyone hurried themselves to wash and dress to accompany them. We were going to pay our respects, and to find out what we should do.

We entered the crowded streets full of people going the same way. The bridge at Castle Sant'Angelo was crowded, so there the flow of people slowed and eventually stopped. Raffaello, Gianfrancesco and I struggled past people who, recognising Raffaello, allowed him to go before them. We got to St Peters Square and found Bramante and Peruzzi there. We puzzled together with the same questions – what would happen to the painters, the builders, the architects? What would happen to us?

The square filled with cardinals in red pushing their way through priests in black, monks in brown and black and white. The noise of the crowd, and the bells of every church in Rome, was tremendous and we had to shout into each other's ears to be heard and understood. The pressure of the people, the pushing as the Cardinals tried to make their way through, the cries of men falling and being trodden on, were immense. Many panicked, causing even more chaos. We saw Michelangelo lumbering through towards us; we could see his mouth forming oaths as he pushed and was pushed in his turn. We were propelled towards the *loggia*, and then into the inner courtyard of the basilica. Gianfrancesco pulled us into the shelter of one of the arches, followed by Peruzzi helping Bramante, who was exhausted by the crowd and the noise. We cleared people away from a seat and made him sit down, standing around him to protect him. We were joined by Michelangelo.

'The doors to the basilica are shut and barred. They are keeping us out, he said.

No-one knew where to go, what to do. Then the doors creaked open and several of the Swiss Guard came out to form a row in front of them. The Pope's secretary appeared on the *loggia* and the crowd fell silent.

'I confirm,' he shouted, 'that Pope Julius died at the third hour of this day and is now with God.' He crossed himself, then the crowd, which, awkwardly, tried to kneel in response.

There was a lot of shouting and hassling as the secretary left. Raffaello and Michelangelo, for once talking together, discussed who might be elected, and their preferences for who might allow work to continue. They threw up one name after another, and it was plain while they were united for the moment on speculation as to the best for us, they could agree on no-one and ended by arguing. Michelangelo then cursed us all and fought his way through the crowd to heaven knew where.

'There's nothing to be done. We should go back to the workshop,' said Raffaello. 'Master,' he said to Bramante, 'we shall see you safely home'. We formed a protective circle around him. A Swiss Captain saw us and made a way for us through the crowd until we were on the edge of the square, where we could breathe and make our way to Bramante's house. There, we settled him with his servants, and were given refreshment, which we took in near silence as there was no more to be said.

CHAPTER TWENTY-SEVEN

CECILIA

The bells woke us. It wasn't yet light. Ginetta woke up in a panic.

'It's war isn't it? Rome is being invaded!' She burst into tears. 'Where can we go?' I tried to calm her; there had been no talk of war in the city, only of the wars that the Pope had initiated elsewhere.

'It's because of those – it's the Milanese!' she sobbed. Serafina heard that as she came into the room.

'Whisht, Ginetta, there is no invasion. The Pope is dead.' Ginetta raised her head.

'What?'

'A bell tolls for death. All the bells toll for the death of a Pope.'

'Yes, but, how do you know?'

'The streets are full of people shouting it.'

I went to the window, opened it and heard feet running through the street and voices calling, 'The Pope is dead! Julius is dead!' some in horror, some jubilant.

'You'll stay inside today. The doors will be locked,' instructed Serafina. 'There will be looting, and, last time a Pope died, the prisons were opened and the city was full of thieves and murderers.' Ginetta started to cry again.

'I'll go out and make sure we have food. They'll not trouble an old woman.'

'No,' I said, 'you'll be attacked for money. Stay here with us and we'll be careful with the food.' Just to make sure, we pulled a large heavy chest across the front door. We sat at the table while Serafina made bread, and I asked her.

'What happens next?'

'They'll take him through the streets to St Peter's where he'll lie in state. I went to see Pope Alexander – he'd been in there three days and the smell was quite dreadful, no-one could get near him –' she screwed her face up at the memory, 'so - I don't advise you to go.' She dropped the dough onto the table. 'Then all the Cardinals will be locked up –'

'Why?' Ginetta looked up astonished. 'What have they done?'

'Nothing – it's just the way – they are locked up in the Sistine Chapel and they stay there until they have elected a new Pope. They will be guided by God.' Her tone made me look at her sharply.

'Well,' she said kneading the dough with relish, 'sometimes God takes a while to make up His mind – sometimes, He forgets to tell the Cardinals and they argue amongst themselves, and sometimes He seems perverse in his choice.'

Ginetta was shocked and crossed herself.

'How can you say such things Serafina?' Serafina shrugged.

'After Alexander, they picked Cardinal Piccolomini who, they said, was too ill even to stand at the altar. He died not a month later.'

'Perhaps God wanted to give him an earthly joy before he took him to his side,' I said, and glanced at Serafina under my eyelashes. She pounded the dough.

'It's said that the cardinals who elected him got their earthly joys from a share of Alexander's goods.'

Ginetta's mouth dropped open. Although she took part in gossip and listened to the chatter around her, she only paid attention to that about her immediate circle and dismissed most of the rest. She ignored that about bribery and corruption in the Papal Court. Although she had spent two years on the streets as I had, and accepted that men could be cruel, and monks and priests could be clients, she never gave up her faith in the Pope as speaking the word of God and thought that Cardinals were just below him in holiness and piety. She would confess her transgressions each week and was pardoned and blessed, so she was able go with her clients in good faith of being forgiven again the following week. I once tried to persuade her that Pope Julius was a war monger and led people to kill, but all she said was, 'God told him to – he is doing God's work to bring people back to the true Church.' I asked Serafina what she meant.

'When Pope Alexander died, his son Cesare took all the money from the Pope's apartments, then locked it, and himself, in his own apartments.'

'Well, I suppose if it belonged to his father, they were his to take.' Serafina raised an eyebrow.

'Then his rooms were stripped bare of everything else, while his body lay there.'

'No! That's dreadful! How do you know?' cried Ginetta.

'Because I saw it, I was there.'

I was startled I knew that Serafina had been a prostitute at the time, and she had been one of those invited to Cesare Borgia's parties. I was curious.

'How?' Serafina continued to fold, stretch and knead the dough.

'Cesare wasn't well at the time, and wanted some girls to amuse him, not in his bed, but he wanted to watch them with each other to take his mind off the pain of his stomach. Three of us were found who were poor enough, and old enough, to agree. We had no idea that the Pope was ill too. We had to wait outside Cesare's room ready for when he wanted us. After a long wait – it was cold – we were called into the room. There he was in this huge bed, sitting up against a great pile of pillows, and we were instructed to remove our clothes and perform with each other in front of him on that bed, and to make sure he could see everything.

'So there we were, fondling and writhing and gasping, when a man came in and whispered to Cesare. He roared and kicked his legs – I remember falling off the bed and taking me with him. He yelled out that the news of the Pope's death be withheld and the doors to his chamber locked to prevent those thieving Cardinals – though the word he used wasn't thieving – from helping themselves. The other two girls slid off on top of me and one of them squirmed round the bed to reach our clothes.

"Get them out!' he roared and we were hustled away down the corridor, hearing shouts from elsewhere – then we had to stand aside while men came past with chests, silver jugs, and all sorts of other objects. We hadn't had time to dress and we cowered together against the wall trying to cover ourselves. The men laughed at us and one caught hold of Verena's clothes and ripped them away. We had only two dresses, no shoes, no cloaks, and were shivering. The man with us pulled curtains down from a room nearby and gave them to us, so we tied these round ourselves. When we were in that room, we heard a lot of noise and the breaking down of a door. We were told to wait, and we saw men passing our door with furniture, curtains, other objects. Several of them wore the livery of Cardinals.

When there was a lull, we were taken outside, given a purse each, and told to say nothing of what we had seen. It was mid-afternoon, and we were jeered at for our 'fine brocades'. We went home, wondering what had happened as the Pope's death wasn't announced then. The next day it was, and we realised the lull was to give time for those men to loot the Palace.'

She quartered the dough with swift cuts of a knife and set them by the fire to rise.

'We didn't talk about it to anyone, not even amongst ourselves. We were too shocked, and frightened.' She turned her head to the window to listen. We were aware of an increase in the noise from the streets outside.

'And that,' she said, sitting with us at the table, 'is what will be happening now. looting.' she grinned. 'The money we were given lasted us quite a few weeks - we made splendid dresses from the curtains - we wore them to a Cardinal's party after Julius was crowned Pope. They were so fine, we could put our prices up!'

Ginetta looked aghast.

'You went to work in the Pope's curtains?'

Serafina moved her hand to pat Ginetta's.

'They were just curtains, fine brocade, nothing holy – just expensive!'

'And Pope Julius?' I asked.

'Well, he was a very wealthy man – he was elected in a day. No sooner had the Cardinals all trooped in, they all trooped out again. It was obvious, then, that God had sent angels to them all overnight –' she winked at me '- with purses full of gold.' Ginetta now realised that Serafina's tone was mocking.

'How can you be so? You go to church every Sunday.'

'Of course I do. To ensure myself a place in heaven. Don't worry, Ginetta, it will all be over soon, there will be a new Pope, and we shall go on as before.'

We set to sorting out the food we had, vegetables, fruit, salted fish, wheat flour. We divided it all into piles so we could eat once a day for four days. Serafina reassured us that that would be enough: the funeral would take place, then the conclave and then the crowning of the Pope, and all would be well. She confided in me that water was low, and we discussed when would be the best time to venture out, but could not make a decision.

'We'll bide our time,' she said.

The noise in the street was such that it penetrated the house, and we could not hear ourselves speak. At one point someone pounded on the door and shouted.

'Bring out the whores for us!'

Ginetta was very nervous and would not leave my side. We hauled mattresses into my room, for her and for Serafina, so we could all sleep together. Ginetta worried about Gianfrancesco: what if he was murdered in the street?

'He will be with Raffaello, and the others. Raffaello's status will protect them all.'

Did I believe that? After all, his chief patron had died. It struck me then how important the choice of Pope would be for the painters. I would have kept these thoughts to myself, but Serafina told me that when Julius became Pope, he had shut up Pope Alexander's rooms, had dismissed the painters and employed new ones, of whom Raffaello was one.

'If the next Pope has not time for paintings and buildings,' she shrugged. 'When Pope's change, we may not be close to them, but what they do affects us all.'

CHAPTER TWENTY-EIGHT

GIULIO

Raffaello had gone to see Tomasso Inghirami, the Pope's librarian and supervisor of the painters' and architects' work. Gianfrancesco was worried about Ginetta.

'They're in the middle of the trail from the Gate to the Vatican - in the middle of the crowds going to St Peter's. I'm going to see if they're all right. Will you come? We'll take food.' I couldn't refuse him, so we filled large pouches to carry on our backs. When we were ready to go, I took out two knives from my room, and offered him one. He protested; it was not legal.

'The law is in abeyance,' I said, 'especially where we're going.' He took it.

We took a route through the narrow alleyways of the Borgo to try to avoid trouble. We could hear the noise from the main thoroughfare, the cries of men, the crashing of steel on wood. We passed women cowering in the alleys, knocking on doors, begging to be let in. Some were, some weren't. We came around a corner to see one woman being molested by a man, screaming. Gianfrancesco and I pulled him off, taking out our knives to threaten him as she struggled to her feet and escaped, while he ran off. We then kept the knives in our hands, and were avoided, being regarded as dangerous looters because of these and our pouches. We reached the house and pounded on the door.

'It's Gianni and Giulio!' he cried. The latch was drawn back and Serafina's eye appeared. We heard the sound of something heavy being dragged form the door, the lock being turned, and the door opened. We slid in quickly.

'Are you all right? We've brought you food,' he said, putting down his pouch. Ginetta appeared and threw herself at him with cries of relief. I put both my pouches on the table, then turned to see Ceci in the doorway.

'Thank you,' she said, without smiling. We unpacked the pouches in silence.

'Is there anything else you need?'

'Yes. We need water, we have only enough for today.'

I raised my voice to Gianfrancesco, and we discussed how to get water and what to carry it in. Serafina told us that the nearest fountain, which they always used, was in *Piazza di San Pietro*. So one of us would carry both buckets, and the other, I, would act as protector. This proved successful, and although some jostling meant a loss of water, we manged to get enough for a further day's drinking and cooking. We agreed together that we should stay at the house, there being no work for us to go to, until the streets were calmer, and, if necessary, until the new Pope was announced.

This plan was greeted by Ginetta with tears of relief. Serafina glanced a question at Ceci, who nodded. We were to be together.

Except we weren't. Mattresses were re-sorted, Ginetta and Gianni together, Serafina slept with Ceci and I slept in the attic where Serafina usually slept. Except that I didn't sleep, or, rather, each time I did, I fell into dreams. Dreams of Ceci, but she as the prostitute I had injured. I woke sweating. I sat up before dawn, pulled on my clothes and went downstairs for water. I sat at the table. What was I doing here? Protecting the women? Or was I just here to be near Ceci?

I picked up an apple, and twisted it in my hands. It had a soft part, the brown forming a loose skin over pulp, and my thumb went through it. I threw it across the room.

At dawn there was a rap on the front door. I went to it and pulled the latch. Outside was Giovanni da Udine, close-cloaked against the chill.

'I've come from Raffaello. Let me in - I'm freezing!' he said. I opened the door, and banked up the fire so he could warm himself. I poured him wine and water.

'The funeral is tomorrow, and Raffaello wants a good company, so we're going the rounds telling people together,' he said, rubbing his hands. 'We're to meet at his house at dawn so we can all go together.'

'Is there any news on the work?' He shrugged.

'Raffaello went to see Inghirami, but he said he couldn't authorise us to continue. The treasury is frozen, so we might not even get paid for what we've done.' This was not good news. 'He's giving the funeral oration, and will include praise for the Pope and his support of art, but can't say more until the election.'

'What are the signs for the new Pope?'

'No-one definite. The French Cardinals are banned from the conclave because of Julius's decree against the French, so there's only twenty or so Cardinals to vote.' Serafina had come down and looked suspiciously at Giovanni.

'Giovanni, one of Raffaello's associates,' I told her. 'Come to tell us about the funeral tomorrow.'

'Then you'll be going?'

'To the funeral, yes.' She turned to Giovanni.

'How are the streets?'

'Calmer,' he said, and grinned. 'The Cardinals couldn't get their hands on Julius's goods as he'd had them sealed up in the *Castello Sant'Angelo*!' Serafina grinned and started to prepare breakfast.

'Will you escort us to the funeral?' I shook my head.

'We are to go with Raffaello. Perhaps we can find someone who can do this if you wish?'

'I will ask my ladies,' she said. Ceci came in dressed in an unbelted gown and loose hair. My heart lurched, and my body stirred inside to reach out to her. She glanced at me, them looked at Giovanni. I explained who he was and why he was there.

'We should be there for the funeral procession,' she said, as Ginetta and Gianfrancesco came in. Giovanni gave him his hand.

'You'll need a protector if you go,' I said. We all sat round the table as Serafina served us food, and discussed who this might be. 'All the painters will want to be with Raffaello; it is necessary to be there in force to remind the Cardinals of our importance to the Papacy, for one of them will be elected Pope.'

'We will find someone,' said Ceci.

Giovanni repeated what he had told me. Gianfrancesco, who had more knowledge through Raffaello of the Papal court, told us that Giovanni dei Medici had been talked of.

'Except that he is young, thirty-seven, and the older Cardinals wouldn't want that.'

'Who else is there?'

'The English want Riario.'

'Either would be good for us, both support new work.'

'Indeed,' said Gianfrancesco, 'let us hope for one or the other. Although the Medici is unwell, the physicians are with him to operate on him. I don't know why, it could be that they'll kill him rather than cure him.' This was not good news.

Ginetta was looking distressed and was about to say something, but Ceci put her hand over hers and shook her head. Giovanni rose.

'I must go, I have some birds to catch!'

I was not used to being without anything to do. My hands itched to draw. Giovanni always had paper and chalk. I asked him if I could have some. He nodded, took out a bundle, picked out some large sheets and added some chalk. I wanted to draw Ceci, but the painter in me also wanted to draw Serafina for her creased, older face.

When Giovanni had gone, I asked if they would model, in the room, as they were. Serafina wanted to know, why her?

'I'm not a pretty face any more.'

'No, but your face is interesting, and I need more than young pretty women for my designs.' She laughed at my candour, and I saw Ceci smile. I caught her eye, and her meaning: she would model if the others did, as long as they were together. She would not be alone with me.

So we spent the day, changing poses and hairstyles and groupings, which included Gianni. I drew them in repose, talking, stretching, moving, preparing food, until the pages were covered both sides with faces, heads, compositions. Every line of every sketch of Ceci evoked a memory until I found it hard to concentrate on the others. At times she struck an attitude that I did not recognise. A way of standing with one hip higher than the other: a pose of flirtation; sitting to show off her breasts, a turn of the head and a smile that was one of a courtesan. I drew these, my hand accepting, my mind rejecting them.

The time passed, the day drew us together. Meals became the background to chatter, stories and jokes. Ceci and I were part of the laughter, and once her eyes met mine as they sparkled with amusement, with the gesture of a hand to her mouth that I knew so well. The sparkle went out, her eye darkened, and seemed to stay on mine for a long moment. Then her eyelids dropped and rose again in another direction to make a remark I did not hear, but which caused more laughter. I wondered if I had imagined her look. If I had, was this because I had wanted to, willed it; that I wanted her? Yes.

I hold his eye. I can't help it. His eyes are dark and still. It seems as if a line of light is starting between us. I have to extinguish it, I say something silly, there is laughter. My insides are churning. I want him.

CHAPTER TWENTY-NINE

GIULIO

The funeral took place. Riario, the *Cardinale di San Giorgi,* was there, Giovanni dei Medici was not. Ten days later, the Cardinals went into conclave, and we waited. For two weeks. Raffaello insisted we carry on work in the workshop, as he was sure we would be able to get back into the Papal Palace soon. He worked on the painting of the Madonna and St Sixtus, and St Barbara. As she emerged under his brush, so did my desire. The downward look of the painted Ceci, covering her eyes, was that of the real Ceci after catching my eye. I was aware of something besides desire which I could not name (would not name), something which filled my whole being with light when I thought of her. Something which made my painting closer to that of Raffaello, not in technique - that I had mastered - but closer to its gentleness and beauty, which I had not altogether managed before. I painted with love.

Giovanni de Medici was declared Pope, Raffaello went to the Palace and returned triumphant. Materials were gathered together to start work there the following week. It was agreed that the figure of Julius would stay on the wall we had almost finished, but his face on the prepared sketch for the next wall of the room was erased until Raffaello could make drawings of the new Pope, Leo X. Joy replaced uncertainty. Preparations for the coming *possesso,* the progression of the Pope from St Peter's to St John Lateran, were immediately started for there was only a month from his declaration to the date of this *possesso.*

For us, there were commissions for triumphal arches to be set up along the way. The main, and most glorious, arches were for the points where the procession would stop for Leo to enjoy a presentation. One of these was to be at the Capitol, near the *Macello*, which excited my sister, Gerolama, who was seven. She was to be a Flower Girl, in the presentation there, with her younger step-brother and twin step-sisters, who would be dressed as cherubs.

The work for these major arches was divided between Raffaello's and Peruzzi's workshops, the latter working on one commissioned by Agostino Chigi. I was put in charge of the work for another arch was composed of representations of the antique, as a sign of the new Pope's interest in reviving the style and continuing the creation of the 'New Rome'. The whole of the preparations engaged all the painters then in Rome, and more besides from Florence, Naples and Siena, made necessary as we had only five weeks to complete these. Gianfrancesco was in charge of engaging painters to help us, numbering more than fifty, with the same number under Peruzzi's supervision. We worked on the floors of several churches to give us room for the large frames covered with canvas. The smell of size and glue overwhelmed that of incense, and caused much anxiety among the clergy, although we tried to be careful. The building of the Belvedere was halted once more so that the men could work on the many rostrums and seating platforms at the twelve stops. My father was in charge of half of these, while those in the *Piazza di San Pietro* were erected by a team under one Giuliano Leno, who would, alas, overtake my father in being the preferred builder of Pope Leo.

Every carpenter was engaged on making these rostra, and the frames for chairs for the wealthy families who would occupy them on the many daisis at the stopping places. The tanneries were busy making leather for the seat and backs of these and every goldsmith and silversmith were engaged on making the family crests to be attached to them. The haberdashers and cloth-merchants ordered cart-loads of fabric from Venice and Naples, while every nun, and every woman in the city who could sew, was given a costume to make. I thought of Antea with sorrow.

Musicians were rehearsing: trumpets and sackbuts blared across piazzas, drums pounded in cross-rhythms from different public spaces, shawms and bagpipes squealed from windows. Choirs practised in churches, monasteries and convents, while dancers and acrobats practised in courtyards and streets - wherever there was space enough for them.

The streets were full of the traffic of deliveries to and from shops, workshops, and houses with balconies that faced the streets where the procession would travel. For those, it would be a delivery of a new tapestry or Turkish rug to hang over balconies and make the streets dazzle with colour. Pedlars were stocking up with ribbons, bells on sticks, small carved wooden objects and any trinkets they could find to sell to the pilgrims, including real or fake ancient fragments of sculpture or mosaic. I thought of Ceci and our times amid the ruins, searching, then selling. The Papal printers were making indulgences for those who sought absolution from the Pope, to be had at a price. For these pilgrims, every inn and tavern cleared its outhouses and made up mattresses from homespun and straw to accommodate the poorer pilgrims, while monasteries and convents did the same for more high-class visitors.

Shepherds and goatherds and herdsmen came in from the country around the city to be ready to sell their meat, and there were many disputes over grazing ground between the city herdsmen and the visitors. Wagons weighed down with wine-jars and barrels got stuck in the narrow streets; many a jar was 'liberated' from the waiting carts, and many a driver and a thief went home with a bruise or two. Families with wall-surrounded villas made sure that their locks were strong, while gardeners, who remembered the damage from the last such occasion, tried to set up fences to protect their just-budding trees and just-planted seedlings. The number of prostitutes of both sexes rose steadily, and the cutpurses sharpened their knives. The whole city was alive from dawn till sunset and beyond with preparations, and nothing else was spoken of.

Gianfrancesco told me that Ginetta and Ceci would be part of the presentation in the Borgo, outside the Castello, for which Agostino Chigi had gathered together the prettiest of the courtesans. The high courtesans represented goddesses, while the lower ones, like Ginetta and Ceci, would represent the Muses, the Virtues, and other qualities. Leo's procession and presentations would mix the pagan and the Christian. He told me that Ceci had chosen to be Peace; Ginetta, Hope. They were to be given poems to speak, written in Latin, of which they were very nervous…one of their clerical clients would be engaged to teach them the meanings and the proper pronunciation. The poems were to be written by Pietro Aretino, a poet sponsored by Chigi and a friend of Raffaello, whom I had met once or twice at drinking parties, and whose preference was, mostly, for his own sex.

Gianfrancesco managed to visit Ginetta once or twice, but most of the time we slept in the church with the other painters and young apprentices, exhausted from the day's work, to be ready to start as soon as it was light. Had it not been March with its sudden showers of rain, we would have worked outside, and would have had one or two more hours of light. We couldn't risk water damage, so every canvas was in line with a window, and every possible hour we were able to see properly was spent working on them. While we did so, we prayed to the saints in our various churches for April to be fine, and dry.

CHAPTER THIRTY

CECILIA

I chose to represent Peace in the *posseso* because, after the wars of Julius, when once we were threatened by a French army camped outside the city, that is what I wanted. Unlike Ginetta, I was of the same opinion as Serafina concerning the holiness of Popes and Cardinals, but had ceased to be puzzled why God had put such people in charge of His Church. I just accepted that it was all beyond me. However, I found it hard to believe that Julius's wars were supported by God, whatever Ginetta said, because that meant God was himself disobeying the Commandment not to kill. I wanted the next Pope to be a peacemaker. I had no idea whether Pope Leo would be one, but I would make my claim on Peace. Ginetta had chosen Hope because she hoped that Gianfrancesco would be as famous as Raffaello and marry her.

We were at the table discussing costumes. We would receive money for material, from the *Maestro di Cerimonia,* but we didn't know how much.

'Or when we'll get it,' said Serafina, 'so we should see what we have that we can use.' As models for the painters, we had a quantity of materials to drape around ourselves as required, alongside veils and headpieces. We went up to our rooms and pulled all these out.

'Green is the colour of Hope,' said Serafina, and pulled out a green velvet curtain and several *braccia* – armslengths – of veiling, which was tinted green. 'We can make a dress with the velvet, a drape across your head with the veil, and you can have a crown and wand of new leaves.'

I wanted Peace to be in white with an olive-coloured drape. Everything white we had was dirty or diaphanous; Serafina held up pieces against me, but we decided that it was all too flimsy for outside in April.

'What about that dress you've got bundled up - behind the cushion on your bed? That's white,' said Ginetta. The dress Giulio had left. I had rolled it up and put it there; I didn't know Ginetta had seen it.

'I saw it when I borrowed that cushion to prop me up when I was ill and couldn't breathe lying down.' I had forgotten that. 'I hadn't seen it before and you've never worn it.'

Serafina knew it had been on the floor when Giulio left. She had asked no questions then, but now looked at me with eyebrows raised.

'I don't know,' I said.

'Look!' She pulled up the cushion and drew out the dress, shaking it. 'It's very crumpled, but it is simple - just right for Peace. It's good material, and you can wear something under it in case it's cold. And you can have the tinted veiling to drape, I don't have to have a green veil.'

If I wore it as Peace, Giulio would see me. He might even... I was tempted. No...

'No. I don't want to wear it.' Ginetta cried out.

'Oh why not? It's beautiful, it's hardly worn. What was it for?'

'I had it for a wedding, an important wedding. It was too good to wear every day.'

'Well, this is the perfect chance to wear it, look how the back of the hem sweeps the floor.'

'Look how it will attract the dirt outside,' I said, glad to get away from the serious discussion. But Serafina would not have it.

'We can make you an underskirt to support the white so if it drags, the dirt will go on that. Besides, if you wear it, we can claim the money for material and spend it on something else for ourselves.' They both looked at me, wiling me to change my mind.

There was no chance Giulio would have forgotten it; not only had he kept it, but his painter's eye would remember me in it. Perhaps with the drape he might not recognise it. If he saw me, saw it, what would he think? Would he think I was offering myself again? *Which is what I want to do.* He didn't have to take me.

No, I would drape it in a way that altered it, that disguised it - I would wear it - it was just a dress. If I took it off for Giulio, I could surely put it on for the Pope.

'You're right, I'll wear it.' Ginetta jumped up and kissed me. 'Now what about Serafina?'

'What about me?'

'You'll be with us, so you must dress up too!'

'With you, yes, as protector - all those men about, perhaps I should dress as a Roman soldier,' she said, which made us laugh.

'No, you shall have a new dress, we will use the money for you,' I said.

'And who will pay for the material first?'

'We'll ask Chigi directly,' I said.

'That's bold.'

We went, Serafina and I, to the Chigi villa. Of course, he wasn't there, but in the garden we saw Salvatore, who organised the parties and knew us. I approached him and bowed. He looked puzzled at first, so I gave him a dazzling smile. Then he remembered and he kissed my hand.

'Tomasina. What can I do for you?'

I explained about us being in the *Castello* presentation, and how we didn't have enough money to buy the good material we needed for the costumes. Although we knew we could claim it, we didn't know when that might be. Would Master Chigi lend us the money?

'You want Signor Chigi to lend you money?' He was amused.

'Yes. There can be interest.'

'You understand interest? Well, then. You don't know how long the claim will take? It might be a long time – it might be never.'

'I am as capable of going to the Papal treasury as of coming here.' He smiled.

'I'm sure you are.'

'Then, what is your rate?' He thought. I was sure he was playing with me.

'It's very little we need, surely that is a sum you can do quickly?'

'It's the time you see, the time – unknown.'

'Then tell us the interest per month: we shall know to make a claim for the cost of the material and interest for, say, six months. That should be enough.' I spoke sharply.

'So if your claim comes through before six months, you will make a profit?'

'Indeed.' He laughed.

'You should come and work for the Master yourself!' He stopped testing me.

'Master Chigi is paying for the arch that will be at the *Castello* – Apollo, I believe, nothing churchy. So I think he can pay for your material – what will you represent?'

'Peace.' He roared with laughter.

'So, we make peace here, how much do you want?'

I told him. I had decided, while we were talking, that I would add on a sum for the expenses of the other Muses and Virtues who were in the same position as us. Salvatore grumbled at the total amount, so I pointed out that it would be to Master Chigi's credit that the appearance of the Muses and Virtues, most of whom were reciting Latin, should be brilliant.

'Then come tomorrow morning and I will give you the money.'

'And the interest?'

'There will be no interest. There will be no loan. It will be part of the Chigi *possesso* expenses, the same as the scene painters. A payment for your work.'

It was more than I expected.

'In addition, you should claim from the *Maestro di Ceremonia* with a receipt for the material - don't forget to add a sum for the making. The Papal treasury can afford to give something to the women of this city, whom we all need. Then you will have made a good profit, which your bargaining deserves. Mistress Tomasina, you should have been a man!'

This was accompanied by a look of amusement and admiration, but I responded with a scowl which quickly changed into a dazzling smile. He noticed, as he was meant to. He gestured in contrition; I curtsied and thanked him. He still smiling as we left. As was I, at the revival of my skills in such a situation, where money was the only concern, not on exchange for my body.

We told the Muses and the Virtues, collected the money, and we all went to the cloth merchant to choose material. The chattering and delight was high and the merchant was flustered with so many young women in his shop at once. I told the merchant the material was for the *Castello* presentation, the most important one, with Latin verses, for which the Pope would definitely stop and listen, and I mentioned the name of Agostino Chigi. Having assured himself that we had money enough, and would pay him that day, he called in all his assistants from the storehouse, and they threw lengths of cloth over lengths of cloth; velvets, brocades, glittering with gold and silver thread, silk, gleaming with tones of colour altered by the light as it moved. I held this new, expensive material against my face, glorying in its softness, in its lightness, in its depth of colour.

I had to get quite tough with the women, who held piece after piece against themselves, to make them decide, as there were other customers and I didn't want to turn trade away for the merchant just because we couldn't make up our minds. I made each one choose, and ordered the lengths as soon as they had, which were cut for us, wrapped in cotton and tied with ribbon. For Serafina, a soft blue velvet, and lengths of olive-green silk for my drape, and light green silk for Ginetta. The merchant made a list of the costs and proffered the final figure, which caused the women to stop chattering and gasp. I said we would spread the word about his excellent materials around our circle. We agreed a very good discount. I poured silver out onto the counter, requested and received a receipt, and found we had some money left. We went to the glove-maker and, guiltily, ordered gloves for us all – 'in case it was cold'.

We were light-headed during the visit, pretending we were fine ladies and did this every day.

'Except that it would be the servants that actually went to the shop,' said one of the Muses.

'No,' said Serafina, 'the cloth merchant and the glove-maker would come to us!'

'But how shall we make the dresses?' said Ginetta suddenly. 'Who will make them?'

I sighed. It was time to tell them something of my past, of my cutting out skills and my reluctant sewing skills. It got round all the Muses and Virtues that I could cut, so my time for the next week was taken up with this; it was good to have a week when we could turn away all but the nicest clients. Ginetta's was a merchant, a widower, who brought her presents of spices, who took her gently and talked of his wife. Mine was a chubby little priest who only wanted to stroke my body, including my pubic hair, but his fingers went no further. He liked to brush the hair on my head and sing sacred songs as he did so. His need, he told me, was spiritual not physical, and that feeling my body gave him a feeling of mental ecstasy. I believed him; he was certainly not sexually aroused, and left with a beatific smile on his face, paying Serafina twice as much as a more demanding client (which was good, because I had forgotten the cost of the thread). We worked at the costumes and ate and slept well.

There was time the week before and the week after the *possesso* to take the best of the pilgrims; our being part of a presentation and speaking Latin would put our prices up. There would not be too much sleep then.

CHAPTER THIRTY-ONE

GIULIO

I had promised to be with my family for the *possesso,* I knew that Ceci would be at the *Castello*. Could I see Ceci and then get to the Capitol? The streets and roads were packed the whole of the route; the short answer was no. Perhaps if I went to the *Castello* early, to see her, if not to hear her, I could manage it. At dawn, I and a thousand others pushed our way across the bridge. Our double triumphal arch shone out between the *Basilica di San Pietro* and the *Castello*, caught in the rising sun. I have to say that I thought it was magnificent. The scene at the back was of arches, climbing plants, birds and fruits – Giovanni's work.

Before the arch was a rostrum, carpeted in Turkish red with garlands of fresh leaves across the front. Musicians were practising their individual parts, and a group of singers were gathering. Around us, and filling the *Piazza di San Pietro*, were Cardinals in their full red regalia, men on horseback, the animals snorting and frisking at the noise, accompanied by their cohorts in family liveries. The smell of horse dung was everywhere. The air filled with greetings, shouting and instructions from harassed, Marshalls responsible for making sure everyone was in the right place. There were family groups, children on their fathers' and uncles' shoulders, squashed into crowds behind men with flags, and rows of the Swiss Guard.

There was a group of children, wrapped in blankets, with women carrying sets of wings: cherubs. Then another group, wrapped in cloaks, the Muse and the Virtues, accompanied by older women and some men. I caught sight of Gianfrancesco, and saw Serafina looking splendid in large brimmed hat and a gown of blue showing under her cloak. I made my way through the crowd towards them, and was greeted by Gianfrancesco, who had a laurel wreath on his head. He had a protecting arm around Ginetta, while Serafina, carrying two veils and head dresses, was guarding Ceci. They all wore gloves, new gloves. I kissed Ginetta's hand and turned to do the same with Ceci, but she was looking another way, fiddling with a scroll and an olive branch. I saw that the dress she was wearing was white, with material in olive green, presumably a drape. She started talking to another Muse, or Virtue, and two more came between her and me.

There was a drum roll, trumpets and shouts. The crowds pushed back to leave a space into which the crush of people, horses and colours suddenly swerved and astonishingly quickly ended up in a line of perfect order, while the Muses, Virtues, the singers and musicians ascended the rostrum. The cherubs were unwrapped, the wings fixed and they joined hands to form a line in front of the rostrum, their mothers cooing at the side. The Muses and Virtues removed their cloaks, adjusted their dresses, put on veils and headdresses, took up their attributes and scrolls and stood waiting. All faces bright with anticipation and nerves. Ceci, olive branch across her from hand to shoulder, holding her scroll, was in the white dress draped with olive-green silk. The sun lit her up, and she smiled, her bright hair loose under the veil, held there by an olive leaf headdress.

I saw what dress it was.

I gazed at her, enchanted, as the fanfares from the trumpets and drums formed an arc of celestial music around her. She wasn't St Barbara, she was St Cecilia, patron saint of music. The music twined with the clatter of hooves, the shouted signals as the procession started and the first groups crossed the bridge. She looked at me and smiled and everyone else faded around her.

'Hey, come away, the Pope!' Gianfrancesco pulled me away from the front of the rostrum as Pope Leo, on a litter under a canopy, stopped and waited while the poems were read out. They had all been taught to hold the scrolls in front, to look up confidently and speak out. The verses of the poem being spoken, so painstakingly rehearsed, were drowned out by fanfares and hooves. Only by their moving lips could you tell that they were making an address. The lips stopped, the Muses and Virtues curtsied, the Pope blessed them, smiled broadly; the litter was raised and he went on his way. The women came off the rostrum, chattering, with mouths, arms and hands – still gloved – to be greeted by their lovers and their guardians. Serafina, who wouldn't have heard a word, praised both Ginetta and Ceci for their clarity. Ginetta believed her, Ceci smiled her thanks. I was so close to them, I could see the sweat on their faces, from exertion, not heat. Ceci shivered, and looked around for her cloak.

'Let me,' I said and went round the back of the rostrum to pick it up. There were several. 'That one.' She was there. She stood in front of me; I pulled out her cloak and held it. She turned into it, and I placed it on her shoulders, and left my hands there.

'It's the dress.'

'Yes.' She raised her right hand to cover my left one and left it there, binding us.

My right hand curled round her hair, freeing it from the cloak, twining it through my fingers. She was still. The trumpets, the shawms, the shouts, the cheers; the clattering of hooves and rumble of feet swirled round us.

'Your hair.' I kissed it. She turned, suddenly, disengaging my hands, leaving them between us, palms facing downwards. Her action made her cloak slide off. My body tensed, ready to pull back, my mind trying to control it.

'Giulio.' She turned, lifted her arms to me and kissed me. I pulled her tight and needed no triumphal music to tell me I was on a painted cloud, looking down at earthly mortals! Around us the women were getting their cloaks: I threw back my head and laughed. I encircled her with my arms to lift her as she laughed down at me, as I swung her round.

'I love you!' We cried together, and I saw Gianfrancesco and Ginetta grinning. I'm not sure if the louder cheers were for the Pope or for us. Gianfrancesco picked up Ceci's cloak, gave it to me and this time it stayed on and she fastened it. She took off one glove, we held hands and stood with the others to watch the wealth of Rome, the monks, the clergy, the soldiers, go by.

My family was forgotten; I had my family, here, my friends, and my love.

For the rest of the day we became as if children again, with Serafina playing nursemaid to the four of us. We weaved our way through crowds of good-natured people, making our way towards the *Piazza del Popolo*. The streets were lined with stalls, and we stopped frequently, tugged by Ceci towards them to examine jewellery, embroidered girdles and sleeves she couldn't afford, which called forth exclamations of delight and envy from both her and Ginetta. Gianfrancesco and I bought ribbons and tied then on their wrists and around Serafina's close-wrapped head veil. We found a stall with various bits of stone and marble. Ceci and I went through them, and found a very nice piece of intricate marble moulding, which she bargained for with smiles and pouts until it was hers for a fraction of the asking price.

'Time to start a new collection,' she said as she tucked it into my pouch.

There were posies of wild flowers brought down from the

hills, which wilted not long after they were pinned to our clothes, and wreaths of laurels for our heads to match those of the women. We bought pastries to cram into our mouths, quenching our thirsts at fountains. I bought Ceci a castle made of sugar, and joined her in licking sugar-crumbs off her lips and her tongue, making us both laugh.

As Gianfrancesco was dripping honey from a spoon into Ginetta's mouth to do the same, we heard trumpets and drums coming towards us. Along the street which would join with the one we were on at the entrance to the *Piazza,* which held the gateway to the North and the church of *Santa Maria del Popolo*, where I had copied the *chiaroscuro* below the frescos of Pinturicchio. Both church and *Piazza* were named after the poplar trees which grew all around it, many of which had been hewed down to form this wide space as a gathering place for travellers and traders who used the gate, and for festivals such as this one.

'Come on!' said Ceci, pulling me and Serafina along, leaving the other two, who seemed to be honey-stuck together, to follow. At the entrance we stood and applauded the procession of musicians and men with flags on long poles: flags in coloured patterns, flags with crests, flags with animals on them. Each set of flags being carried by a group in the same coloured livery, women in colourful dresses mingling with them. They passed by, then everyone followed them, dispersing to the edges of the square.

'Look, over there!' Ceci pointed to where young men were scrambling up ruined walls. We ran to join them. I jumped Ceci up to the first ledge, and she pulled herself upwards, two young men making way and helping her, to sit high above, feet dangling. I hauled myself up and stood just below her so my head could rest on her knee to show the young men she wasn't for them. She fondled my hair.

'There, Giulio,' she said, pointing to where Gianfrancesco,

Ginetta and Serafina had managed to find a place at the front. She waved but they could not see us.

All eyes were on the fluttering company weaving in and out of each other, flags aloft, curving around each other without clashing, making brilliant swirls of colour. Men raised children onto their shoulders so they could see. The musicians took their places on one side of the square, facing inwards, and the flag throwers stood, each group forming the side of a square facing outwards, waiting for the signal to begin.

CECI

My hand was on my knee, resting against Giulio's hair, not believing we were together. Not believing that, by following him behind the rostrum, the wall I had built around his memory had crumbled. The conviction that I was too evil for him, which had prevented me from seeking him out, had hardened me in what I had done to survive. This had softened and blown away as dust when I felt his hands on my shoulders. I felt his hair move on my fingers as he turned his head slightly to take in the sight before us, and I knew that, inside that head, he was noting features and attitudes to draw later. I looked at this head, taking in the individual strands of hair close against each other, marvelling. The hair turned to one side, as he said, 'Look, the leader is ready,' and I raised my eyes to see a man's arm in the air and trumpets being put to lips. The crowd quietened in anticipation, a breath's pause, then the arm went down and the drums sent a frisson around the spectators which increased with the trumpet fanfare. The thrill of the music chimed with the thrill in my heart and I thought I was never as happy as I was that minute, that hour, that day. It was as if every movement, every sound was binding me closer to Giulio, to where I wanted to be. Above the crowd, as if on thrones, watching the performance which was just for us, jubilant in the finding of each other. To be still, within a love that extended to everyone around us, centred on only one. The colours and sounds as vivid and vital as the paintings he made.

There was a roar; the flags quivered as the throwers moved into a circle facing inwards, then they worked rhythmically to the calls of the leader and the accents of the trumpets and drums. The flags were tossed into the air and caught on the beginning of a swing which sent each one to the next catcher on the beat. The flags seemed to travel up and down and sideways of their own accord. The flags changed direction round the circle and with a quickening of the drumbeat, suddenly became an up-down zig-zag as if two sets of flags were being used.

The throwers separated into their groups to wait while a young lad, short in stature, appeared with a flag which seemed twice as high as he. This drew forth laughter and comments about ''is pole is longer than 'im,' and 'what'll 'e do with that pole?' which brought my hand to my mouth to suppress my laughter, while Giulio clapped and cheered. The lad, obviously used to this, swayed from side to side and made as if to topple over, encouraging more and more variations on the theme of his pole, more whistles and laughter. He was accompanied by belches from trumpets and squeaks from bagpipes, which caused even more laughter. Then with a swift turn he went on to make amazing throws. The flag twisted twice and three times into the air, before he caught it. It moved so fast in its swinging that it became a blur of colour as he danced in circles with a final throw where it seemed to hang in the ait before coming down. During the wild applause, he bowed, then swung the pole from side to side, jumping over it once, twice, three times. This made us all gasp and cheer, and coins were thrown in his direction which he swiftly picked up and bowed, grinning widely and doffing his cap.

'He's not so young,' said Giulio, and I realised that his face was that of a fully-grown man while his short body was that of a youth, an athlete.

There was a change of music and eight young women came into the centre to perform a courtly dance. The crowd quietened and swayed with them, enjoying their grace and beauty, the precision of their movements. There were some mutterings about the audacity of these young women performing in public. At the end, the 'women' raised their skirts to the 'ooo' of the audience and revealed themselves, by their breeches and hose, to be young men, who went off laughing and embracing each other to wild ribald shouts and applause.

A final dazzling show of throwers, commanded by the 'young' athlete, was followed by the performers, musicians, and drummers passing round and round each other in patterns across the square. The ended by going through the crowd to march down the street to the next square and the next performance. I sighed with pleasure.

'Where are the others?' I looked across to see Ginetta and Gianfrancesco with a trio of ladies, looking round for us. Giulio stood straight, waving and making a piercing whistle, which I didn't know he could do, and then attracted waves back, and a move towards us. The trio were Serafina and two old friends from her past. She was tired of standing so long, so we found a place under the poplars for all three so they could chat to their heart's content. We four lay next to them and shared pies and fruit, water and wine bought from barrels fastened to each side of a mule following its owners through the crowd. I lay with my head in Giulio's lap, looking at the sky and wishing it to darken so I could reach up and draw him to me.

~

The door closed. We stood in the middle of the room. My ache for him was palpable, but I did not move. I had to lower my eyes from him as my head released the memories, the emotions that had been held back. The torrent filled the space between us with a roar and turned into a wave that passed through, carrying with it all the men who had inhabited this body which was once his alone. The mechanical sex act of no meaning, the melodrama of the pretend gasping and cries, my way of survival, the crushing of any physical feeling was swept up in it. It curled upwards and came forward to topple me. I put up my hands to protect myself from it, gasped and sat down suddenly on the bed. I whimpered as I felt moisture between my legs and the longing to be touched.

I looked up at him, my mouth open, my eyes on his. He was at my side, his arms around me, rocking me, Ceci – Ceci – Ceci. The waves subsided, its torrent became tears falling from my eyes, joining those that were his, as the young Ceci returned. We rocked and sobbed and kissed our tears, our faces, our eyes, our lips. Hands reached clothes which were pulled off until skin met skin, his hand was where it should be, as was mine. We closed together as the torrent dissolved into the feeling between us that rose and rose until we arched and cried out.

We lay, panting, sweating, holding each other tightly; kissing, kissing, whispering our names, such that he grew again within me. It was as if a full moon had shone through the window laying a bright ray of light across the bed which engulfed us. This was love. This...was...love...overwhelming and wrecking my carefully built-up life.

CHAPTER THIRTY-TWO

GIULIO Rome, 1514

The *Orso* became a fashionable place for artists to find female models. Serafina realised quickly that this would allow her best girls to rest and still bring in a fee. She charged by the hour, and would keep an ear and an eye out for any sexual activity for which she demanded more, with a large black slave standing by to make sure it was paid. For Gianfrancesco and I, as Raffaello's favourites, and in turn favoured by her two best girls, Ceci (Tomasina) and Ginetta, the charge was very little as long as we bought wine. There were no money charges for the sex either, provided we made presents of things she could sell or pawn, like lengths of silk, or gloves, or baubles. Raffaello had been a favourite customer, the girls adored him and all of them wanted to pose for him, to be in one of his paintings. Which is how St Barbara came about.

I never asked Ceci if she had done more for Raffaello than pose. I never asked her about the parties she went to. I accepted it when Serafina shook her head at me when I visited and told me when I could come back. I didn't wait to see who the client might be. Gianfrancesco was the same. Neither of us could afford to support a mistress. Our time with our women was what it was, love. The rest was out of sight, out of mind; the way we lived.

The afternoon was still. In her room, Ceci sat on the ottoman under the window, still, but for the slight breathing of the gauze over her breasts. I could see how the light brightened the left side of her face and how it made the strands of hair escaping from her blonde plait shine white against her skin. I looked down at the paper, then up again quickly. Her lowered brown lashes allowed only a slit of green-black iris and dark pupil to show. A second plait was tucked behind her ear and covered with more white-grey gauze, which folded into the shadow of her long straight nose as her head fell to the right. Her lips upturned slightly, but she was not smiling. I traced her body through my eyes onto the paper.

She was confident in the positioning of her limbs, left leg crossed over right, making fabric-folds from knee to toes. Her right foot not quite hidden, her left foot with its misshapen big toe was poised, unshaking, above the ground. The long slim fingers of her right hand curled over the edge of the ottoman, a strong wrist supporting the contrasting chubbiness of her forearm. Her left hand rested on her knee, on the end of an olive wand which rose, like a sceptre, to touch her bare left shoulder with its end-bunch of leaves. Gauze crossed her elbow and drifted to a cord tied under her unsupported breasts. She was Peace once more, this time, in preparation for a frescoed statue required in the Pope's rooms.

The air, like her, was still. Hundreds of dust motes pitched and tossed in slow motion across the sunrays from the window, moving on their own personal air drifts with no reference to each other. I was aware of the sound of my chalk on the grey paper, amplified by the velvet hush in the room.

Outside, chickens squabbled; in the street men called to men, coarse laughter followed a ribald cry. I know she wanted to laugh from the twitch in her eyebrow, but she didn't. She knew I needed her unmoving a while longer. Pico, a recent apprentice addition, brought to watch how I worked, was sitting on the ground next to me, grinning but making no sound. He watched me, watched her, saw her form take shape on the paper. Thick, thin, short, long curved lines make a record of a female shape, a shape that may be used more than once, perhaps in reverse, perhaps mirrored thus on either side of a main picture, perhaps dressed in different colours, or not much at all.

I finished the sketch, grunted and put down the chalk.

'You can move, Ceci.'

She stretched, uncrossed her legs, reached for a length of scuffed gold coloured fabric from the floor and wrapped it around herself. She shivered, not from cold, but from the effect of holding a pose, which slowed the blood and cooled the body. She rubbed her feet. I poured water and wine into three beakers and give one to Pico, nodding towards Ceci. Pico blushed at being close to her body and there was a flutter under his jerkin. I smiled; at eleven years old, he had yet to take control of his cock. She took the drink, smiled and touched his cheek to thank him. His face and ears rushed from pale pink to deep vermillion; he stood not-quite still, then turned and rushed from the room. Ceci looked from under her lashes guiltily, but with a hand over the laugh in her mouth. I grinned and rubbed chalk from my fingers with a rag.

She came forward to kiss me and picked up bread and cheese from a plate. I took a swig from my beaker and stuffed meat and bread into my mouth. Pico crept back in, and sat down close to me, not looking at her. I passed him some food. A mule brayed. Sunrays moved further into the room, the dust motes followed them.

We all chewed together.

Ceci wiped crumbs from her mouth.

'Is it true that Raffaello's painting Beatrice Ferrarese, nude, for a Cardinal…?' I shrugged, threw her an apple and passed her a knife. She sighed.

'I saw her last Sunday at San'Agostino - she had two manservants and a page in front of her, and another four behind, all in rose pink livery - with a fine young man dressed in velvet at her side - hair piled up in gold curls…' Se twirled her fingers over her head; I took up my chalk to make swift sketches of her rapid hands.

'Black velvet and gold robes - gold cords interlaced. The work alone must have cost a fortune! And the jewels, the necklaces and the rings! She could have been a *Marchesa*!' She almost overwhelmed herself, remembering. She looked at the knife and the apple with surprise at finding them over her head. She lowered her arms and swiftly tackled the peel, held up a complete spiral, dropped it on the floor and bit into the apple triumphantly. I added juice running down her chin from an open mouth.

'Oh!' she wiped her hand across the chin and licks off the juice 'Ginetta told me that Katrina was cut – night before last.'

'Client?'

'No, Lucia! The cat!' She made claws in the air, whined strident 'mreeOOOWs' through her teeth, and wiped her mouth on her hand.

'What for?' I threw her a cloth.

'Ginetta says - Lucia says - Annina stole Orazio dei Falcone from her.' She shrugged. I drew the shoulders and the outstretched hands, omitting the apple and the knife. 'Ginetta says it's really bad, her nose took it.' She swished the knife across her cheek '- *Sfregiato!* –', slashed. She flourished the knife and put it back on the table. 'She won't be so attractive to Orazio now.' I raised an eyebrow.

'Or anyone else.'

Ceci mumbled into the apple.

'It happens…' She munched. 'But I know,' she said with her mouth full, 'it wasn't her that took him, it was your friend, *Il Sodoma*.'

Giovanni Bazzi made no bones about his sexual preferences. After all, he'd painted the pretty Orazio as Alexander in the bedroom of the Chigi house, and probably had him there as well. I'd painted Orazio once or twice myself – as an angel. Ceci finished the apple. I drew her parted lips and her teeth, without the gap in them. She stretched again and stood up, twirled round, spread her arms. The golden fabric fell off her, and the light shone through the gauze, showing every part of her body. Pico stared, eyes on stalks, vermilion to his toes probably.

'You're getting fat.'

'It's all the good food I'm having!' and she twirled again, hands on hips, the gauze tightening across her body, showing the dark patch of full, furry pubis. Pico got up, grabbed his trousers and fled from the room. Toxic stuff, vermillion.

Ceci bubbled with laughter, and I pulled her to me.

'Giulio! – Pico.' I shut the door.

'I think he'll take the hint…'

~

Pope Leo loved display. Once again the streets were lined with people, but this time there were no arches or decorations to prepare. We were waiting for - an elephant! Leo had already made a menagerie at the Palace with lions, leopards, monkeys and bears. Their noises could be heard in the square outside. Children were threatened with the lions if they were naughty, but many people were afraid that one day those lions would escape and eat them. Because very few actually saw the lions, their size grew and grew in the collective imagination until they were as big as, well, an elephant…

The Portuguese ambassador's gift had arrived at *Porto Ercole*, some seventy miles from Rome and the poor creature had to travel that distance on foot. His appearance at the villages on the way caused everyone to stop work and crowd round the procession of men on horses, cages of birds and small animals, frightening them all including the poor elephant. There were stories, when the travellers, human and animal, stopped to rest at inns or villas, of people clambering over walls to see it. Stories of an inn roof collapsing, of the gardens of a villa being destroyed. There was destruction all along the route; even the fact that it rained most of the time did not dissuade people. Large groups of horsemen, including Cardinals, impeded the progress of the Portuguese so the Pope had to send out his Swiss Guards to protect them.

Hearing gossip about exotic animals, and men in Eastern costume, made everyone in Rome eager to see for themselves, and on the first Sunday of Lent, the streets were packed well before daylight. Raffaello and other favoured painters had an allotted place under a canopy at the foot of the *Castello Sant'Angelo*, where I stood waiting for the arrival of Ceci, Ginetta and Serafina, protected by Gianfrancesco, Giovanni and Ercole. I saw them just as a thunderstorm started and they rushed towards me to be pulled under a canopy against the fortress wall. The downpour was such that the fabric filled with water and bowed down in the middle, so painters on each other shoulders had to push it up and those of use, me included, who were holding the canopy poles, got drenched. The rain stopped as suddenly as it started. Amid cries and laughter, and exaggerated wringing of clothes, we emerged into the sun to dry out. Raffaello, Peruzzi, and other architects like Benedetto Sangallo, arrived (having waited undercover, probably in a tavern), and laughed at our sodden selves as they passed us. We squashed together so that we could see the Pope at a window in the Castello, from where he would greet and bless the Portuguese and the animals. People who had sheltered from the rain came back and started to argue about the places they had lost when they ran away. The procession was on its way, we could hear the cheers rising, then the sound of trumpets and drums.

'I can't see!' cried Ceci and Ginetta, jumping up and down. So we pushed them, and the other painters' women, in front of us, behind the row of Swiss guards who were there to keep the space in front of the *Castello* clear. The trumpets got louder, but these were drowned in the sound of cannon fire from the roof of the *Castello*, a signal for us to cover our ears and of the Pope's arrival. Brightly dressed people on mules were coming across the bridge and took their places facing the *Castello*, the family and personal friends of the Pope.

'Oh look – look, Ginetta! How beautiful!'

It was a pure white horse ridden by a black man in glorious costume with a cat-like animal sitting behind him. A large shape followed him.

'Oh!' Ginetta squealed 'Look! Is that the elephant?'

'Oh My Lord!' said Serafina, her hand to her breast.,

It was indeed the elephant: a large grey-white animal, with another richly dressed man sitting behind its big ears. A silver tower with turrets was behind him on the elephant's back, set over a finely wrought casket, with brocade flowing over its flanks almost to its feet. 'He's lovely!' 'So big!' Magnificent!' were the cries from our group, all of us clapping our hands in delight. The elephant passed us, almost touching the Swiss Guard so we could see how tall he was, higher than twice, three times a man. Ceci stood with her hands over her open mouth, and Ginetta tried to stretch between two guards to touch him.

'He's a glorious beast!' I said to Gianfranccsco. 'Magnificent! Magnificent!' murmured Giovanni. We were itching to draw him.

He was turned towards the Pope, and bowed down, his front legs kneeling. The Pope and the crowd roared approval. The elephant put its trunk in a large bowl, sucked up water and spouted it up in the air, drenching those near it, delighting the Pope and making everyone exclaim, laugh and applaud.

'No-one can say the Pope doesn't know how to put on a show!' said Giovanni.

We watched the whole procession gather along this side of the river, then turn to go back through the streets to show off to the rest of the city.

A week or so later, I got permission to enter the menagerie to draw the elephant, whom the Pope had called Hanno. It was to appear in a bible painting in the Pope's *loggia*, but by the time it was painted, poor Hanno had died, and was mourned throughout Rome. My painting was copied many times by other painters, and Giovanni made an elephant fountain later in in the garden of a villa built for the Pope.

~

The week before Hanno arrived, Donato Bramante had died. He was just sixty. He had been unwell for some time, his work having been undertaken largely by Peruzzi. We attended the funeral, led by Raffaello and Michelangelo, who buried their differences for the length of time taken by the *Messa da Requiem* and the burial at the old *Basilica di San Pietro*. Soon afterwards, Pope Leo, in addition to completing the inside rooms that we were already working on, requested Raffaello to finish the *loggia* being built on the side of the Palace overlooking the city. The *loggia* had been designed and built by Bramante, using the *tablinarium* in the Campo Vaccino as a model for the high arches crossing the interior. Raffaello wanted to re-design it, to make it more like the pattern of the Amphitheatre, with different capitals on the pillars and a more complicated interior. The Pope agreed and appointed him *Architetto Papale* - Papal Architect - which meant that he would be taking over the construction of the new *Basilica*. It also meant that there would be a new way of working for us.

Gianfrancesco, Giovanni and I met in the *Orso* after we heard the news. We sat down with our jugs of wine and water, and at first no-one spoke. We were letting the implications sink in.

'It isn't as though he knows nothing about architecture,' Giovanni said. 'He's been studying the ruins for years.'

'And he worked with Bramante in Urbino, so he must know about plans and buildings.'

'He's ambitious, what he doesn't know he'll ask. He said that the Pope had asked him to work with Fra Giocondo; what he doesn't know about Vitruvian architecture isn't worth knowing.'

'And Peruzzi, he'll be there.'

'So, how's it going to work, for us?'

No-one could answer that. I didn't speak, as I had already thought of how my training with Peruzzi in measuring and drawing the antiquities and in copying architectural plans gave me the edge on the others. I could move between painting and buildings. My heart leapt at the thought of how I could become Raffaello's assistant in other ways than painting.

'We've still got the rooms to finish, that'll keep us in work.'

'Raffaello won't give up painting surely?'

'Of course he won't, but he'll be weighed down with commissions after this appointment. It'll be down to us, I reckon; he'll design and we'll paint.'

And I, I will help him make buildings as well as paint them.

Gianfrancesco and I met with Raffaello the next day. He came in, eyes sparkling, carrying rolls of paper.

'Bramante's plans!' he said as he threw them on the table and leaned on it looking towards us, sitting opposite. 'Now, I need to talk about how things will be. You know I haven't done much painting on the current project - I shall leave it to you to finish it and go onto the last two sections. Pope Leo wants the Bramante *loggia* painted as well - I'll make the drawings of course. I want the painters all contracted to me and no-one else, and you two will be in charge of both projects. We shall make the 'New Rome' together!' He sat down and grinned at us all. 'I've some ideas about the *loggia* decoration.' He unrolled one of the plans and explained what he wanted to do.

'There are thirteen sections, each of which will be totally painted. Each section will have a scene from the Bible on the vault, surrounded by decorations; each arch will have its own design, birds, animals, figures, imitations form the *domus aurea*. From each end of the *loggia* you will see the series of arches as in perspective - as you travel up the *loggia*, you'll look up to see another scene.'

The scheme was ambitious: a continuous design with each arcade telling its own story. I started to sketch ideas.

'We'll use the *domus aurea* vault scheme for all of it, layout and decorations. So there'll be a lot more visits down there to make more drawings.'

'What's the time scale?' asked Gianfrancesco

'Yesterday!' I said and we all grinned. Raffaello nodded.

'Of course!'

'No surprise then!' said Gianfrancesco

'We'll need everyone on this. Giovanni da Udine can be in charge of the landscapes and animals and birds, you, Giulio, will be in charge of the bible scenes. Gianni, you will paint of course, but you'll be in charge of finding and contracting extra painters. Make sure they're reliable - I want them full-time on this, no slouching off to do other work.'

'What about the Pope's rooms?'

'Who's there today?'

'Tomasso, Luca, Bartolomeo.'

'We'll need more. I think, Gianni, you should manage the *modelli* and *cartone* as usual. Giulio, you can work on the designs for the next walls and rooms, and manage the painters.'

He'd had got us right, Gianfrancesco as *fattore*, managing men, and all the paperwork, in charge of the processes of putting ideas on walls; me the creative, the trainer, the inspirer. But nothing about the architecture – I would have to wait.

Raffaello stood up.

'I'm going over to see Peruzzi and Fra Giocondo -' he picked up the other rolls - 'to talk about the *Basilica*.' And he was off.

'It's going to be like this from now on, like being on galloping horses, trying to keep up with the Master!' Gianfrancesco said. 'Well, we'd better get over to the Palace to look at the work in the rooms, and have a look at the *loggia* as well. Might as well start as we mean to go on.'

'And we'll call on Giovanni on the way back.'

Giovanni, hands covered in plaster, flecks of which were in his hair, did not want to come with us. He was muttering about *stucco*, the plaster forms in light relief, which he wanted to make as white as that in the *domus aurea*.

'It's still not right- I've been mixing plaster – '

'We can see that.' He ignored us. '… with the white lime of ground travertine instead of the volcanic *pozzolana* - but it still isn't pure white – and it is rougher and more granular.' He scratched his head.

'If it's not working, the best thing to do is clean up and come with us to the *Orso*.' He shrugged, and, while he was washing, we bought food to take with us. We tramped up the stairs to the women's rooms, and spread it over the table and talked, telling the women about what Raffaello had said, *San Pietro,* our ideas for the Pope's rooms. We ate and drank, talking over each other and laughing at the prospects ahead. Giovanni was still muttering.

'I've been trying different plaster mixtures but it's not right yet. '

'Perhaps you should try urine – it works for the washerwomen,' suggested Ceci, and giggled. Giovanni looked at her

'I'm not sure Pope Leo will like his new *loggia* walls pissed on…'

'Why not? The ambassadors who'll wait there will be!' Gales

of tipsy laughter and groans, and the passing round of another wine jar. At midnight Giovanni left, to meet Ercole, a sculptor, as strong and as beautiful as his namesake, Hercules.

'I think it's love this time,' he said as he left. We cheered him; he always said that.

I was now alone with Ceci. I drew her by moonlight and by candlelight. I copied and compared the different shadows, first moving slowly, then flickering, onto her clothes and then onto her skin. She started fully clothed, sitting on the bed, then, as the clothes got less and less, she lay back, then down, nude, her back to me. She pulled her braid over her shoulder and unravelled it until her hair fell free to the bed, gleaming in the candlelight, cascading in different tones of gold, ochre and burnt sienna. I put down the chalk and paper. I snuffed the candle; I crossed to her. The moon beams lit her neck and shoulders as she turned over, and made her eyes shine green as glass as she reached for me.

'My painter, my architect' she murmured. Of course, she would know my mind, before I did. I kissed her forehead.

'I will' - her eyes - 'build a house' - her nose - 'just for us' - her lips – 'and I shall paint you on all the walls, my goddess.'

The moon smiled and shone down on us from a clear sky full of millions of stars, like the ceiling in the Sistine chapel before Michelangelo painted over it.

CHAPTER THIRTY-THREE

CECI Rome 1516

Giulio and Gianfrancesco came to visit us after a day's painting in the Vatican *loggia*. They banged on the door.

'Let us in, we have something to tell you!'

Serafina opened the door and we heard her being greeted by Giulio with boisterous kisses on both cheeks. She shut the door, giggling as they swung up the stairs two at a time.

'Whatever is it?' I was brushing out my hair so it was hanging in front of my face and peered up through it. Ginetta was lying on my bed eating apricots.

'We,' said Giulio taking the brush from me, 'are going to paint – a bathroom!'

'What's unusual about that? Ouch!'

Gianfrancesco stretched out on the bed and started to share the apricots. 'It's not just any bathroom, it's in the Vatican, for Cardinal Bibbiena!'

'Ouch!' I snatched the brush back from Giulio, threw back my head.

'You look like Medusa!' He knelt in front of me and took my face in both hands. 'Which means that the bathroom will be erotic...'

'Titillating,' contributed Gianfrancesco

'Full of naked Roman women and ancient satyrs,' Gianfrancesco stuck hand up over his groin and wiggled it.

'With mighty erections...'

'And I suppose -' I rubbed Giulio's nose with mine ' - that we will have to pose for the naked women.'

'For the goddesses, for Venus, for Olympia, for Psiche!' He kissed my nose and snuffled my ear.

'Get off!' I pulled my head back then quickly forward covering his head with hair, kissed his lips and pushed him backwards. My hair got caught in his, over his ears and in his beard and we fell onto the floor entangling the rest of ourselves. We had to get Ginetta and Giovanni to wrestle with my hair so we could come apart. We all landed up on the floor on our backs, with them laughing, and me cross. I sat up and pawed at my hair.

'I will never get this untangled!'

'Let me!' Ginetta grovelled for the brush and knelt beside me. She began to tease out the hair with her fingers. Giulio lay back with his hands behind his head.

'And I've had an idea.'

'Ouch!'

'The Cardinal says he is tired of the same faces –'

'And bodies –'

'And bodies, female bodies, at his plays and parties. And he wants some new ones.'

'Owwww!'

'So I thought we – all of us here could help him.'

'How? We've never been invited to a Cardinal's party – we're not refined enough!' Ginetta pulled the brush through some hair.

'Ow! that hurt!' I snatched the brush from her. 'I'll do it.' Giulio rolled over to face me.

'I thought you said Vanozza was too ill to take much interest here anymore and Serafina doesn't have the clout to attract the better clients.' This was true, we hadn't made much money recently.

'Go on.'

'We could gather up some new young pretty girls, you could train them and we could offer them for parties - for which we would get a percentage.' I pulled hairs from my brush.

'I shall go bald!' I wailed and hit Ginetta with the brush. She slid away and cuddled up to Gianfrancesco who was now sitting against the bed.

'And just where are we to find these girls? And where shall we keep them? And how shall we feed them?'

'Well –'

'Off the streets?'

'Well, yes.'

'Like Serafina found me?'

'U-huh.' He dropped his gaze.

'You want us…' pull 'to go out…' tug 'on the streets… ouch! - and pick up girls.'

'We'd come with you,' said Gianfrancesco, 'You'd be quite safe.'

'And how will we know that they haven't got the pox?' Giulio looked me straight in the eyes and said softly, 'We didn't know that you didn't.'

There was a moment when no-one moved.

'True – ah!' The tangles were out. I pulled the hair back behind me and let it fall. I sat cross-legged and Ginetta knelt behind me and started to plait my hair.

'And where will we take them? There's only room enough for us here.' Giulio got to his feet.

'I thought, rent a house, bigger than this, with lots of rooms.'

'Giulio, I will not run a brothel!' I shook the brush at him. 'Here it is just we two, we look out for each other.'

'No, not a brothel, a house to live in, to sleep and eat in. You'll not conduct your business there, not like here. We'll make arrangements to supply girls to the great - the money will come from the Cardinals and the merchants, from Chigi, from Bibbiena, from the Pope himself! You can train the girls to talk properly, have good manners, be entertaining, and everything else you're good at.'

'I'll teach them the everything else,' offered Ginetta. 'I'm good at that,' she giggled. I waved the brush.

'Who's this 'we'? Rent a house. Where? What with? And who'll do all the arranging? You – unlikely! How will we furnish it – and what's in it for you?'

'Whoa! First, where. Chigi – he's bought that line of houses along the inside wall, by the *Porta Settimania*, next to *Santa Dorothea*. You're good at trading, you know you are. I've seen how you buy the antiquities off your clients and sell them on to others – I've heard you do it – which gives me another idea.' He sat up.

I shook my head at him.

'Stay with this one. So we rent a house from Chigi. It'll take us time to find girls and train them; we might not earn much while that's going on. And there'll be other costs – food, drink, clothes – we'll need good clothes - and apothecary bills... I'll need some capital – and where is that to come from?' I pretended to dismiss the idea, which, truly, I was getting very interested in.

'I'll talk to Chigi.'

I'll talk to Chigi – or at least to his secretary, Salvatore. I hadn't ever told Giulio about the money for the costumes.

'We only deal with the rich, then we can charge good prices – as long as the girls come up with the goods.'

'And how will you persuade Chigi to give money to an assistant painter and a prostitute he doesn't know?' He shrugged.

'I won't always be an assistant. Besides, you haven't let me answer about my part in it.'

'Go on.'

He leaned on one elbow and looked at me intently.

'I can't build you a house yet, I can't support you - if you have a house, and a business, then you won't have to serve other men. The house will be my home, after Raffaello's house, and I will have you to myself - you can be wholly mine.'

He was serious. I was totally surprised, taken aback at this declaration. Yes, we loved each other, we knew that but this, this was different.

'And for Ginetta and Gianfrancesco?'

'It's what I want,' he said. 'It's what you to want isn't it?' He asked, looking at them. The both sat up, looked at each other, and then at Giulio. And nodded.

'Ceci?' My heart beat faster, I felt the hairs on my arm prickle. Yes, it was what I wanted – Giulio, oh yes. But also, I remembered the little girl, the little girl who wanted to do things, who wanted to be as free as a man. To have an ambition, like Giulio: 'I want to be a painter.' 'Then be one'.

I remembered the geese and the bargaining. I remembered finding and selling the little bits of antiquity to pilgrims; I remembered taking orders for garments we made, setting prices, and I remembered having to refuse Adelina; refuse the chance to learn to write and read properly, to learn to be a shop owner. It had all been hidden away, forgotten. Another wall erected against my past life in order to survive. My life now as a whore, parallel to my love for Giulio, totally separate, but both equally passive. This all went through my head like an arrow. They were waiting for me to speak.

The arrow hit its mark. The wall collapsed. Giulio was offering me commitment and the chance *to be*...It was all there: the idea of being able to take girls off the streets and feeding them properly. The idea of living with Giulio, of having a house for me and for Ginetta, of being in charge of my own business, of becoming his equal. I took a deep breath.

'I shall want to choose the girls, and train them properly - they'll work when I think they're ready. And...I want to be able to ban any client who mistreats the girls. You introduce me to clients; I'll give you commission, and a share of the profits. I will organise the service - but it'll be *my* business, *my* house.' I emphasised this with the hairbrush. I said nothing about love, I said nothing about his declaration of commitment. Ginetta gasped, Gianfrancesco at up straight. They waited.

'I shall ask Chigi to invest – he's a banker after all – and he will make sure I get the richest clients. He ought to be interested in the idea now Vanozza no longer operates.' Our eyes met and locked.

Giulio threw back his head and laughed.

'I knew it! I knew you'd go with it! Ceci! My Ceci!'

His eyes shone with admiration and love. He knelt in front of me.

'You are amazing!'

'Yes, I am.' He removed the hairbrush and took both hands. 'And what was your other idea?'

'We'll start trading in antiques. I'll collect them and you will find the buyers among your clients.' I smiled. It was a very good idea. He pulled me towards him. 'The houses have gardens – you'll love them!'

We fell to the floor and were at it as if there was no-one else there.

~

I went, with Serafina, to meet Chigi's secretary, Salvatore. I had told Giulio about the costumes, and said that I would try my luck again. If it came to nothing, I would ask him to intercede with Chigi, through Raffaello. But I was sure I could succeed.

'Ah, Mistress Tomasina, the astute bargainer. What is it you want today?'

I sat without being invited, and told him about the scheme.

'You want Chigi to loan you the money?'

'No, I want him invest money, then he will introduce me to possible clients.'

'I see.'

'We can arrange a percentage when we start to make money.'

'And the house, you will not run it as a brothel? '

'No.' I explained the plan.

'You'll want the house rent free then?'

'No, we will pay rent from the time we start earning. Master Chigi's money will enable us to set up.'

'And Romano, the painter, where does he come in?'

'He will also introduce me to clients, his clients, and he will get commission on that.'

'I see – but I think he will also be getting free food and board.' I did not answer. He sat back, looking at me, playing with his quill pen.

'And you? Will you…?

'No. I will escort the girls, as will Ginetta, but we will not service the men.'

'You may have learned from Vanozza, but I think, Mistress, you are naturally skilled in these matters.' His look was one of admiration. I could get used to this.

'I shall make notes. Let's go through it again.'

~

The smell of orange blossom was intoxicating as I entered the Chigi villa garden with Ginetta. A servant escorted us through the pergola where the vines were starting to grow, with fresh light green leaves opening out into tiny versions of their later palmate shapes. White lilies grew below them, just about to bloom, with violets at their feet. We passed a fountain with marble seats around it, next to them rose bushes tumbling into beds of herbs, with thymes, oregano, and rosemary overlapping the path where they could be brushed to release their scent. Mulberry trees and the pink tamarisk gave shade, below which grew daisies, cornflowers and marigolds with their buds promising colour in a few weeks' time.

We went up the steps into a large *loggia*, to be met by our hosts, Agostino Chigi and his mistress, Francesca Ordeaschi, the mother of three children by him at that time. I had been curious about her, for it was known Chigi had brought her back from Venice where she had been a courtesan, at a level far above myself, for she was from a family quite high up, though poor. Chigi had previously had the great Imperia as mistress, and had acknowledged his child, Lucretia, by her. Imperia had died, some say at her own hand, some years before, and her daughter was in a convent. The banker had wanted to make a marriage with Margherita Gonzaga, the natural daughter of the Marquis of Mantua, but it was rumoured that she refused to marry an 'old man'. He chose Francesca, a woman to love and to give him children; a woman he could talk to as well as make love to. For that, I applauded him as a sensible man.

She was beautiful, of course, and smiled as she greeted us, a smile which did not reach her eyes, which regarded me coldly. Master Chigi insisted that we accompany them up the stairs to see the work being done by Master Peruzzi. We entered the large room and stopped in amazement. Chigi was pleased with our reaction.

'Magical work, magical! See, you thought there was a *loggia* over there with a view out over Rome!' and indeed we did. Pillars seemed to invite us to go between them to stand at a balustrade and take in the view.

'It's exactly what you would see if it was real!' Chigi was very pleased. I noticed that the panels between the windows were painted to continue the view seen from the windows. If you stood in the right place, the paintwork was exactly lined up with the real thing seen through the next window. The fireplace appeared to be in the centre of a landscape, seen briefly through the double pillars on either side. I walked round the room in astonishment. Both the painting and the illusion were very fine indeed. I had not realised the true extent of the talent of Baldassare Peruzzi, who was a very modest man.

'Master Peruzzi is indeed a master,' I said as Ginetta was pointing at one of the cherubs with a curtain over his head and laughing with Francesca.

'Indeed. I brought him here from Sienna, you know. He's as good a painter as Raffaello; he ought to push himself more, I keep telling him.' He wrinkled his eyes and shook his head, standing in the centre of the room.

'He was Giulio's teacher,' I told Chigi.

'Giulio Romano? I have a painting in the Galatea *loggia* by him. Peruzzi told me he would be important, and he is! First Peruzzi, now Raffaello – I started both of them off you know. Perhaps Romano will paint my other *loggia*'. He laughed and leaned towards me, taking my elbow. 'But don't tell him I said so, he'll put his price up if he thinks I want him!' He turned towards one of the doors.

'That will be my bedchamber, and, when this is finished, it will be the next to be painted.' Chigi said with obvious pride and enjoyment.

'Now Francesca, what are you two gossiping about?'

'Fashions, my dear, Ginetta wanted my guidance on her

next dress.' Ginetta was being schooled in the art of flattery, of which I am sure Francesca was well aware.

'Well, she'll have no better mentor than you.' He kissed her hand, playing the game. At that point Salvatore entered the room, and greeted us with a bow and a smile.

'Salvo! You're here. Come, let us eat!'

We descended the grand staircase, its arches above us all in line, revealing the view ahead out to the garden. We crossed the inner hall, through another door, to where a table was set out with silver, majolica plates and dishes of food. I stopped to look around the walls of which I had heard much from Giulio. I turned my eyes to the *Galatea* painted by Raffaello. Giulio had told me about the plan for five paintings, but this was the only one completed. Next to it was a Polyphemus painted by Sebastiano del Piombo. I knew that this character was a giant, but the painting, curiously, seemed far too big and at odds with the delicate, but powerful, sea nymph next to him. The rest of this wall was hung with tapestries.

'The tapestries are temporary,' said Chigi. One day, Raffaello will complete the rest of the wall,' he told us. I doubted that. As we were seated, I looked up. A vault, with a pattern of painted sections which seemed familiar. Suddenly, I was back in a dark cave, with candles and torches, looking up at a ceiling in bright colours, with sections just like this.

'It's the *domus aurea*!' I cried. Master Chigi looked puzzled. 'The *domus aurea* – the old roman rooms below ground, this ceiling is sectioned in the same pattern as the one I s – ' I caught myself just in time. 'The one I saw a sketch of – by Giulio.'

'There you are! I said Peruzzi was a good man. He promised me the paintings would be in imitation of the antique ones. I think he is the first to do this in Rome – this is the first villa of its kind, with its double *logge*. It's based on the writings of Vitruvius, the Roman architect who built ancient Rome, you know…' He took up the stance of a teacher and it was obvious he had given this talk many time. Francesca interrupted.

'Agosto, don't keep our guests from the food with your endless talk of the antique. Please sit down, Mistress Tomasina, Mistress Ginetta, Salvatore.'

We sat either side of the long table, me on one side, Ginetta and Salvatore on the other, with Francesca and Agostino at either end. There were no other guests. Ginetta was quiet, but exchanged quietly flirtatious looks with Salvatore, who concentrated on passing tasty bits to her. Francesca concentrated on me. A lutenist entered the room and started to play.

'We are honoured to be here with you,' I said.

'Tsh – Francesca wanted to meet you and I thought it would be pleasant for her to get to know you – both.' I glanced at Francesca and caught her look. I knew exactly what this was about, not just for Agostino Chigi to test me out as a partner, but for her to let me understand that I should not become her rival. She didn't want me to be among a large party where Agostino might take me to one side. I returned her look. If my business included providing for Agostino himself, well, he would have the right. It just wouldn't be me.

We talked some more about the paintings and the architecture. Francesca watched me, and realised that my conversation wasn't that of a trained courtesan, who asked questions, made compliments and kept the talk moving, but of someone truly interested in both arts. She then joined the talk of the meaning of the ceiling, the astronomical signs of Agostino's birth, with real information about the stories depicted. At one point we were talking together as Agostino left the table to deal with a letter which had arrived from the Pope. Salvatore rose and suggested that he showed Ginetta the garden, which had been lit up by servants setting lanterns among the trees and along the paths, making lines of lights like fireflies. It was enchanting, and I wished to be out there, but knew that the Pope's letter and Salvatore's suggestion even if he was to take advantage of it, were ploys to allow us to be private together. This was an arrangement to leave me alone with Francesca.

She did, though, lead me to seats outside so we moved from a ceiling illuminated by candlelight, darkening its shimmering blues and painted stars, to a place beneath a deeper tone of blue and glittering actual stars. It was well-though out indeed. The lutenist moved to sit on the step pf the *loggia*, and servants served us with sugar shapes and sweet wine.

'I was of good family in Venice, but I became a courtesan to have better life than being the wife of a man as poor as we were,' she said, taking up a sugared violet. 'A good choice, as you can see.' She waved her hand in the direction of the villa and Agostino. 'So I know the ways of a courtesan.' I waited.

'Agostino has informed me of your plans. I wanted to be sure that was what all you wanted – that you weren't planning to take my place.' I crushed a sugar rose between my teeth so that I couldn't answer. I wanted to hear more.

'Agostino has his pleasures, and some have tried to replace me, but I am the mother of his children, and I will go on having them.' She sipped her wine. This was to be a duel with sugar and honey, and my silence. 'You're a courtesan, you're intelligent, you're beautiful. You would be a rival worthy of me.' I picked up my glass, Venetian, very fine.

'I would, if that is what I wanted to be.' I turned the glass to sparkle in the lantern-light. 'This glass is beautiful – the villa is beautiful and, yes, I would enjoy living here, I would enjoy what wealth could bring. But I want to earn it myself. I have a brain, I am good with money and organisation. What I want from Master Chigi is the capital to start. That is all I want.' She smiled.

'Straightforward. 'She beckoned a servant to fill our glasses. 'And to find your own rich lover?' I smiled back.

'Perhaps.'

'Or will the painter prevent that? Giulio isn't it?'

'My private life is not for discussion here.'

She put down her glass, and leaned towards me.

'It will be the first time Agostino has made a financial business deal with a woman.' She sat back. We stared at each other like cats. She curled her fingers. Claws.

'Be sure you are not my rival, Cecilia.' So, she had her informers.

'You can be sure.'

The claws retracted. She sat back and smiled. She signalled to the servant and whispered to him. He bowed. He went to the lutenist, who stopped playing; a purse was put in his hand. He made a bow towards Francesca, and the servant accompanied him out of the loggia. Master Agostino then came out and sat with us receiving a slight nod from Francesca.

I knew I had won the prize.

As if by magic, Salvatore appeared with Ginetta. We were to be dismissed.

Agostino and Francesca accompanied through the unpainted *loggia*.

'We look forward to your presence at our villa,' he said. 'Mistress Ginevra.' He kissed her hand, then turned to me. 'Mistress Cecilia…' Ginetta looked startled as I nodded. Salvatore and a servant led us to the gate where a carriage was waiting to take us home. Salvatore bowed and said,

'Perhaps, Mistress Cecilia, you would like to meet with me tomorrow.' I said that I would.

In the carriage I embraced Ginetta and told her the news. I did not explain the use of my born name; she did not believe spies existed.

'I hope I played my part,' she said. 'I think Salvatore was

pleased with me.' She held up a small purse. We leaned back and giggled all the way home.

~

We moved into the house, taking Serafina with us, and invited Livia to join us. She was twenty years old, had been at the *Orso* for five years, and like us, had been worried about the future. She was overjoyed to be asked, and loved our idea.

'And the banker is part of it? This is a step up for me – thank you so much!' She hugged and kissed us both. We took two of the younger girls, with sweet voices, Annina and Jacquetta, who would specialise in singing madrigals with party guests. We would look out for other promising young women after we were settled. From then on, I relinquished the name of Tomasina. This was the house of Cecilia Arditti.

~

Our first invitation was to a banquet, arranged at the Chigi villa, at which the Pope was to be the main guest. I arranged for musicians to meet us at my house, then we formed a little procession down the *Via Lunghara* so that people, especially the Farnese next door, would know that Chigi was hosting the Pope. We were then dispersed around the garden, making beautiful tableaus of goddesses, who were then to escort the men to the dining chamber after the Pope had been greeted and taken round us all, beaming. The dining chamber was in a new building, decorated with bright tapestries, which, at the end of the meal, were taken down to reveal that the building, designed by Raffaello, was actually to be Master Chigi's stables!

From this came other invitations: to Cardinal's palaces, to poet's parties, to adorn the audience at entertainments.

One such was a play put on for Pope Leo in honour of Isabella d'Este, the mother of Frederigo Gonzaga, with stage sets by Master Peruzzi. I was asked to supply twenty young women, which meant that Serafina and I had to find eight more than the twelve my house held. We went round the shops and markets to find ones with beauty, or ones who could be made beautiful, and 'borrowed' some; sisters of the painters, of the musicians and dancing masters we used. The house was in uproar as they all were there to change into beautiful dresses before we were taken to the venue near the Vatican in decorated carts, accompanied by the painters waving flags. We had to make sure that, after the performance, the painters' sisters were not mistaken for whores, unless they actually were, and discovered just how good Serafina was at guiding my women towards the richest men, while ensuring the sisters were safe. I knew then that my enterprise was good, even more so when my reputation as a supplier of antiquities became known. I was a courtesan to whom men came for beauty and skill in all its forms.

CHAPTER THIRTY-FOUR

GIULIO

Raffaello was trusting me more and more, allowing me to paint parts of the commissioned easel paintings as well as the frescoes. The technique differed in that the paint powders were mixed not with water but with walnut oil, and later, linseed oil, although the former was the best. This meant that the paints themselves were softer and, when wet, could merge into each other to produce blended colours, making more shades and tones available to the painter. I had learned to prepare canvases for Master Peruzzi, with a coat of white plaster and size, followed by the *imprimatur* - a coat of mixed pigment and earth or clay. This was put all over the dried size of fish glue and flattened with the palm of the hand. I had then placed Raffaello's *cartone* on the canvas, over another piece of paper which had been blackened on one side. The lines were then traced by a point of iron or sharpened wood, ready to be painted. I remember my first placing of the brush into the glistening oil, the colour of sky, and moving it across the prepared canvas. I delighted in the different tones which emphasised the folds of a dress or cloak so well, and became adept very quickly.

I learned how to imitate his style, as did Gianfrancesco, and the way he built up the paint on the canvas, so much of the easel and panel paintings which went out under his name were executed by us. In this way he could accept commissions from smaller churches or less important families. In time, he accepted commissions on the understanding that the paintings would be made by his best assistants – myself and Gianfrancesco. For the Pope and higher clients, he would paint most of the work himself. And there were some which he wanted to paint all himself, when he felt the need to draw away from the demands of St Peter's, his concern to protect the antique ruins and make records of them, and the continual round of supervision and inspection and meetings for new projects.

We were working on the Papal *loggia* at the same time as the Papal rooms, when Leo decided that he wanted to send pictures to Francis I, King of France. At the same time, were being held about building a great villa in the style of Vitruvius on land that the Pope had just purchased on the top of Monte Mario, outside the city, to be known as *La Vigna del Pape*. These two large projects would entail a great organisation of men and time. Antonio da Sangallo, the architect who had worked with Bramante, had joined Raffaello in his work on the *Basilica*, and started on drawings for *La Vigna,* much to my annoyance, and I was given charge of most of the work on the paintings for King Francis and his sister, Marguerita de Valois

We sat down to talk about, and draw, the first ideas for the paintings.

'Holy Family - a close group, with St Elizabeth and John, with Joseph and a couple of angels,' said Raffaello, drawing. 'Mary looking at the child, John looking at him. No-one looking out at the viewer. What do we have?'

I pulled a pile of drawings towards us. Paintings were composed of drawings from many sources. Those we had already made that would suit the composition, drawings made especially for that composition underway, single models or groupings of models. Sometimes the female model would hold wax figures of babies for St John and Christ to get the position of the adult models, hands in the right place. These wax models, sketched in outline, were replaced in the painting by drawings of real children. Sometimes, we draped fabric over legs and arms carved in wood or made of clay, to get the correct shadows and folds. The composition was therefore made of many elements, which were brought together by Raffaello for the final drawing. If we knew where it was to be hung, perhaps as an altarpiece, we would go to the place to take note of the surroundings and in particular from where the light came which would rest on the painting. In this way, we would match the painted light to the real light.

Raffaello was choosing drawings and had begun to make a sketch. I watched as the outline of figures grew.

'It will be Our Lady and Saint Elizabeth holding the young children Jesus and John, very close together, with Saint Joseph looking from behind. Our Lady's head will be central, Saint Joseph's higher, so we will need a balancing person on the other side, behind Saint Elizabeth.'

'Angels?'

'Yes, one holding a garland over Our Lady's head. We don't have the attitudes for Elizabeth and Mary that I want; I don't want them looking at the viewer, I want them looking at the babies. And we'll have new angels as well. You need to make some new drawings for those live models.' I nodded - It would be a chance to spend time with Ceci, with Serafina for Saint Elizabeth.

'Is it inside or outside?'

'Inside, on a marble floor that you do so well, Giulio, but no other detail, concentrate on the group. With a window for light, here, from the left, so it lights Mary's face. We don't know where it will be hung, so we'll have to make the decision and hope someone has the sense to put it in the right place.' This last was said without much hope. We talked about a painting for the sister of King Francis,

'Marguerite de Valois, so we'll make a St Margaret...'

'With the dragon?' Margaret was an early Christian woman who was asked by the Roman governor of her town to be his wife, but he wanted her to give up her religion. She refused, and among other tortures, was swallowed by Satan in the form of a dragon, which spat her out because of the cross she was wearing, although she was eventually put to death. She was therefore a martyr and popular because of her piety. It would be a compliment to the King's sister to be associated with her, and the story gave me the opportunity to depict a frightening animal.

I decided to create the dragon as if it were one of the drawings I had seen in books of the last century; a great mouth gaping open with one or more people inside. I would make it truly terrifying.

'But because it's for the King's sister, it should show a beautiful martyr, not a frightened one. She's to be in perfect shape, no torn clothes or spittle, or whatever comes out of a serpent' was Raphael's command. He asked me to prepare the drawings in between work at the Papal Palace. I went to Trastevere to work with Ceci and Serafina, accompanied by the young apprentice Pico, laden with drapes and a wax baby with moveable limbs.

Serafina was busy with washing when I arrived; Ceci was helping her sort it. She was dressed in a plain simple robe, with her hair up, tucked in a cap. She was sitting down leaning forward with the skirt up over her knees, pulling on sheets. The drapes were dropped on the floor, with the wax baby on top, and Pico sent back. She looked up, smiled. 'Whatever have you got there? What's that hideous thing?'

'Stay like that, don't move. Put your head back the way it was, looking at the sheet. Imagine the sheet is a child you want to pick up.'

'Good morning to you too!' I kissed her, rearranged her head, and placed the baby near to her, so that she would have to stretch out to it.

'Look at the child.'

'Is it crying?'

'No, he's pleased to see you – he wants to be picked up.'

I drew her as Serafina pushed all the sheets into the steaming tub and pounded the clothes up and down with a stout stick. We were surrounded by steam and damp air so I worked quickly before the paper became limp. When Serafina called out for help, two of the younger girls, Annina and Felicità, came down to wring the water out of the sheets, and hang them up outside.

'I shall want you two,' I called to them.

'You want to draw us?' Annina was surprised.

'Of course he does. Clothes on or off?' Felicità raised her skirt up her leg.

'Enough!' Serafina made to slap her but missed. 'Wring out these sheets. then you can pose.'

'Clothes on – I need angels.'

'Then Felicità won't do,' said Annina twisting a sheet. Felicità poked her tongue out.

'I can be angelic', put her hands together, and raised her eyes, singing '*Kyrie eleison*' off key. We groaned. Ceci was trying not to laugh. Serafina hit out at Felicità with the end of a sheet, reaching her this time.

'Get on with it, girl!'. Felicità turned with a pout and a laugh to twist in her turn, spraying water on the floor. This pert new girl, I noted, with her fine breasts, would be an irresistible attraction.

I finished the drawing and asked if we could go upstairs, caught Felicità's grin, and said, 'No – for more poses with the drapes. Serafina, could I draw you together with Ceci?'

'An old woman like me?'

'Yes, I need you for Saint Elizabeth; besides, you have an interesting face.' She frowned as if I were mocking her, but realised I wasn't, then looked pleased.

'You two, before you can be angels you need to hang these sheets up,' she said and followed us upstairs.

I posed Ceci winding drapes around her, with her arms stretched out exactly as I had posed her earlier. Serafina knelt, looking down at the wax baby in her arms. Felicità and Annina came to watch us, sitting cross-legged on the floor. When I had finished the group of two, Ceci stood up and stretched. 'Why don't you draw the girls while I have a walk about?' She helped Serafina from her knees. I posed the girls.

'Imagine you are holding a posy over the head of a bride,' I said to Felicità, and to Annina, You are close to her, looking up at her, like that. Now, can you stay still?'

They could, but were so stiff I had to tell them to relax - and remember to breathe. They gasped and started to giggle. Ceci was arching her back and advised: 'screw up your face tightly, then relax it - and Felicità, you don't have to hold your arms out like sticks. Put them down, and Giulio will tell you when to raise them - so you don't get aches.'

'Have you got a wreath or something she could hold?' Ceci looked around, and saw a circular headdress.

'Here.'

'Arms up.' I posed Felicità, ignoring her flirtatious look. Ceci frowned at her. 'Stop that, you're not at a party, you're an angel. This is serious. It's for the King of France.' Felicità stopped playing about and changed her face into that of an innocent child. Yes, you can be anything you want to be, I thought, convincing, facile, without conscience.

When I'd finished they asked to see the drawings. Felicità giggled.

'Perhaps the King will like me and invite me to France!'

'I can see it's me, but you have made me so… I don't know… what about the babies?' asked Annina, seeing that they were only lightly sketched in.

'I've got some drawings of my brothers already, but I shall visit them for some more.' I turned to Ceci. 'Why don't you come with me? It will be good for you to see Graziosa again, and meet the children.' She sat down suddenly, her face changed. Serafina looked at her quickly and ushered the girls out of the room.

'What is it?' I asked. There were tears in her eyes.

'I can't go back, Giulio, not there.'

'But it's where we made love for the first time.' I sat beside her.

'It's where the baby died, Mama died – don't ask me to go back. Giulio.'

I didn't understand, I couldn't see. It was long ago.

'I know, but there were so many years before that when you – we - were happy. Think of those.' I took her hand.

'I do, I do, but – I was different then Giulio – I was a child.' She dropped my hand and got up. 'It was another life – you go back there all the time. I – I have cut it off. I have built a wall around it. I can't let that fall.' I got up.

'I'll leave the drapes with you, for next time.'

'Oh, Giulio, don't go!' She came to grasp my hands. 'Please! I'm being silly!' I tasted salt as I kissed her.

'It's all right, if you really don't want to come.' She smothered my words with her lips, letting the outer layer of drapes fall to the floor.

~

For the next week I was busy in the *loggia*, supervising the underdrawings of the bible scenes. It was some time before Raffaello was free to look at the drawings and agree the composition for the Holy Family.

'The old woman is perfect, but I'm not sure about the angels – this one is too…fulsome.' Lascivious, I thought, how I saw her. 'And the other is too stiff. I like the idea of the wreath, though. Perhaps you could re-do them with the lads?'

I nodded. I had wasted my time, but it was my fault.

'We need a Joseph. Find the Joseph drawings.' These were in a box, men with beards in various attitudes. He picked out one. 'This one – set him behind Our Lady.' He sat down to draw the composition. He changed Ceci's face, made it rounder, softer, sweeter, but kept Serafina as I had drawn her.

I set out the painting, and, in between the fresco projects, I painted it.

~

I was working on the composition of the painting of St Margaret. I made two drawings of the dragon, long curled tail, mouth open with lots of teeth, one with its head on the side, another with its head upside down so that its eyes gleamed out. When I showed Ceci the drawings, she pretended to be afraid of the serpent; she shivered.

'You've made them seem so real!'

'You needn't be scared, he's dead – but if he wasn't –' I crawled over her making what I thought were serpent roars, and tickled her until she pleaded with me to stop. I changed the tickles to caresses...

In the workshop, Raffaello looked at the dragons side by side and decided on the one with the eyes; it had a wing next to it midway between the head and the coiled tail. 'I like this, he really looks as if he has spat out something horrid! She can be standing on the tail, stepping forward, away from the evil...' He drew over the dragon. I nodded. 'So prepare the *cartone*...

The other dragon was not wasted: we often persuaded those who asked us for paintings to have one very like those we were working on so as to use the preparatory drawings we had already made. At the request of an ambassador for Charles V, newly ruler of the Spanish Empire, I made my own version of

St Margaret, using the other dragon, with Ceci as St Margaret, standing inside the dragon's curled tail, looking down at it. I wanted to show the saint's triumph over it. The two paintings were on easels next to each other, so I could move from one to the other, working on the dragon and the background on the one on which Raffaello would complete his Saint, and the other which was entirely my own.

With the two paintings together, I could how my painting, when not under the supervision of Raffaello, was different from his. The forms had harder edges, the colours were stronger, the faces had none of their (his) innocence. His Saint Margaret, leaving the dragon, having no connection with it, was as sweet as his Madonnas, with a little smile, her limbs fluid, an idealised woman, holding just a stick. Mine was knowing: she had a connection with the dragon, she looked at it, firmly holding a cross; she had conquered it, she stayed within it, touching it, her face showed no sympathy for it. Her limbs were strong, her pose confident. She was, of course, Ceci. The women I painted in the frescoes and in the monochromes underneath them were directly from the prostitutes: their poses were bold, hip tilted to one side, hands on hips, faces bold and knowing: many drawn from prostitutes I visited elsewhere, for sex not love.

For another client, I made a painting which closely imitated the composition of Raffaello's earlier Madonna holding the child close in a *tondo* – a circular painting – which he'd painted four years ago, and I found in the studio. I re-painted this with Ceci's face, and the child looking outwards, without the second child, Saint John. This pleased me – I had placed them against darkness illuminated by a single candle light behind them, and as if the viewer was holding another light in front of them. So I achieved bright eyes for both mother and child, and the smile I knew so well.

In other pictures, I painted backgrounds of the Roman ruins, very precise and true so they could be recognised. I used these in a work commissioned from Raffaello, but which I painted totally, a Saint Stephen, being stoned. I used faces from my studies of Trajan's column, and I knew that they were fiercer than any Raffaello himself would have painted, but he was pleased with the result. He sent me to Naples to paint Isabel of Requesens, the wife of Ramón of Cardona, viceroy of Naples. This was a commission made for Cardinal Bibbiena to send to King Francis, who knew how he loved beautiful women (he's not alone in that) and I was excited that Raffaello had asked me to go and paint her on my own.

She sat in the most gorgeous dress I had ever seen, dark red with gold lined sleeves, her hair loose over her shoulder and a red hat with jewels.

Behind her I painted a servant looking out over the balcony and at the side of her, two lion face sculptures. I liked drawing animals, I drew dogs and cats for my step-brothers and sisters, and I made drawings of rams and ewes drinking at the side of Ceci and Ginetta for a bible picture, the meeting of Jacob and Rachel, for the ceiling of the Pope's *loggia*. Animals began to turn up in my Madonna paintings; in one of those I painted with Ceci and Serafina I included a little white lap dog. In another I drew a cat, which I copied to take to Ceci; I thought she would love it, for it was Prettycat. She took it in her hands, and stoked it as if it was real. I remembered how she was when I asked her to come to the *Macello* with me, and was sorry I had brought it.

'I'm sorry I've upset you again.' I tried to take the picture from her.

'No – no – it's lovely. She was so beautiful – it's just like her. She brought her kittens to see us, then took them away. I saw her sometimes on the streets, she used to come up to me, but she never came back to the house.'

'You can keep it – it's for you.'

'Thank you, Giulio.' She kissed it.

A month or so later, I took her a basket. As I gave it to her, the basket mewed: a kitten in the same colours. For a moment I wondered if I had done the right thing, but she laughed and took it out.

'It's a boy –'

'But it's still Prettycat!' She cuddled it, and I realised I wouldn't get her attention for a while, so drew them both instead. I didn't mention visiting the *Macello* again. I had no idea then what she was talking about when she said she had built a wall against it. Now, in Mantua, I do.

CHAPTER THIRTY-FIVE

GIULIO   Rome, 1519

Agostino Chigi, who was rumoured to be unwell, made three decisions: the first, to write his will. The second, to marry the mother of his, now four, children, Francesca Ordeaschi; this was clearly to legitimise his two sons and make sure the fortune, and his villa, stayed in the family. His third decision was to have the unpainted entrance *loggia* decorated, to be ready for the wedding day, for which he, of course, turned to Raffaello. A story was chosen, appropriately centred on the wedding of a god with a mortal girl, Cupid and Psiche.

I went to tell Ceci, who was sewing, and was therefore in a bad mood. She said she hoped Francesca didn't see that as insulting, the story – aping a banker, nicknamed 'Il Magnifico' - the 'god', marrying a courtesan.

'But of course she's with him for the life they lead and wants to keep it for her sons, so perhaps she can suffer the inference.' She broke the thread she was pulling from a spool with her teeth. 'It's what women do,' she muttered, missing the eye of the needle. She cursed, sucked the end of the thread, screwed up her eyes and tried again. 'And which of us will be lovesick Psiche?' She pulled the thread through too quickly and it came out. 'Mother of God!' she swore, threw down the needle and the cloth she was sewing, and glared at me. I raised my hands in supplication.

'I'll let you know,' I said and left her to it.

~

Once more old drawings were pulled out and gone through, but most were discarded, because this vault was to be something new. A pagan theme, gods and goddesses: nude gods and goddesses. Nudes had been painted before, but for private places, noblemen's bedrooms: these were to be something not seen before in a place to where the public were invited. It was daring indeed.

Raffaello's Galatea had been draped superbly to suggest full nudity, but this time we were to dispense with that. Chigi had told Raffaello about the nudes painted in Venice, and as always, Raffaello liked to please his client. He asked me to make new drawings 'of undressed models' and left the clothed Psiche to Gianfrancesco.

We went out to the villa to take measurements and to observe how the vault could be divided. First we stood on the Galatea *loggia* and looked up at the vault.

The vault would be the sky, a continuation of the real sky, and extension of the garden. Festoons of leaves, fruit and flowers would follow the bones of the vault, and in the centre would be a pair of illusionistic tapestries, imitating the canopies that would be set up in the garden for the wedding guests. The work had to be done fast, for a date of the end of August was set for the reading of the will and the wedding ceremony. Gianfrancesco and I spent time at the house of Cecilia drawing the women in pose after pose, mostly nude, for Juno, Venus, Ceres, Psiche. Pico posed for a young Mercury, Zeus was taken from a statue, the cherubs from stock drawings and wax limbs. The 'tapestries' were designed entirely by me, and were groups made out of drawings and paintings I had done before. The angel holding a circlet over the Madonna's head, which I had painted into the Holy Family for King Francis, was repeated, with butterfly wings, hovering over the bride with two companions.

Giovanni drew up a collection of drawings of fruit, flowers, birds, and 'attributes' - the objects associated with the gods and goddesses - for the cherubs to carry. Raffaello was intrigued enough to draw a Venus receiving a pot from Psiche, and chose Livia's face for Venus and Annina for Psiche. The others Psiches were Ginetta. Ceci became a pointing Venus next to Cupid, posed by a beautiful boy found by Giovanni.

There was scaffolding across the whole room, and several painters worked at the same time, including Gianfrancesco's brother Luca, Raffaellino delle Colle, whom I had trained, Vincenzo di San Gimignano. Two or more teams, with their plasterers, and apprentices making paints, worked there at the same time.

I assigned the painters to each of the sections, and worked on the Venus (Ceci) over the entrance to the Galatea *loggia*. Raffaello came in several times to assess the work, to assure Chigi that he was in charge. As each section was finished, Giovanni painted the festoons of leaves covered with fruit, vegetables and flowers: apples, oranges, pomegranates, squashes, aubergines, lilies, daisies. Over one section, where young Mercury's hand is towards the sky, he painted a bottle gourd penetrating a quince - there were other fruits that had equally erotic shapes. He also painted exquisite birds around the many cherubs, who were dipping and diving in the spandrels, making the vault full of movement and excitement.

I took Ceci to see the *loggia* when it was finished. There was Livia as Venus in her chariot, Felicità flirting with an absurdly young Zeus. Annina and Ginetta, for some reason fully-clothed, were chatting with both mouths and hands to a nude Venus. Giovanni's Ercole as a mature Mercury carried a quite content Psiche across the sky. Zeus grasped the face of a Cupid with huge wings, obviously telling him off.

'Oh look, that poor boy!' she laughed. 'and I love the gossiping women, Ginetta is just like that! And Felicità, flirting of course, and Livia, her lips turned down, even as Venus, she's miserable!' She turned round and round, looking up. 'And that's Ercole isn't it? What a handsome Mercury he makes – oh and Pico, a young Mercury – and what is he pointing at? Ooooh!' She giggled. It was the gourd and the fig.

'There are more like that.' I pointed them out.

'Oh Giulio, all this nudity, it will be the talk of Rome! And I am sure not all of it will be in approval – it's so public. '

'What about Michelangelo's work? And the antique statues? They're nude.'

'Yes, but they're statues, they are very still by their stone nature. These are so real, they're moving! Those two women chattering, just like any Roman women.' She had not commented on the Venus with the beautiful boy with wings. I turned her round to face it.

'What do you think of Venus?' She stared.

'It's you Ceci.'

'That isn't me, I don't look like that.'

'Yes you do.'

'No I'm thinner, harder – she looks like…' My drawing had been subtly shaped by Raffaello. He had softened my crisp outlines and made her into the dreamlike, utterly beautiful, entrancing Ceci I had loved in the moonlight.

I could not surpass his portrait of her. I could capture her stance, the brightness of her eyes, her hair, her assertiveness, but the gentleness was out of my reach. This was the portrait I knew I wanted to paint of her, but my style had developed in such a way that I could not. Even the drawing of her when we first made love was brilliant rather than soft.

She had stood there for a long time looking up.

'She looks like someone I wanted to be.' She looked sad. 'Even as a child I wasn't like that – I was rude, I wanted to be a boy. I was tough. If I hadn't been so, I wouldn't have survived.'

'But you are like that, I've seen you.'

'Raffaello hasn't. He has idealised your drawing, she isn't even Venus, the one who bribed Paris to choose her as the most beautiful goddess. This is a beauty, as only Raffaello could create.' I should have been mortified, but she was right.

Raffaello painted women who were unreal, women who had not suffered as Ceci had. If they had, he painted it away. It was Ceci, but not the whole Ceci, not the one I held in my hands. Yet the picture of her, up there, was a painting without flaw, a painting that spoke love. My two loves, Raffaello and Ceci.

She laughed and twisted round to me.

'It's certainly nothing to do with the suggestive courgette! Do they grow them here?' she said archly, and placed her hand on my thigh.

'It's a good thing the family's not here!' I laughed 'Would you like to see the summer house over the river, where they catch the fish?'

We wandered through the garden, passing gardeners, including Felipe, whom I had met at Ceci's house when he was advising on the garden. He waved to us and smiled. Ceci sang all the way, substituting words of love and flowers with sexual words. This was the whole Ceci, this was the real flesh and blood, funny, passionate, tough. We didn't make love, we just sat on the steps down to the enclosure which trapped fish, and watched them swimming in and out.

It was after that I made a visit to the goldsmith, Benevento Cellini, to give him instructions for a commission.

The wedding took place. Ceci was commanded to provide flower girls, dressed in flimsy fabrics with garlands made of real leaves and headdresses. They were to hand out posies to the visiting ladies, and then entertain the single gentlemen. I was invited, with Gianfrancesco and Giovanni, as part of Raffaello's party, and somehow the handsome Ercole was included, to the delight (if not the satisfaction) of the ladies.

The *loggia* design really worked. Festoons of real leaves and flowers flowed out from the arches into the garden along temporary pergolas. Tables were laid out under painted canopies, copies of my tapestries inside. There were huge floral arrangements around jugs which would tip wine into cups at the touch of a handle. Flags and pennants fluttered from poles. Inside, the walls underneath the vaults had not been painted for there had not been enough time, so they were covered with real, rich tapestries. Musicians sat under them, playing, while a group of singers with part-books stood waiting for their turn. The smell of roasting meat, vegetables and spices combined with the scents which were sprayed around by boys employed to do just that, all day.

There was a buzz of chatter and laughter as we waited in the gardens for the Pope, lined up either side of the main path. Chigi and Francesca's children, dressed in brocades, took their places on the steps leading into the *loggia*, each with a basket of rose petals. The wedding couple appeared at the top of the steps, with four trumpeters, two either side of them, framed by the arches. There was a clatter of horses by the stables, and the Pope was helped off his horse onto the ground. This was the signal for the trumpeters, and for Chigi and Francesca to descend the steps to greet him.

The Pope passed between us, two fingers aloft blessing us as he walked, women bobbed, men bowed, as we all crossed ourselves. The flower girls spread rose petals on the ground in front of him as he walked forward. He was followed by eight Cardinals and his usual large entourage of family members and favourites, including his dwarf, Marioana, who walked behind the Cardinals, aping their pompous strides.

Pope Leo was greeted by the couple, and then led up to the first floor room, with the Cardinals, where the marriage was to take place. We all stood around, murmuring and trying not to giggle, until the trumpets sounded and we all cheered. The happy couple, the Pope and the Cardinals all came down the staircase and into the newly finished *loggia*. They reached the tops of the steps, and acknowledged the cheers and the applause. Chigi made a signal and the musicians began, not just the ones in the *loggia*, but groups of them dotted around the tables, which stretched into the gardens on either side of both *logge*. Servants with trays of food came out of the villa: an endless succession of pies, pastries, joints, bread, fruit, sugar shapes. The crowd got noisier, and drunk, as the afternoon turned into evening, and lanterns were lit, to rivals the stars shone above us. The garden was scented, not just by the perfumes sprayed by the boys, but by orange blossom and jessamine and became the top of Mount Olympus itself. The sound of cicadas underpinned the sound of the music, talk and laughter. Ceci and Ginetta floated about, smiling and kissing hands, laughing - and avoiding being groped too grossly.

When the Pope had gone, they came to find us.

This was the moment. I took Ceci by the hand and led her to a fountain depicting two lovers. There were others sitting on the stone benches around it, drinking from superb Venetian glasses which sparkled in the soft lights. They did not matter. We perched on the sides of the pool where the ripples of water were tinged with lights from the lanterns, and in which Ceci moved her fingers.

'There is only you now, Giulio, no others, no clients. Just you.' It was as if she knew; of course she did.

The lantern-light made her face glow and her dress change colour from gold to grey and back again, like shot silk, as her body moved gently in tune with the ripples. The talk of those around us faded as we became one with the water.

I took from my pocket the finished commission from Cellini. I lifted one hand and slid it onto a finger: a gold band with ends forming leaves, which clutched a set of five lapis lazuli stones in the shape of a speedwell flower. I turned her hand so the light made the deep blue lapis glimmer.

'A painter's gift,' she said, moving her eyes from mine to the ring.

'A painter's love – forever – until death.'

She smiled 'Forever. Until death.'

We both believed it was true.

CHAPTER THIRTY-SIX

CECI Rome 1520

Raffaello was ill, Giulio and Gianfrancesco were taking it in turns to be with him, to watch him in fever, and to supervise the workshop.

'He's weak, they've bled him, and he sleeps most of the time - he doesn't eat,' came the message from them. It was the week before Easter, and I led the women into *Santa Dorothea* to pray for him. The church was swathed with black drapes, a painter was touching up the statue of Our Lady which would be carried through the streets, to meet the statue of Christ from *San Pietro*. We could hear the choir practising for Easter Day. I tried to pray, I could see Ginetta's lips moving rapidly as she gazed up at the crucifix. The others, who had only seen Raffaello, had not met him, prayed because they knew he was loved by the painters.

I repeated 'save Raffaello' several times, but I did not believe God would hear me, or do as I asked. I was quite sure that He was there but I also thought He was impassive. He just watched us, making mistakes, knowing that we would answer for these at our deaths; He did nothing to prevent us making them. Holy Week always affected me this way, the meeting of the Madonna and Christ statues brought a lump to my throat, a mother and her dead child. Mary was worshipped, as Christ's mother, but I had never lost that question about why God had used her so, why she was put through that pain. There thoughts were with me, every Holy Week. Such that on Easter Sunday, which was supposed to be the time for rejoicing for everlasting life, the mother of Jesus was forgotten.

I tried to get my thoughts back to Raffaello. I wondered about Margarita, his favourite. Would she be with him? Giulio had not mentioned her. I prayed for her, that she was there, that she was able to be with him. Raffaello couldn't die! I pleaded, but my heart was heavy.

Then Agostino Chigi died. He lay in Santa Maria del Popolo where Raffaello had painted his chapel. I went with Serafina to pay my respects, but I did not attend the funeral. I worried about the investment. Chigi had had a good return so far, and I hoped the family would allow it to continue. The business was well-established enough to carry on, surely. I knew, though, that they might ask for the money back; if that was the case, would I have to sell everything? I started to make an inventory, just in case. I couldn't discuss this with Giulio, he was too concerned with keeping the work going and in looking after Raffaello. I hadn't seen much of him.

GIULIO

The smell of the room was held within its walls, heavy with urine and a noxious stale smell of suppuration. My hand went to my mouth and nose instinctively.

'You need come no further.' The croaked voice was hardly recognisable of Raffaello. 'I know how it smells.'

I dropped my hand and disobeyed him, moving towards a stool beside his bed. The face on the pillow was grey with red streaks of a rash, cheeks sunken. His mouth was covered in sores. The eyes glittered and fluttered back and forth as if he could not see, and his hair stayed on the pillow as he moved his head from one side to side, seeking to know where I was.

'Giulio,' he rasped, 'my will is made...' He stopped to breathe, the sound of bellows in a forge. 'You and Gian –

Gianfranc– you will complete my works – the studio – and all – all -' He coughed up phlegm onto the already-stained sheet.

'Everything is yours'.

'Don't talk.' I could feel the tears starting, tried to control them.

'Don't cry, Giulio.' It would have been a smile. 'I have loved you.'

I couldn't stop the sob; it was covered by his rasping.

'And I you, Master – Raffaello.' I looked for his hand but it was under the covers.

'My hand – not for grasping.' I knew the hands, the rest of his body, would be covered in pustules. It was the smell of the French disease, caught long ago, now in its final, deathly stage. He shut his eyes. Without the eyes, the face was that of a cadaver, the skin sunken into the skull.

'Go,' he said, 'do not come back.'

I ran down the stairs and out of the house, vomited into the street. The smell was in my nose, Raffaello's face in my mind. I tried to cover it with his real face, the laughter, the smile, with the faces of his Madonnas, sweet, gentle, like him. I slid to the ground within the darkness, sobbed and failed to see the stars. The dawn would rise on the Friday of Holy Week, the day Christ journeyed to Calvary with his cross. I pictured him with the face of Raffaello. I opened my mouth to howl. Two men stopped.

'Don't crucify him – take him now!' I said out loud.

'Madman!' said one. They walked quickly away. The street was still, dark grey, silent.

A breath of wind passes over my face, then another; a rustle of leaves, a sigh.

A woman comes out of the door with a boy; pointing in one direction. She watches him go, turns and sees me. I don't look up.

The women - for the washing and laying out.

'He's gone.' She goes back in.

I know. I heard.

CECI

There being no parties or requests for Holy Week, we were at home, and I set everyone to mending their clothes, tidying the house, preparing food for the end of Lent. The younger women, Annina and Felicità, laughed as they swept, gossiping about their clients and giggling. Livia was her usual morose self. Again I wondered how she managed to turn herself into a sparkling companion for work. I once asked her, in exasperation, why she couldn't be cheerful at home.

'The work takes everything out of me, pretending to be happy, even though I know some man is going to crawl all over me and do things I don't want.' She looked away from me. 'I'm entitled to be miserable in my own time, don't you think?' I had to agree that this was a point of view.

'But it makes the rest of us miserable,' I pointed out. She raised her eyes.

'I do this to survive, not because I want to. I would give up the finery just to be on a farm milking cows.' Which wasn't at all true. If any woman fussed about her clothes and adornments as much as Livia, I would like to see her. Besides, I'm not sure she'd ever seen cows being milked let alone a farm. She sighed and promised to do better.

Today she sat mending clothes, which I recognised belonged to the younger ones. I saw her smile at their silliness and realised that she loved them as if they were her sisters, or daughters. She hadn't stopped moaning, but did it more quietly.

The day of Good Friday dawned and the bells tolled. Crowds of people were waiting outside for the procession. We got ready for church, standing in our black veils to follow that procession. There was a knock at the door, and Serafina let in Pico, the apprentice who had come with news before. He was white-faced. I knew what he was going to say.

'Raffaello - he's dead. He started to cry. The sounds of the crowd gathering outside, feet shuffling, muted conversation filtered through the still-open door. The younger ones cried and Ginetta made them sit down. The bell was tolling for Raffaello, not for Christ. Serafina crossed herself.

'God bless him,' Ginetta said. He must be loved by God to be taken on this day'. I took charge.

'Come on, we must go outside to see the Easter procession and send our prayers for Raffaello to God with the Virgin and her son.' I swept them all out. It was hot, the sky blue and bright, the sun's light screaming down. It shouldn't be – or was it welcoming Raffaello to heaven? What superstition; for children. Not us. Raffaello was dead. The drum beat shot through the whispering crowds. As they marched:

Step, step, step – stop, pause – step, step, step – stop, pause - step step - stop, pause, step step... *Ra – pha – el* stop *Ra – pha – el* stop pause *is dead* stop pause *- is - dead*

The beat went through my ears and out of my eyes. I thought of the kind, the polite, the talented man and let the tears flow. The statue of Our Lady, grieving, carried aloft, passed by, followed by the Crucifix. The day after tomorrow, it would be the celebration of the resurrection of Christ. Not of Raffaello.

~

Raffaello's body lay covered in rich brocade on the bier, surrounded by every painter and artisan in Rome. His painting of the *Transfiguration*, on which he had been working, was placed at his head. The body was carried through the Borgo, with Giulio and Gianfrancesco walking in front of it, to *Piazza di San Pietro* where the Pope was waiting.

We walked behind the men, with almost every courtesan

and whore in Rome. I looked for Margherita, the beloved of Raffaello, but could not see her. We crowded into the square to watch the bier stop and Leo came out on the *loggia*. People close to him said he was crying. Cardinal Giulio dei Medici, who was the leader for the creation of *La Vigna del Pape* on Monte Mario, walked with a group of priests to join the procession, which turned to pass the Castello and over the bridge. Raffaello would be buried in the Pantheon as he had requested. The streets were lined with silent people, women throwing flowers, men bowing their heads. Women of wealth were crying openly on their balconies, their men joining the procession. Every church on the way tolled it's bell as the bier passed. It was astonishing and moving to see how well Raffaello was respected.

The Cardinals and the priests followed the bier into the huge building, followed by the crowd. We women stood close together, just outside the portico, like a choir of veiled angels. Indeed, from inside came a chant of great solemnity. The square was full of people, so silent were we at the portico, we could hear the priests, the large interior amplifying their voices. We knew when to cross ourselves during the mass, and the gesture was repeated like a wave through the crowd, right up to and past the great church of *Santa Maria sopra Minerva.*

When the mass was finished, the Cardinal and priests left and passed through the crowd, blessing us as they did; a wave of bowed heads and crossing hands followed them, and the crowd dispersed. The painters were inside watching the internment, some sobbing. Ginetta and I waited, sending the women home with Serafina and Giuseppe, our newly acquired manservant. We sat on the step waiting, in case we were wanted. Gerolama and Catarina, Gianfrancesco's sister, came to join us.

Gradually the painters came out. Perino del Vaga came to take Caterina, his wife away, Lorenzetto and Polidoro came out, greeted us, and walked away with Gerolama. Then came Gianfrancesco and his brothers, Luca and Bartolomeo. Ginetta put her arms round Gianfrancesco, whose face was wet with tears, and the four went off together. Alone, I stood up and looked through the door for Giulio. He stood, watching men finish adjusting the sarcophagus to secure it into a niche in the wall. They picked up their tools and walked away. There were a few people in groups who took their final leave, crossing themselves. Some went up to Giulio to embrace him. I recognised *Il Sodoma* and Peruzzi, and another architect, Benedetto San Gallo. There were one or two others priests and laymen, who were looking round the building, up at the dome. Whispering.

I went into that vast space; the light through the oculus made a perfect sun-shape on the floor. The vault was so high overhead you could fall backwards just looking up at it. The arches of the ancient building enclosed swathed niches, where there once were statues, there were now tall candles. An altar with a cross was inside the arch immediately opposite the great doors. The men inside, and I, were dwarves. The child Giulio had told me this place was built by giants. The other dwarves left. I stood on one side of the marble sun on the floor. Just us, and the vast distance between us. The air between us stirred, shivered and lengthened, its heat-haze made his form uncertain. I saw it shorten. He had gone down onto his knees, was touching the sarcophagus. The air carried his sobs into the niches, into the vault, up through the oculus.

I did not go to him, I was not wanted there. I would not intrude into that circle of grief. I could not comfort him for this, not now, perhaps not ever. I turned away, my tears not for Raffaello but for him, in the knowledge that he would not share his sorrow with me; his love for Raffaello did not include me. I walked out of the building. I walked as if in a bubble which stretched and stretched until it burst, and sprang away to enclose just Giulio. I felt pain in my breast. The love between us would change now Raffaello was dead. I shivered.

There would be no house built for us, no life together, not now. I wept.

Giulio came to the house; he had been drinking and did not speak. His eyes were red. He took me in his arms and his love-making was rough and short-lived, unshared. Unlike any other time; could have been any woman. I held him in my arms as he slept and told myself it was the grief, and I should be glad he had come to me, not a stranger. Yet that is who I felt I was that night.

CHAPTER THIRTY-SEVEN

GIULIO

After Raffaello's death, at his bequest, Gianfrancesco and I took over the work. Part of *La Vigna del Pape* had been built and was being used for parties, even though we were far from finishing the painting. We had to fit this around visits of the Pope's guests, ambassadors and anyone else who wanted to see this great marvel, an imitation with the antique buildings. Raffaello had designed it following Vitruvius's writings exactly, with architectural quotations from the huge, silent ruins. The arches of the *loggia*, leading to a terrace, were as high as those built for *San Pietro* by Bramante, the only part of the new basilica which had been completed. It was the *loggia* of *La Vigna* which needed to be completed with paint and stucco. Giovanni and I worked at it, but we argued. We quarrelled about the scenes that should be painted, how they would balance with unpainted stucco reliefs. Giovanni wanted a great deal, if not all, of the *loggia* to be in stucco relief to show off his fine work. He had finally mastered the technique of the fine white plaster: the white lime of travertine mixed with ground white marble reduced to a fine powder.

Gianfrancesco came in one day to find painters idling in the garden and us shouting at each other. I was accusing Giovanni of starting to place stucco where I had designed a painted surface, and he was insisting that we had agreed.

'I've got all the pieces prepared,' said Giovanni, pointing to the crates of stuccowork, 'why would I have done that if it hadn't been agreed that this is my space – and here and here!'

he indicated areas at the tops of the arches. 'The spandrels as well as the underarches were to be in stucco only!'

'No! The spandrels and are to be painted, and your stucco frames them! The underarches are also to be painted – here! Here are the drawings!' I pointed to the rolls unravelling on the floor. 'These -' I waved at the idlers '- are here to paint, not to fix stucco! God in heaven, who's in charge here?'

'Raffaello always put me in charge of the stucco, the animals and the birds. If you do all that painting, the balance between colour and whiteness will be spoilt.'

'Raffaello put me in charge! Goddamn you – *figlio di puttana!* – sodomist!'

Giovanni raised his fist and would have come at me had not Gianfrancesco come between us.

'For God's sake, both of you! We have enough to do without you taking time to quarrel!'

Giovanni scowled at me and I at him.

'And Giulio, don't mention Raffaello's name in the same breath as an insult.' He turned to the idlers.

'You are contracted to paint, then do so!' They rose and looked hesitantly at each other. 'Come on!' he roared indicating the scaffolding up to the underarches.

'Giulio, Giovanni, I'm tired of your quarrels - you will have to work away from each other. And Giovanni, you start over the other side, on the pillars. Giulio, you work at the other end.' Gianfrancesco rarely got angry, but he was like a lion when he did.

'There is so little time to finish – I came to tell you that Peruzzi has agreed to help us by painting the main dome – as long as he can make the drawing for it. I'm not going to consult you on that, I'm just going to ask him to do it - you two are unlikely to get it done!' He picked up the rolls and began to give them out to the painters, then pushed the waiting boys towards the plaster pots and the paint pots.

'Get on with it! I will not stay, I have a design of my own to work on!'

I left *La Vigna* that evening and made my way through the city to my old home in the *Macello*. My father was ill, indeed, he had made his will, making me responsible for my stepbrothers and sisters. I feared he would die soon, and, as well as grieving, as I knew I would, I would have to take on that responsibility. *La Vigna* was behind schedule and I was eager to get on with a design for a villa on the Janiculum hill at the edge of Trastevere for Master Peruzzi Turini. In addition, there was an anxiety that we might have to find somewhere else to live and work; we were still in Raffaello's house, but already there was talk of us having to move out.

My visits to Ceci became less and less because of the work and the worry. She was busy as ever with the organisation of the girls to parties and accompanying them herself. I became short-tempered with her, and convinced myself that she was hiring herself out too. One of the evenings she went out with the women, leaving me to get myself some food. I was in the kitchen when I heard a sound behind me. I turned. There was Felicità, in a gauzy gown, which left nothing to the imagination. I thought they had all gone with Ceci.

'Oh – I've come down for some milk,' she said opening her eyes.

'What are you doing here?'

'I couldn't go; I have a fever.' She passed a hand over her forehead. 'But it's gone now.'

She passed close to me, and I could breathe in her warm, sweaty smell. I reacted like a dog after a bitch, caught hold of her and kissed her soundly. She giggled, and put her hand on my cock, which needed no excuse to rise. And there, in the kitchen floor, we coupled. It was over in minutes. I dragged myself up.

'Giulio! I have long wanted you, Giulio!' she said, reaching up to me. 'Why not make me happy?'

I turned away, feeling nothing, and left her, returning to Raffaello' s house. I went to work on the drawings for the new villa by the light of one candle, which was all we had as no-one had ordered anymore, and the boys were too shy to remind us. I drew until my eyes ached, and I wanted to sleep. As I lay in bed, I remembered the encounter. Felicità was flighty, she had been easy. There had been no emotion, just relief. This is what I wanted, not the emotion I felt with Ceci, not the overpowering desire for her whole self. It got in the way of my work. I decided I needed to cut myself off from her. From then, I didn't go back. Gianfrancesco asked me if I had quarrelled with Ceci too.

'It's none of your business' I told him, and he didn't mention her again. I worked in the last of the rooms commissioned for the Pope. I painted easel paintings, I drew plans. I visited a high-class brothel when I had the need. There, I paid to draw the girls and the men in different sexual positions, and laughed grimly at how absurd they looked. I became obsessed with drawing as many positions as I could, and asked them to try things that were different, and, often, unsuccessful.

The giggling that followed this often resulted in me taking over from the male 'model'. This pure physicality was my escape from my mind, my work; from Ceci.

No word came from Ceci. Raffaello's house, which had been looked after by servants, became untidy, dirty, uncared for. I often did not wash unless I was to visit a client, but I did. Pico gradually took over and found maids to clean and cook; it was he, acting as my assistant, who made sure that the boys were fed and warm, I noted this, but failed to comment upon it or thank him.

There came a request from Frederico, Marquis of Mantua, the boy who picked up sexual tricks from Vanozza's girls, for the services of Raffaello's assistants at his court. The request came through Master Peruzzi Castiglione, a friend of Raffaello's whom I had met once or twice, Frederico's courtier, his advisor, and his representative in Rome. Castiglione asked me to visit him.

'The Marquis Frederico wants one of you to become court artist at Mantua,' Castiglione told me, and I explained to him that we had too much to do in Rome, for the Pope himself among other high-class people. Castiglione said he would report this to Frederico, who then replied that he wanted one of us, and that he would wait.

'Why would a Marquis wait?'

'Because you are pupils of Raffaello,' he said simply.

'And that is all?'

'He can't have Raffaello, and we know, in any case, that Raffaello wouldn't have been in the least interested in leaving Rome. But he wants someone who can paint like Raffaello.'

'I have my own style – and I'm not just a painter.' I told him about the Villa Lante, the design of which had been accepted by Turini and plans for it were then being drawn up. 'I'm an architect. I want to make buildings, and then decorate them.'

'The Marquis does want to build,' mused Castiglione.

'I trained with Peruzzi and well as helping Raffaello with the *La Vigna,* of which I now have full charge.' It was not altogether a lie, for Gianfrancesco and I had not discussed its progress for many days.

'I will write to the Marquis.'

The result of this was that I was asked to be a consultant for the renewal of a castle in Mantua along the new 'antique' style. This I was prepared to do, but I was not prepared to leave

Rome. I saw my future with Pope Leo, and with creating villa after villa in the building of the 'new' Rome.

CHAPTER THIRTY-EIGHT

CECI

I heard his footsteps on the stairs; he seemed excited. I hadn't seen him for a while, and was pleased when he entered the room, smiling. He presented a portfolio of drawings.

'What are those?' I was arranging flowers in a vase, and just glanced at it.

'Mine!' he put it on the table next to where I was working. I stopped with a lily in each hand.

'Yes, but what?'

'Drawings – look!' He put them on the bed '*I Modi* - the Positions. They'll be exclusive to those who can afford it, not for the general public.'

'What sort of positions?' I added some foliage, thinking it was some sort of architectural term that I'd failed to pick up.

'Sexual.' He threw himself onto the bed and grinned.

'What? Not of me I hope?' I held a stem poised over the vase. He turned the first page towards me.

'No, not of you. I've collected these over the last ten years - in various places.'

'Brothels.' I stabbed a stem into the vase: why wasn't I enough for him? He had told me once that he used others for purely physical reasons – with me, it was different, it was my body and my soul. Was it not the same for me? *Yes – but – but we live together now, and I have no others. I thought, but did not say.*

I looked and saw I had crushed the petals in my hand.

'Yes – and at painters' parties. I'm thinking of giving them to Marcantonio for prints, to make some money. Look!' I looked – a man and a woman on a mattress lying close together, her leg over his, lips frozen together, not doing very much.

'They don't look very enthusiastic - bored really.' I left the vase and flopped down beside him. 'And I suppose you were just there to draw?'

'Of course!' he leaned over to get a pear and started to suck noisily. 'Have a look – go on.' I drew the folios on my knees, turned over to the next one.

'They're a bit posey aren't they?'

'Statues,' he said. 'Classical poses – the antique. There's one with Hercules in there.'

'Oh yes – I should have guessed.' The third one was rather beautiful, a boy with curly hair looking at the girl who was intent on guiding his cock towards her.

'I can believe in these two – as lovers.'

'You and me,' he said, lying on his back. I felt irritated, scratchy.

'Not a bit like you – much more handsome - maybe she's a little bit like me though, at my professional best. I turned over two pages.

'Boring – mechanical - oooh! This is a bit more lively! and this one – except if her hand slips, it'll spoil it and they'll fall off the bed!' The next one was totally athletic in a way that made me turn it to one side and laugh, despite myself.

'Impossible - no human being could do that!'

'That's why he's a satyr – look at his ears – they can do inhuman things, satyrs.' I laughed as I saw he had drawn the bed end having a lionhead with a serpent's tail; the lion was immensely interested in the efforts being made on the bed.

'Will they make it – he's saying. I doubt it! and it's another case of falling over!' The next two I had to turn upside down.

'Yes, I know they're not convincing. I had to draw quickly as the models were trembling with trying to keep their rear ends in the air!' The following one was so subdued that the lion had fallen asleep, then they were off the bed altogether.

'Oh, look, that's not Serafina looking round the door – oh that's cruel! She's much nicer looking than this old crone!'

'My imagination – I've not actually seen Serafina look like that, unless the money we gave her wasn't enough.'

'Oh no, Giulio, you mustn't show her!'

'Already have – she went through it cackling all the way. Said she'd had a go at most of them!'

'Hmm – not sure about these…' I giggled again. A girl leaning on her forearms, the man behind holding her legs. 'Like a cart! If he tries to get into her, he'll drop the legs and they will fall on the floor!'

'I didn't say they were possible positions.' The juice was running down his chin with his tongue chasing it as he put down the core. I turned another page. 'Oh sweet! They're asleep now. You're making them into prints? To sell?' He shrugged and wiped his mouth with his sleeve.

'To exclusive buyers. They're no more than visual expressions of what's said in plays – remember that one for Bibbiena? And what we painted in his bathroom?'

'I know – but – they were only to be seen by him. 'Prints – they're public'

'I need the money, Ceci – look – look at this one.'

'It's a good drawing of a very nice mattress – but she looks very disinterested.'

'Classical statues – they always look like that.' He pulled at the ribbons of my dress. 'Want to try?'

'You're not serious!' I held out one of the more contorted scenes. 'Not a hope – even in hell.'

'Come on!' He tickled me and I collapsed onto the bed where he pulled off my clothes.

'Careful!' I said holding the drawings at arm's length, 'You'll tear them! How much are they worth?'

'Marcantonio -' he pulled off his shirt 'will engrave them, then he can print as many copies as he wants.'

'How much?' I kissed his shoulder.

'Enough!' He kissed my ears and removed his breeches.

'How much is enough?'

'How much is a Pope's indulgence? As much as the buyer will pay.' He threw himself on me. 'Now! Position Seven!' We tried to get into position number seven which was so uncomfortable and so impossible, we did fall on the floor, pulling the cover after us, giggling.

'Right place for Position Eleven!' He cried, turned me over and raised my legs.

'What do you think I am, a handcart?' I moved on my hands over the floor away from him as he tried to pull my legs towards him. I kicked out and he fell on top of me, both of us shrieking with laughter.

'Not erotic at all!' I gasped.

'What about Position…?'

'No – 'I sat up and shook my head – 'no, Giulio, you know I won't do that.' He pouted, then smiled.

'Of course you won't, and I wouldn't ask you.' He got hold of me. 'Back to position one then, the only one the Church approves of!'

But we were laughing so much he couldn't get his cock to rise so we lay there hiccupping. He slapped my back, but it was no good, A glass of water had to be drunk upside down, which seemed so incredibly funny, that we finally lay back exhausted.

'Will the Pope have one?' I asked, toying with his black curls as I lay half on top of him. He raised his eyebrows and I slapped him. 'A set of prints!'

'Of course! Leo will love them! Come here.'

He pulled me across him, and as the sun lowered itself outside the window we embarked on a position which was not only possible but immensely pleasurable. It seemed as if Giulio was happy. I ignored the wildness about him.

I did not know these were to be the last hours of pure pleasure between us.

~

At the end of the year, everything was thrown up into the air by the death of Leo, and the election of a new Pope, Adrian, who was known for his austerity and lack of interest in art, regarding most of Leo's commissions as a waste of money and time, and his court as being degenerate. His mission was to cleanse Rome. One of his first actions was to remove all the sculptures from the Belvedere court and to order veils painted over the private parts of Michelangelo's nudes. Once again, painters started to leave Rome. And brothels were closed.

I Modi got everyone into trouble. Marcantonio dare not print more of them when Adrian was elected Pope, and instead printed fine religious texts and pictures. I think Giulio realised that he should not have given Marcantonio the drawings to engrave, but when he asked for them back, he was refused, and told they had been destroyed. When, after only a few months, Adrian died and Giulio dei Medici was elected, Marcantonio got out the engraved plates and stared to print again. Ghiberti, the Pope's secretary, expressed his horror at the publication of such drawings, at their printing, the production of which that meant no-one could tell how many were in circulation. Marcantonio was jailed, Giulio was not: it was said that Marcantonio had stolen the drawings, that Giulio had not meant them for publication at all. It was demanded that the copies already sold were to be collected from the buyers and destroyed.

What happened to the buyers, no-one quite knew, their names were not divulged although gossip was rife. You would have thought more than a hundred were distributed. I don't think their money was returned either. I hoped they had – it was just a joke, wasn't it? But it had all gone all wrong. Giulio did not admit his part in it, and was quiet when I reminded him it had been his idea.

'If you want me in jail, then betray me!' he shouted, and left the house. The engravings were destroyed by Ghiberti. Marcantonio was let out of prison through the offices of Pietro Aretino, but he must have re-engraved them because they appeared again five years later, with rude – very rude – verses by Aretino, who then had to flee Rome because of them. To Mantua, care of Castiglione, to Frederico.

During Adrian's papacy, I lost business, no parties, no entertainments. I lost girls, who were persuaded to stay on with lovers as mistresses. Felicità died in child-birth, and the baby was taken away by Serafina. Income dwindled until only Ginetta, Annina, Serafina and I were left. Annina was pregnant, once she began to show, I could not send her out. She was quite sure who the father was, and so was I. Silvio Cento, a grain merchant who lived over the river, who had asked only for her for some time after he met her at a party. He sent messages asking for her, but, as she was showing, I was about to send back a message saying we could provide neither Annina, nor another girl, when I decided I would go myself. I thought I might persuade him to take her on. I was not hopeful, men wanted pleasure not family. They often, if they suspected a pregnancy had occurred, did not want that particular woman again.

He was surprised to see me. I was, after all, rather older than Annina.

'Cecilia, mistress of the house,' I said as I removed my veil.

'I didn't expect –'

'You expected someone younger – yes – but I haven't come to give you sex,' he flushed. I've come to talk about Annina.'

'Annina?' He smiled then looked anxious. 'She's not – the plague?' He sat down and I sat opposite him.

'No. The plague hasn't reached us. She's pregnant.'

'Oh.'

'By you.' This was where he would protest that it could be anyone, that I was trying to trick him, and he would throw me out. He did none of those things. 'Oh.' He twisted his fingers together.

'You can be sure it's you because you were the only one she went with during these last months.' It was true, but he didn't know that.

'Really?'

'Yes, really.'

'Will she have it - she won't –?'

'She's too far gone for that, she'll have it.'

'What will happen to it?' This was unusual, I felt encouraged.

'We don't keep them; they go to the hospital or the convent.'

'What happens then?' I shook my head. Adopted or abandoned, ending up in the quarry.

'I would have asked her – but I'm so old and she's – so young and beautiful. I thought when someone else came it was because she didn't want to come to me anymore.' I began to be hopeful. He looked up, frowning. He was probably in his late forties; his beard had grey as did his hair. I hazarded an untruth: well it might not be, I didn't know.

'She liked you.' He smiled.

'Did she?' The smile showed gaps in his teeth.

'She said you were gentle.' She'd said that his breathe smelt sometimes. Well something could be done about that.

'I tried to be. I didn't want to put her off.' Well, that was a new one! But his anxiety was genuine. 'I liked looking at her, but in looking at her –'

'I understand.' I looked round the room, good furniture, brocade drapes, a painting on the wall of a Madonna, quite nicely done. A man of means.

'Since my wife died –' he looked apologetic -'we had no children.' I understood a lot more, that my scheme might come off. He was lonely, he had money, he had no heir.

'Do you think? – no –'

'That she would come to you?' He blushed.

'That she would marry me.' I hadn't expected that.

'Would you like me to ask her?' He nodded.

'Yes. Ask her.' I went back to tell Annina.

'You mean I can keep the baby?' She knew we would have a hard time keeping her and the child, but I hadn't realised how much she dreaded giving it away. I, so observant, hadn't noticed that. Serafina grinned.

'Yes. He wants it – him – her – as much as you do.'

'And he said he would marry me?' She burst into tears.

'Do you like him?' She nodded. 'Yes - he's sweet and shy.' Probably not in his business, or he wouldn't have such a good home. I looked at Serafina.

'I think we should do this properly, a *cassone*, a new dress, a wedding party – just a little one – here.' Serafina nodded.

I went to tell Silvio myself. He was overjoyed, he took my hands and didn't let go while he laughed and cried and thanked me. I told him of my plans, and he agreed.

'You will come with me to the notary and witness a marriage settlement,' he said. 'How soon can this be?'

It happened within the next week. Serafina, Ginetta and I went through the boxes of clothes and made up a pile of clothes and linen to fill a small wedding *cassone*. It wasn't really necessary, Silvio had enough possessions and money to buy clothes, but we wanted it to be done as well as we could, even though we had no money for a dowry. We made her a simple dress, such as a maid would have on her wedding day. The visit to the notary took place, Serafina prepared a meal at the house. Gianfrancesco came, Giulio didn't.

We invited Felipe, the Chigi gardener, and his son Luca, who brought us a large bunch of fresh flowers. Then we all followed them across the river, followed by the men carrying the *cassone* and saw her into her new home, which Silvio had garlanded, had placed a Turkish carpet over the threshold, and had filled with flowers. We were greeted by his neighbours, who congratulated him and drank to their health. It was the one of two joyous occasions that year. The second was the birth of Annina's and Silvio's daughter. They called her Cecilia.

CHAPTER THIRTY-NINE

GIULIO

I was called to see my father, who was ill. Graziosa had sent the children to her family near the Castello, leaving her and my sister Gerolama to care for him.

'It will not be long now – the priest has been here,' whispered Gerolama as we entered the darkened room. His breathing was stilted; it sounded loud in the heavy hot air. I squeezed her hand.

'Go and rest – I'll call you if anything happens.' She nodded. I sat by his side, and looked at the gaunt grey face, so different from the face that beamed as he climbed up scaffolding, that frowned if a workman was careless. One hand was outside the covers, its muscles wasted, the veins standing out like purple cords. This man had brought me panels, chalks paper, had introduced me to Peruzzi, had encouraged me in every way. I thought of my mother, who died in this room, and found my eyes wet with tears. The room darkened, and my father stirred.

'Giulio?' his voice was weak and hoarse. I took his hand. His eyes were flickering, searching for a focus.

'I'm here, Father.' He turned his head slightly at my voice, but the grey, no longer brown, eyes would not still.

'Look – after – them.'

Gerolama must have been outside the door, for she looked in, then disappeared to return with Graziosa. Pietro struggled to lift his other hand over the covers, she came to the other side and took it. As she did, there was a loud exhalation of air and the flickering stopped, his eyes were as frozen wax.

As the women washed him to prepare for the burial, I went outside. I leaned against the wall, looking at, but not seeing, the stars. I wept for everything that my father meant to me, for everything that had happened in this house, in this street. I wept for Antonina, for Antea - for Ceci. There was a shadow beside me.

'Giulio?' I turned. A tall man, muscular with features that once I knew so well. I had seen him once or twice across the street when I had visited but had not spoken to him. I was ashamed of that now.

'Niccolò?' His hand went to my shoulder, then both arms came round me and I was engulfed in his bear hug, his smell of sweat. I was ten years old, I was with him playing stones and watching a girl with blonde hair playing with a cat.

'I found Ceci.' I said.

'Found her? Where? We looked everywhere, we thought she'd – '

'I found her, through a painting.' He looked puzzled. I shook my head.

'Is she – is she all right?' I didn't know. I hadn't seen her for weeks.

'You loved her,' he said. *I still do.*

'Will you take a message to her? She lives in the Trastevere. Will you tell her about Pietro? About the burial?' I thought but did not say.

'Which church will the funeral be? Everyone will want to come.' I stirred myself.

'San Nicola. He wanted that. Everyone is welcome.' Girolama came out. 'He is ready, Giulio'

I went in with her. Graziosa stood beside him. No longer the young girl he had wed, she was round, soft-bodied, and looked older than her years. The look of a woman who has borne many children. I was sorry I had always treated her as if she were a nurse or a servant, or a stranger. I don't think I had ever had a conversation with her. For the second time that evening I was ashamed. She stood aside to let me go to him. I took her hands.

'Thank you for being such a good wife to my father.' How pompous I sounded! 'You made him happy.' I believed that. She nodded, squeezed my hands.

'He was so proud of you Giulio, so proud.' She sniffed. 'That drawing you did in the attic room – where the twins are now – he would never let anyone touch it. It's still there.' I was moved. I hadn't been upstairs since I left. A drawing that was the revelation of what I wanted to be – a painter. *'Then be one,' she'd said.*

I went to kiss my father's brow.

'Thank you.'

Word was sent out the next morning to the workshop, to the Papal Palace, to the family. The children, the twins Sylvia and Laura, Domenico and Francesco, were brought back by their grandparents for the funeral. The bier was carried by myself and the men of my family, most of whom I had not seen since I was a child. I felt apart from them, I did not understand any of the family gossip, any of the neighbourhood concerns. As soon as it was over, I made my farewells to Graziosa, embraced Gerolama and made her promise to come to see me soon.

'Please Giulio,' she held onto my hand.

'What is it?' She blushed. 'Come on – '

'How, how is Lorenzetto?' And the colour went right up to her eyebrows.

'He is well.' She lowered her eyes.

'You like him?' She nodded and held her breath. She knew that in admitting a preference for a person her brother did not approve of, she was open to refusal and disappointment. I liked Lorenzetto, he wasn't a great painter but he worked hard, he was honest and reliable, he didn't grumble.

'Then you shall come soon.' She beamed and threw her arms round my neck.

'Thank you! Thank you!'

I left the *Macello* on muleback, started on the road to the Borgo, but turned left, to Trastevere. I crossed the Ponte Sisto and came to the Via Santa Dorothea. I stopped outside the house. Candles lit up the windows and I could see figures moving inside. I led the mule into the courtyard and knocked on the door. Serafina slid back the latch, I heard the bolts being drawn and the door opened. She did not smile. I hesitated. She stood back.

'Come in Giulio, she will want to see you.' We did not make love. I lay in her arms and slept.

His face is etched with work and sorrow, which I cannot erase. Beneath the eyelids, the eyes are no longer bright. I do not sleep, in case I wake and he is not here. I love you.

~

Gerolama did not come to see me soon. The flood had brought with it the *mal aria*, which had raged through the city. It infected Graziosa's family, it infected her children. Graziosa and Gerolama were kept busy looking after them, bringing in Adelina and Faustina to help. The twins died within a fortnight, Francesco followed them.

Once again, Graziosa followed a funeral, supported by myself and Gerolama. Three small coffins were buried alongside Pietro.

Graziosa became silent and anxious, watching Domenico all the time. Gerolama would not leave her. She took over the running of the house, keeping the accounts. He recovered but was weak, coughing and unable to work. In spite of the care he received, he too died the following year. I had had no time to fulfil my father's request to care for them. Graziosa moved into an apartment near to her family, and relinquished all claim on the house in the *Macello* to me.

~

The work on the final rooms at the Papal Palace had stopped with the election of Adrian. Castiglione tried to persuade me once more to go to Mantua, but I was held back by my hopes in Rome. Now that Adrian had died, and Giulio dei Medici was Pope Clement VII, I was confident that I would be asked to finish these, and the work at *La Vigna*. They were important: as a completion of Raffaello's work, and to keep my name in front of the Pope, beyond every other painter and architect in Rome. I heard that Sebastiano del Piombo had petitioned the new Pope to allow him to erase our work and paint the rooms himself. Gianfrancesco and I counter-petitioned to finish the work we had started and stated that we had the original designs by Raffaello to follow. We won back the contract, making Sebastiano more against me than before.

There was no reason for me to go to Mantua. No reason at all. I was building my own workshop, my own practice. I had my house to myself, I even drew up plans to renew it in the antique style. It would be my base, my home. It was ready for a family. No reason to leave for Mantua at all. And I had Ceci, didn't I?

Ceci had lost Ginetta to the plague. Gianfrancesco was in intense mourning: I could offer no comfort. Ceci did not show her grief, but took flowers to the grave every day for weeks. My love curled up into numbness. My passion into grief. I lay in her arms, and that was all.

~

Using the original sketches, Gianfrancesco and I spent long hours turning them into compositions and *modelli* to show. We used drawings of Ceci and Ginetta we had made before as the

Virtues on either side of the main picture. We also used The Crown. This was an old circlet of metal with spikes pointing upwards painted gold, which went from male model to male model whenever we wanted a King or an Emperor. In time, it could be added on to any drawing by any of us. It first appeared up in the Pope's *loggia*. On these new drawings, on the head of the Emperor Constantine, twice. It had become a running joke and went on being drawn long after it had disappeared.

After the completion of the rooms, Gianfrancesco and I agreed to operate separately and parted company. We divided Raffaello's paintings and possessions between us. I claimed the 'Transfiguration', which had headed Raffaello's bier, and went to the Palace to get a payment for this. I needed this money to make a dowry for Gerolama who was to marry Lorenzetto.

~

As I built a model for Frederico for the renewal of his *Castel Mirolamo*, and worked on the re-building of the *Palazzo Maccarani*, near the Pantheon, I also built walls in my head, just as Ceci had described to me, against the pain of losing my family. She was living in her house with just Serafina, having come to an arrangement with Salvatore, and was letting out rooms.

CHAPTER FORTY

CECI Rome, September 1524

I was sitting down working at my accounts, or, rather, I wasn't; the book was on the table, but I was looking out of the window. The apricot trees laden with their fruit in tones of pink and yellow ochre were glistening next to pale green leaves against a sky the blue of cornflowers: it was a painting by Giovanni da Udine. Serafina was picking up those on the ground, looking them over for insect holes and sorting the unblemished ones into one basket, the damaged ones for *marmalada* into another. Prettycat was flat on her back, head back, paws in the air, at the base of the tree Serafina was shaking to make other fruits fall, one of which caught Prettycat. She leapt into the air, scowled at Serafina and stalked off, tail in the air. I laughed as I watched her. Her progress caused the finches to start warning trills though the orchard.

A bee flew into the room, buzzing gently, then escaped. I sighed in pleasure, trying not to re-focus eyes and mind on the accounts, when there was a pounding at our door. I saw Serafina look in the direction of the house and walk back, one basket in hand. A tradesman probably, I was expecting no-one. I shifted in my seat and forced myself to go back to the figures and pulled an abacus towards me.

'Ceci, you have a visitor.' Serafina looked flustered, and stood back to let in a man in rich black clothes and a hat with a jewel whom I did not know. I rose to my feet, then recalled him from a party at *La Vigna* on Monte Mario some time ago. Master Baldassare Castiglione, the Mantuan envoy, who had been liaising with Giulio about his project for Marquis Frederico, and the request for him to go to Mantua. Was he seeking Giulio? I curtsied and waited for him to speak. He nodded with a slight bow and went to the window.

'A very pretty little garden, some fine fruit trees,' he said. 'The garden Giulio has designed for Frederico Gonzaga will be very fine.' He just stood, looking out. I had to speak.

'May I offer you some refreshment, Your Excellency?' He turned.

'A little wine perhaps, and some of those fruits your servant was carrying?'

I went to give instruction to Serafina. Castiglione sat on the chair at my desk, glancing at the book and the abacus, raising his eyebrows slightly. Perhaps he had not expected to find this skill in the house of a woman. I stood. Serafina came in with our best tray with a glass jug of wine, the Venetian glasses and a bowl of apricots, with plates and napkins. She put them on the table and poured out the two glasses, then curtsied slightly and left, closing the door.

'Please, do sit,' he said and handed me a glass, as if he were in his own home. He was quite at ease. He tasted the wine. 'Hmm, pleasant enough.'

'I believe it came from Mantua, from Your Excellency.'

'Indeed. I gave Giulio a small barrel when we last met.' He picked up an apricot, wiped it with the napkin and split it in two, staring into the centre as if inspecting the kernel for flaws. He placed the half with the kernel onto the small plate left for the purpose, and bit into the other, chewing with relish.

'Just right!' he said and wiped his mouth. What was he doing here? As if he had all the time in the world. I was determined to wait for the reason for this visit, and sipped my wine.

'It is slightly more acidic than the last barrel you gave him.' I said.

'Indeed – this is from the Frederico's main vineyard, the last was from the vineyards of the Gonzaga in Ferrara. The soil is a little sweeter in Ferrara. You have a good palate.' He took up the second half of the apricot, placing the kernel gently on the plate, biting into it. 'It goes well with the fruit, sharpens the sweetness.'

What was he doing discussing wine and fruit with a courtesan in her own home?

He wiped his mouth again.

'Frederico wants Giulio in Mantua.' I nodded. 'He will have told you of course.' I nodded again. 'He is impatient for an answer. He wants the heir of the great Raffaello. His mother, Isabella d'Este, who unfortunately did not receive the picture promised to her by Raffaello, wants him. She was impressed with her visit to *La Vigna*, the decorations, the choice of sculptures.'

'Giulio will be flattered by the interest.' Castiglione leaned forward.

'Giulio would do well to keep that interest, and realise it is in *his* interest to go to Mantua.' He looked directly into my eyes. I felt a shiver over my body. 'He wants *San Pietro* does he not?' I did not reply. 'He will not have it. The Pope will confirm Sangallo in that position. Giulio is more talented than Sangallo, but Sangallo is a solid worker, and little trouble. The Pope is no longer Cardinal Giulio dei Medici, supervising the painters, having to put up with their quarrels. As Pope now, while he would like *La Vigna* finished, he will no longer be dealing with the architect or painters directly as he did. That will be Ghiberti. And Ghiberti does not approve of Giulio Pippi.' He emphasised Giulio's former name.

Was this about *I Modi*? I shifted and regretted that movement, which was noticed by Castiglione. He stood, on the other side of the table, looking out. His body blocked the light, the cornflower blue, the bird sounds. The room darkened.

'The Pope will give permission for Pippi to leave Rome, to go to Mantua. The Pope needs Frederico. He does not need Frederico to side with the French King or Emperor Charles against Rome. He needs to make sure Frederico gets what he wants.' Was Giulio so important? He sensed my thought.

'I like Giulio, I like his work – not as fine as Raphael or Michelangelo, but he is talented enough to serve Frederico. He will not have the opportunity to create the new Rome but he will have that to build the new Mantua. You would wish to see that, would you not?'

'Yes.'

'Then you will encourage him.'

'Of course, but it is his decision.' He turned to face me. 'And yet he will not agree to come back with me. Why is that?' I shook my head.

'He has no family, his sister is married. He has a house,' he paused, 'and he has you.' He put both knuckles on the table and looked directly at my hand, the ring. Then back at me and held my eye. 'Forever. Until death.'

I shuddered.

'Since I knew of Frederico's wishes, I have found out a great deal about your Giulio, about you. I have found, while he has his playmates, it is you who holds him.'

'No –'

'Yes. It is to you he will come and tell you that he has not become the Architect of *San Pietro*, it is you who will comfort him. It is you who will tell him to go to Mantua, to get out of the way of the Sangallos, out of the sight of Ghiberti, and the Pope.'

I was silent. I was cold.

'He will want you to go with him, but that would not be appropriate. A courtesan maybe, but ones whom he loves? No, no. He must be untrammelled, he must marry well, he must have heirs. Frederico can only have *courtiers*' He emphasised the word, the name, I knew, of his famous book, *Il Cortegiano.* 'A mistress, a courtesan, perhaps, but from the court of Frederico, not from Rome.' He paused.

'Not one who is a murderess.'

I felt he was looking into my soul, seeing Giorgio, seeing – no, he could not know about the child.

'Twice,' he said. 'Your sibling – even Giulio's sibling, I believe.' I could hold his eye no longer. 'And I need Giulio in Mantua. Frederico's courtesan, his mistress, Isabella Boschetti, is my niece. I have to protect her. I have to get Frederico everything he wants.' He moved then, away from me.

How can I? How can I make Giulio go? He sat down again, the light behind him.

'You have a very pretty house here, you are not as high in your profession as you were, but you could build it up again, if you had a patron. Giulio could try to find other work in Rome, but he may find the doors have closed - if it is known he is not in the Pope's favour.'

I looked at him. All the gossip about the Papal court, the families, the spying and intrigue, which I knew to be true, was there in front of me, aimed at me.

'If you persuade him he means nothing to you anymore, if you tell him you have grown out of him, then, his pride will take over. He will find out about *San Pietro*, he will find the Pope will not stand in his way. Why would he stay?'

I knew I was shaking. He leaned towards me, took my hand, turned the ring with his fingers.

'Forever. For him, Cecilia.' I dropped my head. He dropped my hand, and turned to the window.

'A very pretty garden. I trust you will enjoy this for many years to come.'

He bowed, and left. I heard the door open, heard the horses outside, heard them go.

I took off the ring, placed it in a little bag, put it at the bottom of my *cassone*.

~

I sat in the arbour next to the aviary. It was warm and bright: the end of summer. My eyes were closed to shut out my sight and I tried to concentrate on two senses, of hearing and of scent, through the birdsong and the late roses and jasmine combined. I leaned back against the trellis and caught snatches of warmth on my face and arms as leaves moved to make gaps for the sun. I was tense, waiting for Giulio.

A shadow fell across me. I opened my eyes. He was standing up, eating berries from his hand. I smiled up at him, shading my eyes, not from the sun but so he would not see the expression in them. He sat beside me. He pushed the berries into his mouth, quickly, one by one. Some fell onto the seat.

'Sangallo has *San Pietro*. It was confirmed yesterday. Castiglione goes to Mantua in October – wants me to go with him.' The birds stopped singing.

'How long will you be there?' He did not reply. I sat up. 'Giulio?'

'I don't know.' He did. 'There could still be work in Rome –' Not with Sangallo refusing to contract him, despite the petitions of Master Peruzzi. Not if it is made known that he is not in favour with the Pope.

'In Mantua, you will be a Master, no competition, no quarrels.'

'Castiglione says that Frederico Gonzaga can give me my art, my chance to build – to re-build Mantua.'

Not Rome.

'He says I will have power. I will control my own destiny.'

'Then you must go.' I fanned my hand affecting weariness.

He looks at me. The world, as they say, stops. Everything for him. 'Forever'. I think but do not say.

'And you, you will come with me?'

His eyes are uncertain. Mine blink and uncover ice. The world turns.

I laugh, my professional laugh.

'Why would I go with you?'

'Because - we love –' I laughed again and told my biggest lie. 'Love? Oh Giulio, that went long ago. I don't love you!' I could have struck him. 'I love your company, you are a friend, but love? Once - I have grown out of that!' He paled, he clenched his fingers.

'And so have you! You have your play-things, and I -' I played the courtesan and kissed his nose. 'Whatever made you think I would come with you to Mantua?'

His face was dark. His eyes filled with anger. I thought he would hit me.

'Go to Mantua, Giulio Romano, make your name.' I held out my hand.

I want you to take it, pull me towards you, make me confess my lie.

He looked at my hand, my ringless hand. I followed his eye.

'Oh, that, I lost it – I don't know where it is.' I dropped the hand so he would not see it quiver. His gaze seared my heart.

He got up and left.

And took my soul with him, to be shrugged off and left in tatters to dissolve in the mud on the road to Mantua and be blown apart in the drying winds.

I have loved you for more than twenty years. Therein is my grief. Therein, my betrayal. I slide on the seat, where my hand falls into the berries he has dropped onto it. I bring it to my face. My eyes and mouth drip red as blood. The birds sing, the leaves twitch, and bees sit on the roses, and I sense nothing. In this deserted garden I fall, and I open my mouth like Giulio's painted people and howl until the darkness silences the birds and the moon takes the colours of the garden away. And then the pain comes like child-birth clawing at the hollowness in my stomach, under my ribs, between my legs but no child comes. Just my moaning, and my hands pulling earth wanting to bury me, the foetus who is dead.

Serafina found me, cradled me in her arms, lifted me up and led me into the house.

CHAPTER FORTY-ONE

CECI March, 1525

It was the first morning that the windows could be left open and I could sit in the garden for longer than ten minutes without a thick shawl and a shiver. A shiver that contained, and surrounded, the void which once held Giulio. Not once, but three times: the child-friend, the adoration of innocence and the adolescent fantasy when my love invented him when he wasn't there, and the consummation and the passion of my life when my invented Giulio took over from what, I ignored, he was.

My recollection of the last time I saw him had been used to convince myself his anger was of pride, my words had wounded his pride, not his love. I persuaded myself that he had loved me once, for a while, in those heady summers of art and love. I persuaded myself that I had only said what wanted me to say, to make it easier for him. He had to go to Mantua, without me, to become the great architect that he was, to make his name, to marry, to be respected.

I shivered again, this time to rid my mind of him. Just as I tried to rid my mind of the death cart with my mother so long ago. But this time, I could not escape my sex. I could not be Tomasso, could not use that disguise and my natural exuberance to enter life again (so quickly) as I had then. Nor could I be Tomasina, that pretty young thing who sold sex, and gave love.

This won't do! Look around you.

I looked at the cherry tree and saw the tiny pale buds that preceded its fruit blossoms and imagined the wide drifts of blossoms that soon would be showing in the Chigi Villa gardens.

Instead of imagining, I should go and see them, next week.

So I kept my eye on my tree, and when the flowers, still with petal closed, showed, I summoned Serafina, with cloaks and veils, and together we went through the archway and up the roadway to that heavy closed door. I rang the bell and listened to its peal, which scared the birds that had been foraging in the branches of the cypress trees on the other side of the wall. We waited. The birds settled again, then the latch slid open.

'It is Cecilia, to see the garden. Please tell Felipe.'

The latch grunted in a boyish tone and shut. We waited. Then we heard the locks turn and the door was opened.

'Master Felipe is in the orchard, Mistress, and will be pleased to see you,' said the lad with a nod of the head. It was Luca, Felipe's son, become a young man now. Already his muscles were developed from the work on the garden.

It was one of the reasons I had liked coming to this garden, one of the few places I could go and be greeted with real, not fake, or sarcastic, respect. Because Felipe appreciated that I knew about the growing of plants for food, that I had increased my knowledge of plants as ornaments while I had been visiting here. I know it is this which kept Felipe from his work when I was there. He liked to share the garden and his knowledge with someone who showed an interest, which was shown by no-one else he knew or met. To the absent owner, he was the person who kept the garden up to date, and in good order. To the rare visitors, who admittedly called the garden 'lovely' as they sniffed and enjoyed the colours, he was unknown. To me he was a source of knowledge and pleasure. To him, I was always 'Mistress Cecilia', not Cecilia, a keeper of prostitutes, but a gardener. A gardener to whom he could give cuttings and seedlings and know they would be properly cultivated and cared for.

Serafina liked our own little garden, but regarded this one with suspicion; it was beyond the outer walls for one thing, and therefore countryside, tamed for the moment but threatening to return to a natural overgrown, therefore, wild, savage, it could return to that state any minute. She whisked through it to sit in the *loggia*, safe within manmade walls.

Felipe greeted me, his brown face smiling and crinkling at the eyes. A pleasant face, with black hair touched with grey escaping from his hat. Although the veil would not have impeded the orange blossom scent which swept over me as we turned the corner, I raised it in acknowledgement of Felipe as a friend, and the better to see the flowers. We searched for the tiny orange fruitlets between the leaves, me taking great lungsful of the intoxicating scent, which entered my head like angels singing. He took me to the nursery area to show me the then-new sweet orange tree given to Chigi years ago by the Portuguese ambassador, and the little trees made from cuttings Felipe had made each year and grafted onto the rootstock of the sour orange.

'These are five years old now, and they have blossomed.' He showed me the brush he used to take pollen form one flower to another. 'I'm hoping for the first fruits to set this year.'If they are as sweet as those from the first tree, you'll be able to eat the oranges straight from the tree. When this one arrived it had fruit and the Master gave me one. It was sweet indeed.'

'No need to boil them up with sugar for *marmalada*?'

'So they say, I'll believe it when I see it! Here -' he gave me a leaf and scrunched it 'smell this.'

'It smells the same as the sour orange.'

'No! It is softer, sweeter, more delicate – like the quality of rosewater – with no lemon afterscent.' Felipe could be very poetic when he chose. He made me close my eyes and sniff leaves he took from all the citrus fruits he was cultivating, lemon, cidonia, sour orange, and in the end I could distinguish between them. I was triumphant.

'I'll save one f'or you,' he said, caressing the new grafts. Luca came up to ask some question, and Felipe left me to wander alone.

I left the nursery with its grafts and its young plants, and crossed to the rows of cherry trees, where swathes of white blossom rose and fell, making their own clouds against the new-blue sky. On to the pink-white cushions of apple and pear trees, and the trio of quinces, which Felipe had told me were old, perhaps from the time of the Emperor Constantine, but his eyes twinkled when he told me this. I touched the gnarled bark of these trees, and buried my nose in the fresh green long leaves among the white cups of the flowers.

To me this orchard is paradise, much more than the formal gardens with the pergolas and the statues. Although they are beautiful, this is a different kind of beauty. The trees in the orchard are in rows and are pruned and managed as much as the formal gardens, but here, in spring, with the blossoms of each tree reaching out to another and, if you squint, touching, there is an abundance of freshness, of tranquillity that was found nowhere else in Rome. In the streets, excrement stands and dries, and does not go away (and stinks), here, it is renewed through the plants. The leaves that drop feed the next leaves. This continuation is what I like; there is no violence, no pain here.

Beyond the orchard is the kitchen garden, with its rows of green different shaped leaves which will become vegetables, all known to me. Felipe and Luca are working there with a young lad. A new apprentice, for Felipe is showing him the right distances between the plants he is planting, and how to keep them in rows. I watch them, intent only on the teaching and the learning.

I go into the formal gardens, for I know the roses will be budding and the violets be in full bloom, and, yes, it is a paradise here too. A paradise with just me and the gardeners and Serafina huddling in the loggia, where she always stays; hating spiders. Where the birds both in and outside the aviary are singing and tweeting and fluttering about, and the sound of the fountains come and go as I walk through the pergolas, just leafing, with the promise of flowers to come, and trail my hand through the aromatic herb-bushes. It is bliss. This is why I come.

I was joined by Felipe, who presented me with a small branch with a rose, its petals white round the freckle-yellow stamens, clear pink on the outside, and a dense pink rosebud.

'This,' he said, 'is my own rose, the first flowering.' I took it. 'May I call it Cecilia, Madama?'

There was a silence. I gazed at the rose. This was the best present anyone had ever given me, and I told him that.

'I will give you a plant when I have propagated more,' he said. And he bowed and left me. I called Serafina and we walked home together, she gently grumbling about the cold and the garden.

'There was this big spider in the *loggia* – THIS big. I had to run away, and then I saw the snails on the path and had to run back.'

But I didn't care. I had my rose. These were the first hours I did not think of Giulio. A new, single rose is not erotic.

June 1525

I had been at the Chigi garden all day. I had joined the workforce there, not just weeding, but helping in the growing house. I learned to take cuttings, to trim topiary, to know when the vegetables were ready to harvest. I learned how to test fruit for ripeness, how to prepare baskets for the absent family, how to look after hens and pigs, how to cook rabbit over an open fire.

~

After a day's work, I was pleasantly tired and was looking forward to a rest and a glass of wine. When I entered the apartment, I called for Serafina. She came in looking flustered.

'What is it, has something happened?' She shook her head.

'Yes,' she said. I laughed.

'Which is it?'

She took my hand and led me into my bedroom. The sun was low through the window. A small shape was on the bed.

'What?' I crossed to it. A child. Asleep, snoring slightly. I stared.

'Serafina? What is this child doing here?' She said nothing. 'Serafina!'

'He's Felicità's child. I've brought him home.'

'What? Why? He went to the convent – '

'No he didn't. He went to a wet nurse, near Montorio. I went there from time to time, to see - ' I sat on a stool.

'To see what?' She said nothing. I looked at the child. He had the look of – my heart thudded. 'To see…who…he looked like.' She nodded. 'You knew.' My voice was dull. As if I hadn't known. As if I had just found out. 'The model for the young apprentices 'to practise' - at the workshop. Here too?'

She sat. 'In this room?'

'No. Not in this room. Not in your bed.'

Felicità and Annina shared an attic room. It would have been easy. Of course it was easy, I heard them go up the stairs – how would I not know Giulio's step?

'Why didn't you stop - ?' She was genuinely surprised.

'I didn't think it mattered – those years when you were servicing men – it made no difference to you, either of you - I thought what you and he had, it was so different, the rest didn't mean anything, his other women, they didn't come between you.'

I wanted to lash out but couldn't. I had done what I did to

live, he had done what he did for pleasure. It's what men do. What we had together was outside all that – wasn't it?

'But why did he choose one of mine? In my house?'

'A whore is a whore is a whore. Yours were more refined, cleaner, prettier.'

I flinched.

'He always paid. She was a hussy, he knew that. She tried for Gianfrancesco, but he refused her.' Giulio didn't. He'd asked for her? 'Cecilia, you have had more that most women - your business – which gave you your freedom – your love with Giulio. For it was love.' She reached for my hand. 'Don't doubt that. It's rare, but I've seen it from time to time. This child is his, so he's yours too. I'm sorry she died, but Felicità was simply a vessel.' I held on to her hand.

'I don't know why I didn't get pregnant, by him or anyone else.'

'It happens. Before I found you, the way you lived, what happened to you – sometimes it wrecks your womb.'

'Yes.'

The child sighed, a hand came over the cover, his head turned. The black hair was silky, the eyes slightly downturned, the nose prominent. If it opened its eyes, they would be dark brown, almost black. It – he – snuffled.

'I don't know how to care for children.'

'He's two years old, he doesn't need a wet nurse any more, we just have to feed him, keep him clean, talk to him.' She was brisk. 'Or I can take him to the orphanage tomorrow, and he'll be in slavery or on the streets in five years' time.' I shuddered – as I was meant to.

'But he's a painter – he's an architect –' I said foolishly.

'Only if you guide him.' I looked at her, then at the child. I had to take him, I had to make sure he followed his fate, didn't

I? I owed a life, a child's life. I owed my brother. I sighed and smiled, a little.

'You know I will - or you wouldn't have brought him here.' She shrugged. 'I couldn't be sure – children have never been in this house, or in Vanozza's – they came and they went…'

Not this one.

'You can go back to making children' clothes.'

'Oh no, not that! We buy them!'

We did buy them, and a beautiful child's bed, and engaged a nursemaid. I called him Giulio.

I took him to Chigi's garden. He loved the pigs and chased the hens, falling over his feet. Luca lifted him onto his shoulders so he could press his nose against the fruit, and got a stream down his back for his trouble. Felipe laughed picked him off and while Luca stripped to wash, he deftly removed the sodden cloth around the child and washed him. I was so surprised. He looked at me and grinned.

'Susanna was ill after he was born, then she died; I had a maid but I liked to see to Luca myself sometimes.' I couldn't imagine any man I had known ever doing that – ever thinking of doing that. I said so.

'Why? I'm a gardener, not a banker. I look after my plants,' He laughed and lifted Giulio into the air, naked, who giggled. He put him down. 'Let him play, the sun will be good on his skin.' And that's how Giulio learned to shit near the compost heap.

CHAPTER FORTY-TWO

CECILA September 1526

There was, of course, no word from Mantua. A man had come with an order signed by Giulio to collect a box of antique coins. He had a large cart with strange shapes covered in hemp cloth. Sculptures.

'Have you no letter for me? No packet?' He shook his head.

Perhaps Giulio would send the money later.

~

Serafina could do very little; I now looked after her. She liked to sit in the garden under the arbour when it wasn't too hot. I found her there, leaning peacefully against the wooden support, eyes to the sky. I sat beside her, taking her into my arms as she had done, so often, for me. And cried. Giulio came to me.

'Serafina?' he tugged her hand.

'She's in heaven, Giulio, with Jesus.' I stretched an arm to include him.

She was buried next to Ginetta. I had sent word to Gianfrancesco, but he did not come to the funeral. It was just me and a four-year-old boy, Felipe and Luca.

~

It was natural that I should move in with Felipe. I sent word to Salvatore, with a list of my tenants. I received a short acknowledgement and my tenants, sad to say, got news of much higher rents.

I was finishing packing my personal things when there was a knock on the door. I thought it would be another angry tenant, so I drew myself up ready for an onslaught. It was Gianfrancesco. I invited him in, hugged him, gave him wine and water. His face was creased, his eyes sad. He sat, looking down at the floor.

'What is it? You've come to wish me well?' He smiled

'Yes, of course.'

'And?'

It was some minutes before he spoke. He twirled the glass; one of three Venetians I had left.

'This reminds me of – how happy we were.' So he'd come to talk about Ginetta.

'Serafina died. She is next to Ginetta – I keep both graves.' He looked startled.

'Oh.' He took a gulp. 'I'm sorry I wasn't at Serafina's funeral. I was…in Mantua.' It was my turn to be silent.

'I saw Giulio, I asked him if there was any work, but - it was as if we'd never been colleagues – friends – I know we agreed to go our own ways here, but, I thought –'

'You thought he would still be a friend.'

'Yes.' He sat back. There was more. I waited. 'I talked to him about – about you, about little Giulio. He said it wasn't anything to do with him - he wasn't the father. I told him the child looked like him, he said how could he? He never had Felicità,' He blushed.

'You knew. Ginetta told you.' Statement, not question.

'Yes.'

'She said nothing to me.' She didn't have to.

'He said he didn't want to hear about the child, about – '

'Me.' He looked miserable.

'Of course he didn't. He's the architect of Mantua – the

architect of Frederico Gonzaga – he will marry into a wealthy family. He will have legitimate children. What need has he of a bastard? What need has he of a whore when he can find one in Mantua? A young one, a prettier one –' I burst into tears

'Ceci – '

'I am going to the Chigi villa, to friends, to be with all my friends painted on the vault. I won't be lonely. Felipe is a very kind man. He loves Giulio, and his son, Luca loves him too.' I couldn't stop sobbing. 'I'm lucky!' I bawled.

He took me in his arms and let me cry. Everything I had held in, every hope I had foolishly had that Giulio might send for me, and his denial of his son, all flooded out of me. All the 'common sense' of his ambition to be a great artist well-connected in marriage, was battered down by the bitterness of the acknowledgment of betrayal - mine.

The storm subsided. I drew part from Gianfrancesco. His clothes were sodden with my tears.

'I'm so sorry!' I tapped his chest and smiled.

'I'm sorry too. I shouldn't have come. I shouldn't have said.'

'Yes. You were right to come – I'm leaving here, I have to -"

'I know.'

'Gian – Gianni – I loved Giulio as you loved Ginetta. I will never have that love again. But I will have a happier love, a kinder love, a peaceful love. I will have this for *my* child.' I touched his hand. 'I wish the same for you.'

He took mine, leaned forward to kiss me.

'Good luck Ceci – be happy.'

He left. There were no other shadows of my past to say goodbye to.

I had a man who loved me, a family, a home – a palace! Felipe and Luca came with their mule, Giulio was sat on its back, laughing. The panniers were loaded, and we travelled the short way to the villa.

But Giulio Romano does not leave me. He is in the garden, by the fountain, in the loggia. Beside me when I look up at Venus; even when I don't. He will always be here. I didn't lose him. He is held inside me; he will not go away.

CHAPTER FORTY-THREE

CECI Rome, January, 1526

Day and night, thunder and lightning cracked over the city. Felipe and I moved the piles of root vegetables into the *Galatea loggia* out of the seemingly ceaseless rain. Every morning and evening he went to inspect the river, and each time, told me that it was higher than the last check.

'We must hope that it doesn't overcome its banks,' he said as we ate that night.

'Couldn't we shore them up?' asked Luca.

'No – that was tried last time, at the house, next door - the strength of the river brought it all down in an hour. We must just wait and hope.'

The villa had been built as far from the river as it could be, Giulio had told me, in the hope that any river flood would be taken up by the garden.

'And did the last flood reach the house?'

'This wasn't built then, but yes, it reached the old farmhouse, and the Farnese house next door.'

'And *Santa Dorothea*?'

'Yes, the church was flooded, and the streets around. People fled up the hill with whatever they could carry. The smell was putrid, the streets covered in excrement. They were clearing their homes for several weeks.'

'And then,' I said, 'the fever, the plague. Should we not move up the hill?'

'And camp in the woods, in this rain? We'd do better to take everything up to the top of the house.'

'Yes.' I realised Giulio was looking worried. 'Don't be frightened.' I ruffled his hair – which he hated '- it might not happen.' But it did.

The river rises suddenly as if a great torrent has arrived from outside the city. The banks cannot contain it. We watch from the windows of the upper floor as water roars and rushes through the trees. It hits the walls of the inner garden, spreads itself until it finds the entrance, then sweeps across the flowers beds and the pergolas, crashing the wooden supports and bringing them down. Giulio is excited and runs from window to window to watch the incessant flow. It rises up the Galatea loggia steps and tips over to flood into it and under the doors through to the Psiche loggia, and the whole of the lower part of the villa, covering the first two steps of the staircase. The hollowness of the logge emphasises the crashing of water against the inner doors; the house is surrounded by water; we are part of the river; it is like the flooded streets painted on the walls of the perspective room on the upper floor. It meets the wall bordering the road, and finds its outlet past the stables, flinging open the gates and making the Via Lunghara into another river. Across the other side we see the water has filled the river gardens and the little streets and flooded the lower floors of the houses. Like us, people are staring out of the upper floor windows, mouths open, gesturing.

The only sound is of water roaring, crashing. I imagine whole shops losing their goods to the river, and indeed, as I do so, I see furniture bobbing past us, more swiftly than a galloping horse. A boat with three people in it clinging on, helpless to steer it, sped past then turned over, its passengers tipped out and swept away. Parts of carts splinter against our orange trees and many young ones keel over. The cypress trees whip back and forth making loud snapping noises as they hit each other and their trunks break. Twigs and branches split from leafless trunks, whirl into the air, join others, and whole trees, to be swept down river, tossed against buildings. The river reaches the underside of the bridges, then over them in huge waves, carrying bodies with them.

'Look!' cried Luca and we look.

Bodies are being carried downstream, arms up, whether in supplication or just pushed up by the water could not be seen. Horses are trying frantically to swim, some still yoked in pairs, some still attached to carts. Some with people caught in their reins. We see their screaming mouths and white frightened eyes as they pass. We see them because the river brings them almost up to our walls. We see them because they are caught between the trees in our orchard. Shapes of cats, dogs sheep, cows, career across our vision, tossing in the mess of broken trees and branches. We see a monkey manage to climb up a trunk, it is then dislodged by the carcass of a cow. It disappears under the water. I realise Giulio is beside me, a frightened child. He is crying now, excitement turned to fear

'Why didn't we build an ark? Then we could save the animals?'

I hold him close, his face buried in my skirt. I see a child smash into a tree, then be whirled away; a woman whose clothes catch on a branch. I realise she is still alive, clutching at the tree. Her head lifts and it seems that our eyes meet. Eyes round with terror: then she slips and is gone.

I can watch no more. I turn and slide down the wall with Giulio in my arms. He puts his head in my lap and his hands over his ears, and I feel him shaking. I hold him close, whisper that the water would not, could not get as high as our floor. Then thunder and lightning come together over our heads; rain blacks out the sky and the ever expanding, restless water. There is only sound. Sounds of inner doors being smashed. Sounds of buildings collapsing. The rattle of window panes adds a treble note to the bass thudding of water, flowing round us, coming down on us. We hear in our minds water creeping up the stairs, flowing up each step towards us, to swallow us. It is the story of Noah, the story of Sodom and Gomorrah, the Fall of Jericho. Luca sits on the other side of Giulio, now as close to me as he can be. Felipe next to Luca, an arm round his shoulders, his hand reaching my shoulder. We all enclose Giulio. We sit in this day-turned-night and wait.

CHAPTER FORTY-FOUR

CECI 1527

The damage from the flood could still be seen. The riverside *loggia* had half collapsed into the river which silently passed by, innocent now of any wrongdoing. Felipe and Luca trimmed the torn branches, dug out the completely shattered trees, buried bodies where the trees had been. We replaced the pigs and chickens, and got a little dog for Giulio as a playmate. He called if Rafi.

Every day we worked as if on our own farm. The owners were not interested in it, except to show visitors the paintings. If these had not been frescos, they would all have been sold by now. All of the movable sculptures had been taken away, only two fountains were left.

There were rumours, passed round the markets and the taverns, of Rome being threatened by the Emperor, Charles V. The Pope took these seriously enough to post guards on all the gates to stop goods being transferred out. At night, we could hear carts travelling up the *Via Lunghara*, to leave the city on a roundabout route, enabled by the transfer of bags of money. I suspect every gate was treated the same. People began to stockpile food, and we, once more, transferred our stock into the house, and Felipe made a cage for the animals to be kept under lock and key safe from looters.

On Holy Thursday, a man called Brandano told a crowd that Rome would be destroyed, by what or whom he didn't say, but everyone got very excited.

'Do you think we should go inside the walls?' I asked Felipe in bed one night.

'I can't leave the villa, not without permission.'

'But if we were threatened?'

'Then we will leave.'

'I'll get packs ready.'

'Do that; you're right, we should be prepared.' He kissed me. 'But it will come to nothing.'

'Remember the Colonna?'

The family of Colonna, the same one which had owned the garden I worked in, had rebelled against Pope Clement and had raged through the city after breaking through (forced by more little bags of money no doubt) the walls the other side of the Vatican. There had been looting and murder in the streets then.

'Yes, but that was internal quarrelling. To have the Emperor raid Rome, well, why would he?'

There were times I wished I was near to the courts as I used to be. I would know how big the threat was. I couldn't share Felipe's complacency; I knew more than he about the way the world ran. I also knew that many would welcome the Emperor; they believed he was strong, unlike Clement, and would bring prosperity to Rome.

I insisted that we move as much as we could upstairs. Not where we were for the flood in a room with windows, but in the corridor between Chigi's bedroom and their children's apartment. This had been fashioned so that the doors on either end shut closely; on their other sides, they looked like part of the walls. It was a trick for the amusement of the owners, but now looked as if it could be a refuge, if we couldn't get away, if we were taken by surprise. I even arranged pens for pigs and chickens. Felipe chuckled at me, but helped with hauling bedding and straw for them. We stacked dried meats, wheat flour, fruit and vegetables up there. I made him and Luca take up caldrons full of water and insisted it be changed every two days. I made the downstairs where we normally lived look as if it had been deserted. Felipe thought I was being far too dramatic, but indulged me by carrying bedding for ourselves up there. Giulio thought the whole thing very exciting, making a camp inside a house instead of outside.

We had three visitors, Annina, Silvio and little Cecilia. They were on their way out of Rome, going south to Naples, where Fabio had business interests. Giulio took Cecilia to see the animals, while Felipe took Fabio to the growing house. Annina and I sat on the steps of the *Galatea loggia* so we could watch the children leaning over pens, trying to reach the pigs ears to tickle them.

'Come with us, all of you.'

'Felipe won't leave the villa.'

'But you can – you and Giulio.' I shook my head.

'No – if he says, I stay.'

'And Giulio – shouldn't you think of Giul io?' I watched him. Why shouldn't he go?

'If the troops come, they'll come from the north – they'll be here first.'

They would not come. I didn't say; I didn't want Annina to think I was suggesting they were foolish to pack up carts to leave. I picked up a straw and started to twist it.

'Cecilia – please. It's why we came here, to persuade you.'

'And is Silvio having this same conversation with Felipe?'

'Yes - you're not his wife, Cecilia, Giulio is not his son.' My eyes went from the children to her face.

'We are his, Annina. I am his wife. We were married at Christmas.'

'You didn't tell us –,' I could hear her thinking *'We are your best friends, why were we not at the wedding?'*

'There was no wedding, just a contract - to give Giulio a name, a father. We are a family now. I can't leave if Felipe stays.'

'He will not forbid you?' I smiled

'No - he will try to make me leave.'

'Then –'

'I can't. He didn't have to marry me. He loves me – he has looked after us. I've promised we will be together.' … *forever…*

We watched the children chasing each other round the orange trees, laughing, as they often had before.

I see another pair named Giulio and Cecilia….

I saw I was twisting my fingers, not the straw. Could I lose another Giulio?

'Would you – would you take Giulio? For a while – until this uncertainty is over.'

'You know we will.' She put a hand over mine, stopped them twisting. The men came back to us.

Felipe said 'You must go with them, you and Giulio'

'Annina says she will take Giulio – a treat – a holiday.' I smiled as little Cecilia took Giulio's hand and they ran towards us, followed by a yapping Rafi.

I got up.

'Giulio!' He ran to me. 'Annina and Silvio and Cecilia are going on a journey and they said you can go with them – won't that be nice?'

'Will you come Mama?'

'No, I have to stay and work with your father. It will be an adventure for you.'

'Can I take Rafi?' I looked at Annina…

'Course you can,' she said…and picked up the dog.

'You'll see places I haven't seen.' Felipe went down on his

haunches. 'And when you come back, you can tell us all about it.' Cecilia was excited.

'Come with us Giulio, we can sit together on the cart.'

'Can I ride the horse?'

'Not now, but later, when we get there.' said Annina.

'I'll get some things ready,' I said and turned so they couldn't see the tears pricking my eyelids. Felipe followed me inside.

'Go with them – please.'

'No, I'll stay with you – and Giulio will be back soon.' He took me into his arms.

'Of course, there will be no war. The Emperor will be stopped.' I sniffled, gulped and turned to make a bundle for Giulio. I went to my *cassone*, took out the little bag with the ring. Downstairs, Luca took the bundle to put into their cart, taking Giulio with him to meet the horse. Felipe and Fabio spoke in low voices. I gave the bag to Annina.

'If anything happens to me, send this to Giulio in Mantua.'

'Oh, Cecilia.'

'Cellini made it – it's *lapis lazuli* – tell him – his son' I choked, turned it into a cough. 'If nothing happens to us I'll let you know.'

'I'll bring him back to you.'

'Of course you will.' I smiled at her. 'We mustn't cry.' Giulio came up to me.

'I've met the horse; he hasn't got a name. Ceci says I should give him one.'

Ceci?

'Time we went,' said Silvio, holding out his hand to Felipe, but then they embraced.

We all went to the cart, their servant turned it round to go back through the gate, where their second cart full of possessions was waiting. I cuddled Giulio for too long – Felipe had to take him from me.

'Up you go!' he said. Giulio sat next to Cecilia with Rafi between them. The cart started off. Giulio waved, Annina and I exchanged looks. We watched them go through the *Porta Settimania*, on their way out of the city.

Ceci -

I clung to Felipe. It was the hottest day of the year so far. Birds sang loudly, bees buzzed as if their lives depended on it. The little fountain trickled and I could hear petals fall from the apple trees. Luca closed the gate, barred it. We were enclosed. The river flowed, through the city, away from Rome - Giulio and Ceci chattered and clattered away from Rome.

Nothing would happen, it was all rumour. He would be back soon. Annina and Silvio and the children, would be back and unpack all their possessions. It would be as it was. The ring would not go to Mantua.

Ceci -

~

An order went out to call people to form a militia to defend Rome. Very few citizens answered this, but wealthy families, in a panic, engaged their own men to defend their villas and palaces if they could not leave. Artisans and painters were forced to leave their work and join these defenders. I knew that Lorenzetto, who had married Giulio's sister, was impressed to protect the family of Raffaello da Montelupo, and Cellini became part of a guard for a merchant. The Chigi family sent no-one to the villa – what was there to protect?

We heard the army was at Viterbo, that Isabella D'Este, on a long visit to Rome, was taking people into the Palazzo Colonna; why had she not left to go back to Mantua? Then we heard that her older son, Ferrante Gonzaga, was leading the army. That put Frederico against Rome, didn't it? Did it put

Giulio Romano against his birthplace – the place whose name he took?

Many people were still not convinced, in spite of all the movement, that the troops would enter in triumph with the Emperor at their head, that there would be no fighting, no bloodshed. Some even prepared to welcome him, to rule them, to replace an unpopular Pope. Rome had not been attacked in most people's lifetimes; why should it? It was the city of God, always protected by Him. Had they forgotten the rebellion of the Colonna family only a year ago, with its looting and savagery? God had put a stop to that, they said, through the Pope. So, when May arrived, the carnival took place. It was said that the Pope would move into the Palazzo Venezia; into St John Lateran, or that he had already left, or that a treaty had been made with the Emperor...

We awoke to a clear sky and the sound of people in the street, running and shouting. 'They're here –on Monte Mario!'

Luca sped to the top of the villa and shouted out of the window.

'I can see smoke!' I ran after Felipe who had gone to the gate. Someone rapped on it.

'Let us in - the Germans are here!' they shouted. And rapped again. Another voice:

'They're on the hilltop, they've have taken over the *La Vigna*.' Felipe and Luca raised the heavy board, never before used, into its brackets across the gate

'You should have gone with Annina.' I gave him a look. 'You can still go into the city.' As we ran alongside the wall to bar the other gate, there was a loud roar.

'Cannon!' Another crash, a second cannon.

'It's coming from the *Borgo* – it's the cannon of the *Castello*!'

The noise the other side of the wall increased. Men and

women's voices and the screams of children. There was pounding on our gate.

'They've shut the *Porto* – they won't let us in!' We heard people trying to climb up our wall, but it was too high, as had been planned.

'Pigs!' I shouted. 'Hens!'

Felipe and Luca looked at me astonished, then realised what I was saying as I ran to the hen coop. With three hens struggling in my arms, and the men with a pig under each arm, we ran up the stairs and put them in Chigi's bedroom. We locked and barred the main door to the house, put up the new bars Felipe had made over the doors to the *logge*, locked and bolted the main door to the perspective room. We went to the top of the house to watch from the windows.

The *Via Lunghara* was full of people, running into each other, going back to climb the hill to *San Onofrio* and beyond. Men who had got over the walls ran through the garden and were banging on the villa doors too. We watched a whole family run past the villa to the stables; they could barricade themselves in there.

'We forgot the mule,' said Luca.

'I don't think we'd have got it up the stairs!' said Felipe. He looked at me but I couldn't giggle. We could see smoke from the *Castello*, then, we saw smoke drifting into the gardens.

'Where?' We darted from widow to window to find the fire.

'It's not smoke - its fog!'

Unbelievably, fog was rolling up the river. It was like the darkness of the storm at the time of the flood.

'God's on our side then – the enemy won't see what they're doing.' Felipe's voice was grim. The fog dulled the sounds of the cannon, made them seem farther away. We could no longer see the street, or the people in it, or the river. We fed the animals. Once more, we waited.

'It's going to get smelly in here,' said Luca, as one of the pigs defecated. Then we laughed – pigs, hens, foul straw, fog, us - we laughed until we cried.

No sense of time.

'Listen!' Nothing.

'The cannons have stopped.'

The fog turned black. It was night. None of us slept, none of us spoke. We listened. We prowled the windows. We heard firing, we heard shouting; we did not hear cannons. When the sun rose, there was no sound at all. The street was empty. We watched the family leave the stables and help each other over the wall.

'The *Porto* is open,' reported Luca, after climbing the roof.

'Then you can go to safety.' Luca shook his head.

'Only if you come too'

'Cecilia – '

'No. Why should we be safer in the city? We don't know that it isn't full of troops.' Felipe could not bear the uncertainty.

'I'm going downstairs.'

We unbarred the door and crept down the stairs. Felipe unbarred the door to the Psiche *loggia*. Nothing. The garden looked exactly the same. No cannons. No shouting. Quiet.

After a while, we lit a fire at the foot of the Psiche steps between the two wings, and roasted a pig. While it was cooking, Felipe and Luca went down to the riverside to see what was happening on the other side. They called out to the boats laden with frightened people and bundles, going in both directions, but got no reply. Across the river, they watched a family board a boat from the garden of a villa. They were rowed upstream.

'They yelled back that they were leaving before an army came,' Felipe told me. I was cutting up the pig.

'So we know nothing.' He nodded. After chewing for a while, he said 'I'm going into Settimania to see what is being said.'

'Don't go any further, will you?' I was anxious.

'Let me go, father, I can run faster than you – I can run up to the Borgo, that's where things are happening.' Felipe frowned. Luca got up. 'Let me go, Father.'

Felipe was reluctant. Then he nodded. He let Luca out of the stable gate, and barred it behind him.

We worked in the garden. My mind was spinning – where were Annina, Silvio? Where was Giulio? Had they got through? I found my hands shaking as I weeded between the vegetables. It was late afternoon when we heard a shout and a whistle. We ran to the gate to let Luca in.

'The Duke leading the troops was killed at the *Castello*. The Pope is making a treaty with the Emperor, but there are groups of men, Germans and Spanish, and Milanese, breaking into taverns, stealing. I just escaped being caught myself.' We were sitting on the steps.

'There's more,' said Felipe. Luca nodded and looked miserable.

'I saw three men drag a girl out onto the street. She was screaming. They pulled of her clothes – and'

'They raped her,' I said. He nodded.

'I should have gone to help her. I was afraid – they slit her throat.'

'There was nothing you could do, Luca.'

'There was a man being attacked. They strung him up on a tree by his feet, and took shots at him. They left him swinging and bleeding.' He was crying now.

'And there were others, lots of others, corpses, wounded men screaming…' He lifted an arm to his eyes and we saw the blood. A sword slash. He had been nearer to the men than he had said. Felipe put an arm round his shoulder.

'They were shouting that they hadn't been paid, that they would take what they were owed. They will come here, Father.'

'They may bypass us if they think the villa is empty and find nothing to steal.'

He kicked the fire out and swept the ashes under the topiary hedge. Luca carried more water upstairs. I picked up the cooked pig and we went up into the corridor. The hens had settled and there were eggs. The smell was fetid.

'The smell – it will give us away.' I said.

'And it will be better if it looks as if the animals have escaped and are searching for food.' Felipe said and I nodded.

We gathered up the dirtied straw, took it down to the garden, pushed over the pig fences and chased the pigs and all but two of the hens down the stairs and into the *logge*. Then we barricaded the door to Chigi's bedroom, and left the other so we could go up under the roof to keep watch, and to let air in.

'We'll take it in turns to sleep and to watch. I'll go first, Luca. You need to rest.' I gave the hens some grain. They settled down together, clucking quietly. We should have chased them out too.

'If they get into the house, we will have to kill the hens.' Luca nodded and lay down. I sat next to him. He fell asleep but was restless; he cried out and sat up.

'Those men – murderers – that girl!' and he wept again as I held his hand. Then he went back to sleep in my arms.

I was woken by Felipe. It was dawn.

'They're coming down the *Via Lunghara*. Hordes of them.' I woke Luca and we went up to look – and to hear.

It wasn't an orderly march, it was groups of men, walking,

laughing, shouting. Not an army, a rabble, helping each other scale walls, including ours.

'They'll open the *Porto*!' There was an explosion and shouts of joy; the *Porto* was breeched. It must have been unbarred. We heard muffled musket shots, men shouting, women shrieking. A church bell rang unevenly, frantically.

'They're in the garden!' Luca stepped back from the window. We went back into the corridor, barricading the other end.

We hear booms and shots, pigs squealing. You would think the walls would muffle the noise, but it seems louder that would be expected. There is banging on the doors downstairs, an explosion. The hens start to flutter and cluck. Luca and Felipe fall on them and wring their necks. We lie still. We hear feet on the stairs, the door to the perspective room attacked by thumps; an axe. We hold hands. There are jeers and shouts, and we hear them in Chigi's bedroom - a wall away - whistling at the wedding picture on the wall. We hear scratching and laughter. Lewd remarks, in a strange language, but it is obvious what they're saying. My heart is thumping so hard I am sure they will hear it. More shouts, more scratching, more laughter, then feet descending the stairs. I give thanks to Il Sodoma for his excellence in painting the wall to disguise a door. We communicate by pressing hands, to make sure we are still there, still alive. One or other of us lets go to roll to the edge of the room to urinate, then rolls back to find a hand again. We don't drink even though mouths are dry. My legs and arms are stiff. We don't know when it is night as it is dark in the corridor. Silence lies over us like fog. It buzzes. It is laden with the smell of us, of urine, of fear. I am hiding in the ruins; I am being passed from man to man in the dark, I am lying in the street in the muck. I am killing my sibling, I am lying beside my mother, in her blood. There are no sounds from the stairs. We hear nothing from Chigi's bedroom or the perspective room.

Felipe stirred. He dropped my hand and unbarred the inner door. Light came in. He crawled upwards making no noise, then came back.

'There's no-one in the garden, there's fires smouldering, broken trees, but no soldiers.'

'Don't go down,' said Luca.

'No.'

We stayed, we drank and ate and plucked hens. We stayed for two more days and nights. Then Felipe unbarred the door to the bedroom. The door to the stair was smashed. Luca and I waited as Felipe crept down the stairs. It was half-light, evening. We strained our ears for his footsteps.

A crack, a cry. 'Felipe!' 'Father!'

A rush down the stairs, into the Psiche loggia. Felipe is lying on the floor, writhing. A soldier with a pistol is standing over him. He turns as we rush into the room, Luca first. The soldier turns, shoots. Luca falls. I stand still frozen. Luca is crying. I step forward. The soldier gets hold of me and I fight. Another soldier is standing in the archway. He comes forward, together they push me to the floor, hold me, rape me, first one, then the other. A third and a fourth. Luca. He stops crying. I am dropped to the floor, my head kicked. A shot and pain in my stomach. Laughter. Clattering of boots down steps. I haul myself over to Luca, who has fallen on top of Felipe. I crawl between them. I pull Luca onto my body, I hold Felipe's hand. I lie back and look up. Annina, Livia, Ginetta; Serafina in a corner, glowering at a spider. A shadow on the steps, Giulio? The shadow holds hands with another – a child. I stretch out my arms, they disappear.

The women I love come towards me, floating from the ceiling. Smiling, talking, beckoning. I drop my head back and see Venus, pointing downwards. To us. To me; not a Venus. I am not modelling for a Venus…

I am modelling for a Pietà, my son across my lap…

The pain is great. Giulio – Romano – I watch him sleeping. He stirs, sits up and reaches out to me…forever…forever… until…

There is the shape of someone under the middle arch. A woman -

I lift my head: 'Mama!'

EPILOGUE

GIULIO Mantua, 1528

The Room of Psiche in the Palazzo on the island of Te is finished, the Marquis comes to see it today. None of the men and women on the walls have virtue. They are not beautiful; they are bodies made for sex. They are dull with sex; they are beyond redemption. The largest figure is the one you first see on entering the room, Polyphemus, muscular, frightening, the lord of seduction: Frederico Gonzaga. The room is unfeeling, cold; Jupiter's penis is ready to penetrate Olympia, whose mouth is open, not succeeding in smiling, rather a grimace of submission and fear. There is the head of a watcher, his hand on the door frame, not conscious of the bird about to peck out his eye.

This room is for a lecher. Frederico, the child corrupted by Leo's court. It is made from the darkness in me. It has not the beauty of the horses or the painted monochrome statues in the reception chamber, nor the gentleness of the little paintings of the seasons in the room next to it. It is not from my lightness, which delights in flowers and trees and birds and animals. A lightness of the panels in the garden *loggia*, until you see the subjects, the abduction and seduction by King David (Frederico) of Bathsheba, the wife of his loyal warrior, Uriah (Isabella, the wife of one of Frederico's courtiers – and niece to Castiglione). A lightness fast disappearing beneath my false friendliness and charm; darkness prevails in me. These creatures in this room of Psiche contain all the sexual wrong in Mantua, in Rome, in the world. Beneath its too-bright colours, the breasts and buttocks, is rape and sodomy. No beauty. No Raffaello.

No Ceci.

I await Frederico.

Frederico arrives, the courtier takes over. I bow and smile and he looks at it all laughing and clapping his hands. He sees only his pleasure. He is pleased with me, and I smile with my mouth.

He had all my (and Ceci's) coins, all my (and Ceci's) sculptures. He took them as a gift.

I am the Architect of Mantua. I am re-making Mantua. I am Frederico's favourite.

A year ago. I was quite sure Ceci was at the bottom of my bed, smiling. I had woken, startled, sweating, but there was no-one.

I will marry Elena Guazzi, with a dowry of 200 ducats. More than Leonardo da Vinci made in a year. I have a house. I will have a son, call him Raffaello. I like the name. A daughter will be Virginia. No-one will touch her until after marriage. She will not see the Psiche *loggia* in Mantua.

In my own room, I crush a letter in my hand. Unread.

The ring lies on the table. 'Forever. Until…'

Neither wife, nor son, nor daughter will replace my soul.

I will have everything I ever wanted.

In 1546, Giulio Romano was offered the position of the architect of St Peter's. He died in November of that year in the Sanità in Mantua. The position was given to Michelangelo.